Joss was born on the borders of East London and Essex. Leaving Essex behind for Cambridge, she went on to have careers in British diplomacy, as a policy adviser for Oxfam, and along the way gained a doctorate in English Literature from Oxford University. More recently she has written for children and young adults, winning awards in both categories. She has published over fifty novels that have been translated into many languages. She lives in Oxford.

🐦 @jossstirling
goldinggateway.com

Also by Joss Stirling

The Jess Bridges Mysteries
White Horse
Red House
Grey Stones

Standalones
Don't Trust Me
The Silence

Black River

Joss Stirling

One More Chapter
a division of HarperCollins*Publishers* Ltd
1 London Bridge Street
London SE1 9GF

www.harpercollins.co.uk

HarperCollins*Publishers*
1st Floor, Watermarque Building, Ringsend Road
Dublin 4, Ireland

This paperback edition 2021

1

First published in Great Britain in ebook format by
HarperCollins*Publishers* 2020

A catalogue copy of this book
is available from the British Library.

ISBN: 9780008422585

Set in Birka by Palimpsest Book Production Ltd, Falkirk
Stirlingshire

Printed and bound in Great Britain by
CPI Group (UK) Ltd, Croydon CR0 4YY

To my friends in my real book club based in my home city of Oxford. Thank you for the years of food, wine and conversation, and a wide range of book choices that have stretched my reading habits. There have been some mountain tops – and some boggy reads – but they've always been fun. We've not yet taken it as far as a swim in the Cherwell, but maybe one day ...

Chapter 1

Jess

I don't know what your book club is like, but mine is the sort that ends up with me stranded naked in the river with a dead man and a murderer on the loose.

Or maybe that is just me?

How did this happen? I suppose you could say it started when Cory told me it would be a great idea for me to join her group.

'Just a few of us mums – our night away from the husband slash partner and the kids. Bring-and-share supper. Lots to drink. Lots of gossip. A bit of discussion about the book – eventually.'

'And if I don't qualify as a mum?' I watched Cory push her three-year-old in the swing in the back garden of her Summertown house in north Oxford. It was a minute patch of lawn edged with lots of planters that Cory confessed to restocking each year as she suffered from an incurable case of black finger. Nothing survived in her care over winter. My hopes weren't high for her scented geraniums. We were both sipping our evening glass of white, a congratulations for getting through another shitty day.

'God, Jessica, you don't need kids to come along! In fact, you'd be our exotic alternative, the one living the life innocent of NCT classes or PTA politics. I bet you don't even know what a traybake is – or pelvic floor exercises?'

That was when I realised that reproducing brought with it almost as many acronyms and codewords as the army. Then again, from what I'd seen, maybe parenthood was a bit like entering enemy territory and you needed some discipline to get through?

I still wasn't sure I wanted to enter this contested area that appeared to belong to professional mothers. What did I have in common with them? I didn't have kids, a husband (or ex-husband), a house or career prospects. On the other hand, almost all the women I knew were in this life stage, what choice did I have if I didn't want to embarrass myself angling for friendships with those years younger than me? 'But you do talk about the books you read?'

'Oh yes. Most of us went to uni. Except for Jasmine. She opted for modelling and has ended up earning more than the rest of us put together.'

I wasn't sure I was destined to like Jasmine and told Cory so.

Cory drained her glass and handed it to me to hold so she could launch Leah more vigorously. 'We all agreed to hate the bitch naturally, but she's so sweet we couldn't keep it up. She'll win you round too.' Leah squealed as the swing hit the point where it made the frame judder; Cory slacked off a little. 'The point is, Jess, we all have dormant brain cells that need stimulating at a minimum once a month. Stave off Alzheimer's. You can never start too soon.'

'Well, that's an optimistic outlook, Cory.'

She ignored my dry tone. 'Believe me, you can only get so far on Disney Princesses and the Marvel Universe.' Cory had Leah and Benji, a boy of five who currently wanted to be Spider-Man when he grew up, so considered herself the expert in both topics. 'I really think you'll like it. Adult conversation and culture.'

Standing by the swing set with the munchkin trying to launch herself into space, I discovered that I'd do anything to please Cory. Even risk an evening of book talk with fecund thirty-somethings. And as real friends do, I agreed to join the book club to keep Cory company. That was why I was now hiding in the bushes without a stitch on trying to work out how I could get home without anyone seeing.

Conclusion? It was not possible and I had the horrible creeping feeling that things were going to get much worse.

Cory said she'd come back once she'd caught up with the dog that had run off with my rolled-up clothes. I'd hoped at least for knickers and bra, but the bundle had kept together surprisingly well in the big jaws of a flat-coated Retriever. I suppose the name was a bit of a clue, though I was not sure what the owner was going to do with his mutt's offering of a Primark polka dot sundress and scanty panties.

She still hadn't returned. I shivered. My head was swimming with too much white wine – and my body from the real dip it had just taken. Our summer book club meeting

– *a picnic by the swimming spot called Parson's Pleasure, in University Parks, it'll be fun!* Our chosen good read, *Wild Swim*, a trendy book by the improbably named Jago Jackson. This travelogue-cum-social-commentary featured him leaping up each day from his lodgings in an Oxford college to discover another hidden treasure in the upper reaches of the Thames, ranging from Port Meadow to Cheese Wharf. Even the swimming places around Oxford sounded like something served in the Senior Common Room. Parson's Pleasure was the oldest spot, famous for its male nude bathing and featured in Oxford folklore, until it was officially shut in 1991. Closure was just a challenge to people like me. Parson's Pleasure lay on a bend in the Cherwell where the water dithered for a while under the overhanging willows and washed against the punt rollers that allowed the flat bottomed boats to progress upstream. By day, it felt a place for *Brideshead Revisited* student picnics with college scarves, champagne and teddy bears. At night, the black waters enticed you to join the desperate and the drunken who had ended their days here.

Jago had now adopted it as his own place for a daily dip. Cory's ex, Brendan, made the documentary that accompanied the book – another reason for us all to come down hard on it. Jago only stopped in his praise of swimming to make acerbic comments about the various new tribes now living in his city, of which Yummy Mummies were, of course, one. His pen did not spare the people who dared to enjoy the same places as him and introduced such abominations as kale smoothies and oat-milk cappuccinos to staid Oxford cafés.

My book club friends howled at his caricature of them, calling out his thinly veiled disdain for their life choices.

'Hey, Jago!' Cory had roared at the picnic, waving a celery stick like a machete, 'I may drive an Audi, job-share and have an *au pair*, but I also have a degree in international development, get paid a pittance at DfID to go on project assessment visits to Syrian refugee camps, and you still dismiss me?' Cory was a civil servant working part-time for the Department for International Development in London.

'I don't think he means you,' said Jasmine. She absolutely was the epitome of the term 'yummy': coffee-coloured hair, big dark eyes, svelte figure. Where her little boy Reuben came from, I'd no idea, but I was voting 'stork' because there was no way that midriff ever housed a baby.

'You mean I'm not young, attractive and still sexy?' asked Cory, ready to rumble even though her wine intake had been modest as befits our designated driver.

To be honest, Cory wasn't really the poster girl for the Yummy Mummies, more the Over-Stretch-Marked Mums.

'No! What I mean is that Jago hasn't bothered to talk to a real woman,' said Jasmine, deftly avoiding a fight. 'All the fellow wild swimmers he interviews about the life are either hoary old men or eccentric lady artist types. The sort who have long grey hair, an allotment and make pots.'

'Or smoke pot,' added Frances, our one-liner expert. An acerbic forty-something with family back in Hong Kong, she now ran the HR department in a law firm – another part-time job-share mum burning the scented candle at both ends.

'And we wouldn't know anything about that,' I said archly.

Their faces were blank.

'You mean, you don't?'

'Not since college,' said Frances.

'Not even then,' said Cory.

Jasmine kept silent.

Right. OK.

'So Jago doesn't like empowered women,' I said, hoping to deflect the conversation from drug taking.

'Exactly!' said Cory.

'Then I say we should claim the riverbank here as our own. We can't let media darlings like him steal our identity as women.' I'd had my fill of media darlings when living with my ex, Michael, TV's favourite psychologist. 'We have a right to the same water Jago swims in. Parson's Pleasure is not just for naked dons!'

'Actually, there's a traditional spot on the river for women, called Dame's Delight,' said Jasmine helpfully, pointing upstream.

'I want to be a Parson not a Dame.' Maybe there's something wrong with that statement? 'Whatever: I'm going in!'

'But you can't!' protested Jasmine. 'The park's about to close. Even if you swim out, your stuff will be stuck on inside the railings.'

'Just watch me.'

'Oh God, I don't want anything to do with this. Jess is going to do one of her crazy things.' Frances was already gathering up her blanket and picnic bag. This was my third book club and she already had my number. 'I've got to get back to pay the babysitter. No time to be arrested for public indecency.'

The others decamped with her, leaving just Cory and me.

'Jess, this isn't a good idea,' said Cory plaintively.

None of my ideas are good. 'I'm committed now. I'm like Eddie the Eagle having left the top of the High Jump at the whatever Olympics.' I rolled up my underwear in my polka dot dress and put it at the bottom of a tree. If I'd thought about that a little more, I would've realised that wasn't a good place because you know who else liked tree-trunks ...? I pushed my way through the undergrowth – not so funny, naked – and kicked off my sandals before entering the icy water.

Ah, Jago, now I understood why you bother to get up for this. It felt sensual and might've been the closest I'd come to orgasm for a while now. I waded in past my lady bits and squeaked when the water reached my waist.

'You go, girl!' crowed Cory, clearly having decided that, as no policemen rushed up to arrest me, it was safe to be supportive.

'Join me! The water's lovely!' I did breaststroke out into the middle of the Cherwell and lay on my back, bosoms saying a perky hello to the unscandalised sky as the current drifted south towards the punt rollers and the next bend in the river. This is the life. I might have messed everything else up but at least I still had the ability to live free and easy under the apple boughs. A wild child wild swimming.

Barking and a scream from the bank broke into my reverie.

'Nooo! Give that back!' wailed Cory, running off after the aforementioned Retriever retrieving my clothes. 'I'll get them for you, Jess!' That was the last I saw of her. When I scrambled out, I saw that she hadn't even thought to leave me the picnic blanket. From skinny-dipping to starkers in the shrubbery.

Welcome to my life.

It's hard to estimate how long you've been waiting when you are alone in a park with no clothes, no watch, no phone.

Even a little while was too long.

Someone was bound to come along soon. A park keeper to check the public hadn't planned on any overnight camping. A last minute jogger. Another dog walker. A creepy guy in a mac ...

Oh hell, I needed something to cover up the bare minimum.

Bare minimum? God, I was even cracking jokes to myself about myself. Focus.

I spotted a punt tangled in the bushes that overhung the river. It must've got loose from the Cherwell boathouse upstream where you could rent them. Thinking optimistically, it might contain a tarpaulin, or a couple of cushions.

I could swim over there, check it out and then be back before Cory returned. Or huddle in it and call across the water to her.

Good plan.

I launched into the water and swam across. I couldn't get into the boat at this angle, not without someone to haul me onboard, so I went to the bank. Somehow climbing out here made me feel even more naked.

Think beach in the south of France, I told myself. You're surrounded by lots of Chloes and Jean-Pauls, all buff and naked. But I couldn't help picturing grandads with rolled-up trouser legs and handkerchief hats, eyes goggling, as I climbed out. Admittedly, this was all a bit *Carry-on Camping* with the dog running off with my stuff like that.

A chill breeze blew away any humour. I was cold and miserable now, and the situation was giving me the creeps. I was just asking for some pervert to attack me, standing exposed like this. I had to cover up. I gave a trailing rope a tug to bring the boat a little closer. I hoped for a tarpaulin. Instead, I found another naked body.

But this one was dead – and not by natural causes.

My heartbeat went into overdrive. I really shouldn't be here – weaponless, no clothes, and a murderer nearby.

Then the bushes on the opposite bank rustled and a man pushed his way through, coming towards me.

I screamed.

Chapter 2

Leo

No police officer welcomed this kind of call. It came through late evening on a rare day off.

'Hello?' Holding the phone in the crook of his shoulder, Leo wiped a hand on his gardening jeans. They were in the middle of a scorching summer, and he'd been repainting the Japanese-style bridge over the pond in his garden in the cool of the evening.

'Detective Inspector George?'

'Yes?'

'Please hold for Superintendent Thaxted.'

His heart sank. He quickly reviewed all the things he might have done to warrant a call this late. He was not on duty, his paperwork was up to date and performance reviews done. He couldn't imagine what had brought this upon him. While waiting, he shook a handful of pellets for the Koi carp, drawing it out of the shadows. The carp had come with the house when Leo moved in six years ago and he had nicknamed the fish Goldemort, giant survivor of what once had been a shoal.

Charitably, he had put its solo presence down to depredations by a heron; but, as a detective in CID, he had to harbour doubts as to whether he was giving sanctuary to a killer.

'Leo?' Superintendent Thaxted's voice was as forthright as ever. Leo held the phone slightly away from his ear.

'Ma'am?' Best not to assume this was for a bollocking, though the formidable Head of the Local Police Area was known to prefer to do her reprimands one-to-one just before Monday arrived. Clearing the decks, she called it, like she was a frigate setting up the guns to blast them all out of the water.

'Sorry to disturb you on your day off, but we've got a situation.'

Ah, so not a telling off. Leo felt slightly less guilty. 'No problem, Superintendent.'

'A body's been found by the river in University Parks.'

'I see.' Where is she going with this? A body in the river was hardly news. Suicides, drunken revellers, cyclists missing the path: he'd unfortunately seen it all. The Cherwell, which flowed into the Thames in Oxford, looked the epitome of a gentle English river, passing through meadows, willow banks and colleges, but the police could tell you that any stretch of water had the potential to be a killer. 'How can I help?'

'I'm going outside protocol because I need someone I can trust to head up the investigation.'

Alarm bells began ringing. This sounded like politics: the police officer's nightmare.

'I see.'

'There are two reasons I'm calling you. First, initial reports are that the victim is well known in the university.'

Leo swore silently. Getting involved with the Oxford elite is like dancing on an ants' nest covered in honey. 'And the second reason?'

'We have a witness who needs sensitive handling; I'd prefer that you, rather than the duty officer, do that interview.'

'Who's on call?' Leo tried to remember who was on this weekend.

'Harry Boston. I've told him already that I want a more senior officer to head the operation and am sending you to take over. He's to stand by and preserve the scene until you arrive.'

Oh, Harry would love that. It was well known at the nick that DS Boston was under a cloud with the top brass for his treatment of students arrested in a demo the previous month. Word was that he'd been a little too handsy with a girl and complaints have been made.

'Any more details, ma'am?' She was being very cagey.

'Boston's initial report is that it looks like murder, not suicide.'

That was why she was keeping the details brief: she wanted a clean investigation with no assumptions. Leo was already in the house, picking up his keys. 'Which entrance, ma'am?'

'You'll be met at the gate near Linacre College. And, Leo?'

'Yes, ma'am?' Putting the phone on speaker, he changed into dark trousers and grabbed a shirt from the clean laundry pile.

'Get this right. If the initial identification is right, Thames Valley Police doesn't want to bring the wrath of the university down on our heads. It would be career-ending stuff. And I'm not talking just about Sergeant Boston.'

And there was the ballsy threat. At least he knew it really was the Super he was talking to.

'Yes, ma'am.' Passing the back of the sofa, as a final thought, he snagged a jacket he'd discarded earlier. 'I'm on it.'

Sergeant Trevor Kent, a uniform Leo knew well from Kidlington HQ, was on the watch for him. He was an older man, approaching retirement, but could be relied on to get the details right. Blue and white tape already blocked the cycle path to Marston and entrance to the park. Getting out of his car, Leo nodded to him.

'Trevor.'

'Sir.' Kent came to attention. All the uniformed officers did this with him. Leo had never developed a knack for setting junior officers at their ease so had to settle for wary respect in all his dealings. It didn't help that in his very first case in Oxford, Leo had torn a strip off an old-timer who mishandled evidence. He couldn't abide any sloppiness; that could lead to the guilty being acquitted.

'I take it that you've got someone on the other end of this path, Trevor?' This corner of the park intersected with one of the main cycle routes between the city centre and one of Oxford's urban villages, Marston.

'Yes, sir. Constable Kennedy is at the Marston end.'

'Good. Any trouble?'

'No, sir. The park was closing when the body was called in, so it was already empty of visitors. I don't know much but Sergeant Boston told me that we've got the person who found the body on the bank, the witness who called it in and a park keeper who did the final sweep for members of the public. They're all waiting for you in there.' He gestured to the black gates that would normally be padlocked by now. Orange light from the streetlamp barely made an impact on the darkness beyond. The leaves rustled as the breeze picked up, and branches tossed against the silver sky. Leo remembered something on the forecast about a storm approaching, which was the last thing he needed for preserving the evidence. They would have to work fast. He took a flashlight out of the boot of his car.

'Is SOCO here yet?' He couldn't see any sign of their van.

'Heading in from Kidlington. Should be here any minute. The ambulance went in a few minutes ago – not that they're needed. Too late for our victim.' Trevor's radio crackled and Leo could hear Harry Boston demanding an update.

'Sir, DI George has just arrived,' said Kent. Leo switched on the torch and began walking away. 'Coming your way now.'

Sergeant Boston's response was along the lines of 'about bloody time' but Leo couldn't stomach beginning a murder enquiry in a showdown with Harry about insubordination. He'd not yet got over Leo leapfrogging him to be made inspector. He'd closed his eyes to the fact that it was not Leo's fault, but his own.

In contrast to the sports fields in the centre, this corner of the park was so densely planted that you couldn't see what lay around the bend. If anyone was going to ambush another person, thought Leo, this would be a great spot to pick: only a short stretch to dump the body in the river and an exit that gave you a choice of directions: south down St Cross Road, east along South Parks Road, or you could even disappear into the warren of buildings in the university science area and make your escape along the alleyway past the Museum of Natural History. That was if the attack happened here and not upstream.

But Trevor had said the victim was on the bank and not in the river. If a murderer had attacked someone on the bank, then he would've done better to tip the body into the water. There it stood a good chance of not surfacing for a few days, weeks even. Maybe they'd been disturbed in their attack?

An attack in a twilit park: was it a sexual crime? Leo hoped he wasn't about to face some poor woman who'd had her life cut short in the worst way.

Chapter 3

Jess

I was fuming. The note of disbelief in the policeman's voice was unmistakable.

'Miss Bridges, if you would explain what happened one more time?'

The officer was a bear of a man with a face only a mother would love – a Tyson Fury gone to seed – and I was standing before him, clutching to my chest and nether parts double spreads from the *Oxford Mail* that I'd fished out of a bin. He'd been summoned by a passing jogger who had seen me on the other side of the river and given me the fright of my life when he pushed through the bushes to offer help. Together we'd brought the boat over to the bank of the river inside the park, as that was nearest the road. I think I had some muddled thought that paramedics might be able to do something, even though the man in the punt was clearly dead. You'll have to forgive me for that impulse; I was in shock, I think. The runner, a man in his late thirties, somehow familiar but don't ask me where from, was now sitting on a bench a few feet

17

away, dripping wet but not seemingly bothered by his state. He also was looking at me incredulously. Or was it ... lasciviously?

'As I told you, Officer ... er ...?'

'Sergeant Boston.' The policeman was not even bothering to keep his eyes on my face.

'I'd been in the river. Swimming. For fun. A Retriever stole my clothes, my friend went after it but didn't come back, so I decided to swim over to the punt to see if I could find an alternative – cushions or something.'

He looked down at the newspaper. Unfortunately, my boobs were currently wrapped in a headline that claimed: 'Oxford named "wokest" place in the country'. I think a few of its citizens might've missed the trend.

'This is my alternative. The local rag. You couldn't possibly call for something for me to wear, could you?'

'The ambulance will be here momentarily.' Did he get off on being pompous? I thought probably 'yes'. 'They'll give you a blanket. You admit to swimming naked?'

He seemed to be missing the point. 'You do realise there's a dead body in that boat?'

'Yes, I do. But swimming naked is a public order offence.'

'So, under public order law, it's OK to murder someone and dump their body but not to skinny dip? There seems to be something a little wrong with that line up of priorities.' Shut up, Jess!

He lifted a brow. 'Did you murder someone, Miss Bridges?'

'No!'

'So how do you know he was murdered?' We both knew

how I was aware it was a he. The victim was lying on his back. I could report that death was not kind to genitalia.

'The head wound was a bit of a giveaway, don't you think?' Half of the man's head had been knocked in by what on TV cop shows they call blunt force trauma.

'Did you touch the body?'

I nodded. Stupidly, in my first shock, I'd felt for a pulse. 'Just the wrist and neck. To see if I should try CPR.'

He rolled his eyes. 'Did you move him at all?'

'No, only the boat.' We'd swum over, tied it up to a tree and then the jogger had called the police on the phone he'd thankfully remembered to leave with his shoes on the bank. What he had made of a naked woman gibbering about a dead man, I had no idea. His eyes had barely left me since.

The flashing lights heralded the arrival of the promised ambulance. Dusk had fallen. The few stars that you could see with the full moon were beginning to spray the sky like a body glitter. Had Cory given up on me? Or would she see the lights and make her way over to this side of the park if she was allowed in? I'd call her on a borrowed phone but realised I'd no idea of her number. The incompetence of the digital age.

The policeman closed his notebook. 'Stay here, Miss Bridges. I'll just show the ambulance where to go.'

Sergeant Boston strode off to welcome the cavalry. But would someone please get me some sodding clothes? I resolved I was not going to talk to anyone until they provided me with something better than newsprint.

19

I looked over at the jogger. He smiled and adjusted his shorts.

Oh great. Lascivious, it was.

I turned my eyes pointedly away.

Chapter 4

Leo

Leo found Harry thanks to the blue lights of the ambulance. That had been parked to one side with its headlamps illuminating a stretch of bank. The river ran black under the willows and alders. Paramedics were huddled around what Leo assumed had to be the punt containing the victim. Harry was standing at the edge of a lawn running down to the riverbank. In the further distance, three figures waited, each sitting separately on a bench.

'Harry.' Leo raised a hand to his sergeant.

Harry turned, but with some reluctance in his stance. 'Leo. Really, there was no need for you to come on your weekend off. I had it under control.'

'That wasn't why the Super called me in.'

'You could've told her I was up to the job.'

He could've but he hadn't. 'Ours is not to reason why, Harry ...'

Harry sniffed at that. He was not a fan of women in authority. According to those that went drinking with him,

21

he suspected all of them of getting their promotions thanks to gender bias. He was not that keen on the new breed of university educated types like Leo either, displacing those who 'learned the hard way' on the beat.

'As per orders,' said Harry, 'I haven't fully questioned the witness who found the body, but I did do an interview with the park keeper, Bill Bethwin. Is that all right?' He said this in a tone that implied it had better be.

Leo really wasn't interested in a fight. He just wanted to get on with this before the storm hit. The fretful trees were already making it hard to hear his report. 'Fine. What did Mr Bethwin have to say?'

'Apart from the jogger, who called it in, and the witness who found the body, there were no other members of the public in the park when Bethwin did his final check. He thinks it's likely that the punt drifted here from upstream, rather than came from one of the hire places near Magdalen Bridge.'

'What makes him say that?' Leo had his own ideas but he was interested in what an experienced groundsman might say.

'No pole. Hard to punt without one so if it moves it will be with the stream, not against.'

'Unless the killer punted it here and dumped the pole in the bushes? We'll need to mount a search for it.' Leo glanced up: it was already dark with an almost full moon that was playing hide-and-seek with the clouds. 'At first light. Can you call that in?'

'Already done. We'll sweep the meadows on both sides of

the river between here and the boathouses – there's the hire place as well as a couple of college ones.'

Grappling for authority with Harry was like trying to catch a bar of soap in a bath. 'OK. Let's concentrate on getting the body processed before the weather changes. The Super said the victim is well known?'

'Yes, the witness thinks he recognises him.' Leo's ears pricked up: connection was always worth a closer look. 'He reckons it's the bursar from Linton College, Dr Kingston.'

Linton College was just upriver from the park, sharing a long boundary on the north. 'Has anything been moved?'

'Unfortunately, yeah. The woman who found the punt moved it to this side of the river with the help of the Good Samaritan who went to her aid. Swam across towing it, can you believe it? To get help, or so she claims.'

Leo gave him a sharp look. 'I thought you hadn't spoken to her?'

'I got this much out of her before I got my orders to stand down.' And Harry was clearly furious about that. 'The girl's a liability, messing with evidence, prancing about buck naked. The victim is starkers too.'

'Do you think she's involved, with the killing? Some sexual encounter that went wrong?'

'God knows, I haven't been able to ask her, have I?' Headlights appeared behind them, casting Harry's craggy face into dissatisfied lines. 'Thank Christ, SOCO are here. They took their own sweet time, didn't they?' And without waiting to ask if Leo had finished with his questions, Harry strode away to greet the scene of crime officers who'd just driven into the park.

Leo knew he was going to have to do something about Harry's attitude, but not now. First, he wanted a look at the body; then he needed to talk to the witnesses, particularly the one who found him. The wild swimmer.

Chapter 5

Jess

From my soggy vantage point on the bench, I could see that Sergeant Boston was now briefing a newcomer who had walked in from the gate. After a brief discussion, another vehicle arrived and the new man walked down to the punt, something draped over his arm. Was he another policeman maybe? They wouldn't let the press in to view the body, would they? He had to be official. Mr Tall-and-too-dark-to-see-if-he's-handsome talked to the paramedics, shone a torch into the punt for a thorough examination, then stepped back. Switching the torch off, he approached me with – yes, thank God! – a jacket.

'Miss, I thought you might need something to wear?'

Not meeting his eyes, I grabbed it from him and draped it over my shoulders. It was a lovely soft linen that smelled faintly of wood fires. As he was a tall man, it hit me around the mid-thigh. 'Thanks. Newspaper was not a fashion statement.'

'I'll see if the paramedics have some scrubs you can borrow. This might take a while. I'll be back in a moment.'

Thankfully the ambulance came stocked with spares, and I was able to face the world without a blush. It wasn't nakedness that bothered me but being naked when other people weren't.

The scene of crime officers were now clustered around the boat with Sergeant Boston and Mr Tall-and-dark, finally getting to the important part of the evening's story. Not bloody skinny dipping. I lay back on my bench and closed my eyes, wishing it all away.

I'd found a dead body once before. That time hadn't been a coincidence as I'd been looking for the man in question, not knowing someone else had got to him first and killed him. And what a can of worms that had opened. This time should be much more straightforward as I had no idea who the victim was or why he met his end here, presumably sometime while we in the book club were discussing Jago Jackson on our picnic blanket on the other side of the river. Trees on the edge of the water had prevented us from seeing anything so, other than being the one to discover him, I was going to be a piss-poor witness. Hopefully the police would see that and let me go. Cory must be worried.

There was a tap on my shoulder. I opened my eyes reluctantly, half expecting the aroused jogger, but instead found that the nice policeman was back.

'I've just got a message from the gate. There's a woman who claims she knows you. She says her name is Cory Reynolds.'

'Cory? Great. Can I go home with her?' I glanced over but there were too many vehicles now to see her.

The policeman had the sensitivity to pull a long face. I could now attest from close up that he was indeed good-looking in an overworked kind of way, straight dark hair, short at the sides and longer on top. Long-sleeved white shirt with a moss green tie completed the look. He was definitely the most smartly dressed person on this crime scene, hitting the note of classy gentleman rather than rumpled policeman, a modern-day Mr Knightley come to take your statement. 'Sorry, but I can't clear that yet. But she says she has your ... um ...'

'Panties?' I suggest. 'Bra?'

He looked away. Great: I'd managed to embarrass him. 'Yes. A dog apparently dropped them and made off with half a dress. I think Mrs Reynolds has the other half.'

I can just imagine the game of tug-o'-war that Cory had played. At least she persevered.

'I live with her – as a lodger – friend – not partner –' I'm rubbish at not spilling the beans to the authorities '– and she drove me here. She's got kids. I don't think she can stay any later.' I'm hoping the nice officer will say that they'll follow up at home tomorrow but I'm not so lucky.

'Then how about I tell her we'll drop you back in a squad car? Do you want your ...?'

'Yes, I want my underwear. I'm not an exhibitionist!' He doesn't have to say anything but we both look at the sodden remains of my newspaper. 'Not normally. God, wasn't anyone here ever taken with the urge to skinny dip?'

'When I was eighteen. Scottish loch. Bitten to death. Learned my lesson,' said the policeman, without cracking a smile.

'That would do it.'

* * *

I went behind a bush to reorder my clothes, hoping no one was getting an eyeful. With the jacket draped over my shoulders, I pulled up my blue panties and matching bra. Mum would be proud. I hadn't been run over by the proverbial bus and undressed in hospital, but this was close. My underwear had been on unexpected parade to various law enforcement officers, Cory and a dog, and I'd managed a matching pair. Point to me. I wriggled back into the scrubs and stood up.

The jogger was standing right next to me.

'Jesus!'

'Not looking, I promise.' He held up his hands, but I was not convinced. 'You disappeared and I just wanted to check you were OK. You've had a shock. We weren't introduced earlier.'

And if I had my way, we'd never be introduced. 'I'm fine, thanks.' I had to wonder if he had anything to do with the body, being the only other person on hand at the time. The sooner I got clear of him the better.

'Good. You're made of sterner stuff than most then. I'm Jago Jackson, by the way.'

I stood up straight, hand clasped to forehead. 'You're kidding me!' It was reassuring to find he was someone well known, less sinister somehow.

'You know me?' He sounded chuffed.

'We were only trashing – sorry, critiquing your book this evening. That's how I got into this mess. Decided to try out the wild swimming thing for myself. This is totally your fault.'

'You didn't like it?' He was talking about the book, not the swimming, but I decided deliberately to misunderstand him. This guy's ego had been stroked enough.

'Loved it – until the part with the dead guy in a boat. That kinda killed the buzz for me.'

'Yeah, I'm sorry about that.' Hardly Jago's fault but he had obviously decided to claim responsibility for all Thames Valley aquatic experiences. 'I hate that your first wild swim was spoiled.' I didn't say it was my first but I let him run with that assumption. 'You know, if you want, I could introduce you to some other great swimming spots? Ones that don't make it into the book – that I've kept to myself.'

'Er ...' How many ways are there to say no?

'Don't answer now but think about it. You might want someone to talk over this experience – someone who understands – who was here.'

What was it about meeting someone naked that made them think you might want to prolong the encounter?

'Mr Jackson ...'

'Call me Jago.'

I wanted to laugh – I couldn't take the name seriously – seems too Polo-and-Pimms to me – but that would be so inappropriate with a murdered man just a few metres away. His accent, I noticed, was trying for London rather than royal enclosure. 'Jago then. Thanks for the invitation, but ...'

He placed a card in my scrubs' top pocket. 'Call me. I'm easy to find as I'm a fellow at Linton College. I like the tattoo.'

I'd got a panther on my butt to match my sort-of-boyfriend Drew's. And, just like that, I was suddenly very sad and a little bit grateful that the Jagos of this world would flirt with me. My honey was yodelling with a yoga guru (she happened to be female and gorgeous – I checked), tying himself up in knots for her, and I was left wrapped up like old-fashioned fish-and-chips in yesterday's newspaper. But someone fancied that. I patted the card.

'Actually, thanks, Jago. I'll call you. Maybe. Really did enjoy the book.' That's not a lie. I had enjoyed arguing in my head with the author. That was a kind of enjoyment, right?

'Great. You never did tell me your name.'

'No, I didn't.' I smiled enigmatically and impressed myself by my restraint.

He laughed and turned away. 'OK then. Surprise me later.'

Wait, he was leaving?

'They're letting you go?'

'Yes. I gave my statement. Not much more to say than I saw you in, you know ...' He waved to the riverbank. 'And called them. Unfortunately, you were right: he is dead. They confirmed it.'

'You doubted me?'

'I thought you might've been a bit hysterical – maybe a victim of an assault or something? Something he did to you?' He gave me a searching look.

True. I hadn't been very coherent. He had come to the rescue, called the police, and helped me wrap the paper around myself, a process I thought he'd enjoyed a little too much. I suppose it was only logical to think I might've had a hand in the body ending up in the punt: a sexual encounter that had gone wrong would've been my assumption in his place.

'No assault, thank God. He was dead already when I found

him and I had nothing to do with it. Maybe they'll let me go too.' I looked around for the helpful police officer.

'Goodbye for now, mystery lady. I really hope you call.' He shook out his legs, stretched so his abs were on display, and resumed his much neglected jog, leaving by the southern gate controlled by the police. He'd have to run all the way round the outside perimeter of the park to get back to his college, not much fun in damp clothes.

It made sense, I suppose, that a wild swimming expert would live near here, one of Oxford's premier wild swimming spots. He probably said as much in his book but my local geography wasn't that good. I might've missed the clues.

A white tent had been set up over the boat for the forensic team to work undisturbed. They were too busy to be bothered by my questions so I turned to look for someone else.

... And walked directly into the tall, dark form of the jacket-offering policeman. But something must've changed since we'd last spoken because he was now shaking his head at me. Usually people took a few minutes of talking to me before they reached that stage.

'Miss Jessica Bridges? My colleague got your name correctly?'

'Yes?'

'Same Jessica Bridges as the one involved in the Jacob West case?'

I nodded warily and hugged my arms to myself. Someone must've run my name through a computer.

'So you've discovered another body. You really mustn't let this become a habit.'

Chapter 6

Jess

'It's hardly a habit.' I squeezed the bridge of my nose in a vain attempt to make life return to something more normal.

Normal? Jess, when was your life ever normal? When your father bullied you? When you ran away from home as a teenager to escape his abuse? When he plagued you with unwanted gifts and messages to win you back? When you got employed by a fantasist? I could go on.

'I'm Inspector George, Thames Valley CID.' He gestured me to take a seat on my bench again as he got out his notebook. 'Do you know how many people find dead bodies more than once in their life? Aside from policemen and fire officers?'

I held up my hand. 'Bet I can beat you there – I worked for an undertaker's until recently. Dead bodies were a daily occurrence.'

'I meant by accident.' I was amusing him, I could tell as his eyes held a glint even if his lips didn't curve. I expect the little detail that I had reported the murder while naked had also flagged up the incident in the control room by now. I

33

didn't begrudge him his humour. Usually a victim stumbling out of the bushes in my condition meant something unspeakable had happened to her; to be that way because of some overzealous pet and an impulse to wild swim provided him with some deserved light relief. I lived to serve.

'Then I think you know the drill by now, Miss Bridges.'

'Jessica, or just Jess, please.'

He still didn't crack a smile. Inspector George was a tough crowd. 'Miss Bridges, can you run through once more what happened here tonight?'

Finally, after the fourth repeat, bored out of my tiny little skull by the very few facts that I had, I was allowed home in a squad car. I was told that it would be helpful if I remained contactable for any follow-up questions. How there could possibly be any was hard for me to see but I agreed cheerily. Anything to persuade him to let me go. He could've asked for me to pledge my firstborn child and I would probably have said yes.

When I got back in at midnight, Cory was waiting in the kitchen. She had a bottle of wine in one hand and a box of camomile tea in the other. The tea made me think of Drew. He believed in the power of herbal.

'Oh, on a night like tonight: has to be wine!' I slumped down in the unforgiving wooden chair. 'What a mess!'

'They wouldn't let me inside the taped-off area or tell me what you found. All they would allow was for me to hand over the clothes I'd rescued.' Cory passed me a generous serving and helped herself to a similar amount.

Of course, they wouldn't. They didn't want the media swarming the place. 'I found a dead body.'

'Wow.'

'Yeah. I was looking for something to wrap myself in and came across a very deceased man.'

'Natural causes or had he had an accident?'

'Option three, I'd say. Very unnatural causes.'

'As in murder?'

I nodded.

'Jess, I have to say my life has become a lot more interesting since you moved in. Don't leave.'

I got up and we met in a hug on her side of the table. 'Thanks.'

Cory Reynolds, my saviour in Oxford, had taken me under her wing three months ago. My boyfriend had, quite understandably, decided that he needed some space. From me. *Just for a few months, Jess. I totally love you but I need to get my head together.*

Didn't we all?

We're not splitting up. Not at all. Drew told me it wasn't about me (*riiight*) but him. He was no longer sure that life in his dad's undertaking firm was where he wanted to put his creative energies. In fact, I'd even helped him come to this realisation, living in the moment as I do. (Yay, me). He'd never had a year off so Ron (Drew's dad) had agreed that time away to investigate if he wanted to become a yoga teacher would be time well spent. Drew talked about juggling undertaking with yoga instruction, which created some fascinating visuals in my head of whirling coffins and chakra symbols.

'If he comes back to the business,' Ron told me after Drew's announcement, 'then Glenda and I will know he really wants it for himself.'

And I supposed Drew's fleeing for the hills had been nothing to do with my total cock-up of Councillor James Cavendish's funeral. *Jess, how could you send the wrong body?* Quite easily as it had turned out. Or my arrest during the Extinction Rebellion sit-in on the Strand (I hadn't even meant to be there but just got carried away – literally in the case of the policemen who hefted me off the tarmac). On a normal march, Drew would have been sitting beside me but we were on duty at a service held in St Clement Danes Church in sober black suits. Apparently it wasn't right for the funeral directors to get sidetracked.

My life was one big sidetrack. I thought Drew knew that about me?

You can have too much of a good thing, he had told me kindly as he went off to the Austrian Tyrol to train as a yoga teacher. *Think of it as a fast – Lent for our relationship. A hiatus for us both will do us good and remind us why we are together.*

A 'hiatus'. Is that what they were calling it now?

And, anyway, who learned yoga in the land of yodelling and lederhosen?

More people than you'd think, he'd explained patiently as he kissed me goodbye at Heathrow.

That left me in the awkward position of being the sole occupant in the flat above the London-based family firm, Payne and Bullock, independent funeral directors. Glenda assured me I could stay, but maybe I should step back from helping out on the front desk? (I refer you to the wrong body debacle.) I should concentrate on my private investigator business. Like that was going so well. Ron said he liked seeing my cheery face around the place and I wasn't to worry that Drew's cousin, who was moving in to deputise for him, had to stay with them in Windsor rather than on the premises. Even I got that hint. So I moved out and took a spare room in Cory's house – *a change of scene will do you good. Give Oxford a go*, said Ron. I'd been alerted to that possibility via one of their neighbours (yes, I know, Ron and Glenda were gently managing me). Cory's husband had just upped and left for his old school sweetheart. Dumped wife needed the money and was happy for the arrangement to be a little fuzzy – or what the Inland Revenue might call 'a totally illegal cash-in-hand arrangement'. If anyone asked, I was a friend.

From fake friend I became a real friend.

Cory patted my back. 'You OK?'

'A bit shocked but I didn't know him so ...' Not like when I found Jacob and wondered for a while if Michael might've killed him.

My eyes went to the under-the-cupboard flip-down TV screen and speak of the devil ... Michael was frozen mid-pontification. I pushed Cory gently away and pointed.

'So, he's back?'

'Your Michael?'

'Not mine for well over a year now.'

'I saw this on catch-up while I was waiting for you. I thought I'd see what he was like.'

'And?'

'He's a bit of a dish, isn't he? Such a shame about the spinal injury, but somehow that only makes him more interesting.' Seeing my expression, she turned the screen off and it folded obediently away, hiding from view the chiselled jaw and auburn locks of my former partner. His looks were the best part of him, the Michael Fassbender of Oxford's Psychology Department. No, actually, it was the sex, then the good looks, then at the very bottom of the list, his character.

I slapped my forehead. 'I forgot the important bit!'

'Hmm?' She was getting the kids' bowls out for breakfast, ready on the side for her early-morning wake-up call. Life carried on despite murder.

'I met Jago Jackson.'

'You're kidding?'

'That's exactly what I said when he introduced himself.' I quickly explained the whole screaming to a passing jogger thing and our subsequent conversation. I played down the creep factor and decided maybe he was just being understandably intrigued by my Botticelli figure arising out of the Cherwell.

'I'm putting this on our WhatsApp group.' Cory grabbed her phone from the charging station.

'Isn't it a bit late?'

'They'll see it first thing. They'd never forgive me if they see it all on the news first and I haven't tipped them off.' She typed out a quick summary of my post-book club adventures and even took a quick snap of me in my scrubs. 'Do you think he'd come and talk to us?'

'I thought you all hated his book?'

'Not hated. Loved to hate,' she amended. 'Don't worry: we'll be really nice to him.'

'I'm not sure if I'm even seeing him again. Drew and I are still a couple. I think.'

'Exactly! You think but you don't know. I'm not saying sleep with Jago but he said he'd show you a good time.'

'He said he'd show me his secret ponds.'

'Same thing.'

I wasn't not sure it is. 'Cory ...'

She topped up my wine. How had I emptied my glass so quickly? 'Jessica, did your boyfriend not say he needed space to work out what he wanted?'

'Yes.'

'Then use the space to work out what you want.'

'I want Drew.'

'Do you? Do you really?'

I thought I did. I felt happy when I was with him. We were a team. Bonnie and Clyde. No, not Bonnie and Clyde – they went down in a hail of bullets. Mulder and Scully? Why aren't there more male and female partnerships to cite? 'Yes, really.'

'Then you won't leap into bed with Jago – or try water acrobatics with him. You'll just have a few fun dates and be confirmed in the feeling that Drew is the one for you.'

That sounded so reasonable but ... 'You just want to meet a semi-celebrity.'

'Yes.'

'You're not even hiding it?'

'No. Have another drink.'

* * *

I woke up to find it was Monday and I was supposed to be working. I did have a business that I was growing from a very modest beginning: a private investigation agency specialising in a lost-and-found persons service. It just about covered some of my overheads. I also had a part-time job as an office temp because I was realistic about the chances of making a go of finding missing persons as a full-time occupation. I was actually surprisingly good at working out where people hid once they vanished from their old lives. My method was a mix of research into their private lives (thank you, social media), psychology training, and gut instinct. Once you'd done this a few times, you saw patterns emerging. People were never really random in how they chose to disappear. If they chose to that is. I was also quite good at spotting the more sinister cases and persuading my clients to go to the police.

I had a deal with my clients. When the runaway was an adult, I promised when I found them to pass on news that they were safe and well, and offer a conduit for messages, but I wouldn't give away the location without the permission of the runaway. With minors, I asked for a contact in social services to act as intermediary. I knew from my own experience that you could never be too careful. My father had been good at acting the perfect parent to authority figures while being a complete bastard to Mum and me. His manipulation skills and use of terror tactics such as mysterious injuries to my pets or damage to belongings had made my teenage years a nightmare.

The work that I was waking up to today was of the office temp kind, rather than investigating. That had gone quiet over the summer but I expected it to kick off again when people realised their loved one wasn't coming back from that camping trip, holiday with friends, time at the other parent's, or what other lame excuse they'd been given. With a sigh – I hate you, Cory, and your wine supply – I tumbled out of bed and practically crawled into the bathroom. I stepped gratefully into the shower. I'd had one last night, but I didn't yet feel clean of the river. I closed my eyes in the stream of water, and couldn't stop recalling the face I'd seen yesterday. White male of about forty, maybe fifty. Close cut hair. Not in the best physical condition but not overweight either. Tan lines where he once wore shorts – too much pale skin for Speedos. Patches of dark body hair. A complete stranger to me.

I was only half an hour late when I managed to get to work. I was doing a few weeks of filling in while the PA to one of the partners at my book club friend Frances' law firm, Renfrew and Jakowitz, was on holiday. Frances had put in a good word for me and I got the job without sacrificing the cut to the agency who normally placed me.

I slid into my chair outside Grace MacDonald's office and hoped she hadn't noticed my tardiness.

'Jessica?'

Oh hell. 'Yes?'

'Can you come in here a minute?'

I went to the entrance of her private office. Only the juniors got to sit in open plan; all the partners had their own dens.

'Shut the door, please.'

Shit. That was it – I was fired.

'I'm sorry—'

'Are you all right?' Her enquiry cut across my lame apology.

'Yes?' I didn't sound very sure about it.

'Frances told me.' Mrs MacDonald wrinkled her freckled forehead. She was an extravagantly red person – red hair, red freckles, and even dressed in maroon suits in an 'eff-off' to the universe.

Thank you, book club grapevine.

'It did come as rather a shock.'

'Thank you for coming in, but we'd pay you for time missed under these circumstances.'

'That's very kind. Other than being a bit tired—' and hung over '—I'm really fine. In fact, I prefer to keep busy.'

'Good. At least he wasn't someone you knew.'

I nodded but I'd like to know who he was, just so I could put a living face to the dead one I'd seen. I'd also like to know who killed him and why.

But it was none of my business.

I could, though, do a little poking about if I got a name from the police or press. No harm done. Just a little shaking of the social media tree to see what dropped out.

Chapter 7

Leo

Leo sent a request down to records for a list of like crimes from the database before getting up to stretch. Looking around him, he noted that the incident room was humming with activity as the murder enquiry got under way. In these days of mobile policing, it was never the same station used for an enquiry, just where there was space for the team in the district. This time room had been found at the Kidlington HQ as the brass wanted to keep a close eye on proceedings. Great: the senior officers would be breathing down his neck. Just what he needed.

He brushed his fingers over his desk plant, checking the soil for dampness. It was fine for now. The bonsai, one of the first things he'd carried in from his car on top of a pile of files, was his sign to the team that he considered they had moved in and he expected it to be for some duration.

Leo would have been efficient in any case, even without the eyes of his bosses on him. He had already made sure his officers were fully briefed as they came on duty, the murder board with its timeline set up, and the search teams combing the rain-washed banks of the Cherwell, park and surrounding roads. Superintendent Thaxted had come in early for a full rundown of the situation and offered to inform the head of Kenneth Kingston's college once the family had been told. That grim duty Leo had already performed with Sergeant Boston at one in the morning – a bleak memory to add to the many bad nights he'd had as a policeman.

An email came into his inbox. Forensics weren't happy. The storm had blown through Oxford as forecast so that made trace evidence unlikely, and the body had been touched by Jess Bridges in her attempt to give first aid. A fuck-up but there was little anyone could do against Good Samaritans and nature. It was now midday and Leo hadn't slept, but he counted himself fortunate that he'd had the chance to go home and change mid-morning. Having flirted a few years ago with becoming the cliché of the policeman with a terrible diet and alcohol problem, he'd made sure he spent ten minutes over a late breakfast, granola and fruit, washed down with green tea. He only had to look around the office to see the health problems that could be his in the near future if now, in his mid-thirties, he slipped back into bad habits.

Leo's colleagues, at least the ones like Harry, considered him a 'wuss with fancy habits'. His defence? He wanted to live. He wasn't telling them that he'd only just survived his teens, thanks to some poor choices and worse parenting. Instead, he let his charge to conviction rate speak for itself – and the fact that he didn't get breathless if pursuing an offender. Everyone got mocked for something in CID. Some of the older ones probably thought him homosexual because they couldn't imagine a straight man acting as he did, taking care over his appearance and diet. Harry had even insinuated it to his face a couple of times, expecting Leo to be insulted. His expectations had not been met.

Not that it mattered, but he wasn't gay, as his reaction to the witness last night had made plain. He couldn't carry on a conversation with Jessica Bridges, 'small, blonde and built' as Harry so helpfully put it in his verbal report to the squad, while she clutched the *Oxford Mail* to her chest. She needed more than mail; she needed a full set of armour to stop unprofessional thoughts edging into his questioning. So he'd left her to get dressed in scrubs before embarking on an interview. It was as well that he'd done so because it had given him time to look her up and discover this hadn't been her first time as a witness in a murder enquiry. The mishandling of the Jacob West case by the Met had been enjoyed by all rival police forces eager to see the big boys fall. It had been fresh in Leo's mind as he'd actually met one of the victims, the psychologist Michael Harrison, at Hendon training college a few months ago. Superintendent Thaxted would not want her division to repeat any of those errors.

Stifling yawns, Leo assumed the noon report. The boss would want another update for the lunchtime newscycle.

'Come in, Leo. I hope you got some rest?' Superintendent Claire Thaxted was a slim woman with ash blonde hair well cut in a bob around a long, slightly gaunt face. She did triathlons for fun, which said everything you needed to know about her. Leo had gone running with her when they were on a senior officers' course and he'd had to pull out his best game to keep up.

'Not yet, ma'am. We've not had much luck with our searches this morning thanks to the storm that hit in the night. SOCO aren't getting much from the riverbanks. Fortunately, we were able to lift the punt off the river before the rain. They're going over that now but it looks like a college boat, available to everyone at Linton to hire, including conference visitors. DNA swabs will be basically useless unless we're very lucky. I'm pulling like crimes but it's too early to generate a list of suspects.'

'And the victim? What have we found out about him?'

'Kenneth Kingston. Forty-two. Former city financial wizard who took a job as bursar at Linton with resulting pay cut so he could spend more time with his young family. Worked four days out of five to do his share of childcare. Universally liked and admired.'

She tapped the blotter on her desk with her reading glasses case. 'Evidently not, as someone murdered him.'

Leo disagreed, as often people killed the ones they loved, but he left that thought unspoken. 'His wife couldn't think of anyone who held anything against him – not at work, not in his old employment, not in his private life. We'll check that but, from the early enquiries we've made, he's something of a local hero, volunteering for the local food bank in his spare time.'

'Spare time? That must be nice.' Thaxted got up and walked to her window which had the view of the gardens of the neighbouring estate. 'The family?'

'I left a victim support officer with them and have a constable on the door to keep the press away. Mrs Kingston appears to be alibied – at home with the children, putting them to bed.'

'And did Mrs Kingston have any idea why her husband was found naked in a punt?'

'No. They'd had a normal day – church, lunch with friends, a walk in Shotover country park and then he got a call. That wasn't unusual and she didn't ask for details. He just said it was some problem with the crew that's filming at Linton College this summer. He didn't think he'd be long.'

'His phone?'

'Not yet recovered.'

'You're going to the college, I assume?'

'Yes, ma'am. That's my next stop.'

'Tread carefully. The Master of the college is Norman Wiseman, former head of the Police Complaints Authority. I've rung him already to tell him about Kingston. He was audibly shocked and says you can expect full cooperation from all his staff.'

Her concerns that this must be handled sensitively made even more sense. 'I'll do my best.'

'I need better than best, Leo. I need perfect.'

It was rather a relief to find Harry hadn't yet made it in so Leo didn't have to tell him that he was taking DS Suyin Wong with him to the college. She was a highly competent young officer who had been tipped for the fast track; in fact, Leo could sense her nipping at his heels as they shared many of the same strengths. He could trust her not to put a foot wrong at Linton.

He brought her up to date as she drove down the Banbury Road. The houses got progressively larger and more expensive the closer they were to the centre of Oxford. Many of the Victorian mansions had become colleges, institutes or private schools. Their gardens were beautifully kept, croquet lawn standard, with lush borders bobbing with summer flowers. Perhaps they were too perfect, mused Leo, too much money spent on immaculate presentation, suggesting a professional team of gardeners, rather than the old style don taking a breather from his studies to deadhead his roses. Oxford was losing some of its charm to the influx of serious money.

'Saintly man ends up naked and dead: the papers are going to love that,' Suyin said acerbically when he'd finished profiling the victim for her.

'So far there's no hint of anything sexual in the crime.'

'But you have to go there, don't you, considering?'

'Let's just go there with an open mind, sergeant.'

'Yes, sir.' She turned into the residential street leading to the castle-like entranceway to the college. The Oxford under-graduates were away for the summer and had been replaced by flocks of language learners and conference goers. Linton was experiencing a different summer from the usual, as they had attracted a film company and were currently pretending to be living in the 1920s. The vintage Rolls Royce parked on the forecourt, women in flapper dresses and men in Oxford bags and blazers, made the illusion almost complete, if it weren't for the scaffolding holding the lights. They parked on a side road rather than risk getting entangled in that business.

'One of our witnesses is from this college, isn't he?' said Suyin.

'Yes, a don and a celebrity author. He's near the top of the list of people we want to talk to, but first I think we should tackle the porters and Dr Kingston's office.'

'Which one do you want to do, sir?'

'I'll do the porters. Let's get the key for the office from them. We need his mobile.'

'You think they already know he's dead?'

Leo glanced at her, surprised she'd even had to ask. 'Suyin, this is an Oxford college, and the university is a very small world. Everyone knows everything within five minutes of it happening.'

They entered into the lodge under the archway. A man who had the unmistakable bearing of a head porter, which Leo thought of as Mein Host crossed with Rottweiler, came to greet them. His stomach was straining against his mustard waistcoat under his black jacket. He was not in costume, but he might as well have been as porters had not updated their image since the nineteenth century.

'Can I help you?'

Leo held out his badge. 'DI George, DS Wong. Do you know why we are here, sir?'

'I do, Inspector. It's about poor Dr Kingston. I've been instructed by the Master to make sure the college offers every assistance. I'm the Head Porter, Robert Field.'

That made things a little smoother. 'Mr Field, my colleague

would like to see Dr Kingston's rooms in college and I have some questions for the porter on duty last night.'

'That would be me.'

'Is that right?' Leo hadn't expected the top man to pull the Sunday night shift.

'They were filming.'

Now it made sense. He didn't seem the sort to risk leaving such important matters to an underling.

Field cleared his throat. 'I had a cameo.'

Crystal clear.

He turned quickly away from Leo. It was too frivolous a topic to be dwelt on when a member of college had just been murdered. 'Bernard, please take the young lady up to Dr Kingston's rooms.'

'Right away, sir.' Another porter came forward and selected a key from a hook on the wall.

'Is that the only key?' Leo asked.

'Dr Kingston had a set, of course. And the cleaners,' said Field.

'So no.' Leo gave the nod to his sergeant and Suyin followed the porter out and across the quad, leaving him with Mr Field.

'Is there a place we can talk in private?' he asked. Outside a bus delivered a new batch of extras to the forecourt. They spilled like streamers from a party popper when the front door opened. A lighting crew, an older man with a young red-headed assistant, set up a bank of lights near the Rolls. A couple of sound technicians, one male, one female, rigged some microphones. 'What's the film?'

The Head Porter frowned. 'We're not to say.'

'Right.'

'To protect the stars.'

'Understandable.' Leo was guessing an Agatha Christie – the period felt about right.

'Very big names. They won't want any association with any of this.'

His attitude was irritating but Leo remembered his lecture on sensitive handling. 'Then we'll try and be in and out of here as quickly as possible then.'

The porter jingled the keys at his belt a little nervously. 'Inspector George, there is something I wanted to ask you. Your men are already in the boathouse and the film makers want that for a scene they planned to shoot today.'

The forensic team feared a far more dramatic scene had already played out there last night. From the early results on the blood splatter marks, they believed they'd found the site of the murder before the body was set adrift in the punt.

That made Leo wonder: why bother pushing it out in the punt rather than just leaving it there? He'd have to puzzle that one out later as he had more immediate questions that needed answering.

Mr Field was still speaking. 'They'd got it all rigged but I've had to put them off. When will they be able to get back in there again?'

'I'm afraid that depends on what we find but I can assure you that everything will be done as speedily as possible without prejudicing any evidence that might be there.'

'Of course.'

'I think it is safe to tell them that it won't be today.'

'Lad, pass on the bad news, will you?' This comment was lobbed to the scrawny young man, most junior of the porters, who had the frightened-rabbit look of someone terrified of his superiors.

'Yes, Mr Field. Right away, Mr Field.' He picked up the phone.

As the head porter led Leo to his office, Leo saw the junior porter smirk at his back. He revised his opinion that the lad was a rabbit, more a sly fox. There was something not quite right about the young man's attitude in the wake of a murder, just a slightly off note. Maybe the porters, with their access to all areas, would be worth a closer look as suspects?

'Mr Field, did you see Dr Kingston last night?' Leo asked, getting back to more immediate business.

'Not personally.' Mr Field offered Leo a chair but he indicated he preferred to stand. Even with all the windows open, the porter's office felt airless. 'I knew he was around. His bike was chained up in its usual place.'

'If you could show me that next?'

'Of course.'

'Any idea why he was here?'

'None. Everything seemed to be running smoothly and I was here if there were any college related enquiries.'

'But if you were involved in a scene, maybe someone thought they shouldn't bother you?'

He rubbed his chin. 'That's possible, I suppose.'

'Who else was here?'

'Simon – that's the lad on duty now. He didn't see Dr Kingston, I've already asked him. But he did admit that he was very busy, so Dr Kingston could've walked in without Simon noticing. We don't have a formal signing in process for college staff, only visitors.'

'May I see that list?'

'Of course, but you'll want the film crew's records as well, which we don't keep.'

'I'll ask them myself, don't worry about that. Mr Field, you'll understand I have to ask difficult questions as part of my duties.' This was the right button to push with this man.

'I understand.'

'Was there any suggestion, no matter how slight, that Dr Kingston was involved with anyone, anyone he might arrange to meet here to go on an evening punting expedition?'

Mr Field went to the wrong part of the question. 'None of the punts were signed out last night.'

'But one was taken?'

'Well, yes. Students have been known to copy the key to the padlocks. It isn't unheard of.'

'But you still have the master key?'

'Yes, and it remains in the lodge.'

'Hanging behind the counter?'

'Yes.'

'So if, say, a porter was distracted, it would be simple to take it and return it without anyone noticing?'

'Not simple, but possible.' Mr Field adjusted a pile of letters on his desk, ill at ease.

'Do you have CCTV in the lodge?'

'Of course.'

'I'd be grateful if you'd give this to us so we can check what was going on last night.'

'It only covers the front door and the desk.'

'That's better than nothing. Mr Field, about Dr Kingston and his ... er ... friendships.'

The porter puffed up. 'Dr Kingston was a happily married man. There was never anything like that about *him*!'

Whereas there was about other staff members? They'd check this through many conversations with staff and academics over the next few days.

'Was he particularly friendly, would you say, with Dr Jackson?'

'Dr Jackson?'

'Jago Jackson. He was there when the body was found.'

'Oh. I didn't know that. I wondered why we hadn't seen him yet this morning. What a shock for him.'

'Were they friends?'

'Dr Jackson and Dr Kingston?' Mr Field scrunched his forehead in thought. 'Nodding acquaintances only, I'd say. They move in different circles – the academic fellows and staff.'

'Would you mind showing me to Dr Jackson's rooms? I have some follow-up questions.'

Pleased to have something he could do without holes being picked in his procedures, Field got to his feet. 'Not at all. Follow me.'

Chapter 8

Michael

It's not every day you get sent a baby bird through the post.
A dead one.

Michael Harrison had been a little suspicious as he took
delivery from the DHL driver but persuaded himself that it
might be a book to review – the dimensions were correct and
it was about the right weight. Instead, he found inside a
wooden box – the kind cigars came in at Duty Free – and a
baby bird nestled in white tissue paper. Deceased, of course,
eyes blind before opening, scrawny wings ragged with black
feathers, obscene pink, grasping feet trying vainly to hang on
to life. It was easy to imagine how it had fallen from the nest
in the merciless way that nature has of wasting so many of
her offspring, favouring just the few to survive. His admirer
could have scooped it up off the pavement anywhere in the
last few days to wrap up for him.

Or killed it themselves?

A maggot crawled out of its beak. Michael considered

himself tough, but even he flinched in shock and threw the box away from him as if it were radioactive.

In a way, it was – broadcasting a fallout of hatred from some madman who thrived on spreading his brand of twisted hatred to those he probably didn't even know.

Michael felt a little better now. Over the shock, thanks to a stiff talking to and an even stiffer drink. As a psychologist, he knew that such things didn't come out of the blue. Only two days ago, he'd gone head-to-head on a discussion programme about the causes of social violence. His leftie opponent, Anushka Kapoor, had been one of those short-haired female warrior types with an ethnic background that made her a popular sign-up for BBC panels. She thought violent crime could be mitigated by reduction of violence in video games and on screen. That had led him to make some acerbic comments about those who take their violence from their bedrooms out into the real world, the ones who approach games to feed their existing propensity for violence. They watered the seed that was already there. He laid the moral responsibility for their acts squarely on their shoulders. That no doubt had annoyed a few haters, prompting today's offering in the post.

He went through his list of possibles from his social media crazy file. He'd lay good money on it being this joker:

Duckweed58 @Radsor16893 Aug 9
Replying to @DrTypeM
Harrison, you're a fucking fraud. You deserve to die.
Duckweed58 @Radsor16893 Aug 9

Replying to @DrTypeM

Your woman is going to suffer. I will spend a very long time explaining to her what a fuckup you are. She will pay for it. Then I'll come for you and kill you like a dog.

He poured himself a second Scotch and continued scrolling through the comments left on his recent Twitter posts. This made messages 250 and 251 from the same critic. He could be called Michael's most persistent admirer.

He was not impressed by the invective coming his way from Duckweed58, whoever he was. Or she, he supposed, but the tone sounded masculine to him and women still made up the minority of trolls online, thanks to their lower propensity to narcissism.

Michael glanced through the other messages in the thread. Duckweed was not the only one to write to him and there were many more contributions like this sent since his return to the TV but he was beginning to feel that Duckweed needed flagging with the authorities. Michael really wasn't happy that the man had his home address. How had he got that? Michael didn't advertise it and was ex-directory. He supposed the creep could've followed him home – that was easy enough to do and he hadn't been very vigilant recently. Oxford didn't feel a threatening kind of place. Not a very comfortable thought, though.

It would be as well to have this on file somewhere so no one could ask why he hadn't reported it.

He swirled the Scotch, enjoying the rattle of the ice in the cut-glass tumbler. His wife Emma had bought a set for him as a Christmas present – a his and hers – so they could drink together and compare notes on their days. Taken by cancer, she hadn't lived long enough to enjoy very many sessions. Jessica, of course, had broken one within a few months of them living together, leaving Michael with a solitary 'his' glass. There was probably a metaphor of widowerhood in there somewhere.

Michael had never used to feel physically at risk but his recent experience had changed his mind on that. He should probably report this bottom feeder. He would. In the morning. Duckweed could keep swimming in his invective for a little longer.

As for the 'she' encompassed in his ravings? Who did he mean? He couldn't mean Anushka Kapoor? They were only connected by virtue of the fact they'd been on the same programme. Michael decided that he would mention something when he next saw her. At the end of the programme, she'd predicted that the trolls would be coming out from under their bridges for him. It was annoying she was right.

The only other 'she' that had been linked to him in public recently was Jessica. Should he warn her too?

Hey, Jessica. It's me, your not-so-fondly missed ex-partner. I thought I should let you know of an unspecified threat, from an unspecified source, about an unspecified grievance. And it might not be for you in the first place.

Great.

He'd tell the police that she could be a target and let them decide.

Glass emptied, he put the Scotch back into the cabinet and locked it. Michael left a wry observation on the day's news on Twitter, letting his opinion prove overnight and gather the yeast bubbles of other people's reactions. He used to have to go into secure wards to find examples of deviant behaviour. Now they were screaming at him on a daily basis, rage unfiltered, freak flag flying. He sometimes wished he had Anushka's optimism that we could make it better, but someone like Duckweed? He was already on the reject pile and knew it. That was why he was so angry.

Michael pitied him. A little. Duckweed was even bad at being an inadequate.

His inbox pinged. A message from his publisher. The one good thing about the events of last year was the fame it brought and the subsequent boost in sales for his book about psychopathic crime.

> *Michael,*
>
> *Great news. Type M for Murder is shortlisted at the Frankfurt Book Fair for the European Non-Fiction award. The organisers want to know if you can come to Frankfurt on 17th October for the ceremony. They will cover the cost of your travel, plus a companion, should you wish to bring someone to help out.*

He had to grit his teeth. He didn't need a nurse.

> *Your German publisher will arrange a dinner and make sure you meet the key media contacts while you're there.*

Let me know if you can attend. I'll be there too, of course.
   Best wishes
   Petra

He'd go, there was no question, but he didn't want to appear too eager. He typed his reply but scheduled it to be sent after lunch the following day.

   Petra
   October is a particularly busy time but I will see if I can fit it in between speaking engagements. Luckily it is a Saturday so I'm hopeful it will be possible. I'll confirm if I will bring a plus one with me nearer the time.
   Regards
   Michael

Chapter 9

Jess

'Let me get this right: you go skinny dipping and find yourself in the middle of a murder hunt?' Drew's voice was lovely and warm, amused rather than shocked. 'Only you, Jess, only you.'

I hugged the phone to me. It was my lunch hour at the law firm and I was pleased I'd made the decision to call him.

'It could've happened to anyone, Drew.'

'You tell yourself that, sweetheart, if it makes you feel better.' There was a sound at his end. 'What's that?' He wasn't talking to me, but someone in the room with him. 'My friend, Jessica. She's fallen into another situation.'

He said it like he'd discussed my habit of stumbling over trouble with Nel already. And why wasn't he calling me his girlfriend, or partner even? We'd been living together for almost a year, after all.

'Nel says "hi" and hopes it all works out.'

I didn't want to say 'hi' back to Nel Addison, the gorgeous instructor with legs like a giraffe and bum like a peach (she wore orangey pink leggings in the promo video so I couldn't help the comparison). 'Thanks. Give her a cobra pose from me.' So I could spit venom in her eye.

Drew chuckled. 'I will.'

'So how's it going? The training?'

'Good, Jess, so good. I'm feeling more centred than I've ever been before. Do you know what deep peace feels like?' Of course I didn't. 'I really think there's something in this for me.'

He didn't mean to, but I was translating that into the subtext that I knocked him off-kilter, made his life too chaotic and fed him spiritual Big Macs. My slightly edgy undertaker, lover of bands Killing Joke and Metallica, tattooed so that every limb told a story, on a vegan kick for the last few months, had been destined to find Yoga. I'd have to let him work this out.

'I'm glad.' I was trying to be.

'The pace of life here is so restful. The views are incredible – mountains, alpine meadows ...' Peach bums, bendy giraffe legs, apple breasts ... 'I think it can teach everyone something, even the most sceptical eventually see the benefit. I've got so much I want to teach you. Hey, I tell you what: you can be my first student!'

Well, that sounded hopeful.

'If you sign up for my evening class, that is.'

That didn't. He was saying it like a joke but was it really? Was that the only way I'd get to see him?

'So you're serious about this?'

'Very. I'll need to look for somewhere with a studio space so I can take students at home, like Nel does here. She thinks if I keep up the training I'll be able to qualify as a trainer myself – keep spreading best practice.'

As long as that was the only thing he was spreading of hers. 'And what about your job at Payne and Bullock, Drew? What will your mum and dad say?'

'I'm thinking of going down to part-time, until the yoga takes off. I won't be leaving them in the lurch.'

I imagined Drew sitting in a rocket in a Buddha pose zipping off into space. It really didn't sound as if there was any room for me onboard, did it?

I wasn't one to beat around the bush. Tact was not my middle name. 'Drew, be truthful: do you see me as part of this new venture of yours?'

'Do you want to be? I thought you liked your missing persons work?'

'I do. I wasn't saying I wanted to join you in yoga teaching. I meant, us. Together.'

There was silence. 'Don't you want to live with me if I teach yoga?'

'It's nothing to do with the yoga. It's whether I fit in with your new life. I'm not exactly a soothing presence, am I?'

'I'm learning these techniques so I can be calm with you.'

Oh my God. I'd driven some men to drink with my ADHD impulses; this was the first who had been driven to yoga.

'Are we still together? Officially?'

'You know I don't care much for labels.'

But I found that I did. I very much wanted to know that I still had a label around my neck saying, 'If found, send back to Drew', and vice versa.

'I mean, if you wanted to date someone else, or I did, would we be free to do so?'

'We're on hiatus, Jess. You're free to do whatever you like.'

So that was what it meant! The sneaky bastard split up with me and didn't even tell me! He'd crept up behind and snipped off the label so I no longer had anyone to claim me.

I didn't know if I was infuriated or hurt – probably both. Whatever the storm of feelings raining inside, the result was that my voice choked. 'And when you come back? What happens then?'

'We'll pick up where we left off, if you want that.'

'Do you?' I could hear Nel calling again in the background and I lost what little control I had. 'Are you sleeping with her, Drew? Is this about her?'

'Jesus, Jess, do you have to be so suspicious?'

Yes, I did. But I found myself apologising. 'Sorry.'

'Look, I love you. Nothing changes that.'

But he didn't say whether he had slept with her or not. And I feared that Drew had the capacity to love a lot of people.

'I know you need reassurances – that's your character – but you mustn't worry so much about stuff. I've got to go. Next session starts in five and I need to focus.'

'And I need you,' I whispered, tears of frustration forming. Why did my relationships always go like this?

'What's that?'

Have some dignity, Jessica. 'Nothing. Speak later.'

'Yes. We'll talk this out. There's really nothing to worry about. Love you.'

I ended the call for the first time without reciprocating. I couldn't be a bloody parrot. *Love you, love you too.* Not when someone else clearly didn't.

What do I do? Get on a plane and drag him back from Austria kicking and screaming? That was my preferred option but I knew it was a doomed one. Go and join him to remind him what I can offer that Nel can't? Like an untoned body and chaotic lifestyle? I'd be better off staying far away so he could romanticise me.

What did that leave? Have such an awesome good time to report back on our next call that he was the one who began to worry that I might be moving on without him? I might have fallen into my old habit of making my partner too sure of my devotion to him, leaping on his texts and calls, never playing hard to get. I never learned, did I? I needed him to need me.

Michael used to do this thing where he would schedule replies to messages so it looked like he dealt with them much later. He explained it added to his professional cool. I sorely lacked a bit of personal life cool.

So I messaged Jago. Not a date, I stressed, but a dip.

Jago didn't play the professionally tepid. He replied immediately. *Send me your address and I'll pick you up 6.30 tomorrow for the first part of your magical mystery tour. Bring your costume – or not, as you prefer ;)*

I wouldn't normally send a man my address on a first date but I comforted myself that Jago was a public figure, not some scuzzy guy met through Tinder. The first thought I'd had in the bushes that he was the attacker had to be way off target. He was famous – sort of.

I went with impulse. When did I not?

6.30 it is, I replied, sending details of how to find me.

Summertown? Very nice. I'll be driving a white Nissan Leaf.

An electric vehicle – that seemed to fit very well with the public image. *OK. Sounds fun.*

And I even can promise everyone you meet will be alive. Jago

Maybe not in the best taste but that reminded me. I did a search for updates on the Parks Murder, as the press were calling it. The victim was still being referred to as 'the unidentified male' and the police were appealing for anyone to come forward who had any information to help with their enquiries.

I trawled through the most popular message boards where people appealed for information about family members who had gone missing, just in case I could spot anyone resembling what I remembered of the body. It was odd how quickly details blur. Pointless. I was not even remembering what the needle looked like in my haystack.

'Jess, do you have my tickets for the trip to Paris?' called Grace.

I'd been following the holidaying PA's system and had these printed off. Grace preferred that to an e-ticket. 'On my desk. You're catching the seven-thirty flight.' I glanced up at the clock. 'In fact, hadn't you better be going?'

Grace whirled out of her office like a matador's cape, snatched up the file, and headed for the door. 'Thank you, Jess. Good work. See you the day after tomorrow!'

With her gone, I no longer had to pretend to be doing her tasks. I'd got all that squared away already – except for that presentation for next week, but I had all day tomorrow to worry about that. With a quick look around the open plan to check no one was monitoring me, I tapped open my personal email to check for messages.

There was a new one from my website.

> *Dear Ms Bridges,*
>
> *I am a neighbour of Glenda Payne and an old friend of Cory – in fact, I'm the one who put you in touch with her. I understand from Glenda that you specialise in finding people. I'm writing to ask you if you will help finding my daughter. Angelica is a vulnerable girl of fifteen. I've appealed to the police but they say there is little they can do. They know where she is but she has told them she doesn't want to come back and wants no contact with me. Now they are saying my son isn't safe with me either and threatening to take him away. It's a nightmare. Please, please, help me contact Angelica so I can sort this out and prove to them that I am a good mother.*
>
> *Amy Mason*

Interesting. It begged the question: what made a 'good' mother? 'Good enough' seemed so much more achievable. I rang Glenda.

'Jess! How lovely to hear from you! How are you, dear?'

'Fine, thanks.' Apart from the dead body in a boat adventure – and the fact that her sneaky bastard of a son had broken up with me without letting me know.

'You must come to dinner at the weekend and tell us your news. Have you heard from Drew lately?'

'Yes, I spoke to him at lunchtime.'

'Lucky you. He only rings home once a week. He must be missing you.' Glenda at least believed we were still together, partly because she was on a mission to become a grandmother and I was her best bet.

'Not so much. He and his teacher Nel seem to be aligning their auras.'

She laughed. 'Don't be silly – she's no competition. He loves you. Anyway, she's forty, far too old for him.' And Glenda had had the same thought – and dismissed it. Had she never heard of cougar women? 'He's just excited by learning something new. He's always been like that.'

Like sixteen new positions for incredible sex? 'I was ringing because I had a message from Amy Mason.'

'Oh, Amy. Poor Amy. Yes, I mentioned you to her this morning. I remember how good you were with that runaway I met with you and thought you might be able to help.'

'Her daughter has run away?'

Glenda cleared her throat. Oh, we were entering awkward territory, were we? 'Not exactly. She's left, but with Amy's old partner, Roman Wolnik.'

I made a note of the name. 'Are they ...?'

'I don't know. I thought he was like a father to Angelica but you never really know, do you? He's a cold kind of man under the charm. Never stopped to talk unless he wanted something. Anyway, Angelica has cut off all contact with her mother and is now accusing her of child abuse. It's the first any of us have heard of it. Amy has a son with Roman – a sweet boy, Pawel, about seven, I'd say. Roman is now kicking up a fuss, claiming Pawel isn't safe with Amy and trying to get the boy handed over to him. Amy is terrified to let him have access in case he snatches Pawel and goes back to Poland with both children. It's all headed to the courts but Amy also has to prove to her social worker that she isn't abusive – all one horrible knot of problems.'

I clicked my ballpoint pen. I had to wonder, allow myself to think the worst. 'How well do you know Amy, Glenda?'

'She's a neighbour in Windsor. Across the cul-de-sac from us. Your Cory knows her – or at least their partners know each other from work. TV, films or something.'

I made a note to ask Cory for the low-down on Amy. 'So not that well?'

'I suppose not. How well does anyone know their neighbours these days? But I can't believe she would do anything so terrible. And Pawel seems such a happy little child. He doesn't seem to miss his sister very much, but then again, she is fifteen and he's only little, so I doubt they spent much time together.'

'Who's the father of Angelica? Not Roman too?'

'No, no. He was a soldier – an officer. Died in a roadside bomb in Afghanistan. Horrible tragedy – happened soon after we first moved in. Everyone was so devastated. And then Amy met Roman through grief therapy. He lost his first wife – to cancer – back in Poland. We were all so happy for her, especially after Pawel arrived.'

I found the situation interesting – that would be enough usually to take the case – but there was the added pressure here that I didn't want to let Glenda down.

'You know my rules – about not telling the one searching where their loved one is without permission?'

'Of course, dear. Roman's working in Oxford this summer – another reason I thought of you. I was expecting that Angelica might still be with him. Amy just wants someone who isn't Roman or the police to pass on a message for her to Angelica.'

'I can do that. Where's he working?'

'Amy and Roman are both employed by the same production company, which is making a big budget film set in Oxford.'

There couldn't be many of those happening at the moment. It should be easy enough to locate. 'OK, I'll see what I can find out. I'll offer her mates' rates as she sent me to Cory.'

Most of my cases were mates' rates as I found it hard to talk money with distressed clients. I needed to toughen up. This was my business after all. Doing what I do, I was hardly going to meet a happy customer, was I?

'Thank you. I knew I could count on you, dear. Dinner on Sunday? You could meet Amy then.'

I realised this had been Glenda's plan all along. I didn't mind as her scheme suited my purposes. It would give me a chance to form an opinion of Amy. 'OK. Sunday.'

'Don't do anything I wouldn't!' Glenda said brightly as she put down the phone.

Too late for that.

Chapter 10

Jess

A double-tap toot, in defiance of the early hour, announced my ride. What an idiot. It was like Jago thought everyone in Squitchey Lane should be up at 6.30 just because he was. I waved to him from my window at the front of the house to show I'd heard, then headed down to the ground floor.

Cory was already way ahead of Jago. Marshalling her children was a tightly scheduled operation that would put military commanders to shame. Her alarm was set for 5.45. She still managed to fold me into her planning as she scattered Cheerios on the children like fairy godmother blessings. Last night she'd told me all she knew about Amy – a neurotic, always on a new diet, but essentially a kind woman. Cory didn't believe the accusation of abuse. *Roman's a difficult man to like*, she'd said. *But then he gets on with my ex so that tells you everything.* She'd described Angelica as taciturn, like many teenagers faced by a well-meaning adult, and unimpressed by life.

'Got your costume this time, Jess?' Cory asked.

'Yes, Mum,' I teased. I was wearing a one-piece under my Looney Tunes T-shirt and black shorts.

'A towel? Water shoes?'

Benji was gazing at me from under a Zorro mask. Perhaps his hero crush had shifted? I was with him on that one: Tom Holland was cute, but Antonio Banderas ... Maybe I should get him a fencing sword, kid-sized?

I looked at Leah and considered the possible damage. Maybe not.

'Cory, I'm thirty-one. You don't need to fuss.'

'I'm three,' piped up Leah.

'I know, Lee-Lee.' I ruffled her hair in passing. She batted my hand away, as was our custom.

'Are you going swimming with your boyfriend?' Leah asked.

'Yes – but with a friend who is a boy. Not a boyfriend.' Such distinctions were lost on the under-fives. I said it more for Cory's benefit so she didn't spread the rumour on the book club WhatsApp, though I suspected I might be too late.

'I wanna go swimming.' Leah's face crumpled.

Cory presented her with a slice of apple as a distraction. 'Later, sweetheart. I'll ask Maria to take you to the pool later.'

Benji miaowed. I changed my mind about Zorro – Puss-in-Boots might be the intended reference. Still Antonio, but not quite as sexy.

'Have fun, you crazy people!' I called, remembering not to slam the door behind me.

Running down the path, I realised that I loved the whole silly lot of them. Very quickly they'd wormed their way into my heart and I'd do anything to make them happy. If not a sword, I could perhaps swing by a toy store later and see if I could get a cape. Black capes were so useful. Come Halloween I could dress Benji up as Dracula and persuade Cory to let me loose on trick-or-treating.

Did that mean I thought I'd still be there in October and not back with Drew? That thought shook me as I got into the car.

Jago was at the wheel of the Leaf. Until today, I would've expected someone looking like Legolas to drive a vehicle of this name, but Jago was more hobbit than elf, if the hobbit was played by Ben Whishaw. His curly dark brown fringe tipped over his forehead like a low diving board did a pool. I noticed that his forehead was scored with parallel lines like swimming lanes, not so much from age as he was about the same vintage as me, but from scowling while thinking. All those annoying tribes, no doubt, had hammered in those lines of displeasure as he sat in front of his Mac computer to insult us. He was definitely going to be a Mac user rather than PC, wasn't he?

But this morning he was all smiles. Jago slid into gear. 'Good morning, mystery lady.'

Oh goodness, I hadn't yet told him my name. He knew practically everything else about me, including that I was a natural blonde (think about it). That seemed wrong somehow. 'Hi, Jago. I'll put you out of your misery. My name's Jess. Jess Bridges.'

He chuckled, maybe thinking I was making a James Bond joke, but it was entirely unintentional, I promise.

'You can google me later.' I really hoped he didn't. He'd find the Michael thing, and possibly, if he dug deep, mention of the Eastfields disaster where I behaved very badly. I was hoping to put all that behind me. 'Where are you taking me?' I looked up at the blue sky. A weather front was coming in from the west but the morning was supposed to be pleasant.

'That would be telling.'

'So you want to keep your secrets secret?'

'And enjoy keeping you in the dark – as you did me.'

'Do I have to close my eyes or something?'

He indicated to pull out onto the Woodstock Road, heading back into town. 'I'll let you know when we get nearer to our destination.'

He was a surprisingly aggressive driver, bullying his way in front of other cars whenever he saw an opportunity. There was a wiry kind of survival instinct to him as he thrashed his way through the urban jungle paths that I hadn't expected from an electric car owner. I added that to my profile of him as considering Oxford his exclusive territory. I decided to probe a little more.

'Were you born in Oxford, Jago?'

'No, London. Can't you tell?' He sounded as if he hoped I could, a small city like Oxford not being big enough for his greatness. 'Born and bred. St Mary's Hospital, Paddington.'

I thought that was where the royals had their babies so I was assuming he had drawn first breath in the private wing, despite his London lad accent. He aimed to sound street but little bits of posh kept leaking through. 'Where did you grow up?'

'Kensington mostly.' I was correct. 'Dad works for the Albert Hall and we have a grace-and-favour apartment.'

I didn't think I'd ever heard anyone string those words together. He clearly moved in very different circles to me. 'And where do you live now?'

'I've a set of rooms at Linton College but I've also got a house in one of the villages nearby. I like living in college so I rent it out for the moment. I was lucky when I bought. Worth a fortune now.'

I headed off this property conversation. Not being on the housing ladder by thirty-one, or even formally renting, it was galling to hear my contemporaries congratulating themselves on their achievement of making the first few rungs. My position felt rather like missing the last lifeboat off the *Titanic*. 'And why wild swimming?'

'I wrote a book about hidden cycle ways.' He gave a cyclist a wide berth. 'This seemed the next logical step. Have you read it? It sold quite well. Picked up after *Wild Swim* hit.'

'Afraid not. Are you preparing for a triathlon then?'

'You would think, wouldn't you?' He overtook a bus just as it indicated to pull out from a lay-by. 'Might be a good idea for the next – to end the trilogy. Wild Running.' He was giving the bus driver cause to add to his own worry lines.

'I hope I'll be suitably acknowledged?'

'How about a dedication to my mysterious naked lady. That should get people intrigued.'

'You're never going to let me live that down, are you?'

'And why would you want to? It was the best moment I've had in ages – shook me out of my rut.'

Oh God, I could see that I was going to be an anecdote in his next book. 'You were in a rut? You, the wild swimmer?' I couldn't hide how incredulous I was at the idea. He sold himself as the opposite of rutted-ness.

He nodded as he reluctantly slowed for a pedestrian crossing by Oxford railway station. I was pleased to see his eagerness to get to our destination didn't include knocking a guy off a scooter.

'Hate those things,' he muttered.

'Hate what?'

'Motorised e-scooters. Ridiculous. Get a bike,' he shouted as we passed the scooter rider. The commuter didn't hear because he had headphones clamped over his mass of curly hair. He stood straight and still as the scooter whisked him along the pavement, like he'd been about to be teleported to his mother ship. To me, he looked blissfully happy. How could Jago hate him?

'I take it that scooterers – is that a word – are another tribe you despise?'

'They aren't my favourite social group,' Jago agreed. He gunned through an orange light.

'You don't like a lot of people, do you?'

'It's my trademark now. I'm unsparing with my criticism of pretence and fakery.'

'Aren't pretence and fakery the same thing?'

'No.' He didn't explain. 'Don't you find it irritating living surrounded by so many sodding people?'

'Not really.' Why live in a city if he couldn't bear it? As a writer, he did have a choice; he had even already admitted to owning a house in a village. I pointed this out.

'Why should I let them chase me away? It's therapeutic to

let it all out on paper. My publisher says that's why the books
sell so well. People either agree with me and enjoy seeing their
own moans put down for them, or they disagree and entertain
themselves with tearing me down – same process, just in
reverse. And we all go home happy – or happily unhappy.'

'So you know that you're outrageously prejudiced against
perfectly decent people just going about their own lives?'

'Oh yes.'

'Like Yummy Mummies.'

He pretended to shudder. 'The worst.'

'Where would the next generation come from if not from
the mums? We felt very got at when we read your book.'

He grinned. 'Good. I hope you ripped me apart?'

'We did.'

He braked for a red light. 'Hang on – you don't have kids,
do you?'

'No. Everyone else in the book club does though.'

'Good. I'm not great with kids. I rapidly run out of conversation.'

I was interested that he thinks this detail of my private life
might matter, as if this might be some kind of relationship
we were beginning that went beyond swimming. 'Hasn't
someone explained you don't have conversations with kids,
you play with them?'

'I think they forgot to mention it.' He tapped his chest.
'Only child.'

Why was I not surprised?

The car turned into a little lane leading to Binsey. 'Close
your eyes now, Jessica.'

When we got out, I discovered that he had brought me to the western bank of the Thames as it runs through Port Meadow, a huge water meadow that floods every year to become one vast lake. In the summer it is usually dry, and grazed by herds of cows and horses who wander among the buttercups and clumps of nettles. Picnickers, drone flyers and birdwatchers all vie for space on fine days. To the south of where we left the car was a marina for canal boats, little yachts, other water craft, owned by people living the kind of off-grid Bohemian life Jago extolled in his books (ironic considering there were few places more on-grid than an Oxford college like his). The spot he had found for our swim belonged to a defunct boating business. He even had the code to the gate.

'Don't worry about that.' He pointed to the sign warning that the premises were patrolled by guard dogs. 'The yard used to belong to a mate of mine. It's just a deterrent. He's thinking of redeveloping it – having a nightmare with the planners – so at the moment we've got it to ourselves.'

Once away from the empty boat showroom, it did get wild very quickly. The dockside on an inlet was beginning to fill up with rushes and willows but there was a little jetty that took us out clear of the undergrowth.

'Why do you like this, Jago?' I asked, looking a little doubt-fully at the slate green water.

'It's the freedom, I think. Most of the time we spend our lives inside bricks and mortar, sitting on upholstered chairs, staring at screens, not interacting with the natural world that honed us as a species.' He knelt and felt the water with his fingers, lifting them up to let them drip in a move that probably played well on camera. 'This stuff – this has been here since before humans, if not exactly in this spot, but somewhere close by. We get back in touch with that primitive self when we immerse ourselves in it.'

I spread out my towel. 'Here?'

'Right here.' He stripped off with the efficiency of a man who made a habit of this. He jumped in the water before I even had had time to bundle up my clothes and weigh them down with my sandals. I headed to the edge.

'Don't dive in,' called Jago. 'In wild swimming, you never know how the river or lake bed might've changed since you were last there. Feet first is much safer.'

I had been intending to slither in from the side but now felt obliged to jump. I did this with a kind of step out, arms spread, not wanting to go under. Water swiped up my body in a great Tinder 'yes!'.

'Oh!'

'Surprisingly warm, isn't it?' Jago was swimming strongly away now he'd seen me in safely. 'Gets that way in mid summer. Freezes your balls off in winter though.'

This was divine. I followed him with my reasonable breaststroke. I was not a bad swimmer. It was one of the few sports I had liked at school.

Jago turned back and swam right up to me. 'Living up to your expectations?'

'Going way beyond!' Then, foolishly, I splashed him – which gave him permission to splash me back. Our water fight moved on to some dunking which involved more bodily contact than we'd yet had and I thought that I might've made a mistake.

This was mixed signals territory. Too late now that hostilities had been started. Anyway, I lost the match as he was like a fish in water. No wonder he loved this so much.

'I surrender!' I declared, holding up both hands, then both feet to make my point.

He shook his head to clear the hair from his eyes, reminding me of an otter. If he had whiskers they would be triumphantly pricked. 'OK. We'd better call it a day – with me the acknowledged victor.'

I swam to the jetty. 'I came second – don't forget that.' I pulled myself out, conscious that he was not far behind me.

'Hmm-hmm, I won't.'

That sounded a little too appreciative. I wrapped myself in the towel. 'Thanks. This is a great place. It'll be a shame when the developers move in.'

'That's a city: you have to grab the good bits while they're still yours. Nothing lasts.' He got out effortlessly and shook off before reaching for his sports towel. I had a chance to admire his lean frame. He wasn't big like Michael, more like Drew's sinewy body, perhaps a shade shorter. He had the build you saw on cyclists in the Tour de France – strong legs and arms, no extra ounces.

'Thanks for coming with me. I enjoy swimming even more when I have someone to share it with. Makes me see it again with fresh eyes.' Jago hung the towel around his neck then showed he is a major planner when he pulled out two flasks from his backpack. 'Tea or coffee? I made both.'

'Happy with either.' Fully dressed again, I sat at a picnic bench outside the derelict showroom.

He poured me a tea and got out a little bottle of milk.

'What else have you got in there?' I asked hopefully.

'A full English?'

'You're joking!' I seemed to remember an anecdote from the book about a fry-up next to a reservoir.

'I am today – but I do have croissants. Will that do?'

'Amazing. Even better. Can I take a photo?' I raised my phone.

'Sure. But let's make it a selfie.' He took the handset and put his arm around me. I raised my cup in a toast as we both grinned into the lens. Oh my God, we looked a bit ... cool. Young and out there – whatever that meant. 'Left a bit so we can get in the jetty and inlet. There. Who are you sharing it with?' he asked as I sent it out.

'My book club. I've got so many brownie points for actually swimming with the author of one of the books we've read. The others are going to have to up their game.'

'Send me the photo, would you? Tell your friends that they could swim with me too if they want.'

'I was thinking more that they'd have to find one of the authors and do something with them, like have dinner or play tennis. Tough for our next book though.'

'What? Why?'

'*Great Expectations.*'

'Yeah, I don't think Dickens would appreciate being dug up to play tennis.' He presented me with a croissant.

'But he wouldn't mind dinner?'

'He was always fond of a good feast.'

I liked an intelligent man. 'Tell me you studied English Literature?'

'With Psychology. UCL. A lifetime ago.'

'Oh my word, I was a grad student there, five years back!'

He added some grapes to the breakfast spread. 'I'd left by then. Got disillusioned with academia for a while and went travelling.'

I had to ask, didn't I? 'But you'd know Michael Harrison – Dr Harrison – if you were at UCL?'

His lip curled. 'That fuckwit? Shagging on the shag pile was his preferred way to teach.'

Actually it was the couch but I kept silent, hoping he didn't look my way and see the confession on my face. 'Really?'

'He tried to pass me on to one of his more junior colleagues but I'd decided by then that it was a waste of time. Who needs an MA in Psychology?'

I did. 'Hmm.'

'I left London and went to India. Never looked back. Travel writing is my thing now – the psychology of place, you could say. It's what I did my doctorate on.'

'Psychology of place?'

'Like here: it's all in layers if you can see them – the meadow that used to be open countryside before the ring road crept too close; the canal that used to carry goods from Birmingham now carrying those after an alternative lifestyle; this boatyard with its short time as part of the leisure industry, now in that in-between state, like a relationship between engagement and marriage, before it becomes a housing development.'

I sensed I was getting a preview of the draft of his next article. 'So who are the planners in this scenario? The lawyers drawing up the prenup?'

He gave me a startled look. 'That's good – very good! May I use it?'

'It's your simile, not mine.'

'Thanks, Jessica.' He poured me another cup from the flask. 'So, do you know Dr Harrison as well or are you just mentioning him because he was the one who got out from under a murder charge?'

'Hmm?' I tried to sound non-committal.

'He got his name splashed everywhere last year – great marketing for his book.'

'Oh, yes, I know him. A little.' This really wasn't a good subject, not for a first date, er, *dip*. Moving swiftly along ... 'I was wondering, do you know if they identified the body we found yet?'

He made a gesture as if to hand a parcel back to me. 'That *you* found, you mean.'

I wondered why he was so eager to duck any association. Worried for his brand of clean living? 'OK, my guy.'

'They have identified him, yes. Didn't the police call you? I even had the press come round to interview me.'

'Why?' I went to my missed calls log. I was not very good at checking up on my notifications and I never listened to voicemail. Sure enough, there was a number that had been withheld, probably the police.

'To ask me if I knew him.'

'Did you?'

'Yes. He was bursar in my college. I came across him a few times, at college events and the like.'

He didn't seem that upset that a work colleague had been bumped off. 'You didn't say anything yesterday.'

He looked away. 'I did, to the police. But I wasn't a hundred per cent sure.'

I was suddenly very aware that coming to a desolate swimming spot with a guy I hardly knew wasn't my best life choice so far. 'What was his name?'

'Kenneth Kingston.'

'Any other details of what happened to him?'

'None. But I imagine the press will have got some by now, if you're interested.'

I scrunched up the napkin he had given me to go with the croissant. 'I'll read up about him later.'

'Why?' Jags slipped his polo shirt back on and we gathered the rest of our picnic.

'You'll probably say it's silly but I feel connected to him.'

He chucked his bag in the boot of his car. 'Not silly, but you do know that you're not connected by anything but death?'

Chapter 11

Michael

The bedside alarm went off and Michael lay looking at the ceiling for a long moment. Sunlight was dancing as branches tossed outside in a fresh breeze. He didn't like the summer very much. Life had more purpose when he could be someone of importance at college rather than that man in a wheelchair next-door, the one you nodded to when you put out the bins. Whereas at college it was *Good morning, Dr Harrison. Interesting seminar, Dr Harrison. Lunch in the pub, Michael?* These days, he was even more of a someone at Oxford, having been through the spin cycle of disgrace and rapid rehabilitation. There was nothing like a bit of notoriety to make students and colleagues sit up and notice; it got him this prestigious post after all.

He missed his ease of movement. He could now stand for short periods on crutches, though for difficult journeys outside the house he didn't want to risk a fall. L4 break – the doctors told him that it wasn't the worst spinal injury and he might one day be able to walk again. Not yet though.

He pulled himself up and considered his day. He had to remember that his situation had improved over the last year. Fortunately, the maddeningly unfair accusations of inappropriate behaviour with female students had been left behind at UCL. In his defence, there had only been one graduate – Jessica – and they went on to have a relationship of almost five years. Hardly a fling. Two consenting adults agreeing to an affair, then to live together. Before that, he'd been married and there had been only Emma. Before that? Well, he'd been younger and more foolish but nothing that stepped over any lines. Not as society understood them then.

These days you had to be so careful. You couldn't comment on someone's appearance or touch any part of them, even as a gesture of comfort. They could've lost their parent/partner/child and you had to commiserate from afar like they had an infectious disease. It was very bad for the human psyche – all people were animals under all their layers of civilisation. Touch was essential.

He noted, though, that he was something of an exception. People assumed they could touch him – lay hands on him might be a better description.

'Oh, Michael, you're so brave.' This said with a heavy hand on his shoulder.

'You've done so well coming back to full-time work.' Hand on his thigh in a disappointingly asexual pressure.

'I admire your courage.' That accompanied by a chaste peck on a cheek by a fellow psychologist from California whom he'd been hoping to persuade to come back to his hotel room with him. That ambition went down in flames.

God, Michael, don't you get sick of yourself sometimes? Enough moping. It was getting late and the best of the weather was forecast for the morning. Once in the chair, he decided today was a crutches day – until he got tired. Carefully getting his balance – a fall could set him back months – he propped himself on these and made his way to the kitchen. Fernanda had been in yesterday so all the pathways were scrupulously clear of clutter and every surface gleamed. There were some compensations living alone.

With the help of a designer friend, he'd given a lot of thought to how he wanted to arrange his kitchen. Everything was within reach: a small countertop fridge, the cereals, the fruit bowl. The bowl, spoon, chopping board and knife were already waiting. He made breakfast methodically, selecting what he ate with care. He needed his strength, particularly upper body strength, to get around. He couldn't neglect lower body either. It was much harder to get back what you had let go. Wise words that covered more than just muscle tone.

Breakfast made, he switched on the morning news to keep him company while he ate. Christ, world politicians were an evil crew, fiddling while Rome burned. It was almost a relief when the anchor moved on to ordinary crime. A stabbing in London. A murder much closer to home in the University Parks.

'... Police have identified the victim as Kenneth Kingston. Dr Kingston, bursar at Linton College, a church warden in Headington, husband and father of two, was found dead on Sunday night by a late-night swimmer. The body had been left in a punt moored at the popular Parson's Pleasure swimming spot in the park. The swimmer who came across the body raised the alarm with passing local celebrity author-, Jago Jackson, author of *Wild Swim*, who was jogging in the vicinity.'

The name caught Michael's attention and he looked up from his diced melon. Jago Jackson. He couldn't seem to escape his old student. Jackson's profile had been growing since he had appeared in a documentary and published a couple of books on the joys of catching Weil's disease in the dubious rivers and ponds of the Thames Valley. The man hadn't mentioned that? Why was he not surprised?

The reporter cut to an interview they'd done in the author's home. He'd got some cushy rooms in Linton College, with a view of the river. Copies of his books were arranged casually beside him, like he'd just put them down when surprised by a call from the press. Poseur.

'Dr Jackson, you were jogging in the park on the night of the murder?'

'Oh yes.' Jago hadn't aged well – already had lines on his forehead. Kept his curls though. Michael had rather thought he'd lose them by thirty as he always had a high hairline. 'I was following my usual route. Just a quick five k before it gets too dark.'

Michael had never liked the guy as a student – too arrogant by far – and he saw that he hadn't grown out of it.

'And then what happened?'

'I heard a woman screaming, and I thought, well, you know, that someone must be attacking her? So I ran towards the noise.'

'You ran *towards* her?' The implication was that Jago had been so brave.

'Well, yeah.' He managed a sheepish look from under his fringe that reminded Michael of Princess Diana. Bashful calculation. 'I find this woman, er, a naked woman, dragging a punt onto the bank. I gathered from what she said that she'd been skinny dipping and stumbled over the body. I went over to comfort her –' *I bet you did, mate* '– we pulled it ashore and I called the police. That was the end of my involvement.'

'You didn't know at that time that you knew the victim?'

'I only had a few dealings with Dr Kingston but I know enough to say that he's a great loss to the college.'

'Have you anything else you'd like to say?'

'Yeah, thanks. I've swum in the river many times before and I've never heard of anything like this happening. People shouldn't give up the chance to discover the joys of wild swimming just because of one random and tragic death.'

The piece cut back to the studio and the anchor filled in a few more details about the victim. Michael's suspicious mind thought that someone so blameless – churchwarden? – must have been hiding some dirty secrets. Else how would he have ended up dead in a boat?

Another familiar face came on screen. DI George, the policeman he'd met at Hendon earlier in the year. He'd come across as far more intelligent than the average senior officer, but so buttoned up that it was hard to know what was going on inside. He gardened like it was his religion, his superintendent told Michael.

'We are appealing to anyone who saw Dr Kingston on the

night of the murder. Dr Kingston had been called away to a late meeting at college. We believe he was lured to the college boathouse. There he was attacked. Robbery is a possible motive as none of his personal possessions have been recovered despite the best efforts of our divers searching the riverbed.'

A reporter got in a question, interrupting the statement. 'What personal effects might the public be on the lookout for?'

'Dr Kingston was carrying a black messenger bag containing a laptop, wallet, keys and papers. He was wearing dark grey chinos, white shirt and no jacket. His shoes were black leather slip-ons. He also had a plain gold band wedding ring and a FitBit style watch on a black strap.'

When George had said no possessions, he really had meant none. The poor sod must've been stripped to the skin. A sex crime? Had the call in to work been a lie to disguise the fact he was meeting a lover? Maybe he had been a closet homosexual? He wouldn't be the first.

Michael had seen enough. He turned George off and put the bowl and chopping board in the dishwasher. He was aiming to go down to the end of the garden and back but, before he could attempt this, the cat-flap rattled and Colette appeared. She'd been off her food recently and he suspected some other neighbour was feeding her. In response, he'd improved his offer and moved on to an expensive tinned variety rather than kibble. It seemed to have won her back.

'Been having fun?' he asked as he loaded up her dish. She now ate on the counter as it saved him tripping over her bowl on the floor.

She gave a purr and dived in, gulping it down as if she feared he'd snatch it away from her. Emma, who got the cat for him shortly before she died, would've told him off for indulging her; Jessica would just laugh and tease him that he was an old softie.

As he stroked Colette, he realised that he was missing Jessica. He always missed Emma, of course, but she was far out of reach now. Passed away six years or more. But Jessica was still very much alive. He missed her presence in his life; he was missing her today as a friend. She had come through for him when it counted and she had kept in touch during his recovery, as well as looked after Colette for him. She was living with her undertaker boyfriend now – strange bloke, alternative, he couldn't see that lasting – but Drew wasn't the jealous kind. Michael decided to send her a text, just to touch base. Not because he was crushed by a feeling of loneliness. No, not that.

Michael, you're such a fraud.

His twenty steps could wait. He'd message her now.

Chapter 12

Leo

In the incident room, Harry shoved the laptop away in disgust.

'There's nothing there, Leo. Simon Potts, the porter, may be an annoying git but he's got no previous, no opportunity if the CCTV feed is to be believed.'

Leo nodded. He'd put Harry to checking the footage from the front desk, a thankless but necessary task. 'OK. At least we can eliminate him.'

Harry reached for a biscuit from the team's tin. They all contributed to a communal refreshment fund but Harry always took the lion's share. 'That Field man, the head honcho, now he's in and out of the lodge like a randy man at an orgy. What about him?'

Leo went to the coffee point and poured hot water on his green tea brought from home. The office teabags would strip the enamel right off your teeth. 'I've interviewed the director of the film unit. Field was on set for his cameo as he claimed. I'm not saying he couldn't have slipped away while going to and from the location in the college, but I don't think it's likely. Also, I can't see a motive. No one reports the porter having any beef with the bursar.'

Suyin came in with another stack of interviews and placed them on Leo's desk.

'Anything? Please say there's something.' Leo sat down to read through the reports. There were scores of conversations that would've taken many police hours to gather.

'Nothing stands out, sir. Some aggro with the catering staff about overspend on their budget but nothing worth killing for. The Master of Linton said he'd never known a better financial officer.' She poured herself some fizzy water from a bottle she kept in the fridge. 'He is very keen we come up with a result.'

As if they weren't.

'Picked up anything between Kingston and the man who was there when they found him?'

'Jago Jackson? Nothing, sir. Cordial but distant – that's both how Jackson describes their interaction and the impression I got from others who know the two men.'

'Still, the fucker was there when the body was found. Convenient if he left DNA during the attack to be there to haul the body ashore,' said Harry cynically.

'We'll take a close look at him,' agreed Leo.

Harry circled in his chair to look at the photos on the board they'd created. 'What about the naked bird?'

'Jess Bridges? I can't see a connection – she's new to Oxford, was with her friends until shortly before finding the body. I think we can rule her out for the moment.' Leo leaned back and laced his hands behind his head, thinking. 'Unless something else crops up during interviews, it looks like this wasn't a workplace grudge or argument.'

'Stripping him naked suggests something personal,' said Suyin.

'Humiliation?' Harry frowned. 'Or sex?'

'No recent sexual activity according to the pathologist,' said Leo.

'Poor bugger.'

'Nobody I spoke to had any idea of anything extra-marital going on, so if the boathouse was some clandestine assignation, then he kept it very quiet,' said Suyin.

Leo shook his head. 'No, it doesn't feel sexual. A single blow over the head – that feels efficient. Calculated. One blow, job done, no further damage to the body. Someone with an emotional reason to hate him would've done more.'

'Who else do we have?' asked Harry, brushing crumbs off his shirt and over his computer keyboard. 'No students at this time of the year.'

'The film crew and the actors,' said Suyin. 'We've interviewed everyone on set that night. The production account, who did know him, was at home in London. She's not needed on set during filming. Everyone else who was there didn't know him, even by sight.'

'Or said they didn't,' said Leo. 'Let's see what we can find out about the cast and crew. Kingston worked in the City before coming to Oxford. Maybe this goes back further than last Sunday?'

Suyin handed him the list of those involved in the shoot.

Leo's eyebrows winged up. 'That many?'

''Fraid so, sir.'

'We'd better get started then. Spread the names out among the team and see if we can find any connection to Kingston. He was in finance. Maybe he pulled funding on a film, or lost someone's savings way back, ruined a career?' He rubbed his hand over his face. 'No, that doesn't feel right. That would have been revenge – more personal.'

'We still have to look though, don't we?' said Suyin.

'That's right. We still have to look.' Leo pulled the list towards himself and marked off the As.

Chapter 13

Jess

I was still feeling the rush of the wild water swim as I sat at my desk. With the boss in Paris, I was enjoying going through the motions of being gainfully employed, opening post, watering the office plants, tidying up Grace's PowerPoint presentation. I felt a little as if I was acting a role, like a girl trying on her mother's high heels for size and smearing lipstick inexpertly across her lips, but no one else seemed to notice. My acting had to be good enough to pass. I'd read about this in my psychology books – imposter syndrome. Apparently many of us suffered from it, especially women. It was that moment in the meeting where you suddenly thought, 'what on earth am I doing here among these grown-up people?' Or 'how can they possibly entrust me with this million-pound budget to spend?' Each of us carried that little girl around inside us who sneaked out and tripped us with her skipping rope at unexpected moments.

I'd just completed a search on Kenneth Kingston. There were more photos of him online than I expected as he was active in his local food bank over in Headington, volunteering as a driver to collect the contributions from Oxfordshire churches. *A lovely man.* The phrase came up over and over. The way he had been murdered tainted all that. Somehow being found naked rather than just bashed over the head undid years of being above suspicion. It was extremely unfair as it might well have not been his choice. Mind you, it had to be hard to undress an unwilling person. Held at knife point maybe?

I closed the search window as another of the partners in the firm wandered my way.

'Everything all right, Jessica?' Terry leaned against the filing cabinet that separated my area off from the rest of the open plan. I didn't feel crowded: a jovial butterball of a man, he was friendly and very gay.

'Fine, thanks, Terry.' I looked busy, flicking open the printout of the presentation I'd already finished.

'Got enough to do? Because I know Linda would like some help with a big archiving job I've just given her.'

'Right. I'll go over to her when I've finished this. Grace's presentation next week.'

He gave the cabinet a little tap as he went. 'Ah yes – the famous presentation. Put in some jokes, will you? She tends to keep it very dry.'

I actually found myself considering that suggestion – there were plenty of lawyer jokes on the internet, after all. What was I thinking? Grace telling a joke was like asking the Queen to tap dance at the opening of Parliament.

That would be awesome though and give the final season of *The Crown* something different to write about.

I pressed my knuckles to my eyes. Was anyone else's brain like this? I missed my Ritalin. That had helped me focus but my doctor, Charles, had weaned me off all medication and stressed the importance of mental exercises to achieve the same effect. I'd been abusing them a little – OK, a lot. I'd become a complete chemical stew, lost touch with reality, and fallen into what he called negative patterns of behaviour. I called them self-harm and slutting around. Now look at me, almost a year later, living a blameless medication-free life, keeping my libido in check, and only indulging in impulses that didn't harm others.

Mostly.

He was talking about reducing our sessions as he knew I couldn't afford them. Somehow he had it in mind that I'd cope on my own, that I'd crossed the tightrope and come to rest at the other side. In fact, I was swaying in the middle, clutching on to the balance pole for dear life – and he was thinking of walking away and leaving me to it. He was my balance pole.

Not a good idea.

My phone pinged and I saw to my surprise that I had a message from Michael. It had been months since we last communicated. I'd been keeping quiet the fact that I'd followed him to Oxford. I didn't want him to get the wrong idea.

Hi Jessica. Michael here.

He seemed to forget that his name was stamped at the top of every message he sent me.

How are you? Would you like to come up to Oxford for a drink and catch up?

Would I? I knew Michael hated the holidays as he now lived alone and could go days without seeing anyone. If I went, it would be another thing to tell Drew about my amazing social life. He never liked Michael, for a good reason seeing how Michael once hit me. A spur of the moment thing, but it still stood between us.

In my pause for thought, Michael had added a sentence.

I've got something I need to tell you.

He could always get me with curiosity – we both knew that.

OK. When?

Busy tonight?

I wished I could say I had plans but I was in fact at a loose end.

Fine. 7?

We agreed a time and place and I put the phone aside.

A little bored and not ready to succumb to the grunt work that Terry had dumped on Linda, I ran a search on the woman whom Glenda had referred to me. Amy Mason. She appeared on a business network site. I belonged to all of them as it was the easiest way to see someone's work history. Glenda was correct: she was currently working as an assistant to one of the big productions. Reading between the lines I thought she was basically the personal assistant for one of the actors, a rising star called Jonah Brigson. He'd been around a lot recently in that way that success breeds more success. With a face that wouldn't launch one ship, let alone a thousand, and chequered past, including a long stretch in prison, he had become the directors' darling. He oscillated between bad guy and misjudged hero. I wondered what he was like to work for. I supposed I could ask Amy about that at the weekend.

Deciding to dig further, I looked up the partner who now had her child, Roman Wolnik. He joined Jonah in the looks department rather than Michael, more bruiser than beauty, and I was surprised to find that he was a set designer. I'd have him down as trucker or bouncer. Never judge a book ... He too worked for the production company, specialising in set dressing. Need a 1920s train ticket? No problem. Want a recruitment poster for World War Two? Coming right up. How about packaging for dragon feed? My pleasure. That sounded a great career! If I could draw, I would totally train as a set designer. My imagination was wild enough to supply the ideas; such a shame all technical skills were lacking.

Concentrate, Jessica.

The film was being made at Linton College. That was a fortunate coincidence as I now knew someone who had rooms there. I'd have to persuade Jago to invite me. So they were both going to work at the same place each day with this between them? That had to be super-stressful for Amy. I supposed they could go without meeting each other if they wanted to avoid it, Amy sticking with her A-lister, Roman with the techs. But would you avoid the man who had stolen your daughter? Wouldn't you want to sink a knife into his back and kick the body? I mean, come on! I couldn't be the only one.

I ran the daughter's name and found she was active on Instagram. Naturally she was – she was fifteen. I clicked to follow her. It really shouldn't be so easy to get a ringside view of someone's life, not when they were that young. There were lots of pictures of her with Roman and none with her mother. Roman and Angelica kite-surfing. Roman and Angelica at a football match. Going back a bit further, Roman, Angelica and little brother Pawel fishing. This must've been taken by a fourth person. Amy? It was the only suggestion that Amy existed as all other traces had been wiped off Angelica's news-feed.

I posted a cute picture of a kitten to my own account in case Angelica followed me back. My Instagram was purposely anodyne so as not to alarm anyone who found me shadowing them. And besides, I liked cats. Maybe the worst thing about breaking up with Michael had been losing Colette?

I managed to avoid the archiving task and leave on time. The lawyers' office was in Botley, so I took the bus then walked the last half mile to Michael's. He lived in a new housing estate called Waterways, built by the old iron works on the Oxford canal. We met at a nearby gastro pub, The Duke of Wellington on Walton Street. This had gone so far with its old vibe to have passed out on the other side into an uniden-tifiable period in history. A Platonic ideal of a pub. Food on chopping boards? What was with that? Didn't they realise plates had curved edges for a reason?

I shouldn't mock. Michael liked it, even the tartan uphol-stery on the pew style benches. And the food and drink were first rate as long as Michael was paying.

Should I let him pay? It had been his invitation. But we're no longer a couple and we're not dating ...

Michael settled that dilemma for me. 'Jessica, thank you for coming. Let me get the first round. What'll you have?' He scooted over to the bar and got served immediately. He always managed to command the attention of barmaids the world over. She brought the order over to the table for him, all smiley hair flicking and Ukrainian cleavage. He would be in there with a chance if he only noticed but he was keeping a respectful distance, even flinching back when she patted his arm. I wondered if he'd lost some of his old confidence?

'You're looking well,' I said. 'How's everything?'

'Not good. I think Colette's two-timing me.'

'What a bitch – or whatever the female cat equivalent is.' I paused as I consulted my mental dictionary. 'Weird – there isn't one.'

Michael toasted me with his beer, used to my little digressions. 'Cheers. I think I've won her back – bribed her. And you? You're looking happy.'

'Am I?' I didn't feel that way, not with Drew yogic flying out of the picture. 'I guess that must be due to my early morning swim.'

'Christ, don't tell me you're risking Weil's disease too? You can't move this summer without people jumping into ditches.'

'Actually, Michael, for your information, I was taken to a hidden swimming spot by the world expert no less. Jago Jackson. He's an old student of yours, he says. Did you see his documentary?'

Michael pulled a sour face. 'Making quite a name for himself these days is our Jago, preaching his gospel of getting back in touch with your primitive nature. How did you meet him? Through UCL?'

I laughed and shook my head. 'Hardly. We didn't overlap. It was very weird but—'

Michael's face changed and he went very still. 'That was you – finding the body?'

'Um, yes.' I sipped my Peach Bellini. 'How did you guess?'

'Saw the news. And it seems like the kind of thing that might happen to you.'

I wondered why all the men in my life thought I was particularly likely to stumble over a murder victim while naked. I mean, it *was* my first time.

Michael took my silence the wrong way. 'Sorry, Jessica. That was thoughtless. It must've been upsetting, particularly after last year. Bad memories.'

'No offence taken. It didn't feel the same at all. Very surreal. And I didn't know the victim.'

'Why were you in Oxford?'

'I ... er ... I'm working here for a while. On a case.' This was kind of the truth.

'So you meet Jago in the park and decide to strike up a friendship?' He spun a beer mat. 'United by a shared experience.'

'Jago was a total gentleman. He helped wrap me in the pages of the *Oxford Mail*.'

Michael laughed. He actually threw back his head and guffawed. I grinned. Most of the time I liked making other people laugh. 'Now that does sound a classic Jessica moment. God, I've missed you.'

'Don't lie. I drove you crazy.'

He grew serious. 'But you were always able to make me laugh and I miss that. My life is far too serious.' He took a sip. 'How's Drew?'

I wondered if I should hide what was going on. But why? I was never, ever, ever, getting back together with Michael as a certain Pop Princess would sing. 'We're on a hiatus.'

'Bullshit.'

'He's training to be a yoga instructor in Austria and taking a break from everything.'

'Including you?'

I shrugged.

Michael nodded as if I'd confirmed something for him. 'So that's why you're working here. I told you he was a prick.'

'He's a guy. It goes with the XY territory.'

He saluted me for that riposte. 'And you're in limbo. Should I read anything into the sudden decision to go swimming with Jago Jackson?'

Probably. 'No.'

'Jessica?'

'Maybe a little. I don't want to look pathetic.'

We moved on and chatted about his book tour and return to the screen. I reciprocated with an edited version of my news and told him about the family Glenda had asked me to help. Michael had always been useful in the past as a sounding board. He spoke the same psychological language as me.

'What's your reading of the family dynamic?' he asked.

'Don't know yet. I've not met Amy. You have to feel for her though, don't you?'

'Unless she did abuse the kid?'

'Or Roman has got his claws into the girl and is weaponising Angelica?'

'True. That's more common than you'd like to think. Jessica, I did have something I wanted to tell you.'

I hoped it was nothing like he wanted me back, or that his treatment had encountered a setback. 'Uh-huh?'

'I'm being trolled.'

It was funny hearing that sentence coming from Michael's lips. I associated it more with feminist commentators or celebrities. I supposed he might be one of the latter by now. 'Why?'

'Does there have to be a why with a troll?'

'I suppose not.'

'My troll has recently upped his insults. They now include not just me but anyone who knows me.' He paused. 'Or loves me.'

There was an awkward gap. I didn't love him any more but I did care. 'I see.'

'He's threatening a female who he thinks is close to me. It could be a colleague, someone on the same programmes as me, or it could be you.' He paused again but when I didn't add anything, he went on. 'Anyone who really does know me would understand how far off target that threat is but he might not be up-to-date with my living situation.'

'I see.'

'I'm telling the police but I thought I'd tell you first.'

'It's not much to go on. A vague threat. How am I supposed to react?'

'Be more vigilant? That's what I'm doing. Not opening post

unless I know who it is from – that kind of thing. He sent me a dead bird.'

I felt a complete worm. I hadn't really thought but he was far more vulnerable than me. 'Michael, are you going to be OK?'

He finished his pint. 'Is anyone? Another round?'

Chapter 14

Michael

How did one go about reporting a troll? Contrary to popular belief, he wasn't an expert on police procedures, only on the behaviour of deviant personalities in police custody, so he wasn't sure how they would handle this. He didn't want merely to ring his local community support officer and have his complaint shuffled into a file somewhere to await further attention in the mythical day when police resources became sufficient to the task they faced.

He put a pre-prepared meal into the oven for lunch. Fernanda was also a good cook as well as cleaner and liked to leave him with fresh overflows from the bounty of her own family dinners so she knew he was eating properly.

'You must eat meat, Dr Harrison! Good ground beef from best butcher!' she had declared as she left it in his fridge that morning. He was getting used to a spicier diet and made sure her weekly pay included extra for this unasked-for service.

Who to call?

There was one local policeman whom he knew a little. Not wanting to get passed around from receptionist to junior officer, Michael got through to him eventually by sweet-talking the assistant to the Deputy Chief Constable, whom he'd met at a fundraising dinner one evening earlier this year. He now had a direct line.

'DI George.'

'Inspector George, it's Michael Harrison here. We met at Hendon.'

There was a brief pause in which he could hear the sounds of a busy station behind him. 'Dr Harrison. It's interesting that you rang.'

Michael recalled that George was working the case of the body Jessica had found. Had George linked her to him by now? 'It's nothing to do with anything you have on your desk. It's about another matter entirely.'

'Go on.' He was wary. The police had probably been warned that Michael might be trouble, seeing how he threatened to sue the Met after the fiasco last year. The case would've still been rumbling through the courts if he hadn't decided to drop it when he got the job in Oxford.

'I've recently returned to taking a more public role – television appearances and so on. I've always been bothered by trolls, even before my accident last year –' it hadn't actually been an accident but he didn't want to go there '– but I've got one that is worryingly persistent. His threats have escalated to include people in my circle and he's started sending offensive objects to me.'

'And what would you like my advice on? I expect you will

110

have made your own professional judgement as to the serious-
ness of this man's behaviour?'

Thank God, he was taking him seriously. 'I was hoping
you would steer me towards the people who will actually do
something about this for me – try to trace the individual, for
example?'

'You've reported his behaviour to the social media plat-
forms?' There was something sharp about his delivery, like
he had a mental checklist he was running down for Michael.
It was a little unnerving, suggesting DI George was somehow
more efficient than even Michael, who prided himself on his
structured approach to life.

'No, no, I haven't. I prefer to give him his outlet. I never
reply, of course.'

'But he'll know you are reading his messages?'

'I suppose, yes.' The inspector was right: that was a kind
of feeding, but there wasn't much he could do about that.

'Normally blocking him is the first step to take. Send me
the messages and any other information you've compiled and
I'll make sure it reaches the right hands.'

'The dead bird is by the outside bin. And I kept the envelope.'

'A dead bird?'

'A chick, fallen from the nest. In a cigar box.'

'How unsettling.'

That was a good word for it. 'Yes, I'm not opening parcels
at home any more – not unless I know the sender and am
expecting it.'

'Right. My colleagues in cyber-crime can see if he is active elsewhere. If he is bothering you, he's likely to be doing the same to someone else. And if alarms are ringing for you, I don't suppose I have to tell you to think carefully about your own routines and personal safety? Would you like me to send one of the Community Support Officers to check your house?'

'OK.' He might as well do that, though he'd already installed alarms on windows and doors, even before the bird was delivered. He was cautious that way. Michael gave George his address. 'Actually, Inspector, what really worries me is that the threats have expanded to include others. He seems to think I have some close female associate – which I don't. Not at the moment.' Christ, he sounded such a sad case. 'I'll alert colleagues, of course, and I've told Jessica Bridges, in case he thinks of her, but it is a concern.'

'Indeed it is. I have to talk to Miss Bridges later today so I'll ask her if she would like a home security review as well.' From the total lack of surprise in his voice, Michael could tell he had already linked them from the West case.

'You need to talk to her about the boat body?'

'Correct.'

'There have been developments?'

The inspector paused. 'In fact, Dr Harrison, do you still consult with the police?'

Michael felt a rush of pleasure. Not since the West case last year. He wasn't sure if their silence was respect for his recovery period or lingering suspicion that he was a trouble-maker. Having the investigating officer on a new matter call him in would be a complete rehabilitation of his reputation. 'Happy to help if I can. I always have been.'

'Would you be willing to come in to our incident room and talk to my team? It appears our killer is a little more complicated than first appeared.'

Michael contemplated a day eating ready meals or being at the centre of a murder investigation. 'I think I can fit you in. I can shuffle a few things in the diary and come today if it's urgent?'

'I'm afraid it is. I can send a car for you.'

'That's fine – I'll drive myself if you can reserve a spot for me.'

He gave Michael the location of Kidlington HQ, an unlovely modern building in an unlovely satellite village of Oxford, a few miles from Michael's house.

'I'll come right away.'

Michael switched off the oven – that could be supper – put on a clean shirt rather than the T-shirt in which he started the day, and headed out for his car. He loved this – this sense of purpose.

Inspector George came down to reception to escort him up to the incident room. Michael had the pleasant sensation of falling back into old routines – this all felt familiar down to the faint smell of male sweat and lighter floral perfumes of the women, the bad coffee and industrial cleaning fluids, sugary residue of too many crisps and biscuits eaten to keep going on a long shift. Way back, when he'd first started out, there used to be cigarette smoke to add to the mix. Now that was banished to one distant corner in the yard and only carried inside on the jackets of the die-hard nicotine addicts.

Despite this, the overall health of the police didn't seem to have improved. They all looked a few burgers and beers away from a coronary.

Maybe he was being unfair. George was in truth quite slim and athletic looking, standing out for the sharp cut of his suit. Michael guessed the overweight desk officers who greeted the public weren't going to be the most impressive specimens of what the police had to offer.

They went up in a mirrored lift. At least it didn't play muzak.

'In here, Dr Harrison. I've booked out the conference room,' said George.

They entered a room mostly notable for its interactive board at one end and white board at the other. A timeline of the victim had already been neatly drawn across that in multi-colour pens. From the handwriting Michael would lay money on it being the work of one of the younger female officers. He could already project back the spotless homework she'd turned in at college and school.

Don't get him wrong: he wasn't sneering. He valued organisation and, though being neat wouldn't find a killer, it was surprisingly helpful for keeping enquiries from collapsing under the weight of extraneous information.

He studied what they'd found out so far. It was odd to see Jessica's name up there, coupled with Jago's. Had the Met made a board like that for his case last year? From the looks of it, Jessica and Jago must've come across the body not long after the victim had been murdered.

'Spot anything?' asked George, seeing how Michael was spending some time in front of the information.

'Nothing you don't already know. It's a narrow window, isn't it, between the last report of someone seeing Dr Kingston and the body being found?'

'Very. Rigor mortis hadn't even begun when the paramedics arrived.'

'So possibly Jessica found him only an hour or so after death?'

'Could be less, according to the pathologist.'

Michael wheeled away and placed himself near the head of the table where George had courteously already moved the chairs apart to accommodate him. 'But that isn't why you've called me in. Something else has happened?'

'Yes. Have a read of these.' He passed Michael two reports. 'Our assailant has turned up masquerading as the victim.' The first was from a food bank on the Curtis Industrial Estate that had reported its van being stolen early in the morning. Nothing special there, you would think, until you read that the same vehicle had been seen driving the route that Kenneth Kingston had followed every Thursday collecting donations.

Michael skim read, getting the gist of what had happened earlier that day. 'And St Matthews was the only place where he had a sustained conversation with a witness?'

'Yes. It just so happens that at the other places he was able to walk into the buildings without being challenged. Muriel Busby, the witness who talked to him, is different because she has been doing the role long enough to notice that something was off about the delivery man.'

'And he acted as if he were Kenneth Kingston?'

'We think he was even wearing his clothes.'

Well now, that was interesting.

'CCTV?'

'Sadly not.'

'Ah.'

'We did get a partial from a camera across the road from St Matthews.' George showed him a still of a man standing with his back to the camera, putting a crate in the back of the van. His dark grey trousers and white shirt were clearly visible.

'Young? Thirty or thereabouts?'

'Mrs Busby puts him at not less than twenty-eight but no more than thirty-five.'

'That's precise.'

'Retired schoolteacher. She's a good witness. Unfortunately, even though we moved as fast as we could, he'd left that van back at the food bank before we could trace it. He was wearing gloves so no prints and as a communal vehicle it is going to be a fool's errand to isolate DNA.'

'Clever then. A planner.' Michael was beginning to see the man more clearly from these details. 'Enjoying the near miss, I would guess. That might be why he risked a conversation on what he knew was his last stop on the round. He probably wanted her to call you.'

'These insights are exactly why I called you in, Dr Harrison. I was thinking I'd leave these with you for a few minutes, gather the team, and then you can tell us what you think might be going on with this person.'

From the picture on the CCTV the man's outer garments were very generic. They didn't have to be Kingston's. Michael couldn't even be sure of the gender from this image so he'd have to believe the witness on that. 'He may not be the same person as the killer, you know.'

'We've considered that angle briefly. Might be something we can discuss with my team. Before I go, what can I get you? Coffee, tea? I can bring you some of my own stash as I don't recommend the canteen.'

Michael smiled. 'Coffee, black, no sugar then. I can see why you make a good detective, Inspector George.'

'For bringing you in?' His hand was on the doorknob.

'No, or not just that. For seeing to the details.'

The inspector laughed grimly. 'Believe me, sometimes that can be a problem.'

Chapter 15

Jess

The first person to greet me when I got to Drew's parents' house was Flossie, the Cocker Spaniel that Drew and I had taken on after her owner was detained. I would've loved to have her with me at Cory's but her enthusiasm for humans was a little too much, possibly overwhelming for small children. If she were a kitchen appliance, she would be a microwave full of popcorn, spinning about on the point of bursting. As I was only a short-term lodger, Ron had offered to take her on for us until I moved back to the flat. He was assuming that Drew and I would just pick things up where we'd left them. That was an unwelcome reminder that I'd have to work out what to do about Flossie on a more permanent basis.

'Hey, girl.' I knelt down beside her and enjoyed a vigorous round of yips, licks and demands to be stroked. 'You have no dignity, you know that?'

Dignity-smignity, or at least that was what I thought she said with her full-on body shiver.

'Yeah, dignity is overrated.'

Initial fireworks over, I went into the house. I could see from the hallway that Glenda was finishing up preparations for the meal while Ron served drinks to Amy in the living room. I looped my bag over the bannister and left my jacket on top.

'We're in here!' called Ron.

Glenda appeared in the doorway and beckoned me over. She was a woman I once cast in my mind's strange fairground as the fortune teller, scarves, kohl eyeliner and blood-red nail varnish, but in actual fact she was a very grounded individual. Perhaps she was more Russian peasant woman of the Tolstoy kind, surviving the winter on cabbage and still having a smile to share with the neighbours as the invaders died in the snow outside. I was thinking she wanted a quiet word but she merely handed me a tray of hors d'oeuvres. It might've been a subtle message that she still thought of me as family whatever else might be happening.

'Wow, you're really pushing the boat out.' I popped one in my mouth. Maybe that was the wrong image to employ, considering my week. 'Pâté?'

'Mushroom. Amy's vegetarian and allergic to nuts.' She nudged the little triangles of toast into order so my scavenging wasn't so noticeable. 'Thank you, love.'

'For what?'

'For coming. She could really do with a friend.'

'I thought I was being a messenger-cum-detective?'

'That too.' She nudged me towards the front room.

I had the odd sensation of having a part in some Mike

Leigh play about suburban couples – Jessica's Party. The decor in the living room was a little dated. Glenda still believed in chintz.

'Here's my girl!' said Ron. He was below average height and neat, like what I imagined the Fat Controller's slimmer brother might look like. 'I see Glenda's roped you in to work already?'

'Hello, Ron.' I put the tray down on the coffee table and kissed him on the cheek. 'Missed you.'

'And I've missed you too, love.' He kept his arm around me, a gentle corral. 'Amy, as you've probably guessed, this is Jessica, our Drew's partner.'

I now turned my attention to the woman sitting nervously at one end of the sofa. Her strung-out looks and plain grey dress made an odd contrast with the riot of flowers on the upholstery. Her dark hair was lanky and tucked behind her ears. Dark shadows ringed her eyes – how Neil Gaiman's Coraline would look grown up. I'd seen that face before – on myself when my own life reached a particularly low point.

I held out my hand. 'Hi, Amy. Cory sends her love.'

She didn't shake, just waved from the security of her retreat. 'Hi.'

I obliged by making my outstretched hand into an awkward wave. 'Great to meet you.' Hardly that, but this was difficult for us both, like two new kids at school told they were going to be the best of friends. 'How do you know Glenda and Ron?'

She frowned as if I was trying to trip her up. 'I live across the road.'

'Oh yes. Glenda did tell me that.' I needed to find some easier ground for us to share or we were never going to get anywhere with helping her. 'You've got a little boy, Pawel?'

'He's perfectly safe – I've got a babysitter.'

Whoa, I wasn't accusing her of neglect but she'd gone right there. 'I'm sure he is. Probably running the sitter ragged and avoiding going to bed if he's like any normal boy of his age.'

She took this as an insult. 'He's a good boy. He'll go to bed when told. Nine-thirty.'

'Then you're very lucky. I was a horror – never did anything my babysitters told me.' I had been so used to jumping to every order from my father, I'd always acted up with the sitters who to me just weren't that scary.

'I can believe that,' said Ron, trying to prolong the jokey tone. 'Drew was the same but devious about it. He'd say he was going to bed but you'd find him hours later, pillows under the covers to make it look like he was asleep, and he'd be round the corner in his den playing games well after lights out. Jessica, what would you like to drink? Gin and tonic?'

Is that where we were now? Drew making a pillow-heap to stand in for himself in our relationship while he moved on?

'Sounds perfect.' I sat at the other end of the sofa from Amy so that she didn't feel I was cross-examining her. 'It's been one of those weeks.'

'Oh yes, the boat incident. Drew told us.' Ron handed me

the drink. 'Our Jessica stumbled over a body in Oxford on Sunday night. Poor man.'

'That was you?' Amy unfurled a little from her defensive huddle. 'How distressing.'

'Yeah, it was grim.'

'We were talking about it at the shoot – the man came from the college we're using. Do you think we're in danger?'

'I don't think you need worry – hardly something that will become a habit – you know, bodies turning up. No matter what TV dramas suggest, Oxford is a peaceful place. I think I was just unlucky.' I took another triangle. 'You should try these – they're lovely.'

'Vegetarian,' she said, as if stating her nationality.

'These are fine for you – mushroom.'

Ron took one. I could tell from his grimace that he was missing the savour of liver or duck but he chewed manfully. 'Not bad.'

Amy reluctantly took one and nibbled a corner, just to be polite.

'Do you want to tell me about your situation now or after dinner?' I asked.

'Could we get it over with now?' she asked with a look at Ron.

He got the hint. 'I'll see if Glenda needs any help.'

Once we had the room to ourselves, Amy didn't immediately begin to speak. Her fingers were knotted in her lap and she was squeezing very tight. In fact, she felt like a wound spring about to leap from its compression if I wasn't careful. How to smooth the way, reduce the tension a little?

'OK, shall I go over what I've got so far and you can fill in or correct any details?' I waited for her nod. I summarised what I'd learned, including Glenda's information about Angelica's father and what I'd learned about her shared work-place with Roman. 'Did you meet through work?'

'Actually, no. I got him the job. He was looking for work when we first met.'

I remembered now that Glenda had mentioned a support group for people who had lost their partners. Roman seemed to have got quite a lot out of his relationship with Amy – a home, a job, a son, and now he was trying to run away with all of that and more.

'Anything you'd like to add?'

Amy twisted her fingers so hard I could see the red marks she was leaving. 'You need to understand that Roman is a monster. Oh, he's charming when you first meet him. He makes you believe his version of events so that you no longer know if up is up or maybe it is down like he says? I didn't realise this was what he was doing to us all until it was too late. Once he left, it was like a fog lifting. I'd been trapped inside his mirror-world for the eight years we've been together.'

'When did he go?'

'Four weeks ago, just as the school term ended.'

'He took Angelica with him?'

She gave a jerky nod. 'They said they were going rock climbing together in the Lake District. I think they did actu-ally go. I didn't hear anything – usually they'd send photos or messages but I noticed that Angelica had left the family WhatsApp group – she does that when she wants to punish me. I only started to panic when they didn't come back.'

'They contacted you then?'

'Roman did. Eventually.'

'And did he say why?'

'Oh yes.' Her laugh was hollow. 'Apparently, while they were away, Angelica finally told him of the years of abuse I had subjected her to. In his story, I'd been inventing illnesses for her, treating her like an invalid, playing mind games until she began to believe she actually was ill.'

'Munchausen's syndrome,' I supplied.

'There's a name for it?'

'Yes. It's a well-known claim of illness either on the part of the person or by proxy for their child to gain attention.'

'So he might've read about it and got the idea?'

I shrugged. 'That's possible.'

'But Angelica *was* ill on and off during her childhood. Roman knows this. Cory can tell you how I struggled. Angelica was premature and that caused issues for some years – granted that was before Roman came along, while John was still alive, but I made no secret of it. I told him how much easier a baby Pawel was by comparison. Then she had a difficult time when her father died – sleeplessness, bedwetting, mood swings and withdrawal, all to be expected with grief when a child can't process what they're feeling. And at the age Pawel is now—'

She broke off. 'It does sound quite a list.'

'Go on. I'm listening.'

'At Pawel's age, she developed asthma, so you can see we

were in and out of hospitals and clinics, but I promise you I never, ever invented a symptom or encouraged her to believe herself ill when she wasn't. Then she got to secondary school and I thought we'd come through all of that and that she was feeling so much stronger in herself these last few years. I relaxed too soon because then she got an eating disorder and we were back at the doctor's again.' She paused and shook her head. 'And Roman had the gall to tell me this was all me and never Angelica. But he was right here!'

I looked across the road to the house opposite. A little boy was jumping on a trampoline in the front garden. 'Is that Pawel?'

She got up, went to the window and smiled for the first time as the boy did a somersault. 'Yes. Little monkey, isn't he?'

'And how does he get on with his father?'

Amy shrugged. 'They're fine together – kick a ball about, go cycling.' She frowned, realising something for the first time. 'I suppose all their activities are action-based and outdoorsy. Roman subscribes to the old-fashioned view that emotions and soft stuff are my area and his job is to teach Pawel to be a man.'

'But you've cut off contact?'

She raised her hands in a helpless gesture. 'What else can I do? The man has already taken my daughter and no one has lifted a finger to help me get her back; I can imagine if he gets Pawel, he'll never let him go.'

It sounded a pretty poisonous Mexican stand-off they'd got themselves into. 'And how would you describe Angelica's relationship with Roman?'

'Now or before?' She straightened a family photo on the

windowsill – Drew, his sister and his parents all wearing ridiculous Christmas jumpers.

'Before?'

'If you'd asked me two months ago, I'd've said that they were fine – friendly. They liked doing activities together but that was as far as it went – nothing that worried me.'

'And now?'

'I really don't know. I can't understand it. My relationship with Angelica had its ups and downs like any teenager, but she would talk to me. She'd say which boys she thought cute, or what she was planning to wear at her friends' parties. And then overnight, I became the wicked witch from whom she had to be saved. All I can think of is that Roman was slowly turning her against me and I didn't see it.'

'Was there a trigger?'

'I don't know.' But she did – I could tell from the tone. I waited her out. 'I think it might've been the last visit to the GP. I was worried Angelica was losing weight again – heading for anorexia. She really didn't want to go but I made her. She sat in the clinic like I was holding her at gunpoint. Our GP was talking about referring her to a specialist. The next weekend Angelica went climbing and that was it.'

I wondered why Roman didn't back the mother up for taking the sensible step to get help for an eating disorder – why he swung so quickly around to the nuclear option of keeping Angelica away and why had the girl gone along with it? He had to have been angling for this outcome for a while – chipping away at the foundations so that this final doctor's visit made the tower topple.

There was no delicate way of putting this. 'Do you think there is anything between them – anything sexual?'

Amy buried her face in her hands. 'Oh God, I hope not but I have to ask myself that, don't I? Why else would she not see me – her mother? What have I done to deserve this? I've tried to be the best mum that I can be – tried so hard after John died when I just wanted to die myself.' Her anguish rattled around the room like a trapped bird – *let me out of this, let me out.*

'I'm really sorry, Amy. It must be difficult.'

She sniffed and wiped her eyes on her forearm. 'But the worst is that Roman is trying to get Pawel from me.'

There was a car drawing up outside. Amy turned to the window and watched on tenterhooks until she verified that it was just one of the neighbours. Pawel was still bouncing, obviously happy as he tried an ambitious back somersault. He saw his mum watching and waved. She waved back.

'You think Roman might try and snatch him?'

A teenager came out – the babysitter – and took Pawel in for dinner. I couldn't help sharing Amy's relief that he was no longer exposed to the street but inside four walls. We both slumped a little.

'Think? I know he would if he could. But he's trying the legal route at the moment. He's started court proceedings. I'll have to grant him access, I know that. Pawel needs his father – I don't want it to be this way. But I'm worried he'll work on Pawel and persuade the social services that his story about Angelica is true and that Pawel isn't safe with me. I'm worried – worried sick – that I'm going to lose both of my children.'

She wrapped her arms around herself. 'Do you know what that feels like?'

'I can't claim I do. I don't have kids.'

'It feels like I'm dying. You've got to help me.'

Chapter 16

Ruby Lonsdale was running late – and really running as she was rigged out in fitness wear and trainers, haring down Binsey Lane for her weekly meet-up for a five-kilometre circuit run. Her high ponytail beat time as she tried to catch up with lost minutes spent with a printer jam. Her boyfriend was waiting for her by the Perch so they could go around Port Meadow.

It was madness to try and fit this in this evening before dinner at Val's, thought Ruby, but she had foolishly declared her ambition to run the marathon next year and, as Danny said, she wouldn't be anywhere near race fit if she didn't start now. One week missed would set back their timetable for both of them getting super-fit. He was such a dweeb sometimes, with his schemes and his graphs. He'd even plotted out their fitness path on his computer and printed it out so it accused them both every time they went to the fridge at his place for a snack.

That was better. Ruby's body was warmed up now and she'd fallen into a rhythm. She tried not to think about the marketing meeting she had to do tomorrow – major tension time. It was for the launch of a new range of sports drinks for which her firm was doing the advertising campaign. Her entire Sunday had been spent head down over her presentation and she was sick of the sound of her own voice practising. Whites and greens – her own favourite colours. Lots of mention of electrolytes, mint and freshness – those were the keynotes. It was like blending a wine getting the messaging right. An organic alternative to all those sugar-and-caffeine packed ones that were sending kids loopy. First trial group: a Muay Thai class at the Oxford Martial Arts Academy in Templars Square – an all women's beginners session. Danny had actually made the suggestion as he worked there and got permission from his bosses. Her research suggested these women would be an ideal market for the drink. Nice to represent a brand she actually believed in, unlike that SUV campaign she'd helped devise last month.

She arrived outside the Perch and looked around, breathing heavily. No Danny. What the heck was he playing at! To think she'd busted a gut to get here only five minutes late! She checked her phone. No message either. How far away was he, she wondered? Tapping on Find Friends she saw he must be very close – practically on top of her. She looked both ways on Binsey Lane, and then wandered a little down in case he'd gone that way. Though why he would when they'd arranged to meet here ...?

She decided to ring him. The call went to voice mail. She was about to end her call when she registered that she heard a phone vibrating somewhere nearby. She rang it again. Yes, she wasn't going mad – right by her right foot, on the verge.

She toed aside the long grass and saw his phone nestled in the stalks like a strange oblong flower and distinguished by the silver case she'd bought him for his birthday.

'Danny, you idiot!' Smiling, she picked it up, thinking how relieved he'd be when he saw that she'd found it. He was probably retracing his steps right now, believing he'd dropped it on the way from his flat. Give him a few minutes and then he'd realise that he could locate it from her phone. All he had to do is come and join her and she'd have an even better surprise for him.

Ruby perched on the fence that bent around the corner, backing on to a ditch and wooded patch, and thumbed through her messages. She told her best friend Yvonne about Danny's phone and Yvonne sent back a facepalm emoji.

A few cars passed. A dog walker headed down the lane to the river. She decided she'd ask the next one who passed to look out for Danny for her.

After twenty minutes it didn't feel so funny any more.

What should I do? she asked Yvonne. *It's getting dark.*

Go home and wait for him there, suggested Yvonne.

I'm so angry with him. He could at least get a message to me!

He's probably frantic about phone.

True. Ruby tucked Danny's phone securely in the waistband of her sports leggings, took a final look around, and was about to leave, but there was someone coming up the lane from the river. A man or stocky woman. As he came closer she saw that he was about her age. Unthreatening looking – close cut dark hair but not so short as to constitute a skinhead. He was smiling as he listened to his music. Seemed friendly. Might as well ask.

'Excuse me, but did you see a jogger down there? He might've been looking for something? It's my boyfriend – he dropped his phone.'

The young man slowed and took earbuds out. 'Sorry, what was that?'

'Did you see a jogger down Ferry Lane? My boyfriend's lost his phone.'

'Oh, actually, I think I did.' He clipped the earbuds together so they formed a little noose around his neck. 'He was in the bushes near the old boatyard, thrashing about with a stick. Is that what he was doing?'

Relieved, Ruby laughed. 'Must be him. Idiot. I found it right here, on the corner. I needed to tell him. How far down?'

He turned. 'I'll show you.'

Ruby hesitated, her suspicions raised. 'Don't bother. I'm fine to find him myself.'

'Really – it's no trouble. You must be Ruby?'

Ruby stopped. 'How do you know my name?'

The guy gave a groan, then laughed. 'Oh God, that makes me sound like a stalker, doesn't it? You've got it round your neck. My aunt has a dog called Ruby.'

Her hand went to her gold necklace with her name on it – something her parents had bought her when she was sixteen and she wore for sentimental reasons. 'Oh. Well spotted.'

'Sorry. Didn't mean to freak you out. He's not far. Just down here. I'm Ken, by the way. So, how long have you been running? I've been thinking of taking it up. Do you have any tips?'

Chapter 17

Jess

I was standing in Amy's kitchen, having walked back with her after the meal at Glenda and Ron's. I surveyed the neat row of herbs on the windowsill. How did she get hers to live whereas any I ever bought from a supermarket died after a few days?

'Jess, I have an idea as to how you could track down Roman and Angelica,' said Amy, back from having put Pawel to bed. 'I'm due to take a few weeks' leave during the school holidays. Why don't you take my place as Jonah's personal assistant on the production?'

Me – on a film set? That would need careful consideration – or not. 'Yes, please!'

She smiled at my eager tone. 'Don't you know what you'd have to do?'

'Go on.'

'Deal with admin, do the day-to-day stuff he doesn't get to – shopping, bill paying, bookings etc – work with the crew so he makes all his calls for hair, makeup and to the set.'

'Admin?'

'Nothing complicated. His agent deals with the contracts. Just fan mail, social media and so on.'

That nudged me into raising a subject that I'd been revolving in my mind all evening. 'Amy, I was wondering: do you think you might need a solicitor?'

'You're right. I do, don't I?' Amy rubbed her face with her palms.

I'd moved from one of her chorus of accusers to someone she believed was on her side.

'This firm I've just been temping for – they're nice.' I noticed the row of medicine bottles on a high shelf and the repeat prescriptions stuck on the fridge with a magnet and wondered about Munchausen's again.

'A nice solicitor?' Amy stacked Pawel's bowls from supper in the dishwasher.

'They do exist.'

'OK, leave me the number and I'll give them a call in the morning. Who should I ask for?' She began the wash programme even though to my eyes there would be plenty of space for breakfast things.

'Renfrew and Jakowitz. Ask for the family division.'

Saying goodnight, I left her to sort out the details of me stepping in as her replacement and headed back to say farewell to Drew's parents. I meant just to put my head around the door, but Glenda drew me inside.

'Let me make you a drink before you go.'

I was conscious of the time. 'Really, I need to catch my train.'

'Nonsense. Ron'll drive you back, won't you, Ron?'

Ron woke up from his doze in front of the TV news. 'What's that? Oh, yes. Too late for a girl on her own to be travelling.'

'I do all the time! I'll be fine.'

Ron pointed to news that the body of a young woman had been found on Port Meadow. 'Not with a madman like that on the loose.'

A sickening feeling gathered as I saw that the victim had been found at a business that had once been a boatyard. She had been dumped naked on a jetty. A secluded swimming spot, an inlet of the Thames, the press were speculating that it was a sexual encounter that had gone wrong, but they were also linking it to the Parks murder. They were appealing to the public for witnesses and wanted to speak to her boyfriend, Daniel Peverell, also missing. Police divers were searching the river.

'Oh my God, I went there earlier this week.' Warnings flashed as I realised this was the second time I'd been too close to a murder. If I'd been a few moments earlier, or a day or two later, it could've so easily been me.

'To Port Meadow?' asked Ron.

'To that exact boatyard.' I remembered how you couldn't just walk in but that Jago had the code. Jago had said it was a secret swimming spot but he had been trying to impress me. For all I knew, everyone in that part of Oxford could be aware that it was a good place to go for a private dip. Once one person knew the code to the gate, then everyone potentially did.

That wouldn't stop me telling DI George when I got back to Oxford.

'Yes, I'll take that lift, thank you, Ron.'

On the way home, I got a message from Jago.

Did you see the news? Another body but this time at the boatyard where we went swimming.

Was it good that he was texting me? That was what a normal person would do, wasn't it? Like I would've thought to message him if I hadn't had a little panicky moment.

Yes, horrible. Poor woman.

I'm going to tell the police that we were there earlier in the week. It will look odd otherwise.

Odd?

Our DNA will be on the jetty. We towelled off there, remember?

And if you wanted to hide that you had returned to kill someone, how better to do so than to go beforehand with a witness.

You're being ridiculous, Jessica. You've watched too many CSI shows on TV. Jago is just doing what an innocent person would do in his shoes.

But he'd been where two bodies had turned up …

I'll contact the police if you like, I wrote.

Let's both do it. Then they know we corroborate each other's story.

That was perhaps not such an innocent thought. What had he been doing earlier tonight? Did he have an alibi?

OK. I'm just heading back home from dinner with friends in Windsor. Will do on my return. You?

He didn't take my bait to describe what he had been doing.

I'll call now. Do you still want to go for another swim next week? I can understand if you're reluctant, what with bodies turning up in your wake.

And yours, I thought grimly.

I'm working for the film crew in your college next week.

That's great. We can meet up. Maybe make plans for next Saturday?

By then, the police should have more of a handle on the killer. It couldn't be Jago – could it? – that was just my imagination running wild.

OK. Let's make plans for that.

I'd certainly make sure the next place we went swimming wasn't in a river and I'd stipulate that I wanted others around me. I could say to Jago that my recent experiences had spooked me, not that I'd been having bad thoughts about him.

'Everything all right, love?' asked Ron. Lovely, sane Ron, sacrificing his Sunday evening to drive me back to Oxford.

'Yes, fine.' Just messaging your son's would-be rival, who may or may not have something to do with these bodies turning up in swimming spots.

'Just that I can hear the wheels in your brain turning. I'm expecting steam to come out of your ears next.'

'Nice that you think I belong to the steam age, Ron, not digital.'

Talking to Ron was as good as a valium. I was feeling far less jumpy and able to cope with my suspicions by the time I got home. I kissed his cheek.

'Look after yourself,' he said, squeezing my hand in parting.

'I'll be careful. I'm working on a film set this week. Filling in for Amy, working her case.'

He waited to see me go inside. Cory must already have been upstairs because I had the kitchen to myself. It was in its ready-for-breakfast state of perfection. I looked in the fridge, intending to make tea, but was sidetracked by an open bottle of white. Cory wouldn't care, not if she knew what was on my mind. I'd tell her in the morning.

I poured a glass and caressed the smooth bulb. It was like a young child's cheek – cool to the touch – like Leah when she emerged shivering from the paddling pool. OK, time to call the police. Scrolling through the numbers I found DI George's. If they'd only found the body tonight there was a good chance that he'd be on duty.

'George here.'

'Inspector George, Jess Bridges. You know, she of the inadequate newspaper clothing?'

He coughed to clear his throat. He remembered.

'Sorry to disturb you – I know you must be busy. I just wanted to tell you that Jago Jackson and I were at that boatyard on Wednesday morning for a wild swim.'

'You were? How did you get in?'

'Jago knew the code. He says it belonged to a mate of his.' What to say next? 'I just thought it odd that both bodies are found where we've been recently.'

I knew what Ron meant about hearing the wheels in someone's mind turning, though in George's case I'd bet they were zippy microchips engaged in data analysis. 'Where will you be tomorrow?'

'I might be at work – I'm hoping to have a job lined up, not yet confirmed.'

'Then I'll come round early or late, how would that suit you?'

'Could it be late? I'll probably be working on the film set and they start early.'

'Film set? You mean ...?'

'At Linton College, yes. I'm working there on the basis that lightning doesn't strike twice.'

'Statistically that's not true.'

Merry soul, aren't you, Gorgeous George? 'Still, I think I should be safe. Everyone will be super alert. So after work then?'

'Seven o'clock, at your home address?'

Someone was planning on pulling a long shift. 'OK. I'll warn my ...' not landlady ... 'friend.'

'One final thing, Miss Bridges: have you and Jackson been anywhere else swimming together?'

'No, not yet.'

'And have you had any cause for alarm recently, the feeling of being followed, for example? Have you noticed anyone who seemed out of the ordinary in the places you routinely visit?'

Way to spook me, DI George. 'No, but I'm not exactly a creature of habit. Anyone would have a hard time working out where I'll be next.'

'I suggest you keep it that way. If you do feel unnerved at any point, ring me and I can have a squad car with you in minutes.'

Wow, he was imagining I might be a target. I had just been thinking I might've inadvertently been hanging out with the killer.

'Are you telling Jago this too?'

'I will – as soon as I get off this call to you.'

I took the hint. 'I hope you find him before he gets a third.'

'Fourth. We found another body in the river an hour ago.'

'Oh my God!'

'The missing boyfriend, so I hope you understand that you should take my warnings very seriously. We don't know who this killer is but he might well know who you are by now if he's watching you and Jackson. Don't underestimate him.'

It was only when I ended the call that I realised Inspector George hadn't mentioned Jago having already contacted them.

Chapter 18

Leo

L eo was still looking at his phone screen as he ended the call to Jess Bridges, not quite ready to put her away in his back pocket. Funny how just talking to her seemed to make things just a little more bearable. She was irrepressible, with her ham-fisted attempts to hide from him that she was an undeclared tenant of Cory Reynolds.

'Glad something's finally amused you,' grouched Harry. 'Though you pick a strange time to show it.'

'It's not connected.' At least, he hoped it wasn't. He had a bad feeling that Jago – and possibly Jess – were deep in this. He was still looking hard at Jackson. He'd read the man's book and got Suyin on the documentary but so far they had only been helpful in proving a link after the fact. There was too much content to anticipate where the next strike would come. Short of posting officers along every stretch and inlet of the Thames, he couldn't keep the public safe.

And so they were standing in the boatyard shed, watching as yet another SOCO tent was erected over the dead. Geraldine

Jones, the police pathologist, had just arrived, wading in with her black wellingtons and white jumpsuit. She was the best in the Oxford area so they were lucky she'd caught the case.

'What do you make of our killer, Harry?' Leo asked.

Harry patted his pocket. He was considering a smoke but knew Leo wouldn't allow it on the murder scene. 'He's a fucking pervert. I bet he's spying on people coming for a bit of how's-your-father and then does them in. His way of getting off, I suppose.'

A dog walker had found Ruby Lonsdale naked but her boyfriend had been dumped fully clothed into the river. Leo couldn't see the sexual element that Harry was quick to assume. His gut said this was different.

Geraldine beckoned them over.

'I see you're doing a two-for-one sale, Leo,' she remarked with her usual gallows humour.

'I'm afraid so. What can you tell me, Gerry?'

'My initial analysis is that both died of head trauma as you've no doubt ascertained.' She pointed to the crushed area of the skull over the left ear of the victims. Water had washed Danny clean, but Ruby's head was a mess of blood, bone and brunette hair. 'Our killer has perfected a quick sharp blow to the skull, incapacitating or killing his victims with one strike. He keeps it tight, probably close to the body so he isn't detected making his move. Left to right which suggests he attacked from behind and I think delivered like a backhand in tennis – that makes him right-handed. He will have practised this. Weapon is probably metallic with a hooked end, like a crowbar, similar or the same to the one used in the Kingston killing. Further blows, if there are any, will just be window dressing, or a sign that he wanted to make sure he'd done a thorough job.'

'Any sign of anger, or passion?' Leo asked her.

'First impressions? Too methodical for that. I'd say he'd set himself a task and got on with it. You'll need a psychologist to give you the full picture but, from these wounds, and the way he's left the face alone, he's not scared, he's not angry, he's just driven.'

Did Jago fit that description? The man in the book was enthusiastic about immersing himself in nature, but he sounded sane. If he was this attacker, then he was hiding it superbly.

'Then we have ourselves a psychopathic serial killer?' asked Harry, rather too eagerly for Leo's taste.

'Believe me, they are much less fun in real life, Sergeant Boston,' said Geraldine, 'than in the offerings you get on television. No fun at all, particularly when the press get hold of that angle. Batten down the hatches, Leo: there's a shit storm heading your way.'

Leo knew this already but he thanked her and made arrangements for a full briefing once she'd had time to process these victims.

Harry had wandered further off and was looking under some tarpaulin that covered a motor launch. 'I always wanted a boat as a kid. Tried to get my dad to buy us one. You can imagine how that went down, him working all hours as a plumber and his son wanting to go off sailing.'

'I can understand the urge though. Cutting loose.'

Harry tucked the tarpaulin back in place. 'That's it exactly. And maybe for someone, killing other people is their fantasy – their cutting loose. I bet he feels fucking powerful right now.'

And this was why Harry was a good detective. Many of his attitudes might appal, but he did come out with these insights.

Leo nodded. 'It's wild, rash even, killing three people in such quick succession.'

'And so far getting away with it. He won't settle for three, will he?'

'No. This one is going to keep going until he gets caught. We'd better find him before he picks out his next fantasy.'

Chapter 19

Jess

I had to admit to a ridiculous thrill as I approached Linton College and the film set. I was just that little closer to fame. This production company had made two of the last Oscar-nominated films, known for their quirky take on historical subjects. Amy had already filled me in on the general layout of the site in our early morning briefing phone call and told me where Roman could be found.

'Does he use the canteen?' I asked.

'There's a mobile catering unit but I can't predict when he'll take a break.' Amy sounded tired.

'What's the film?'

'Set in the 1930s – working class grammar school lad falls under the spell of a right-wing femme fatale. Think *Lady Chatterley's Lover* with Nazis.'

Intriguing.

'Any other clues how to get alongside Roman?'

'Roman smokes. You'll find him in the corner of shame with the other addicts.' Amy's disapproval was plain. With her clean food, clean living ethos, I imagined smoking was one of the deadliest of sins.

'I presume on a big site they have more than one designated area?'

'Yes, but he's most often lurking in the one out front, just past the Porter's Lodge. I avoid it, for obvious reasons.'

'Thanks. It looks like I'm going to have to take up smoking again.'

I checked my handbag for the little packet I'd bought at the newsagents in Summertown. Smoking had been a vice as a teen (I'd tried most things I shouldn't then) but I hadn't succumbed to a tobacco habit for over a decade. These things were dangerous for me. My lack of impulse control meant that flirting with an addiction could be a slippery slope that I didn't try very hard to climb back up.

I reported to the lodge to pick up my pass.

'Name?'

I'd reached the front of the queue without even noticing. 'Jessica Bridges. I'm filling in for Amy Mason, executive assistant, while she's on holiday.'

'Oh yes, I had a message about you an hour ago.' The spotty lad not much out of his teens checked my passport against the name on his list. 'Do you know where to go, Miss?'

'I'm supposed to meet Jonah Brigson at his trailer.'

'Then you'll need the staff carpark.' He handed me a map and drew a dotted line across the site. 'I can call them and get them to send someone for you.'

'Thanks, but I'd prefer to find my own way.'

'Keep to this path. If you spoil a take, the director might

shoot you.' He winked at me, which felt totally wrong as he was way too young for me.

'I'll try to duck all bullets coming my way.'

His expression sobered as one of his colleagues, a tubby man in an unfortunate waistcoat, sent him a disapproving look at our banter. 'Don't get lost and ... er ... also, don't go near the boathouse at any time for any reason until further notice.'

I could guess why. 'Trust me, I'll keep to the path. I don't want to be sent home before I even start work.'

'You wouldn't be the first.' He printed off my pass and fastened it on a lanyard. 'You won't believe the number of undercover reporters we've had to chase off, all wanting to get shots of where it happened.'

And I was just an ordinary undercover missing persons detective. 'Oh wow. The murder. I bet.' I avoided mentioning my small part in this as the one that had found the victim.

'We'll be keeping an eye on you.' He pointed two fingers to his eyes and then up to the CCTV screen.

Ushered out of the door, I turned my map upside down so it faced the same way that I was going. I kept a lookout for the smokers' corner, which I found easily as it was marked by numerous dropped butts. I'd be back later. Entering into the first quad I took a left and worked my way past chapel and dining room to the ancillary areas of the college where the kitchens and bins were to be found.

The staff carpark had been partly given over to a little huddle of trailers for the lead actors, their home-from-home during the long hours of shooting. I knew from Amy that

Jonah would already have been in since dawn for his makeup and wardrobe call. There was always a big rush just in case he was needed but more often than not he was left waiting. He knew to expect his assistant at nine if he wasn't on set and I was only five minutes late. I knocked.

'Yeah?'

I opened the door. 'Mr Brigson, I'm Amy's holiday cover.'

Jonah, early thirties, pale-skinned with hair buzz cut, was lounging on the couch in ripped T-shirt and jeans. A scar – courtesy of the makeup department – slashed across one cheek and one eye was eerily clouded – again an addition for this part and not something he was likely to be born with. He looked very scary – definitely the kind of man that would encourage you to cross over if you saw him coming towards you late at night.

'What the fuck? I told Carol I didn't need an assistant. Didn't she tell you?'

So much for expecting me. 'Carol? Um, no. Who is that?'

'My agent.' He got up, irritable, and stubbed out a rolled-up cigarette in a saucer. 'Amy's bad enough, hovering around to tend to my every whim like I'm some posh boy who doesn't know how to wipe his own bum.'

This was going so well. I refused to be daunted. 'And I'd be very good at that, seeing how my landlady's kid is at that stage and I'm often called in to deputise.' That was probably too much information.

'I don't need you, love. Carol only made me have an assistant so I look like I'm getting equal treatment to Ronnie Merchant, but, fuck, I was looking forward to my couple of weeks with no one hanging around watching me as I scratch my balls or pick my nose.' He reached for his mobile and I just knew he was going to call to have me fired.

'You haven't tried me yet. Scratch, pick and even fart as much as you like, Mr Brigson, I don't care – I wouldn't even notice. And who knows? I could just be that missing ingredient to your dull stew of a life – your chilli pepper.'

His thumb hovered over the call button. 'My chilli pepper? Are you crazy?'

'Definitely. It must be boring hanging around waiting for your call to come to set. My craziness will at least make the time pass more quickly.'

'My life's had enough crazy.' He opened his contacts to find the number to get rid of me.

'Then do it for Amy!' I grabbed the phone from him and held it behind my back. It was such an audacious move he was momentarily dumbfounded. So was I. I hadn't thought this through. What next?

'What the fuck are you playing at?'

Oh God, I was going to blurt it all out, wasn't I? I'd just met one of the hottest tickets in cinema and I was going to spoil it all. 'I'm here for her – to work out what her ex-partner is doing with her fifteen year old daughter, all right? It's not about you.'

That knocked him down a peg or two – being told he wasn't the most important story in British tinsel town. 'You what?'

'Amy's partner, Roman Wolnik, has gone off with her daughter and is trying to get their boy too. Pawel's only seven

– he's a cute kid and likes bouncing on his trampoline. He doesn't need to be hauled away from home just because the grown-ups can't get their shit together.'

Jonah put up a hand to stop me – at least he wasn't using it to place the call any longer. 'Back up a bit, Mary Poppins. You are here for Amy. Explain.'

'Her partner Roman Wolnik—'

'Yeah, I got that part. A dickhead. He stole the girl and is after the boy.'

'But he also works here for Pegasus Tree Productions. Set dresser. Amy wants me to find out where her daughter is and see what's going on.'

'Is he the girl's father?'

'No – but he is Pawel's.'

Jonah sat down and started rolling another cigarette. 'Why didn't she say anything to me? We've been working together for a month, for fuck's sake.'

'Probably too busy wiping your bum.'

He grimaced and tapped the roll-up on the tin. 'And I never asked, did I? Shit, I'm becoming one of them.' He jerked his head towards the other trailers. 'Did she go to the police?'

'Yeah, and they did nothing. They said the daughter was happy where she was with her stepdad. Old enough to decide for herself and all that.' I had run away for the first time at around that age – you were never old enough. You might think you knew what you were doing until life slapped you in the face. 'They won't even pass on a message.' I avoided mentioning the daughter's accusations of abuse. It wasn't fair when Amy came back to find that rumour had soured where she worked.

He didn't look surprised by her predicament. 'Bastards. What does Amy want you to do?'

'She wants me to get into Roman's confidence and find out where he's living at the moment. Her ultimate aim is for me to pass a message to her daughter as everyone else has refused to act as intermediary. I think she wants me to persuade Angelica to come home – and at the very least check she's safe.'

He lit his cigarette – no designated zone for him, unless the whole trailer was one. 'And what does she think you can do about it? You're what? A friend of hers? Moonlighting social worker?'

'No, I'm actually a private detective.'

He let loose a full belly laugh and stood up, heading for the door. 'That's a good one, Poppins. OK, you had me up to that point. Well played. Tell Amy you were worth the ten-minute distraction. Say I'll see her in two weeks.'

He didn't believe me! 'I am – I really am! Not a detective ...' maybe that had been overplaying my hand ... 'so much as a seeker of missing persons. Look – here's my card.' I had a business card these days, thanks to Drew's influence. It just said *Jessica Bridges, Personal Enquiries Agent* and then my phone number and website.

Jonah took one look and tossed the card into the ashtray. 'You're serious? You, Mary Poppins, go hunting for missing persons? You wouldn't last five minutes in the kind of places runaways end up.' He breathed out a plume of smoke and looked at me through the fumes. I noticed his nails were bitten short and knuckles tattooed with the cheap ink of ex-cons and bikers. He was no plastic Hollywood star, this guy.

'You'd be surprised. And I do find them. If you still don't believe me you can contact the Metropolitan Police. I helped them on a case last year.' I really hoped he didn't though, as they might not have many flattering things to say about me. 'Please phone Amy – hear her side.'

'Stay here.' He went into the second room in the trailer. I thought it was just a bathroom but he closed the door before I could peek inside. That gave me time to look around his den. It might be my one and only chance to see inside the life of someone famous. There was a thin spiral-bound script on the table with the name of the film he was working on – *Knives Edge*. It'd got 'confidential' stamped all over it, which, of course, invited me to glance inside. He didn't have much dialogue and that which he had was mostly swearing. He should be good at that then. By contrast, he did have a lot of action, including in the sack, with his co-star, Ronnie. I read a section. They're going to do that on screen, are they? Definitely going to be an 18 certificate. I could feel my cheeks heating just thinking about the logistics of filming that. I put the script down and wandered to the window to take a closer look at the photo on the sill. It was of Jonah with his arms around a gorgeous girl with a cloud of black hair. She was holding a violin. Oh yes, I remembered now: the press linked his name with that classy musician, Jenny something. They liked the contrast between the rough London lad and the cultured classical violinist.

'Like what you see?' He was back.

Guiltily I put the photo down. 'What's the verdict?' I crossed my arms, prepared to argue some more.

'Amy persuaded me to give you a chance. Sounds like she's having a rough time at the moment.'

'Yeah, the roughest. She's terrified for her kids.'

'You can stay and see if you can help her out by getting a message to the girl.'

'You're letting me stay!' I was afraid my relief made my voice a little too close to a squeal, not the professional tone I'd hoped for.

'Yeah. Chilli pepper, hey?'

'That's me.'

He sat down and shoved the script aside. 'So, Jessica Pepper, what's the plan?'

Chapter 20

Isla Shore set out the free samples of Minted on the table in the women's locker room. The pyramid of green and white bottles looked amazing, particularly coupled with the yellow irises in the white vases. She took a picture for the company's Instagram. *Get ready for our exciting new product reveal!!* She dredged up some more emojis – hearts and stars to make it stand out on the increasingly ecstatic newsfeed everyone saw every day, but her heart really wasn't in it. Ruby should be doing this. The whole look of the brand, the marketing materials, even the idea to trial the packs with enthusiasts for the newest fitness trend, Muay Thai, had all been down to her.

Why, oh why, God – fate – whoever was in control up there, did it have to be Ruby that came across the killer? And Danny – lovely Danny who always had a smile for everyone? Isla couldn't pretend she and Ruby were the best of friends. Isla wasn't fashionable or fit enough to have front-of-house roles in branding exercises like those that Ruby led. Each to their own, her boss had said, before promoting Ruby over her. Ruby had hung out with the fast-track managers looking for a job in London eventually. They went for drinks together and batted about ideas for new campaigns while Isla went home to deal with a two-year-old who wasn't impressed by any idea she had if it didn't involve Paw Patrol. Still, Isla had liked Ruby as a colleague and they'd got on well enough.

Maybe I feel worse because we didn't become friends? she mused, rearranging the spiked fronds so they didn't fall into an unintended 'v' sign to the heavens. Actually, sod it, let that stand. She was feeling pretty pissed off with the universe at the moment.

The class was due to finish in five minutes but an early bird entered the changing room, towel around her neck. Isla perked to attention behind her table. The newcomer had her dark hair clipped high and was wearing the same distinctive green and white fitness strip from Gymshark that Ruby had favoured. For an awful moment, Isla thought she was hallucinating, wishful thinking bringing her colleague back from the dead, but then she realised the woman's face and figure were very different. She was barrel-chested for one thing and – oh my God – it was someone transitioning or gender identifying as female. What was the PC thing to do in these scenarios? Don't look. Don't make any comment.

'That looks lovely – as good as I imagined!' the woman said. You did call them 'women', didn't you, even if they hadn't finished the treatment? Isla knew it was a linguistic nightmare – a lawsuit waiting to happen if she offended the wrong person.

'Yes, it looks very refreshing and tastes even better. Have you tried one? These are free samples. We've enough for everyone in tonight's class. It would be great to get your feedback.'

'You want me to try one!' The woman gave a very tenor laugh. It was so hard to think of her as female. 'Isla, I hardly need to do that, do I?'

What? Isla took her first proper look at the person's face. He – and it was a he no matter how PC she was trying to be – was staring at her intently. 'Don't you?'

'You've done a very good job realising my vision for the display. Sorry I couldn't be here earlier. Got held up, you know how it is?'

She really didn't. 'Held up?' And how the hell did the man know her name? Is he ... is some sicko pretending to be Ruby?

'Danny called and I didn't want to make my sweetie wait so we had a chat and I lost track of the time.'

Oh. My. God. 'He did?'

'I think he's going to pop the question soon.' He tweaked one of the irises, coming far too close. 'How long have you been married now? Three years?'

'Ye-es.' How did he know that?

'Shine off the romance yet with, what's his name, Tony?'

'Er ... no.' Could she get by him and get help? But he was standing between her and the door.

'And then there's Julie, of course.'

Leave my kid out of it, Isla wanted to bellow, but found she was speechless.

'Are you staying to help me hand this out? I've got the feedback sheets here. Did you bring the clipboards?'

Isla had printed out her own sheets as the ones Ruby had

prepared were at her flat and no one, of course, had wanted to disturb the family in their grief. 'In the crate,' she said faintly.

The fake Ruby went to the box and took one out. He tutted. 'Oh no, this won't do. Isla, you haven't been trying to take my job from me, have you?' He wagged his finger at her. 'I'll have to tell Susan.'

Remember details, Isla told herself. And – no! – he was wearing Ruby's gold name necklace. 'Of course not. Sorry – I just wasn't sure you'd remember to bring them.' What with being dead and everything.

Don't get hysterical, Isla, she told herself. She could feel her chest tightening as stress-induced asthma caught up with her horror at the situation. It was the killer, wasn't it? 'Do you need a hand swapping them over?' Did that sound ordinary or a terrified squeak?

He was busy, head down now, over the crate, necklace swinging. 'No I'll be fine. Go check on the class. I thought they'd be finished by now.'

'Will do.' Isla dashed out and, she had no idea why afterwards, hit the fire alarm. She scrambled into the middle of the kick-boxing women, somehow seeing them as protection, and collapsed.

'Don't go in there! Call the police!' she gasped before succumbing to her asthma attack.

Chapter 21

Leo

It was getting extremely serious, not just for the victims, but also for Leo's team. The killer had turned up again, this time pretending to be his female victim, Ruby Lonsdale. The press were criticising the police for failing to catch him on this second post-murder appearance, but how exactly had they been meant to know which part of Ruby's life he'd pick? The pattern was only just now emerging. Leo struggled to contain his frustration: the killer was moving so fast Leo couldn't anticipate, couldn't pin him down through painstaking detective work, which was his usual way of handling murder cases. SOCO were hopeful that there would be some trace elements at the scene of both crimes and the murderer's subsequent appearances in character that would match. Nine out of ten times it was forensic evidence that clinched a case but they'd not even had time to get the full DNA profiles through, even with a rush on the samples. Not that the brass were going to accept that excuse. With the heat from the media, they wanted the killer caught yesterday and were looking for someone to blame.

At the moment, however unfairly, the buck was stopping with Leo.

Methodical took time – that was why he was taking a more creative approach and involving an expert. Leo had called in Michael Harrison as he realised they needed his expertise to get ahead of this man. The psychologist was absorbing the information they'd gathered at the sites of both crimes, and the subsequent appearances. They'd got visuals from the gym because, unlike the church, it had CCTV on its entrance. The image showed a slim androgynous figure letting himself in, with a white sports bag slung casually over one shoulder. Face was partially shadowed by a hoodie with the gym's logo on it. There was no CCTV in the changing room for privacy reasons and it was only in there that he had taken off his hood. The witness got a good look, though, and was working with a police artist but the man so far sounded Mr Average – average build, medium height, brown eyes – no killer detail for her to hang onto. No helpfully identifying scar, birthmark or tattoo. Added to that on this occasion he had been wearing a dark wig and lots of makeup, overplaying his hand as a female.

No, not overplaying, Leo realised. Relishing.

'Obviously, we're getting a pattern,' Michael told the audience of the investigative team. 'The killer has to be stalking his victims in advance to learn their routines. I imagine he obsesses about them, following them from work and poking into their private lives. That will be part of his ritual. I suspect he might've broken into their homes when empty before he assaulted them. Did Ruby report anything like that in the weeks before her death?'

'No, but the flat doesn't have sophisticated locks. Anyone with rudimentary skills could be in and out without leaving any sign,' said DS Wong.

'I'm sure you're getting it in the neck, not having anticipated that he would turn up at the gym.' Michael gave Leo a sympathetic smile, showing he knew how police politics worked. 'But I hadn't thought it was possible either for him to move on so quickly from Kenneth Kingston. I assumed, as no doubt you did, that Kingston was the intended target all along. I thought he'd spend longer enjoying that identity – the local saint, college bursar. This changes that. My theory now is that it isn't so much the individuals themselves but the possibility of living different lives that is driving this man. It makes him very hard to predict. It will all depend if he's taken a fancy to something about you – not sexually as there's been no sexual assault in either case.' Leo glanced over at Harry who frowned in disagreement. 'It's just a ... a whim to be you. Or a yearning. Local saint. Rising star at an advertising company, probably heading for the bright lights of London in her next job. They are living successful lives, loved and appreciated by those around them, and it might well be what he wants for himself. Whoever he is, he won't be like either of his victims.'

'Either? There are three,' challenged Harry.

'Sorry, I misspoke. I think Daniel Peverell was collateral damage – someone he had to get through to get to Ruby. I imagine Daniel was killed first, am I right?'

'We've been unable to pinpoint time of death to that extent,' Leo explained. 'One left in cold water, the other on the jetty, so bodies cooled at different rates. But they both died within an hour of each other, we think. He doesn't keep them alive long.'

He nodded. 'This isn't a torture-murder. He wants them out of the way so he can take over. I read him as a thrill seeker. The audacity of pretending to be someone so unlike himself is the attraction, like a role he covets. He knows he isn't convincing as a body double but enjoys the power trip of getting others to acknowledge him in that guise. Both times he has interacted with women on their own who have had the good sense to play along. I doubt it would have gone so well for them if they had baulked or challenged him in any way.' Michael moved away from the whiteboard to take a place at the conference table.

'I don't think either of them feel it went well,' Leo said.

'Oh, but it did. This kind of man – the illusion is very important to him. He'll strike out like a petulant but deadly child if they don't play his game. You should tell them they did exactly the right thing – I hope that comforts them.'

'The right thing – apart from hitting the bloody alarm,' muttered Harry.

Michael waved that away. 'He would've been long gone in any case. I would bet he left as soon as she did, his little cameo performance over.' He rubbed his chin. There was shadow which told Leo he'd left in haste without stopping to shave when he'd called him. He would have to remember to tell Michael that he mustn't push himself too hard for their benefit. 'Have you checked the flat?' Michael asked. 'Was it left empty after Ruby died?'

'We had someone on the door but yes, otherwise it was empty. According to the witness, Isla Shore, he knew about

Ruby's printouts – some special feedback form she had created.' Leo was wondering now if his officer on the door had let someone past him.

'If you look back at the timeline, my betting is that he went in immediately after killing Ruby and Daniel and before the bodies were found. He'd have the keys after all.'

Leo went to the new chart on a second whiteboard. 'You're right. We didn't recover those. It's not so easy to get past a man on the door even if the locks are inadequate. But before the alarm was raised, he could just waltz right in. Who would even notice?'

He turned to DS Wong. 'Suyin, get your team to canvas the neighbours again on this specific point. Let's hope for a Neighbourhood Watch type keeping an eye on the street. I want to know what this man looks like without his disguise.'

Michael shook his head. 'You can do that but he might still have been dressed as Ken Kingston. I believe we'll find he doesn't inhabit his own identity for the crimes but pretends to be the last victim.'

That prompted Leo to a new thought. 'We're assuming this started with Kingston but maybe he's been active long before these attacks? We need to check there haven't been similar cases elsewhere, focusing on this specific detail of reports of a man turning up later claiming to be someone who has recently died. Those first deaths might have looked like accidents so would not have come into our initial sweep for like-crimes. This could be an escalation, or at least a more blatant stage. Going where there's CCTV, he wants us to know what he's doing.'

'So we need to look for someone still dressed as Ruby?' asked Suyin.

Michael turned to her. 'Our killer is savvy, Sergeant Wong. He has only exposed himself when and where he thinks it is safe to do so. It therefore depends where he goes and what he does with his fantasy life. It might be a part-time thing for him, like a job.'

'But it's something to go on. Thanks, Dr Harrison,' Leo concluded. 'We've spent as much time as we can on this. I have to send you back out into the field. OK, people, you've got your tasks lined up. We'll meet again at eight a.m. and hope by then we've got a solid lead on our target.'

The detectives and uniformed officers filed out. Leo lingered, waiting for a post-briefing check-in with Michael, and to thank him for his help.

'That was very helpful, Dr Harrison. Thanks for coming in. Any other insights you have – don't hold back.' Leo couldn't help it. He had to yawn and stretch a little. He'd been deskbound most of the day, completing the reams of paperwork a case like this generated, and reporting up the tree. 'Sorry.'

Michael checked the time. 'Shit – I'll be driving home in the rush hour.'

'I'm afraid so.'

'Don't apologise. Murder doesn't wait. I'm sure you're putting in a lot of overtime on these killings.'

'High profile case like this? You can barely breathe, what with the top brass being at you, the press, your own people. I sometimes wish they'd all just go away and let me get on with my job.' Leo rarely shared but tiredness had worn him down and he risked a little confidence. He didn't talk much to people within his department so it was good to have someone on the outside who understood so much of what went on.

'Only sometimes?'

Leo smiled ruefully. 'You've got me there. Before you go, any more news from your troll?'

'Your colleagues from Community Support came round and approved my home security. Apparently I'm a model citizen.'

'Glad someone is. Have you heard any more from the troll himself?'

'I took your advice and blocked him. I expect he'll pop up again with a new name and account but I've not seen any sign so far.'

'Good. I think it's best to choke off his interest so he moves on.' Leo accompanied Michael to the door. 'Watch your back – but I don't need to tell you that.'

Michael paused. 'Did someone have a word with Jessica?'

'I had a brief word with her the other night, but actually we're more worried about her proximity to these murders than about the troll. In both cases, she'd been on the scene either shortly before or just after the body turned up.'

That came as an unpleasant surprise for Michael. 'I know Jessica is a magnet for trouble but normally that's of a lower order than murder. How is she connected to Ruby Lonsdale's death?'

'The second time, that wild swimming academic from

167

Linton College, Jago Jackson, took her to the swimming spot a few days before. It could be coincidence ...'

'But you don't think so?'

'There may be a connection via Jackson.' Leo had been reading Jackson's books and watched clips of the TV series Suyin had pulled out for him, the parts in Oxford. All left him reflecting that it was amazing what people got paid to do, and for which they had an academic post. He couldn't take it seriously, this modern nature writing. Hardly a trip up the Amazon. He had learned that Parson's Pleasure had featured prominently in the documentary, but he'd not yet come across a reference to the boatyard, not by name at least. Jackson liked to hide his favourite spots, dropping tantalising hints without giving plain directions how to find them. 'The link could be that the killer is using Jackson's book or documentary as a primer for where to find people near wild spots in Oxford, maybe shadowing him. But if that's so, we've been asking ourselves why these two places in particular? Jackson goes out most days but Jessica hasn't been to any of the other spots – it's a hundred per cent match on her record.'

'Which means he's what? Watching her too? Christ, that's all she needs.'

'We know the killer obsesses about people.' Leo was still pondering the possibility that Jago might be playing a double game, posing as victim when in fact he was the murderer. He had no alibi for the time of either killing spree or subsequent appearances.

'Are you thinking ...?'

'That the killer might've lined one of them up as his next

victim? We have to consider that. We'll be speaking to them both more seriously along those lines later today. Jago Jackson is also a suspect – not high on the list but I have to consider him. He had means and opportunity – I just can't see a motive.'

'Fuck.'

'Yes. Not a conversation I'm looking forward to. How do you think Jess Bridges will handle it when she learns she's possibly a target?'

'How? She'll either make a joke of it while panicking inside, or she'll run screaming for the hills. She might try to do both at the same time.'

Leo nodded, agreeing with that sentiment from his slight knowledge of her. 'The good thing is that she's living with a family at the moment in Summertown.'

'She's living in Summertown?'

'Ah. You didn't know?'

Michael looked nonplussed. 'I assumed she was still in London and just commuting here for work.'

'Sorry, I think I might've spoken out of turn.'

'Still, I needed to know. It's here that the killer is active, not London.'

Leo couldn't unsay those words so he had to carry on and make the best of it. 'We've had no indication this individual has got into a house with an au pair and children constantly in residence.'

'Don't tell her that – she'll leave to protect them.'

'I don't think anyone but his intended victim is at risk.'

'Unless they get in the way – like Danny.'

'Yes, there is that.' Leo sighed. 'Hell. I'm going to have to put people on Jessica Bridges and Jago Jackson – and keep that family safe. It's going to blow my budget for the year.' He switched off the lights as they exited the room, one money-saving step he could take.

'Better that than one of them turn up dead.'

Leo ran the numbers in his head. 'Tell that to my commanding officer.'

Chapter 22

Leo

There was one person at the centre of this that Leo was yet to re-interview after the second appearance of the killer: Jago Jackson. He didn't want to alert the man that he was looking hard at him as a suspect so he made an appointment to meet Jackson where the first murder was discovered. He gave the excuse that he wanted to find out more about wild swimming in Oxford.

Jago walked briskly up to join Leo on the park bench overlooking the river. It was a windy day of fast changing sunlight and shadows as the clouds raced each other across the sky. The aspens were dipping and shivering, leaves flashing their paler undersides. A swan swimming upstream struggled with the indignity as the wind blew its tail feathers the wrong way.

'Thank you for coming,' Leo said as Jago reached him.

'Better out here than in my college at the moment. Normal life is suspended thanks to the film crew.' Jago unbuttoned his jacket and sat down, completely at his ease. He was an athletic looking man, pale considering how much time he spent outdoors. Dark hair, dark eyes, forehead furrowed: he would've fitted in among monks in a medieval scriptorium with that earnest academic air he had, thought Leo.

'I can imagine. Any change since we last spoke? Have you noticed anyone following you or being where they shouldn't?'

Jago shrugged. 'Nothing. I lead a quiet life of libraries and college. It's hard for anyone to get close to me unless they catch me outside and then I'm usually moving pretty fast, either running or cycling.'

'Or swimming?'

'Not so much of that going on at the moment.' Jago smoothed his hair back but it flopped over his forehead again. 'It's annoying. I should be swimming each morning but the attacks have stopped that. I love this place.'

Leo followed his eyes to the gentle current of the river. It looked much less threatening in the daylight, almost inviting as the light sparkled on the wavelets the breeze kicked up. 'Yes, I can see that you might miss that.'

'Do you know the stories?' Jago asked, turning to Leo with a light in his eyes of someone eager to convert another to their passion.

'Stories?'

'About Parson's Pleasure. It's been in use since at least the sixteenth century. There are lots of anecdotes, like the one about the Warden of Wadham College, Maurice Bowra?'

Leo gestured for him to go on.

Jago grinned. 'Imagine a gaggle of portly dons swimming in the noddy, sunning themselves on the bank. A punt of ladies went by. The other men covered their genitals with their hats whereas Bowra covered his face. He was said to have quipped that he didn't know about them, but he for one was known by his face around Oxford.'

Leo laughed. 'And you? Do you swim naked?' He wondered if stripping the bodies was connected to this wild swimming folklore.

Jago shook his head with a wry smile. 'I'm not that uninhibited.'

Though Leo would call himself an evidence driven detective, he also believed in checking his gut about his suspects. Nothing this man was saying so far was setting off any alarm bells; but he also had to remember the murderer prided himself on pretending.

He sat forward, signalling a change in tone. 'Mr Jackson, I'm asking all my interviewees for their movements to help me exclude them.'

Jago's forehead lines deepened. 'You're looking at me as a suspect?'

Leo thought it best not to get into that. 'It would help us if you could tell us where you were exactly on Sunday evening between six and eight; Thursday between eleven and one during the day; Sunday again between six and eight; and yesterday between five and six p.m.'

Jago rolled his shoulders, uneasy now. 'That's a lot to remember. Hang on. Let me see. The first one is the one when the bursar was found here, isn't it? I've already told the officer who took my statement: I was in my rooms in college and then went for a run along the river.'

Leo nodded. They'd checked that out first. There was no corroboration of this, no cameras on his riverside route.

'What happened last Thursday?' Jago asked.

They were keeping the details of the appearances of the murderer out of the public domain as far as possible. The press knew they had happened but neither witness was giving interviews. 'If you could just answer the question.'

'I guess I was in the library. The librarian might remember. I have a favourite seat in the Radcliffe Camera.'

They'd checked that already too. Jago sat in one of the aisles of the circular building, out of sight of the librarian's desk. She said she recalled seeing him a lot over the last few days but wasn't sure of exact hours.

Jago tapped his fingers on his knee. 'I know where I was on Sunday. That was the day the poor couple were found at the boatyard. I was at home, reading and making notes. I rang Jess. She'll be able to confirm that I made a call at that time.'

But not where he was when he rang her. 'And the last one? Yesterday?'

'Christ, I don't know. What was it? Five? On the way home from the library, I guess. I don't lead a very exciting life, Inspector, particularly not at the moment.' Jago paused as he thought back over what he had said. 'I don't have an alibi, do I?'

Leo said nothing.

'If I were this killer, I think I would've planned better to at least make it look like I wasn't anywhere near the kill zones.'

Maybe.

'You can't believe that I'm responsible for this?' A panicked note edged into Jago's voice.

'Why not?'

Jago got up, his emotion too strong to keep seated. 'Because I love these places! I wouldn't defile them with this stupid crime!'

'Stupid?'

'Yes! Murder is asinine – a crude proof that you were momentarily stronger than someone else. But it is ugly and brutal – it spoils the place for others, making them think dark thoughts when they should be enjoying the amazing gifts nature has given us.' He swung round to face Leo. 'I hate this person, whoever they are, hate him for spoiling all this for me and for others. And if he's using my work to pick his locations, then I hate him all the more for perverting my hard work like that!'

His indignation sounded genuine to Leo. 'If you were this man—'

Jago opened his mouth to object.

Leo held up a hand. 'I'm not saying you are, but try to think like him for a moment. If you were this man, where would you strike next?'

Jago deflated, sitting back down beside Leo and dropping his head into his hands. 'I don't know, Inspector. Look at the river.' He swept his hand to the Cherwell. 'There's all this and the Thames too, not to mention the reservoirs and lakes that allow swimming. Pick your poison – there are hundreds of possible places along the banks.'

That was very much what Leo feared.

Chapter 23

Jess

I stood at the side of the set with Jonah's cigarettes, water bottle, phone and script – his four best mates as he called them. Joseph Flanagan was with me; he was the personal assistant to BAFTA Winner for Best Actress in a Leading Role, Ronnie Merchant, as he enjoyed telling me with a sparkle in his eye. A dapper older man in his sixties, he claimed he used to be the dresser to Laurence Olivier. Thanks to Joseph, I had been shown where it was safe to wait, out of the way of the lighting people and cameras.

If you didn't know what was going on here, you'd assume that the guys holding the equipment were in charge and the director their servant, waiting on them to be ready. Jonah sprawled on a bed for what he had gaily called his post-fuck scene with Ronnie. In this screenplay, the woman, Diana, was the hard right devotee, one of the Mosley Blackshirt gang, and Kev the one dragged in by his love, or lust, for her.

'And ... action.' Each time the director, Harris Underwood,

said those words, I got a little thrill. Everyone else just looked tense.

On the call to start the camera rolling, something inside Jonah switched on. He projected a charisma that made you want to look at him, bug-eye, scar and all. I'd got to know him a little in the few hours we'd spent together. He made me laugh and how he talked to his Jenny on the phone was simply too cute. He was head-over-heels for her and thought she was far too good for him.

It would be nice to have someone think you're too good for them, rather than a hook-up with a mass of drawbacks.

But then I'd have to be at a level to earn that, wouldn't I? At the moment, I was bumping along the bottom of desirability. *Issues, I have outstanding issues* – I could hear Charles saying it to me at our last appointment. Outstanding, not in a 'well done, you' way but as in intractable. Unsolvable. Never to be cleared level of student debt.

Diana was now screaming at Kev that he didn't love her if he doubted the cause to which she'd given her life. I reckoned she'd gone to full decibels too soon. There was another half a page.

And the director agreed with me. 'Cut. Let's try another take. Ronnie, peg it back a little. Don't let rip until "up your arse", OK?'

She frowned. 'You mean after the second c-word? But it seems such an explosive word.'

'Not in the world of Kev and Diana – it's a normal noun. That's right, isn't it, Jonah?'

Jonah had flopped back on the bed ready for a second go

at the scene. 'Yeah, Harris. Nothing was too shocking for the far right guys inside. And I guess the same might've been true of their fascist grandparents.' Jonah had warned me that this would happen: just because he did time a few years back for drug offences, everyone expected him to be the expert on rough characters. He found it easier not to argue.

The director was happy with takes two and three so the crew broke for lunch. They were filming the sex scene on a closed set. I thought this a perfect chance to go find Roman as I might have to stake out the smoking spot for a while.

This was why I was heading across the carpark with a couple of lighting guys and a sound lady – all of whom shared a nicotine habit and had been told they wouldn't be needed for an hour. I was duly welcomed to the club as we clustered under three umbrellas against the burst of rain that had struck Oxford like a slap.

'This is going to fuck with the guys erecting the outside set,' said one lighting man cheerfully. Ben? Len? I hadn't quite caught his name. I assumed his pleasure was because he'd pulled an indoor job this week.

'I worked on Bond. Serious nightmare keeping the sound sweet and clean. Fucking low-flying aircraft. They had to do a lot of ADR for the back lot scenes, despite our best efforts,' said the woman. I thought she had said her name was Leanne.

I didn't want to spoil the idea that I might actually be a professional so tried to work out what ADR stood for. There was always Google, of course, but later, when I was back in Jonah's trailer or on the way home.

'I hand it to those actors – they're really good at repeating a performance in a studio months after they filmed them,' said the youngest of the trio, Elijah something. Ellwood, I thought he said – sounded like an elf, an impression cemented by his sweep of shoulder-length red hair that was conditioned to an unreal state only seen in shampoo adverts. 'You remember that wet set for *Pirates of the Caribbean*? Where the lights in the boats kept fritzing out?'

The smoking zone had a canopy of a tree in full leaf so we could fold the umbrellas. We stood stoically, like foot soldiers in a dugout in World War I as the barrage rained down a few feet away.

'It's like being in a fucking war zone,' said Ben (or Len). He was a short-statured man with biceps like a weightlifter.

'Crazy summer we're having,' said Leanne. She shrugged. 'Climate change, I suppose.' She was a jeans-clad, plaid-shirted thirty-something who appeared like she might know how to hold her drink.

'I got arrested on the Extinction Rebellion march,' I volunteered, thinking this would cement my street cred with them.

'You daft cow,' scoffed, let's call him, Ben.

'Aren't you outraged by what we're doing to the world?'

'I am,' agreed Elijah.

'I think it's too late already,' said Leanne.

'But we can't give up because we don't know that it is,' I protested.

'That's right!' echoed Elijah, flicking his hair. I could totally imagine a wardrobe of cosplay outfits and an elven sword somewhere in a closet.

'What is it you do again?' I asked, attempting to change

the subject. I was supposed to be hanging out with these guys, not prompting a punch-up about climate science.

'I'm best boy electric. He's the gaffer.' Elijah nodded to Ben.

'You position the lights, gaffer?' I asked Ben.

'Basically that's right. We design the onset lighting.'

'So why does it take so long?'

Leanne pointed her cigarette at me. 'Thank you, Jessica. That's what I've been asking for years.'

'The gaffer and me, we're actually some of the quickest in the business,' said Elijah.

Ben just smiled in a way that suggested I couldn't possibly understand how complicated his job was.

'Well, thank God for that – or they'd never shoot anything.'

'Aye-aye, here come trouble.' Ben shuffled aside as a little group from the set building team joined us. Brilliant – the plan had worked. I spotted Roman immediately from the family photos. In the flesh, he was shorter than I'd imagined, more like five nine or five ten. His hairline was high on his forehead but then gave way to loose curls a couple of inches long. His dark eyes were small for his face, narrowed as they scowled at the world, not generous. With his boxer's nose set a little off-centre, he didn't seem to have the ingredients for handsome but oddly there was something roughly attractive about him. I could see why Amy fell for him in a big way – before she fell out again, obviously.

'Hi, I'm Jess,' I said brightly to the newcomers.

Roman lit his cigarette and looked at me over the top of the glowing end. 'Is that right?'

'She's new,' said Leanne drily. 'She's not been here long

enough to lose the stars in her eyes.'

'That'll come soon enough,' said one of Roman's colleagues. None of them had offered their names. The guy had really short hair so I nicknamed him Buzz.

'I was just asking these guys what they did.' I gestured to Elijah and co. 'What do you all do?'

'Jess, they're on their break,' warned Leanne.

'Oh, right, is there some etiquette here about not talking about what you get up to? Sorry, I'll keep my mouth shut then.' I took a puff on my first cigarette for a decade. I got a head rush.

My enthusiasm appeared to be wearing them out. Maybe I needed to tone it down a little but it was so difficult. I loved being on location: it was so Hollywood.

'Do you remember when everything was that exciting?' Leanne asked Roman wearily, with a look at me.

'Yeah. The Potter days were the best. Could do with more films like that. We made real money then.'

I wasn't going to say it. I wasn't. I did. 'You worked on those films? Oh my God, that's a big part of my childhood right there!' Well, teenage years to be honest. They had been a great escape from the muck that my father spread in our household.

'One of my first gigs,' said Roman, 'as an apprentice. It needed a huge team of designers. I was in the first wave coming over to work after Poland joined the EU. And now look.'

None of us picked up on that particular leading remark. What could we say? Brexit? Bleurrgh!

'And don't you just love what you're doing now? Working

for a film with Ronnie Merchant and Jonah Brigson?' I asked.

'Stars in her eyes?' Roman said to Leanne. 'She's got whole solar systems. However did she pass the vetting?'

'Good question. How did you get in here?' Leanne opened the umbrella, preparing to return to the set. 'You're not going to be one of those souvenir hunters, are you? Stuff's being going missing from wardrobe for weeks now. We're all getting it in the neck.'

I crossed off my to-do list the trophies I'd planned to take. 'No! I'm not like that. But this is the most exciting place I've worked in months. Last week I was in a lawyers' office counting paper clips; now here!'

Roman extinguished his cigarette on the metal receptacle for butts. 'Still counting paper clips?'

This was tricky territory. I didn't want him to suspect a connection to Amy. 'Someone's on holiday so everyone got shuffled around. I've been brought in as assistant to one of the actors.'

'You'd better watch yourself. My fucking ex is one of them. She's fallen for the fantasy life around these actors and tried to live it out at home until I caught her at it. Everything a drama with her as the star.'

Could he be right? Was Amy doing all this because she was a fantasist? 'Right, well, I'd better get back. I might be needed.' Highly unlikely as Jonah would be feigning coitus with a nubile brunette. 'See you guys around!'

'Not if we see you first, you won't,' called Roman, and the others laughed.

Tempted to give him a single finger salute, I resisted and

dashed under Leanne's umbrella. We hopped, skipped and jumped our way across the forecourt puddles. Simon the porter held the door for us.

'Everything all right, ladies?' he asked, his tone hitting smarmy in the bullseye.

'Yes, thanks,' I replied. I didn't like the way his eyes followed me.

Leanne scowled. 'The porters here are a joke.'

'I thought Roman was much worse,' I muttered.

Chapter 24

Jess

I'd almost forgotten in the excitement of my first day at work that I'd agreed to see DI George at Cory's that evening. Barely had we wiped up the splattered avocado mush on the booster seat, when he rang on the door.

Cory clapped her hands. 'OK, kids, upstairs. Jessica has a friend round.'

A friend? Well, I supposed it was more child-friendly than 'policeman on a murder squad asking about the body she'd found.'

The kids thundered upstairs, Benji in the lead, Leah clumping up behind in some plastic clogs I'd found her. She'd refused to take them off since because they had floating glitter in the gel. I think I've hypnotised her by mistake.

'Hi, come on in.' I stood back to let DI George and a female colleague enter. 'Is the kitchen table OK? The living room is a disaster zone, like someone has exploded a bomb in Legoland.'

'That's fine. This is Detective Sergeant Wong.'

I quickly wiped the table where the constable was going to sit, having noticed that Benji had crushed his peas under his plate to fool his mum that he'd eaten them. The police-woman brushed one off the seat before she sat down.

'Sorry – you've caught us at clean-up time. Amazing how much mess two little people can cause.'

Sergeant Wong gave me a deadpan look. 'That wasn't you – hiding your greens?'

So she was OK then. 'Nope – though I wish I'd thought of that when I was his age. Right – tea, coffee?'

'Miss Bridges, please don't trouble yourself,' said George in his lovely rumbling voice. He was wasted on policing; he should be announcing programmes on Radio Four. 'There's a couple of things we need to ask you.'

'Fine. OK.' I dumped the dishcloth in the sink, washed my hands, then sat down. There really was no delaying this any longer.

'The first is the easiest. Have you seen any sign of contact from the person harassing your former partner?'

'Michael's troll? No, nothing.'

'No packages?'

I grimaced, remembering Michael's dead bird. 'I don't think anything has come but I could check.'

'Please – and let us know. But that sounds promising. And are you varying your routines as we suggested?'

'Yeah, I'm working in a new place this week, on a film set – on a case.'

His eyebrows shot up. 'Oh? Something we should know about – to do with the film crew?'

I remembered how unhelpful the police had been to Amy. She wouldn't thank me for involving them. 'No, no, just a family thing. Helping a mum get in contact with her estranged daughter.'

'OK, keep alert to any strangers taking an interest. You have my number.'

I noticed that I'd left Leah's sippy cup on the table. I didn't like sitting still for long so I got up and dumped the water down the sink, then washed it out. 'You had another question?'

'Yes. This is about the two murders. Did Dr Harrison tell you he was consulting on the case?'

I stacked the cup on the drainer and leaned with my back to the butler style sink. Cold enamel pressed against my butt. 'Er, no. We only communicate sporadically.' But I bet he liked that – right back in the midst of things, where he always wanted to be.

'We've confirmed that they are connected. Our killer has a bizarre pattern of pretending to be the people he kills. To do so, he must watch them for some time to learn their routines, the details of their jobs, the people they work with.'

I rubbed my arms. 'Creepy.'

'We have some CCTV images we want to show you. Can you tell us if you recognise him?'

Would I see Jago in the pictures? Then again, the police had met Jago and could do their own identification. 'OK. I'll try my best.'

Sergeant Wong set out five printouts in the very spot I'd played snap with Benji before supper. In one a man stood at the back of a van, not much of him visible. In the second, a woman – no, a man – was coming through a door in a hoodie, sports bag on his shoulder. Same man? The build looked similar but the definition didn't really tell you much other than he was white with relatively small hands. I couldn't rule out Jago but there was nothing that suggested him either. He could be any of the average sized white guys I'd met today, from the porters at Linton College to half the people in smokers' corner. No visible facial hair. Expand that to the population of the Thames Valley and we were swimming in suspects.

'Not much to go on. Do you have him moving?'

Wong got out a laptop and played the footage of the guy going into what seemed to be a fight club.

'Where is this place?'

'A gym in Temple Cowley,' she said.

The guy appeared to be walking on his tiptoes. I pointed. 'Why's he doing that?'

'He's pretending to be his last victim, Ruby Lonsdale.'

'And he thinks women walk like that? Terrible actor.'

'Recognise him at all?'

I shrugged. 'I'm sorry. I can't say I've never seen him before in my life or that I've met him. He's just so ... unmemorable, isn't he? Unless he's playing dress-up and killing people.'

Hearing the sounds of bath-time being concluded upstairs, George collected in the pictures.

'Here's the difficult part. We're not saying that he is circling either you or Mr Jackson, but, as there has been a connection between you and the murder sites, it is worth considering that possibility.'

My blood chilled.

'You mean I might have a second stalker?' The desire to break into my emergency cigarette supply swept me, something to occupy my shaking hands. I couldn't though, not here. 'Oh lucky me. You wait for one psycho to come along and two come at the same time.'

Sergeant Wong snorted, then covered it with a cough. And had even George cracked a smile? It was so faint and then gone-, that I might've been dreaming.

But then something struck me. 'Wait! If he is watching me, does that mean Cory and the kids might be in danger? Oh my God, I'll have to move! Cory didn't sign on for this when she took me in.'

'It's only a very slight possibility, nothing we can build a case on. We don't have any evidence, only coincidences. Talk to your landlady—'

'Friend,' I corrected him a little too quickly.

'Friend, but don't exaggerate the risk. We think you are safest here. We'll keep an eye on the place, naturally, but we're not worried for their safety.'

Was he telling me the truth? I couldn't tell. 'And Jago? Are you warning him?'

There was a strange look in George's eye. 'We have. On that note, I wanted to ask you if you have noticed anything about Mr Jackson's behaviour over the last week?'

Oh my God, they were looking at him too!

'I don't really know him all that well.' I looked back at the printouts in George's hands. They didn't feel like Jago to me. They weren't, were they? 'Do you think he's ...?'

189

'We are following up all leads. If you're worried,' continued George, 'then we would advise you not to go anywhere alone.'

I ran my fingers through my hair and scratched at my scalp, my last ditch move to bring myself to sanity when I was feeling strung out like this. 'OK, let's recap. Troll, doesn't seem to be interested in me. Good. Murderer, maybe is but we can't tell. Bad. Have I got that about right?'

'Yes.'

'So I definitely shouldn't go swimming with Jago?'

'You have plans?'

'For Saturday.'

'I wouldn't change them just because of this, but perhaps you shouldn't go somewhere off the beaten track.'

'I think we'd worked that one out already. Jago's talking about a lido.'

'Then please keep us apprised of your plans. We'd like to keep a close eye on you.'

'Shit. I'm bait.'

The inspector met my eyes. I realised that there was toughness below the quiet exterior. 'It would be one way to flush him out, yes.'

Chapter 25

Michael

Jessica had texted saying she wanted to chat. Hardly surprising as she must've been reeling from the news the police delivered. Michael was aware that he was one of the few people she knew whom she could talk to about being in the crosshairs of a killer and who would not think her crazy.

The doorbell rang. Michael checked the video intercom. Jessica was frowning at the screen, then realised it was a little camera and started to pull faces.

He laughed and buzzed her in. Typical.

The door slammed and she hurried into the open plan kitchen-diner, white linen shirt flapping like wings over a hot pink tank top. 'Cool place you've got here, Michael.'

'It suits me.' He was feeling tired this evening so was in his chair. He rolled towards her and she met him halfway, dropping a friendly peck on the cheek. Her fragrance surrounded him for a moment – some tropical body wash, not perfume. He wished they'd left things in a better place than they had when they'd broken up. Intimacy-starved, he sometimes felt he could do with a friend with benefits and Jessica was the type who would be up for novel arrangements. The thought that she might be persuadable crossed his mind. She was on the rebound from Drew, wasn't she? They knew each other. It would be safe for them both to scratch that itch ...

He gave himself a mental slap. She was here to talk about a killer, not about climbing on his lap and going for a ride.

'Didn't take you long to get here?' he said instead.

'Oh, I ... er ... kind of live in Summertown now. Temporarily.' She blushed.

'It's OK. The police already spilled the beans. Inspector George told me in one of our consultations.'

'The sneaky bastard!'

'Not on purpose. He was embarrassed by the slip, I think.'

'I seem to have the knack of embarrassing him.'

'Can I get you a drink?' He backed away smoothly and went to the fridge where he had an open white wine waiting for her. 'I got in your favourite.'

'Please.' She was prowling, as was her habit, checking out his adaptations to the room, picking up ornaments, running her fingers down the spines of the books. 'Russian translation, huh?'

'Yes. They're very interested in the subject in Moscow.'

'Hmm. Murder. Where isn't? Bhutan maybe. Iceland – can't imagine much happening in that country.' And there she went, riffing off into her own world of speculation.

'Iceland certainly comes out well as a safe place to live,' he agreed, passing her a full glass of wine. 'So?'

'Yeah, so. Chin-chin.' She sipped her wine. 'You're not having one?'

'I'll stick to water.' He wheeled over to the kitchen table. 'Take a seat.'

She sat opposite him and spun the glass, watching the reflections on the surface.

'Jessica?'

'Charles is cutting me off, did you know that?'

Michael had seen Charles last week at his club but they didn't discuss Jessica any more. 'Actually, I did not. Why?'

'He knows I can't afford him and he thinks he's done enough.'

He knew exactly how expensive Charles was, having footed the bill for her care when they were together, and that had been at Charles's reduced rate, which he would've extended to her after they split up. He was a decent man. 'And what do you think?'

'That I'm scared I'll mess everything up.'

'That's natural.' This might not be the best time for Charles to step back, thought Michael, what with the concern that a killer might be interested in her. 'I could have a word if you like?'

She laughed sadly. 'Sorry, I didn't mean you to think you needed to intervene. I can tell him myself.'

'Explain to Charles what's going on. He might give you a reprieve. And if you need a loan ...?' Was he really offering to pay for her treatment again? He must be crazy. Would he never learn?

'That's fine – but thanks. I don't have many expenses and I'm earning so ...' She shrugged.

Michael was relieved. He hadn't meant to get entangled again. No strings is what he liked. He was caught up in enough complications of his own to take on hers too.

'You sounded stressed when you messaged. What can I do to help?'

'Simple really. I just need to know I'm not risking the family I'm living with. The kids are three and five, Michael: I can't endanger them.'

'You're not to blame for this situation.'

'I know that, but I still have to consider them first. I want your professional judgement. Are they in danger?'

'I don't think this person is interested in them – and probably not in you. It's just a slight possibility and it's wise to take precautions.'

'And if I let the police use me as bait, I'm not inviting some creep to decide he is interested in them after all?'

'I think not. Look at his pattern: he didn't touch Kenneth Kingston's family.'

'Of course he touched them – he killed their dad.'

'I don't mean to imply that he didn't harm them; I meant he just didn't think about them. They were irrelevant to him. I think he wanted the local saint aspect of his victim's life, not the everyday stuff. And with Lonsdale he wanted to play at being the upscale brand manager. That was his focus – not her friends or family. Her boyfriend was only killed because he was there when the killer struck.'

'My home isn't the target then?'

'That wouldn't fit his pattern. He likes his victim alone and outside.'

'Why is he doing this?'

'Aside from being a violent man?' She waved to indicate that they could both take that as read. 'He is collecting experiences.'

She gulped her wine. 'OK, I can see that.'

'I wouldn't live my life trying to second guess him.' He nudged the wine bottle towards her and she refilled.

'Let me try this one on you. I did wonder, just for a few seconds, if Jago might be behind it. He knows both those places far better than anyone.'

That was actually an interesting suggestion from Jessica. It was wise never to forget her intelligence. He considered it for a moment. 'I didn't think of him when I saw the CCTV images but then again, the man is in disguise. We really have very little knowledge of what he looks like beyond average height and build. His eyes might be altered by contacts, he might be playing with other theatrical effects on hands or face. That would fit with his methods.'

She grimaced. 'Am I completely running wild even thinking of this possibility?'

'No.' He said it firmly. 'You know that he was a student of mine? Before your time. It's safe to say that we didn't get along.'

'That's what he says, but less politely.'

An unpleasant thought struck. 'Does he know about our connection? Could it be that was why he's taken an interest in you?'

She shook her head. 'Can't be. He didn't know my name to start with. I think the appeal at first was that I'd read his book and not been that impressed. He saw me as a challenge.'

The circumstances of their meeting would also have helped. Jessica had an admirable figure. 'But Jackson as a killer? I don't think he is my top pick.'

'Who is your top pick?' She looked relieved. Michael realised that she wanted to like the guy.

'A killer who has also read the book or seen the programme and is retracing Jackson's footsteps. He'll have seen the news that the police and press have talked to Jackson about being on the scene soon after the first killing and that would've thrilled him – a brilliant coincidence. Actually, he might even have known that Jackson would be running at that time and set it up to increase the chance of him finding the body. Even if Jackson hadn't been in his pattern before, it might've convinced him to include it in his methods. He's arrogant. He likes to give us clues, but not enough to nail him.'

'So you think I'm safe to go to a swimming pool with Jago?'

'No one can tell you that.'

'I think Inspector George wants to use me as bait.'

'You shouldn't let him use you.'

She plucked nervously at her shirt. 'But maybe I can stop another attack?'

He reached out and gave her hand a squeeze. 'No, Jessica, no matter what you do or don't do, this guy isn't your responsibility to catch. He's dangerous and he's having too much fun to stop.'

'Hmm.' But from the mutinous look on her face, Michael guessed Jessica was too careless of her own safety to heed his warning.

Chapter 26

Jess

O n the way to work the next day, I messaged Jago.

Did you get the same creepy pep talk from the police? That the murderer might be after us? Yes.

Michael's assessment that Jago was an unlikely killer had settled my fears somewhat that I might be texting the attacker. *And?*

Let's just say I'm not going very wild with my swimming this week. I'm making a start on research for my running book instead. I won't be in college today.

I guessed that was better but I would've thought that places to jog could also be isolated.

Be careful, OK?

And you. How's the new job?

I sent a string of emojis.

That good, huh? Us little old book writers won't impress after you've met the movie stars.

It's OK, my star is already taken. Why was I telling Jago this? It felt very much like flirting. *Gotta go – my stop.* It wasn't but I was worried what I'd do on impulse if I carried this on.

Instead, I opened a message to Drew. *Hey, there's been some developments.* I quickly summarised the case I'd taken on – Drew would know Amy from the cul-de-sac – and concluded with the news from the police that the killer might be shadowing me.

There was a little ellipsis as Drew contemplated his answer. I was rather pleased by the tack he chose. *Who's Jago?*

I smiled a little smugly. *The author of Wild Swim. He was with me when I discovered the first body. We've become friends.*

The smugness was knocked back a bit by his next message. *Cool. Are you being careful?*

I presumed he meant about my personal safety, not the sex talk. *What do you think? It's really not in my life plan to get murdered.*

You, Jessica Chaos-is-my-natural-element Bridges, have a plan?

Cheeky bastard. *How are you?*

All good. Missing you.

Why did he do this? Send the mixed messages? *When are you coming back?*

I have an assessment at the end of the month, then we'll see.

So this is like a proper qualification?

Yeah, duh!

Well, how was I expected to know? I wasn't exactly an expert in yogic practices. *Good luck with that.*

Nel says I'll walk it. I'll then have to decide about staying on for Part Two. That will really improve my professional qualifications.

My heart sank. *And how long is part two going to take?*
Another few months.

I didn't have anything to say to that. He wasn't asking me
if I thought he should do it but taking the decision entirely
on his own shoulders. It was what you did that revealed the
truth, not what you said. I closed down the message so he
didn't see the ellipsis of me thinking. I'd prefer him to believe
I'd just shelved him for my far more interesting life in Oxford.

And then impulse struck. I reopened the chain to Jago
Feeling spooked here. Do you want to meet up tonight? And
I could dig a bit deeper to find out if he was hiding anything.
Yes! Great idea. At mine at 8?
Sounds good.

There was a problem with one of the sets – police were still
examining the boathouse – so Jonah was left twiddling his
thumbs. He'd had an interview with a magazine, answered his
emails (here my typing skills proved an asset), and read
through some scripts he'd been sent. That meant he was bored
and wanted to shoehorn himself into my investigation.

I grabbed my bag. 'OK, I'm off. Cigarette break.'

He got up with me and picked up his tobacco tin. 'I'm
coming with you.'

'Really?'

'Yes, really.'

It was an overcast day but the rain was holding off. I'd
noticed that Roman was fairly regular with his breaks – every
two hours – so I was hoping he'd show up while we were
outside. Would having Jonah here help or hinder?

I grabbed Jonah's elbow. 'Don't mention Amy, OK?'

Jonah patted my hand. 'This ain't my first rodeo, Miss Jessica.'

I groaned. 'That's a truly terrible American accent, Mr Box-Office Hit.'

We huddled together out of the wind in the forecourt. The sound lady and the lighting guys must've been caught up with the problems on the set as we didn't see them even though it was the usual time for a coffee break.

'How did the sex go yesterday?' I asked.

'It was phenomenal – oh, you mean the filming?'

I buttoned up my jacket, feeling a chill breeze from the river. 'And you don't find it awkward, being naked in front of a camera crew?'

He shrugged. 'Nah. I'm nothing special. It's a job.'

'But don't you worry that what you think is sexy might be laughable to other people?' That would be my hangup.

'Jess, the first thing you have to know about sex is that it is funny, no matter what you do. And anyway, I just take direction. I don't improvise. I've too much respect for my female partner for that – or male.' He licked his cigarette paper to close it around the thin line of tobacco. 'You seem very interested in the mechanics. You should've stuck around.'

'Anyone would be interested – don't believe them if they say they're not. Maybe I will next time.'

'But, seriously, Jess, it's also about revealing character.' Jonah lost some of the brash act which was his default mode. He was committed to his craft even if he joked about it. 'Kev is the passive one in the relationship so takes more than he gives – the sex can show that.'

'So that's why he ...' I twirled my fingers in the air to indicate the sex act described in the script.

'Yeah. It's not gratuitous – not a porno.'

'Oh.' I took too deep a drag of my cigarette, then coughed.

'Not used to sucking?'

I elbowed him in the ribs.

'Help, Amy, I'm being beaten up by the horrible lady you sent to mind me this week!' he exclaimed in a falsetto.

The little smoking delegation from set design emerged on the dot of eleven. They did a double-take to see Jonah had descended from his star to rub shoulders with them and weren't sure at first how to react.

'Don't be such fucking pussies,' Jonah crowed, which broke the ice.

Roman still hung back. He must've known who his ex-partner had been working for. Jonah pinched the end of this roll-up to extinguish it and tucked it in the tobacco tin. He pointed to his eye.

'Hey, mate, this isn't real, you know. No need to keep your distance from the scary dude.'

By making it a challenge about bravery, Roman, of course, had to come nearer. The chat continued for a bit, all general stuff, the up-coming football season, who was filming what, which productions they were scheduled to join.

I was beginning to think this would all pass smoothly until Jonah intervened. 'Aren't you Roman Wolnik?'

My target looked up, surprised. 'Yeah. How do you know?'

Jonah got right in his face. 'My assistant told me what a pile of piss you are.'

I tugged his arm to get him to stop. 'Technically, piss can't be in a pile. Let's head back.'

He shook me off. 'It can be a pile if you're pissing on shit.'

'Lovely image, Jonah. Thanks for that. I'm sure that's brightened everyone's morning. Oh, look at the time.' I was really angry with him now. He was messing with my investigation – doing exactly what I'd asked him not to do. 'I'm sorry, Roman. I didn't mean to expose you to my prima donna here. They don't let him out much. He's forgotten his manners.'

Roman gave me a nod. 'That's OK, Jess. You aren't responsible for who you work for.'

'Come on, Mr Brigson.' I dragged him away. 'Sorry, everyone!'

We left to a muttered chorus of 'fuckhead' and calls of 'that's all right, Jess'.

Once back in the trailer, Jonah took out his roll-up and relit it. He grinned at me. I wished I could have slapped that expression right off his face.

'Do you know what you've just done?' I fumed.

'Yeah. I've given you an in with the set design guys.'

That took the wind out of my very self-righteous sails that I'd reefed to be all billowy and speed me across the ocean of indignation. 'You did that on purpose?'

'You aren't going to make any progress just being nice to them. They'd never trust that.' He changed his T-shirt for the black shirt his character wore in his next scene. He had a sixth sense about when he was about to be called. 'You showed them you were on the side of the working guy against the arrogant actors who waft around here like their shit smells of honeysuckle.'

He was right. I'd come away with a much better standing with the smokers than before. Yesterday I had been an annoyance; now I was their Captain Marvel, removing the asteroid before it hits earth.

OK, that was going a little far, but a star like Jonah could cause a lot of trouble for the ordinary workforce if he put his mind to it.

'Say "Thank you, Jonah".' He did love playing dangerously, did Jonah.

I reached for the next fan letter for reply. 'Go stick your head in your honeysuckle effluent, Mr Brigson.'

Chapter 27

Jess

I made my way to Jago's at seven. I was early so I stopped off at a metro supermarket in Summertown, opting for Marks & Spencer to show I was a classy girl.

Do you want me to pick up something for supper? I asked Jago.

No need. I've cooked a Thai.

There are laws against that.

He sent back a laughing emoji. Lots of guys found my humour tiresome but this week I'd found two – Jonah and Jago – who seemed to find me funny – for the right reasons. He had made no mention of dessert so I picked out a punnet of strawberries and cream.

Waving to the porters, I passed quickly through the college. Filming was over for the day and it seemed very quiet. Jago buzzed me in and I climbed the staircase – oak bannisters and whitewashed walls – all very Gothic revival. With this Victorian atmosphere, I would not have been surprised to find Charles Dickens coming down the stairs the other way. Jago opened the door for me at the top.

Joss Stirling

'Do you want me to take off my shoes?' I asked, hovering in the entrance. His trainers were lined up there. How many pairs did one guy need? Six apparently.

'No, it's fine. I don't believe in carpets.' He headed back to the kitchen whence delicious smells were wafting.

I followed with my carrier bag, wondering when was a good moment to offer it. 'That's a weird religion. The Carpet Sceptics.' I put the strawberries on the granite countertop. 'I bring cream too.'

He shot me a quick smile, a wrinkle of his already wrinkled brow. 'Thanks. I don't usually think of dessert.'

'But you do believe in it, I hope?'

'Oh yes. No worries on that front. Do you want to prepare those?' He got out a bowl and a small knife.

'Sure.'

We chatted about how his research was going. Contrary to my imaginings he actually started his books in a library, working out the history of urban areas and old rights of way. He admitted to nerdish tendencies. He had spent today in the Bodleian; he'd be safe there.

'Did you know that six people went to jail in 1932 trying to protest the right to roam?' he said.

'The Kinder Scout mass trespass.' I dipped a crisp in some salsa he'd set out.

'You know about that?'

'I have a mind stuffed full of trivia. So that's what you were researching?'

'In the newspaper archives.' Taking off the lid, he stirred the rice to see if all the water had been absorbed. 'And what's

206

it like working for bad boy Jonah Brigson?' he asked, finally getting off the subject of himself. I accepted that he was a little narcissistic. Most of the guys I knew seemed to be that way inclined.

I remembered how I'd planned to ask Amy the very same question and never got round to it. Now an insider, I was reluctant to brag so I deflected. 'Really nice. As much as I like the job, I'm actually doing this for a client with family issues.' I explained about the situation with Roman, without using names.

From out of the download of information, Jago picked up on Angelica's odd behaviour. 'Children – that's complete foreign territory for me. I have no hope of understanding what's going through a fifteen-year-old girl's mind.'

'Yeah, their thought processes can do your head in.'

He tapped the slotted spoon on the side of the pan. 'This is ready. I'm starving. You?'

'Yeah, I'm feeling really hungry.' I decided not to spoil his appetite by bringing up the suspicions the police had. I mean, how would that go? Hey, they think you might be a killer? But there was something else I could confess. 'Um, Jago?'

He was snipping fresh coriander over the top of the meal. 'Hmm?'

'I haven't been quite straight with you about something.'

'You wouldn't be the first. Don't tell me: you're married?'

I laughed nervously. 'No, nothing like that. Well, maybe it is a bit like that.'

'Uh-oh, this sounds ominous. Shall we sit down?'

I took my plate to the little table by the window overlooking the river and meadows. He'd put a rose in a long-stemmed vase and there was a candle, but he hadn't lit that. That was what the evening felt like – poised between romance and us not going there.

'I am – or was – in a serious relationship, but my partner, Drew, has called a hiatus.'

'Meaning?'

'It's off for the moment.'

'You're free to see other people?' He offered a basket of poppadoms.

'Yes. I think it might even be expected.' Drew was likely to be exploring his options with Nel so why not me?

'Sounds very civilised. I wish more couples would try that rather than flog a dead horse of a relationship.' He crumpled his crisp bread over the top of his meal. I'd never seen anyone eat a curry this way.

'I had been hoping it was a Derby-fit racehorse we were both riding.'

He poured out the wine. 'Your guy might've felt differently?'

'Clearly he did. But that wasn't what I wanted to tell you.'

He raised a glass to me in a toast. 'Cheers. There's more?'

I took a sip. 'Yes, there's more. It's about me and Michael Harrison. I didn't mention when I could've done that we were actually together for a long time – five years. It ended about thirteen months ago.'

His fork hovered between plate and mouth. 'You – and Michael Harrison? That was you?'

I knew what he meant. The stories had circulated last year in the press and as an old student I imagine he would've followed them. I was a little surprised he hadn't googled me already. Or was he only feigning surprise? 'It depends which version you read?'

'That he seduced you in his office – took advantage of you.'

I snorted. 'That sounds so dated. We were both adults and we had a relationship. Why doesn't the press just grow up?'

'Because they thought Michael was a murderer?'

Which reminded me that suspicions were often wrong. I couldn't believe Jago had a violent bone in his body. 'And he wasn't. Clearly. I've kept in touch with Michael. Getting on better now than we ever did.'

He chewed for a while, then took another forkful. I decided to sacrifice my wine appreciation to start eating before he thought I didn't approve of his cooking. It felt a very long silence.

'How's the curry?' He leaned forward and lit the candle with the waiting matchbox. I took that as another hopeful sign. My confession had been successfully made and received. Time to move on.

'Great. Is this lemon grass I can taste?'

We carried our strawberries and cream out onto his little balcony. There wasn't room to sit so we stood among the pot plants enjoying the view over the meadows. The sun was setting behind us so we just got an impression of darkening clouds and shadows growing under the trees. Joggers and cyclists in neon darted along the towpath across the Cherwell, glimmering like fireflies.

'How did you get into the missing persons business?' he asked.

There was so much behind a complete answer that I went for a partial truth. My past history was much easier to package up than the recent one. 'I ran away a few times as a teenager – once for months.' I'd ended up seeking answers in alcohol and sleeping with the wrong kind of men before I was able to turn myself around.

'Problems at home?' guessed Jago.

'My father. He's a terrifying man who turned the phrase "to rule with a rod of iron" into a daily reality. I survived but barely so I feel I should help others who find themselves in the same, or similar, positions.' And he never really let me go, chasing me to various student digs and flat shares, so I had to be clever to avoid seeing him. That was why living with Michael had been the first time I'd felt really safe. My father had backed off when he saw there was a man in the house who looked bigger and stronger than him.

'That's admirable, Jess.' Jago took my empty bowl from me. 'I bet you're really good at it too?'

'I'm not bad.' And I felt that little rush of pride I got when I remembered the people I'd reconnected to a better life.

He took the bowls inside and returned, holding out a hand to me. 'I hope you don't want to rush off?'

'No. I'm not expected anywhere.' I'd messaged Cory where I was.

'Want to watch some TV together?'

I stepped over the threshold, deciding to trust him. 'What are the chances of us finding something we'd both like?'

'Ah, a challenge! Let's see if I can come up with the perfect programme.' He turned his computer screen to face the sofa and opened up his Netflix account. I kicked off my sandals and sat beside him on the sofa. We started watching, feet up together on a pouffe so that our bare toes looked like twenty little spectators for the film. He had very long toes compared to my piggy ones.

He dropped an arm around my shoulders. 'Is this OK, or too much?'

I turned to look up at him and realised that I wasn't going home that night. 'Not too much.' I closed the gap and kissed. His response was at first shy, then he got with this very different programme for the night.

'In that case.' He looked sweetly bashful for a second, then hit the off button for the screen. 'I have a Jacuzzi in my bathroom. Paid for it to be fitted myself.' He wiggled his eyebrows in jest.

The made me laugh – of course he did! It almost spoiled the moment.

'Seriously – I need it in winter after swimming outdoors.'

'I can imagine.'

'Want to go skinny dipping again?'

'Only if I get to play with the bubbles.'

He took my hand. 'It's not everyone I let fiddle with my controls.'

'I should hope not.'

I woke up and stretched, awareness returning that I wasn't at home.

Oops, I'd done it again. Not that I had regrets.

I groped on the floor beside the bed and looked at the time. Five in the morning. The sun was coming through the white curtains – that was what woke me. Jago was beside me, lying on his front completely limp like I'd just dragged him half-drowned from a river.

Thankfully I'd remembered to text Cory that I wouldn't be home, or she would've had the police looking for me by now. I found her response which I hadn't read last night as I had been *cough* otherwise engaged. It involved lots of emojis for eggplants and swimming so she'd got basically the right idea, the cow.

I flopped on my back and tried to decide what I thought about my impulse. Could I scrape together any guilt? Not really. I didn't think Drew imagined I'd so quickly find someone else but he did say I had his full permission to do so – in fact, that it would be more accurate to say that I didn't need to ask. We were – what was it? – free to do what we liked.

Well then, Drew, I had liked sleeping with Jago. Sex in the Jacuzzi was harder than you might imagine without drowning your partner, but we managed. And then there was the bout on the floor of the living room in front of the open window (he's not overlooked by anything but squirrels). He described that as taking advantage of the summer night air, poking fun at his own words earlier. Once in bed I described the sex scene Jonah and Ronnie had been filming and we had a go of that too – without the cameras. That probably explained why I didn't feel any guilt. I was too full of satisfaction hormones.

In fact, I could probably blame Jonah, as envy of his own happy home life had made me particularly horny last night.

Would I tell Drew?

You bet. If that didn't bring him back to win me, then he was not mine, and I might as well enjoy myself with an eligible man.

'I can feel you thinking from here,' said Jago sleepily. 'Stop it.'

'I wouldn't call it thinking so much as reliving.'

He turned over and smiled at me. 'Oh yeah?'

'Hmm-hmm.'

A tug brought the sheet off my torso. 'You know, I knew I had to have you when we first met. I've been thinking about that a lot.'

'I could tell. Your running shorts don't keep your secrets very well.'

'And yet you still agreed to go swimming with me?'

This was probably not the best time to admit that he was my rebound guy, was it? 'I'm reckless that way. Oh, I perhaps should've made that part of my full disclosure.'

'I thought you gave me a very full disclosure right from the start.' He kicked the sheet down and to the end of the bed. 'I think we should swim naked together more often. I've still got lots of favourite places to show you.' He nuzzled my breasts. 'And now I have some new ones.'

Chapter 28

Leo

The order Leo had given for an increased police presence around Jago Jackson had quickly paid off. The patrol had caught someone spying on Jago's college rooms from the other side of the river, behaving in a manner that fitted with an obsessive stalker killer. His team was ready to celebrate but Leo wasn't so sure it would be this easy. They thought they'd got their man. Had they? It would seem a very fast turnaround for someone whom Leo had down as a careful planner. But then again, murder was fundamentally a reckless act, as well as a morally repugnant one. He shouldn't give the killer too much credit for intelligence.

Leo placed a call. A second opinion from a psychologist might give his gut a little more backing.

Michael was shown into an office which had a screen displaying the interview room. In there, a confused-looking young man in a running strip was sitting at the table, studying his fingers which were clutched together. He had short brown hair, medium build, small hands – nothing that discounted him as the perpetrator but also nothing that separated him from a thousand other men who used the towpath each day.

'Michael. Thanks for coming – and sorry for the early hour.' Leo indicated a place for him to position his wheelchair and put a coffee down in front of him.

Michael took in the participants inside the interview room. 'DS Boston is taking this? That's generous.'

'Not generous, no.' Leo kept his smile tight. He'd imagined the interview and decided this was his best team to field.

'Who's the female officer again?'

'Suyin Wong.'

'Ah yes, the neat and sharp one.' They both fell silent to hear the rights being read.

'Lucas Crouch, do you understand what you've just heard?' asked Harry with his usual bullish tone.

'Yes, but I don't understand what I'm doing here!' Crouch turned to Suyin, mistaking her for the softer of the two officers. 'This is crazy. I was just out jogging. There's no law against that.'

'Indeed, there isn't,' said Harry. 'But perhaps you'd like to explain, Mr Crouch, why you were jogging with binoculars and a camera with a telephoto lens? I imagine that's a recipe for damaging some expensive kit.'

'I have them in a padded rucksack – I always carry them.' He hunched up a little defensively. 'Do I need a lawyer?' He was still looking at Suyin.

They had to be careful here. If he called in a solicitor, the delay would lose them the momentum.

'You have the right to call a lawyer,' she confirmed. 'If you do so, we'll suspend the interview and continue when they get here. That will take some hours.'

It was the right aspect to emphasise. 'You mean take even longer? I'm due at work at nine.'

'What is it that you do, aside from taking photos?' asked Suyin, picking up the opening.

'I'm a caretaker.'

'Where?'

'Ferry leisure centre.'

'Does that mean you clean the pool?'

He was relaxing. Bad move, Crouch. 'Among other things. I keep the changing rooms clean – tidy the public areas – people can be absolute pigs, leaving their rubbish everywhere. It'll soon get out of control if I'm not there. I've got to be there.'

Leo noted the OCD tendencies. That might work with the killer's mentality. He seemed a little mentally deficient too, which could be a problem. From Michael's frown, Leo could tell the psychologist had noted this.

'I don't think he's unfit to answer questions,' Michael murmured, answering Leo's unasked question. 'Not the brightest bulb, but not unable to reason.'

Leo nodded in thanks.

The interview was continuing without any such doubts being raised.

'Then we'll try and clear this up as quickly as possible, shall we?' Suyin gave him a gentle smile. 'We wouldn't want to keep you unnecessarily.'

Joss Stirling

'I like her style,' Michael commented. 'She takes the right, calming tone with him.'

'Yes, she's very promising – very good when a touch of empathy is what is needed. A little surprisingly, she and Boston have a good rhythm together. If I were there with Boston, I think we'd just shut him down – two men seen as ganging up on him.' And Leo had wanted to take a more distant view so he could keep his objectivity.

Harry reached down and pulled a camera out of a black rucksack.

'Hey, that's mine!' exclaimed Crouch.

'Thank you, Mr Crouch, for confirming that this is your camera. Would you like to tell us what were you doing with your camera last night?'

'Taking photos.' Crouch's tone was grumpy, almost childish. Leo could imagine the killer being like that when challenged. Was it him?

'Care to show me?'

Crouch folded his arms and glared.

'OK then. What about these?' Harry drew out a pair of binoculars. 'You were seen using them.'

Crouch licked his lips. 'I was bird watching.'

'You see a lot of birds at ten o'clock at night in the direction of Linton College, do you?'

'You'd be surprised.'

'I'm sure I would.'

'What kind?' asked Suyin patiently, as if helping him.

Crouch couldn't produce an example so stayed silent.

'The problem is, Mr Crouch, that a member of the public

218

saw you using these binoculars to scan the student houses on several evenings recently,' she said, carrying on the almost apologetic tone. 'They told us that you are in the habit of taking pictures of people through their windows.'

'There's no law against it.'

Harry leaned forward, ugly face gleeful. 'I'm afraid there might be, Mr Crouch. Invasion of privacy.'

Harry was fudging that a little. It was very hard to prove a photo taken from public land was an invasion, but they'd agreed this was a tactic to scare the suspect. And Leo didn't think it would take much to frighten this man.

That was where Suyin came in. 'In fact, Detective Boston, I think Mr Crouch could argue that he was on the towpath, not on private property.'

'Yes!' said Crouch, not seeing this for the trap it was. 'I just take photos – I never set foot on anyone's property.'

'It could be argued that it's not his fault if he catches people in private moments.'

'Exactly!' said Crouch, grasping onto Wong's suggestion. 'I'm not doing anything on purpose.'

'You might think that, Detective Wong,' said Harry, ignoring Crouch's self-defence. 'But I believe it shows an unhealthy obsession with one of the inhabitants of Linton College. What interest do you have in Jago Jackson, Mr Crouch?'

Crouch smirked. 'The swimming guy?' He had heard of him. The likelihood of him being their man went up a little. 'Until last night, nothing. The only action he ever got was watering his plants. Very boring.'

Hopes diminished. This didn't sound like the killer after

all. He thought he was being funny, not something Leo would expect from their schemer.

'And what happened last night?' asked Harry.

Crouch suddenly sensed danger. 'I can't get into trouble with this?' he checked with Suyin.

'Not for taking photos, I'd say not,' said the detective.

'Lucky guy pulled for the first time in ages.' He grinned, which had the effect of making him very ugly. 'Pretty woman – well built, if you know what I mean?' He checked this with Harry, sensing another male chauvinist, then looked down. 'Sorry, Miss. I'm just a guy. I like tits.'

They all knew he didn't mean birds now – and he appeared unaware of the pun.

'You like taking photos of them?' asked Harry.

Crouch had the sense to take care with his answer. 'Not on purpose. But if they get in the shot while I'm taking pictures for my birdwatching collection, then fair play, hey? I challenge you to find a red-blooded male who wouldn't agree with me.'

'Did you recognise the woman he was with?' asked Harry, keeping his tone casual. 'The busty one?'

'No. Should I?'

'You haven't seen her before in your life?'

'No, she's not been at his flat before as far as I know.'

Harry had got him. 'But you would know? You've been watching Mr Jackson for weeks now.'

'What? No! Well, not him especially.' Crouch looked shifty again. 'Look, it's like this. I take a lot of photos. But I haven't taken any of him because he's never been –' he searched for a word – '*interesting* before, not like others in his building.'

'Fucking makes him interesting?' Harry dropped any euphemism and got to the heart of the matter. 'You take pictures of people engaged in sexual acts without them being aware of it? That is an offence.'

'No, no, I take pictures of birds, and sometimes people forget to close their curtains and I end up getting more than I mean to.' The man was sweating now.

'Our interest here is in Mr Jackson, not the other inhabitants of that building,' said Suyin. 'Mr Crouch, are you able to prove that it isn't Mr Jackson who has provided you with subject matter before last night?'

Their suspect looked at the camera, considering his options. 'I suppose I can. You're not trying to trap me, are you?'

Of course they were, thought Leo.

'I could get a warrant to search the SD card – that will delay things,' said Suyin, 'or you could just let us look.'

Crouch thought for a few seconds. 'All right.'

Leo's hopes were finally sunk.

'It's not him,' said Michael.

'We have your permission to look at the contents of this camera's memory card?' persisted Harry. Leo could tell from his expression that he too was beginning to feel they might not be on to a killer here. The pathetic far outweighed the potential for violence in this man.

'Yes. I said so already,' Crouch grumbled.

The two officers suspended the interview and took the camera with them.

Leo turned to the psychologist. 'Impressions?'

'Doesn't seem clever enough to be our killer. And, if he lived up to the profile I've generated for him, I would expect him to have been dressed as Ruby Lonsdale last night if he was working up to his next kill.' Michael smoothed back his hair; he must've rushed to the station after the call because his chin was showing more stubble than usual. 'But I might be wrong about that. He might save that for the killing rather than the surveillance.'

Leo wondered if the real killer had jogged by while they were arresting this pathetic individual. He could just imagine him in the twilight, dressed in his green-and-white exercise clothes, high ponytail bobbing, running past with a smirk. Their target knew the police were after him and he'd like the close brush with the law.

'I really don't think it's him,' Michael concluded.

Leo agreed with him but they had to play this out to the end. 'Let's see what the camera tells us.'

Leo's interview team came in with the SD card already slotted into a laptop. They started with last night's images.

Harry laughed. 'Well, look at that. The naked chick.'

Leo scowled at him and blanked the screen. 'Sorry, Michael, not something I anticipated. Do you want to take a break while we check the rest?'

'I'm a professional, for fuck's sake,' said Michael. 'I need to see the whole collection to gauge our man's predilections.'

Fortunately the images were pretty grainy as they were taken from some distance. Enough to tell that Jago and Jessica had had a fun time last night but not in HD quality. The images changed to other windows on other nights. Not a bird among the shots but plenty of students walking around naked in their rooms, unaware of the peep show they were providing. Crouch did prefer women, as he said, restricting his pictures of naked men to when they had company.

'Either he's Britain's most incompetent wildlife photographer or he's a world class creep,' said Suyin.

'Not our man?' Leo asked Michael.

'The killer is a voyeur but the sexual element seems wrong to me. The man you have in there is seeing people as sexual objects; the murderer sees them as lives he can possess. He wants to be them, not look at them. If he were tracking Jackson with a view to taking over his life, then I'd expect more images of him going about his daily business.'

Time to accept they'd got the wrong man. 'You'd better let him go, Sergeant Boston. Warn him that we may still charge him under Section 67 of the Sexual Offences Act 2003 and that the offence is aggravated if he chooses to share any of these images. But basically he is small fry. We'll pass the details on to the sex crimes unit and let them deal with it.'

Harry didn't hide his frustration. 'I wanted it to be him, the perv. Who does that in their spare time?'

'More people than you can possibly imagine,' Michael said. 'People are as twisted as pretzels.'

At least that made Leo laugh in his disappointment.

Chapter 29

Jess

'Someone is looking very pleased with herself,' mocked Jonah. He was in a funny mood as he lounged on his couch like some sulky sultan. Too much time on his hands today, he was looking to scratch and growl at me, but I was fine with that. He never promised he'd be the ideal employer, and in fact warned me he had days when his past made him feel sick of life. Clearly I'd happened upon one of those.

I'd been humming as I answered his fan mail and updated his social media. 'Jenny away?'

He checked his phone. 'Yeah, on tour. Fucking Barcelona.'

Source of bad mood revealed.

'It's supposed to be a great city.' I could tell my upbeat tone was winding him up but he needed to let it out at someone and I was obviously up to bat. Thanks to my dad, Jonah's fast balls felt like pitches from a seven-year-old kid with co-ordination issues.

'And are those the same clothes you came to work in

yesterday?' He rested an arm along the back of the couch, eyeing me with a little malign smile.

'Experts say we shouldn't wash our clothes so much.' I poured Jonah a coffee and dug out the emergency biscuits. 'Save the world.' He looked like he was about to throw a chocolate digestive at me so I reached down and snatched it from his hand and ate it in one big bite.

'Gross,' he said admiringly as crumbs fell from my not-quite-closed lips.

I swallowed with difficulty. 'Yummy.'

He reached for his script to refresh his memory on the next scene. 'What did I do to deserve you?'

'I am exactly what you deserve, Jonah.'

Despite his bad start to the day, Jonah remembered to usher me out at cigarette break time. 'Go catch the bastard,' he growled.

'Eat some biscuits,' I told him. 'You'll feel better.'

I picked my way across the carpark, dodging the drying puddles. The designers had already gathered, joined by the lighting team. It happened to be an all male gathering, which changed the dynamic. It took a little more boldness to go breezing into the centre in my normal fashion.

'Hey, Jess, got rid of Brigson yet?' said Roman as I joined them with a chirpy 'Hi, guys!'

'Not permanently, but I told him he'd worn out his welcome so shouldn't come with me again. God, wasn't he embarrassing, throwing his weight around like that?'

There was a murmur of agreement.

'I think actors like him forget what normal people are like

once they get a taste of stardom.' Sorry Jonah, but I knew this was what you'd like me to do with my opportunity here. 'And I'll make sure he doesn't make any trouble for you – for any of you. I seem to have a knack for handling him.'

'How can you do that, love?' asked one of the men whose name I'd not yet caught, the one I nicknamed Buzz. 'He's got a rep as a hard man but he's good box office. I can't see the studios standing up to him.'

'Jessica's very good with him, we've all seen that; she has the knack,' said Elijah, the elf-like best boy electric with the improbably groomed red hair. I hoped he hadn't developed a crush, but he did keep looking at me and echoing everything I said to earn my approval.

'Yeah, Jess here pokes fun at him between takes – makes the sullen bastard smile,' added Ben. 'Could've done with you on set this morning, love. You're better at cheering him up than the stuck-up cow who normally looks after him.'

Roman smirked at the insult flung at his ex. 'I bet.'

'Jonah says Amy is very efficient.' I trailed my defence out there to see what nibbles I got at the bait.

'Ms Mason doesn't have a sense of humour though,' said Ben.

Meaning she didn't laugh at his misogynist jokes – yeah, I'd heard you, Ben. You made millennial Elijah cringe with your personal comments and quips.

'She's a deceptive, sour bitch, that's for sure,' said Roman.

'Come on, guys, this isn't fair. She isn't here to defend herself,' I said.

'I know what's she's really like.' Roman offered me a cigarette from his pack, a gesture that seemed an unsubtle bribe to get me on his side. I took it, tacitly accepting the compact, and we found ourselves a little to one side of the others. 'She has a history of making false allegations.'

'Really? How do you know this?'

'I used to live with her – until I found out what she was doing to one of our kids.'

'How awful!'

'All the guys in my department know what a liar she is.' He seemed to welcome a new audience for his grievances.

I hoped I looked suitably scandalised. 'You mean, like, mental or criminal damage?'

'Both.'

'What did she do?'

'Everything.'

'Like?' I searched in my handbag for my lighter.

'For one, she made Angelica think she was ill when there was nothing wrong with her.'

'Shit, that's pretty serious stuff.' I brandished the lighter in triumph and lit the cigarette. 'I only know what other people have told me about her and she sounded nice to me.'

'Your source being that fucking actor?'

'Are you sure that ... what's her name? Your daughter ...?'

'Angelica.'

'Are you sure she isn't really ill?'

He smiled grimly. 'Here's a fact for you. Since leaving home to live with me, she's been fine. Not a single health scare – not even a headache. I just need to get my boy out of there and then both of them will be safe.'

'You've got somewhere for them?' That did sound a little too nosey. 'I mean, that's great. I found it really hard to get a decent place.'

He breathed a plume of smoke into the air. 'Got something suitable through a friend here. They really came through for me.' He was looking at the guy I'd nicknamed Buzz.

'It's connections, word-of-mouth, isn't it, that gets you places? Pretty cramped where I am at the moment.'

He pulled a face in sympathy. 'If you were staying on in Oxford, I'd say look in one of the villages nearby. I only have a twenty-minute commute.'

'Oh, that sounds perfect! Where?'

'Elsfield – a couple of miles away.'

'If you hear of anything, let me know.' I stubbed out the cigarette. 'Just need a single room.'

Roman slipped his cigarette packet in his back pocket. 'Taking to this life, are you? Even with the pig of a boss?'

'Yeah. Jonah's OK most of the time. I'd stay if there were an opening.' And that was actually the truth.

'Don't let Amy know you're after her job. She'll see to it that she ruins you.'

'Oh come on, she can't be that bad! She doesn't even know me.'

He shrugged. 'Take it from me, she's devious. And if you don't believe me, check the court record in Cancun. I'm looking forward to telling the judge in the Family Court.'

And that didn't sound ominous? He headed back to work and I started walking back to the trailer, planning on making an immediate internet search. Elijah caught up with me, falling into step. I might as well use his – what? – puppy love for my own ends.

'Elijah, do you know by any chance the name of the older man with the buzz cut – the one with Roman?'

'Pete Murphy. Real old timer – been here since the 90s. Why do you want to know?'

'Apparently he rented somewhere to Roman. I was just wondering if he had any other properties, you know, in case I stay on in Oxford.'

Elijah seemed to be winding himself up to ask me something and I feared I knew what it was. 'Jess, I was wondering ...?'

'Yes?'

'Would you like to go out for a drink after work one night? With me and the rest of the crew, I mean?'

Oh, that actually didn't sound too bad. I could sound them out about Amy. 'What night is crew drinks?' I asked, making it clear I wasn't taking it as a personal invitation.

'Friday.'

'I'll just check with my boyfriend.' Jago had just been officially elevated to the position, my Elijah deterrent. 'But I think that would be nice.'

'You've a boyfriend? Oh, well, I suppose he could come along too, if you like.'

I climbed the steps of the trailer. 'I'll see what he says. Thanks, Elijah.'

I shut the door on him, feeling relieved I'd skated around that encounter.

* * *

I waited for Jonah to head off for lunch then typed in Amy's name and Cancun, Mexico, into his computer and wait for a response. Her name was not so unusual for there not to be three or four Amy Masons active on social media when I'd last checked – and none of them had been her. My Amy kept herself to herself. Nothing.

But if it was old, then maybe it was under her maiden name? Her deceased husband was a John Mason. Her maiden name was ... I checked through my notes ... Sibert. That combination pulled up new results. Add the location and some references to news items that hadn't made the first page now zipped right to the top of the list.

Woman denies making false rape claims in Cancun nightclub
I clicked on the link and discovered a news item that hadn't got much traction back in 2001, thanks to 9/11. The woman, later revealed to be 'Amy Sibert', was found guilty in absentia of making a false accusation of rape against an ex-boyfriend. The bare bones of the case, according to the press that covered it, was that she got her ex thrown into Mexican jail in retaliation for him breaking up with her – I bet that was no picnic for him – then retracted the accusation once she was out of the country. The authorities naturally wanted to penalise her for that but she didn't go back to defend herself and any extradition proceedings ran into the sand. Her sentence, passed in a local court, was still waiting for her, if she ever went back to Mexico. The follow-up article with the unfortunate ex – a former army private – was not complimentary to Amy. Fantasist. Unable to take rejection. Started a process out of spite but got scared when she saw that she couldn't back up

her words with any evidence. In fact, all the evidence was to the contrary from the messages on the phones proving their relationship was consensual.

I was left wondering how that ex-boyfriend related to the one she had gone on to marry – John Mason. Both in the army. Did she have a habit of hanging around with soldiers at that age? She'd been, what, twenty-two? Her home address then was over in Colchester, a garrison town.

Maybe she had good reasons for not following through, but it did go to a pattern of claiming something false – rape or illness – and then getting scared when the consequences came home to roost.

I wondered if I should warn Amy of what Roman had planned when the family matter came to court. She was my client.

And yet, maybe she was the villain of the piece, not him? The already shaky tower of faith in Amy's honesty had taken a serious blow.

When I got home, Cory was waiting. I could tell from the glint in her eyes that she wanted the full details of my night away and I was not going to escape her unless I came up with a very good excuse. Fortunately, things were delayed by the presence of two small chaperones. Leah evidently had been waiting for me all day, just to break her own little bit of news.

'You got present!' she declared excitedly. 'Can I open it?'

From my initial excitement, caught from her, that something nice might've unexpectedly arrived in the post, I suddenly remembered the other creep Michael had picked up and possibly sent my way.

'Really? I thought I told Maria that I wasn't accepting deliveries.' I said this looking at Cory who was aware of the issue.

'It was on the doorstep when they came home,' she explained. 'Leah found it first.'

'She didn't touch it, did she?'

'No. Leah knows better than to open other people's presents,' said Cory with a look at her daughter. 'Maria put it on top of the washing machine in the utility room. Out of reach.'

'I'd better go and deal with it then.' With a smile that said everything was fine (when it really wasn't), I took some washing up gloves, dustbin bag and scissors with me. It could just be a parcel from my mother. She lived out in the country with my big sister, Miriam, and occasionally sent me offerings of books she'd just read or produce purchased at the Farmer's Market. I faced the parcel. It was about the size of a shoebox and quite light, so no Dundee cake, marmalade or stack of paperbacks inside. My name and address was written on a typed label and the packaging was generic brown paper. I lifted it carefully. No sender. It didn't seem like my mum's style.

But I could check.

'Hey, Mum?'

'Jessica! How are you? Your father hasn't been in touch, has he?' She got her question in before I could ask her anything.

Why would she think that? 'No. Why?'

'It's nothing.'

'Mum?' It was never nothing.

'He's just been sending me messages.'

'What kind of messages?' My skin crawled.

'Nice ones. He found me on Facebook and he said how sorry he was our marriage ended the way it did.'

Yes, like a fox was sorry for the chickens it carried off. 'Don't trust him, Mum.'

'That's what Miriam said – and I'm not a fool!' No, just soft-hearted.

'If he keeps on bothering you, maybe you should come off Facebook?'

'Don't worry about me, dear. I was the one who left him, remember!' Yes, but after over a decade of suffering. 'Tell me all your news? How's Drew?'

I realised she was way behind on the Jessica updates and I couldn't go into all that now.

'Everything's fine.' Not. 'Got a really interesting temping job on a film set this week.'

'Ooo, you are moving up in the world!'

'Just two weeks – but I like it. Actually, Mum, can I call you back later for a longer chat? Fill you in on all the gossip.' Carefully edited. 'I've only this minute come through the door and just wanted to check something with you: have you sent me a parcel?'

'No, dear. Why do you ask?'

'A mystery present has arrived.'

'Oh, you've got to be careful about those! I was just reading about a scam where people buy new phones through identity theft using your address.' My mum read all the horror stories about elderly people losing all their savings, or being defrauded by unscrupulous callers. I was pleased she did because she would otherwise naturally be the kind of person to be taken in.

'Yes, yes, I'll be careful.'

'Don't give it back to a courier! That's how they work the scam!'

'Yes, fine. Love you.'

I finally got her off the line after a string of extra warnings. I contemplated the parcel again. Ring the police? And find it is some free sample, or something I'd forgotten I'd ordered online?

Michael had got a bird – gross but not explosive.

Gingerly, I cut the Sellotape and removed the brown paper sheet. The shoebox was old – the Clarks style I used to get my school shoes in at around this time of the year. This had been in someone's wardrobe for many years. Had to be the troll, didn't it?

'OK, you creep, what've you sent me?' I used the closed ends of the scissors to lift the lid off.

Yellowed tissue paper. I could cope with that.

'You all right in there?' called Cory.

'Yes, but keep the kids out for the moment, please.' I nudged the paper aside.

A doll lay in the paper, facedown. I recognised it immediately – or at least the brand. It was a Teeny Tiny Tears – a baby that cried and wet its nappy, someone's idea of a suitable toy for a little girl two decades ago. I remembered I'd begged for one when I was around Leah's age.

But the facedown was a bit of a clue, wasn't it?

Still using the scissors, I levered her over – then let her drop back on her front. Her eyes had been gouged out and she was leaking red liquid. It had collected under her in the shoebox.

I think it's fair to say that Michael's troll had found me.

Chapter 30

Michael

M ichael put the phone down after finishing the call from Inspector George. At least that settled one matter: the mysterious 'she' in the messages was indeed Jessica. Both Jessica and George were coming to see him. The inspector wanted him to look through Jessica's social media accounts to see if the troll had also been rampaging there and he also was keen for Michael to see the contents of the package before it was taken into police evidence.

Jessica arrived first. She was carrying a dustbin bag, holding it in front of her. As he moved back to let her past, she processed inside with mock solemnity.

'Behold, a wise woman came from the south, bearing her gift of mutilated baby. Where is the expert that I may consult him?'

How perfectly Jessica.

'Thank you for ruining all future nativity plays for me,' he said, following her into his kitchen-dining room.

She grinned in a slightly manic way. 'Where do you want this? Outside? I warn you, it's pretty gross.'

'That's not a bad idea. Would you mind unwrapping it on the patio?'

'Your wish is my command!' He knew her chirpiness was Jessica's defence against a world that she realised was cruel so it didn't annoy him any more. It also helped that they were no longer living together; he thought he'd had less patience when he'd had to face it every day. She was relentless in her sunshine and he'd sometimes felt burned by it.

She donned Marigolds and unwrapped the layers to reveal the baby doll. She lifted the face so he could see the empty eye sockets. 'Not blood, you'll be relieved to hear, but some kind of red gel or paint. I think the doll is old,' she said. 'I checked online and they don't make them quite like this any more. I had one just like it as a child – most of us did. It was the must-have present if you were three.'

'What human beings find desirable never ceases to amaze me.'

She contemplated it for a moment, cocking her head to one side like a robin. 'I think it's the fact that you're in charge of the toilet training after having just mastered it yourself – some kind of power play thing. But weird, right?'

He thought her theory about the age was correct as the plastic limbs had that grubby stain that came with a toy that had already been clutched in many sticky hands. 'How would my troll know that this doll was important to you?'

'Important? I wouldn't go that far! I think I abandoned mine at the play park on more than one occasion – I didn't like the way her eyes followed me at night.' She leaned towards him confidentially. 'Dolls are really creepy. Sadly people kept running after me to return it.'

Michael had to agree with her about the eyes, but then he never was given one as a boy, not even an Action Man. His parents had been into wooden castles and pirate ships, thank God. 'But he knew you'd had one?'

'Not necessarily.' She shrugged, a roll of her shoulders in her thin T-shirt and he was reminded of the Peeping Tom images. She probably didn't know that the police and he were aware of her new relationship through the most intrusive of means. Should he tell her? Weigh her down with yet more embarrassment and concern when the policeman arrived? He didn't hate her enough for that – in fact he didn't hate her at all. He was feeling something like protectiveness towards her, which surprised him.

'Why not?' he asked instead.

'This doll sold in the millions – it's the go-to baby doll for toddlers if you like. If you want to mutilate a toy – and what self-respecting stalker slash troll doesn't want to do that? – then I guess this is the one you'd pick up on eBay for a couple of quid.'

The front door rang. 'Could you get that for me?'

As she went, Michael wondered what this particular doll meant. There was a common theme – baby bird, baby doll. Dead and blinded. They were meant to be symbolic, else he would've gone with the more traditional dog-turd or mysterious white powder route. Michael ran through the common associations with the objects – cuckoo in the nest, flee the nest, hand that rocks the cradle, cradle snatching, rock-a-bye baby. Ah – there was the connection. At least, maybe. He might be forcing it. A bird fallen from the nest and a baby doll made up to be like the victim of the nursery rhyme. *When the bough breaks* ... All very well, but what was the link to Jessica and him? His most recent outspoken comments had been on the moral responsibility of perpetrators of violence – it would be a Byzantine series of associations to connect these with that.

Or had he got this round the wrong way? Was it Jessica's involvement in this case – the wild swimming murderer? Was it a threat to keep out of it? No, that didn't work because he'd got the first package and the abusive online messages long before any of that had entered into his life, or Jessica's. There was no baby in their lives now or before. Apart from his wife's child – but that was ancient history, not something some online hater would've been able to dig up very easily.

Jessica guided George through to the patio. From the way he was laughing at something she'd said, they seemed almost pally, which was strange for the reserved inspector.

'Dr Harrison, sorry for disturbing you at home,' said George.

'No trouble. Thank you for coming out.'

He stood next to Michael. 'So this is the parcel.' It was a statement, rather than a question. 'Same person?'

'Yes. I'm more sure about that than the message we are supposed to receive. I did wonder about a falling from the nest or falling from the cradle link but it seems very ... well, Gothic.'

'Whatever the intended message, the threat is very apparent. What do you anticipate he'll do next?'

'He's unlikely to plateau at this point.'

'So he'll escalate? To what? More personal violence?'

'Inspector George, I'm afraid I can only tell you the kind of behaviours to expect, not predict for an individual who is only showing us very limited parts of his nature. If I'd been able to draw up a full psychological profile, even then I wouldn't speak in certainties but only likelihoods.'

'We need tea,' muttered Jessica. 'Or something stronger. Michael, do you mind?'

'Please.' He waved her towards the kitchen and heard the fridge open. 'There's no wine – and I think I've run out of milk,' he called.

She returned with his brandy glass and two ordinary ones for her and the inspector. She put them on the patio table. 'I'll be right back.'

'Hang on – you'll need a key!' He chucked her the little gold one for the drinks cabinet.

'Are you one of these policemen who don't drink on duty?' he asked George.

He smiled but it didn't quite reach his eyes, the tension in his shoulders giving away that he was concerned not to have clearer answers or a way forward to protect them. 'I see this more as an after-hours professional consultation.' He was looking at Jessica. Is this man sweet on her? wondered Michael.

'Good for you.' Jessica gave him one of her warm smiles and brought back one of Michael's less expensive whiskies and gin for her. 'I saw you had tonic.'

'Do you want me to get rid of that for you?' George asked Jessica, pointing to the box.

'Please.' She handed Michael a generous serving in his favourite glass.

'Thanks.' His throat felt oddly constricted. It'd been a while since anyone had been in his home, knowing his routines and preferences. God, he was getting maudlin. Drink your whisky, Michael, and buck up.

Neither of his guests noticed his momentary abstraction. They seemed rather too involved with each other.

'I'll send it to our labs,' said George. 'I take it neither of you touched it without gloves?'

'Michael didn't touch it at all and I used gloves,' confirmed Jessica.

'I'll put it by the front door. I think we've seen quite enough of it for now.' He took the black sack away.

'I think I have ice and lemon too,' Michael told Jessica.

She did a little shimmy on the way to the fridge. 'Now you're talking!'

It was on the tip of his tongue to tell her that he missed her, but what earthly good would that do? She might have got rid of Drew but she had already moved on to Jago. He had nothing to offer her, less than when they had been together. He needed to get over her.

He cleared his throat. 'Do you want me to look through your social media messages to see if I can spot him there?'

George heard the offer as he returned. 'Please do that – if Miss Bridges doesn't mind?'

'I wish you'd call me Jess.' She laughed. 'But this is so embarrassing!'

Michael exchanged a glance with George, then looked away. No, they were not mentioning that.

'Jessica, I'm sure nothing you've put online will shock me,' Michael said.

'Not that.' She rattled the ice in her glass. 'I've only got Instagram and it's a front.' She caught George's puckered brow. He was probably worrying how he could save her from a criminal charge. 'Not for anything illicit, like drugs and stuff, but for my clients and the people I'm looking for. If they follow me back they find a cutesy person with a fondness for cats.'

Michael chuckled. 'That's not far from the truth.'

She grinned. 'What have you done with Colette, by the way? Where is my princess?'

'Probably curled up on my bed.'

She laughed with glee. He'd never used to let the cat in the bedroom when they lived together. He'd let quite a few old rules lapse since the accident. He'd told himself it was because he lived on one level but he feared it was a sign of his drift from old standards. Perhaps it was a good thing not to be such a stickler for the rules? What had that got him but heartache?

He beckoned her closer. 'Show me this front of yours, Jessica. I'll promise not to be shocked.' Ouch – *double entendre*. He didn't look at George.

She logged into her account and as he thumbed through he found himself oddly entertained by her quirky mix of cats and their antics.

'You've got yourself quite a following. You're in danger of becoming an influencer,' he said.

'I know, I know, I'm turning the pet food advertisers away in their droves. Joke.' She sipped her gin and tonic. 'Ah, that's just what the doctor ordered.'

George was making his way through a generous serving of the whisky. Just as well Jessica hadn't brought out one of Michael's prized malts. He was warming to the man but he didn't like him *that* much.

'This all looks innocent,' Michael concluded. 'Your followers are a pretty nice bunch. My troll doesn't seem to have linked CuteCat4567 with you – and why would he? Any other accounts?'

Jessica grimaced. 'Just some profiles on professional sites. These are factual and give an email but I rarely get messages, mostly the usual spam about hot girls in my area that ends up in my trash. If he's been there to look, I wouldn't know.'

'And you've no public listing of your home address?' asked George.

'Not the one where I'm staying now. I suppose I should've switched over from the Feltham address but I'm still on the electoral roll over there. Mrs Payne – Glenda – forwards my post. I didn't bother to change because I was thinking I'd return.'

There was a little pause as she briefly acknowledged the unlikelihood of that.

'But the parcel was sent directly to your present address so he knows enough about you to be able to locate your home.' George's tone was calm but they all could tell that this was the fact that bothered him most.

'You think he followed me home?' Jessica rubbed her upper arms.

'I can't think how else he would find out.'

'Any chance it's the same person as the killer?' she asked, a little panicked if her darting eyes were anything to go by.

'Jessica, it isn't,' Michael said gently. 'It's just a wretched coincidence.'

'I'm not a fan of coincidences,' said George, 'I will be considering if there is any connection.'

They didn't need Jessica to be scared out of her mind by the inspector. 'The timing doesn't work. It doesn't feel right – and that's a professional opinion, not a personal one.'

'Michael, I know you're trying to make me feel better but I'd prefer there to be one creep rather than two,' said Jessica.

'But if the messages were from the killer then I'd suggest you leave Oxford immediately – just think of the violence inherent in the symbols! But I really don't believe that. Our killer is about play-acting, killing to get his targets out of the way; our stalker is about scaring and taunting. They are two completely different personalities.'

'Split personalities, same person?' asked George.

'Very unlikely – in my view. Though perhaps you'd like to call in a second opinion? I don't see myself as infallible.'

'Really, Michael?' If Jessica was back to teasing, then she was recovering.

'No.' He let a little of his regret seep into the single word and she patted his shoulder in passing.

They sat on his patio enjoying the night. The ring road hummed in the distance. An unmuffled motorbike rattled the

Waterways, prompting every householder to a flare of rage against the rider.

'People like him should be shot,' Michael muttered.

The inspector pulled a wry face. 'Best not to say that when I'm here.'

She laughed. 'Michael, you sound exactly like someone else I know. He hates the people who aren't like him.'

She was talking about Jago, of course. Michael had thumbed through his books – a litany of moans in the main.

Then the idea came to him.

Jago? Could he be the troll? He knew them both. He certainly hated Michael enough to send him abuse online and in physical post. But would that stretch to Jessica? And why? If he thought Michael suspected him, then perhaps he would do that to confuse the trail? These thoughts came in a rush. How much they were driven by a desire to find something wrong with a man he detested, it would take a less biased head to decide.

It was hardly something he could raise with Jessica but he would mention it to George when she wasn't there.

Unfortunately, the inspector stood up, first to go. 'Miss Bridges, can I give you a lift home?'

'I won't say no.' She leaned forward and kissed Michael on the cheek, enveloping him in a sweetly scented fall of hair.

He took her hand and held on a little too long. 'Stay safe, Jessica.'

'You too, Michael. You too.'

Chapter 31

Jess

The inspector was quiet as we drove the first few roads and I wondered if I should fill the gap with a joke or some lame comment. I got like that sometimes, mood set to 'bright and fine' like a faulty barometer ignoring the storms outside. I was surprised nobody tapped me on the forehead to settle me back down to more reasonable levels.

'Miss Bridges, there's something you should know,' he said at last.

'Uh-oh, that sounds ominous,' I replied.

'We detained a man yesterday—'

'Oh, that's good news!'

'Not our killer, we don't think. But he was caught outside Jago Jackson's rooms taking photos – intrusive photos.'

He let me join the dots. 'You mean ...?'

Eyes on the road, he nodded.

'How bad?'

'Not something you'd want to see published. We confiscated them. Hopefully, this is the last you'll hear of it.'

I pressed my knuckles into my eyes. 'Who saw them?'

'We're professionals, Miss Bridges.'

I thought of some of the glances I'd intercepted. 'Did Michael?'

Inspector George nodded. 'He's consulting on the case.'

'Damn.' But nothing could be done. 'Well then, I hoped I looked good – a goddess?'

The inspector cast me a surprised look.

'Well, did I?'

He pulled up outside Cory's. 'This is yours, isn't it?'

'Inspector, I hope they were flattering?' I put my hand on the door handle. 'I have a reputation for appearing naked to maintain, after all.'

He wasn't going to comment, was he? I got out. Yet as I closed the door, I thought I heard him say:

'You looked perfect.'

The car drove off before I could reply.

Cory was folding laundry when I came in, basking in the glow of the LED-lit kitchen, a sprinkle of inset lights across the ceiling in a geometric constellation. I could smell the faint odour of supper – I thought it involved baked beans and fish fingers – all wonderfully normal things. And why shouldn't life carry on as usual for some of us? She knew about the unpleasant parcel but I hadn't let her see the contents. Who needed that in their head?

'Everything OK?' she asked, a tiny white pair of socks in her fingers. Children were so vulnerable.

I sat down at the kitchen table and rested my head on my tote. 'I should go, shouldn't I?'

'Go?'

'Leave here – find somewhere else.'

She was silent for a moment. She owed it to her children not to take the offer lightly. 'I'd like you to stay. The policeman who talked to me on the phone said he thought we offered you a kind of shield. You're safer here than stuck in a flat on your own.'

'But the kids. I could probably go to Glenda and Ron's.' I was almost sure they'd make room for me if I explained.

'If you want to, then of course you're free to do so, but I don't feel you endanger us, I really don't.'

Was she just saying that? 'But is even a small risk acceptable?'

She couldn't say 'yes', could she? 'You're not putting us in danger.'

Neither of us could know that. 'Let's both sleep on it. Let me know if you change your mind – no hard feelings. Really none.'

She nodded and moved on to unicorn panties and vest. 'Besides, I'm still waiting for the details. If you move out, how will I ever get to hear of your night of passion with Jago Jackson? I hope he was suitably limber?'

I wanted to put behind me the knowledge that our private moment had been captured. I wished the brain came with a delete function. 'Swimming does seem to build stamina.' I put the kettle on for us both and threw two herbal teabags into mugs.

'Oh lord, that's just what I wanted to know.' She patted her chest. 'Not getting any action here, so I'm going to have to live through yours.' She added to the mountain of small person underwear that was growing in the basket. 'I think that's the worst thing my ex did to me – taking away my identity as a sexual being. I'm left as just Mum. Thirty-six with my most attractive years behind me.'

'Oh Cory, he didn't take it!' I put the orange and cinnamon tea down before her.

'Feels like it. Moved on to the firmer flesh of his childless old flame. No droopy jugs there. No flabby buttocks.'

'But she doesn't have two beautiful breastfed kids to show for it. Anyhow, why are we talking about this?'

She snatched a towel off the dryer airing over the radiator and flapped it like a matador distracting a bull before adding it to the basket. 'Because I'm feeling horny and frustrated and you are the only outlet.'

I grinned. 'So sorry, but I don't swing that way.'

She threw a balled pair of grey socks at me. 'Stop teasing. Tell me how many times and for how long? You can add in positions too.'

Laughing, I blew steam from my tea. This was just the antidote I needed after the tensions I collected from a visit to Michael.

'I was a goddess,' I told her teasingly. 'He couldn't get enough.'

'I'm jealous,' she concluded. 'I'm not sure I ever had a night like that, not even on honeymoon.' She flashed me a wistful smile.

Bearing the laundry upstairs, she left me alone with my tea in her quiet kitchen. I noticed a spot that hadn't been wiped on the table. Yep – baked beans. I got up and gave it a quick squirt with an antibacterial spray that smelt of fake apples, then wiped it clean. Cory might be going through a date desert but there were definite compensations in her life with the buzz of family around her and the unconditional love of her children. Her Brendan had walked out on the best part of life. I'd met him a couple of times at the handover on access weekends. He struck me as an ordinary kind of guy of middling stature and acceptable looks. He used to be big news here in this small world but now he'd been reduced to giver of treats and outings, losing contact with Leah and Benji's day-to-day interests and little events. His part in their life would become smaller and smaller, like slices taken from cheesecake by a dieter with no willpower. OK, that image was more about me than Brendan, but I thought my point was fair. He seemed a nice enough bloke but he'd proved not to have the staying power that was required to get past the fact that this person you've married was it for you, that the grass wasn't greener on the other side of the fence, just another kind of green.

Inevitably, that brought my thoughts around to Drew. Wasn't he nibbling on Austrian pastures right now? Time to let him know what had been going on in his absence on the home farm.

I drafted a long message, leaving nothing out, from my sleepover at Jago's to the baby-in-a-box today. It was a kind of test, I supposed, of how much he cared. If it was enough to fight for me, then maybe, just maybe, there was some hope left. I sent the message then powered off my phone – something I rarely did. I was determined not to spend the night checking to see how long it was until he read and responded to the news.

I woke up at four-thirty and switched my phone on.
I'll fly home today for the weekend. Drew
I did a little fist-pump. Result!

I reached Friday in what had felt a very long week. Jonah was feeling chipper because his lady-love was due back from Spain. I was nervous but happier as my love life was going to get settled one way or another. My biggest problem was how to sort out the rights and wrongs of the Amy and Roman case.

I took my usual smoker's break to coincide with Roman. I didn't say anything when I joined the group, just gave them a nod and a smile. These tactics worked better than overly friendly as it brought Roman over to my side. His curiosity was getting the better of him. He had his hair scraped back today in a bandana which reminded me of a late 80s film star look.

He offered me one of his cigarettes, which I accepted. 'Did you look her up?'

He didn't need to clarify who we were discussing. 'Yeah. Nasty.'

'That's what I thought when I found out.'

I blew the smoke away from him. 'When did you find out?'

He rolled his shoulders. 'She told me early on she'd had some legal trouble with a guy but I thought she was the victim. I didn't follow it up. I only found out the truth after Angelica started talking to me and I began to question things.'

'Poor kid.' That was true, whatever the details actually were. The children always ended up the victims.

'Have you told your boss?' Roman's gaze was now shifty.

'No. Why?'

'I just thought that maybe, you know, if she was exposed and lost her job here that ... well, it makes it all much easier for me to get Pawel out of her clutches.'

His motives for his not-so spontaneous confidence were now revealed. 'You want her to lose her job?'

He gave me a shark's grin. 'She wouldn't be able to afford her fancy lawyers then.'

I was glad Amy's at least had the sense to contact the legal firm this week. She'd need them however this turned out.

'I dunno. Do you think I should say something?' I asked, giving him my best wide-eyed stare.

'I don't like the guy you work for but an assistant needs to be trustworthy, doesn't she? That's the first quality they look for. Wouldn't you say so, Elijah?' he called over to the young lighting assistant who had been smoking within earshot and probably heard the entire exchange.

Should elves be smoking? I wondered. It somehow didn't go with the glossy red hair.

'It's difficult for Jessica, Roman. She's only been here a few days and doesn't even know Amy.'

Thank you, Elijah. 'I suppose it would seem odd – like I was after her job or something!' My laugh sounded a little forced.

'I thought you were,' said Roman.

'Not like this. It feels underhand.'

Roman gave up on me and checked the time on his phone. 'Just think about it, Jessica. It might work out best for you if you do.'

Elijah and I hung back as the set designer team returned to their onsite workshop.

'I don't think it was fair of him to ask you,' Elijah said. 'Still coming for drinks tonight?'

I'd completely forgotten – and I'd already arranged for Jago to drive over and meet the gang. Could I do that *and* talk to Amy *and* see Drew? Nothing else for it: I'd have to.

'Yes, of course!' I said breezily. 'Looking forward to it.'

Elijah knelt down to retie a lace. 'Is your boyfriend coming?'

Which one? 'Yes, he'll be there. He says he might've met some of you before.'

'Oh? How?'

'He made a series on wild swimming a few months ago. Same production company.'

He stood up. 'That guy's your boyfriend? Wow!' Elijah shook his head in not totally flattering disbelief. 'He's the reason half the girls on set have taken to swimming in the Thames. I think Leanne even went there with Kirstie and Marie the weekend that poor man was found dead.'

'Yeah, poor guy.' I wondered how the bereaved family were getting on – it had to be unbearable right now for them.

'Wrong time, wrong place, I suppose.' Elijah tucked his cigarette packet in the back pocket of his jeans.

'I suppose. Life's a bitch that way.'

'See you later. Six. At the Rose and Crown.' He strolled back to work, leaving me to some frantic rearranging of my evening plans.

Chapter 32

Leo

Leo logged the doll-in-a-box with the evidence officer, telling her to cross-reference it to the river murders as well as the online abuse case. As he'd told Jess and Michael, he didn't like coincidences.

When exactly had he started thinking of her as Jess? She was Miss Bridges to him. Anyway, she was clearly in a confused set of relationships, no room for a lonely policeman. He couldn't quite fathom what was going on between her and her threesome of Michael, Jago Jackson and the absent ex-partner she'd talked about, Drew Payne.

Don't even think about threesomes, Leo. He didn't usually have a gutter mind, but Jess brought what latent potential he had out of him

Once home, he shed his jacket and went out into the garden to think. Lost among the trees and bushes he could feel as though he'd left Oxford altogether, entered some realm of his own creation, like Tolkien's woodland Lorien or the secret garden of the children's tale. Here he could breathe.

He knew to his colleagues he was an enigma but he found it so hard to show any of his true self to people. What was that, anyway? As he pruned a withered tendril off the climbing rose, he wondered if Michael Harrison had profiled him yet. If he did, he would be interested to know that Leo's mother had been all about exposure, running her life in the public eye when she could attract attention to her small-time acting career. He used his absent and unknown father's surname to avoid people making the connection to Haven Keene but even that didn't seem enough. Some would still remember the weepy confession from his media-hungry mother before the daytime TV cameras that her son had been abused by an ex-partner. She claimed ignorance and the programme hadn't named him, but there was enough information for some kids at school to make his life hell. Their relationship never recovered. It was far better to keep all that out of sight and mind.

When his shadow fell across the water of the dark pool, Goldemort slipped out from the weed to nudge Leo into feeding him. He obliged. God knows what extremes he would turn to if Leo didn't keep him satisfied. He'd probably sprout legs and chase him into the kitchen.

The carp content, Leo sat on a bench under the Japanese maple. It glowed orange all summer, then flared up in a red blaze in autumn. He relished the way the fallen leaves spread like tiny crimson hands on the black surface in autumn. It was one of the markers of the year that he looked for, like the first celandines in late winter. There was no longer a completely dormant season in the garden, the last late blooms hung on in rose and hebe until December, evergreen clematis took over in a peal of white bells, and crocus edged up among the snowdrops when January came.

. The murderer was like that: always busy, never dormant. You thought you were tracking him in one place and another area of activity cropped up unexpectedly. So far he had chosen riverside locations with privileged entry: the college boathouse, confirmed as the scene of the first attack; the boatyard accessed by a code. How did he get two people to go in there? He must not look particularly threatening. Oxford was a relatively low crime area, at least for serious ones like murder. Most inhabitants felt safe walking around at dusk or even at night. Create the right story and unsuspicious people would fall for it. *I've lost my cat and I think I can hear it in there. Will you open the door? My child is trapped in the boatyard, can you help? My friend's got into difficulty in the water and I can't swim. What do I do?* That would be enough to lure fit twenty-somethings, and Dr Kingston, away from their own business. That led to the depressing conclusion that they were killed by their goodness of heart, not because of some sexual predilection that Harry Boston preferred to blame. He'd worked in Vice for too long.

The killer passed unseen, like the carp beneath the weed. People assumed he should be where he was. That suggested to Leo that he was possibly a familiar face in the college, either on the staff or one of the visitors. Jago wasn't completely out of the frame but Leo was thinking he needed to look elsewhere in the college. He was thankful for that as it reduced the pool of suspects from hundreds of thousands to a hundred, and bearing in mind his age and physical type (male, late twenties or early thirties, medium build, white), they were probably talking more like tens. He'd ask Sergeant Wong to whittle down the lists they had, though she was probably already working on that. They'd been asking for alibis but the film set was full of sudden stops and starts and nobody kept tabs on the crew if they weren't needed. The college was also relaxed during the summer, fellows and staff coming and going in irregular patterns. These difficulties weren't understood by Leo's superiors; they didn't want excuses, only results. But this was a pig of a case. If only they had some DNA to compare, they could then ask for voluntary tests from the men who fitted the description.

Leo picked a leaf from the maple and cast it on the black water.

Come on, life, I need a breakthrough, he thought.

Chapter 33

Jess

Following Elijah's directions, The Rose and Crown wasn't hard to find in North Parade. It had a pink frontage hiding a rather surprising number of bars and dining rooms beyond. It looked genuinely old, with a slightly wonky roofline, which made me instantly like it. Not sure why. I think I just like survivors. The crew had developed the habit of pitching up for happy hour and some stayed on to eat if they wanted to make a night of it. I'd already excused us from the second part of the evening, still uncertain I could keep all my appointments tonight. I wasn't the world's best timekeeper but I tried to make an effort not to let down a client. Jago had offered to drive me to Windsor for eight, saving me hours on the train. It might be a bit risky in case he coincided with Drew but hopefully Jago wouldn't stick around.

'What have you told everyone about me?' Jago asked as we entered the bar. The hubbub of voices wrapped around us so I had to go on tiptoes to reach his ear to answer.

'Not much – just that we're seeing each other.' I didn't want to admit I'd claimed him as my boyfriend to put off puppyish Elijah. Jago might find that a bit too heavy a description for what we'd so far only pursued as a casual thing. And besides, he didn't yet feel like a boyfriend. I wasn't sure what he was, but not that, not with Drew flying home right now.

Jessica, what are you doing? I got very frustrated by myself so often. I managed to screw up all my relationships and this one seemed to be heading that way. One man at a time. Decide!

In the midst of self-recriminations, I felt a buzz on my leg and dug in a pocket for my phone. A message popped up on the screen from my sister, full of uncharacteristic exclamations marks: *Call me!!!!!* I now noticed I'd a couple of missed calls earlier.

I angled it towards Jago so he could see. 'Sorry – I've got to speak to my sister. Can you get me a drink?'

He looked a little unnerved heading into a crowd of strangers without me, but then gave me a brash smile. 'Fine. What do you want?'

'Surprise me.'

'I'll wait at the bar for you.' He headed off into the press of Friday night drinkers as I turned back to the street.

'Hi, Miriam. What's up?' I rested with my back against Jago's car, shivering slightly. The evening had a nip in the air that reminded me summer was fast going. The recycle bins smelt of rancid wine.

'Jessica – at last! I've tried you at least five times. It's Mum.' In the background to my half-sister's robust voice I could hear a Labrador barking. Her Cotswold farmhouse was always busy and I imagined, now I recalled that it was six, I'd picked a bad time to call. The evening meal would be underway if she was keeping to her usual schedule.

'I thought it might be. She's OK, physically, I mean?' Neither of us judged her entirely sound on the emotional level – never had been, never would be.

'Yes, yes, she's basically fine.' My sister wasn't coming right out with it, which either meant she had someone on her end listening that she didn't want to hear this, or she felt unsure how to introduce the topic. Neither was typical of my outspoken sister.

'Do you want me to call back?'

'No. Look ... God, this is difficult.'

I was now getting worried. Up until this point, I'd been telling myself that it was just one of Miriam's occasional flaps about something my mother was doing, some local homeless person she'd befriended, or a cause she'd been conned into giving too much of her time. 'You'd better just tell me before I start imagining all sorts of horrors.'

'Yes, of course. Sorry.'

Miriam, apologising? It had to be bad. 'Please, put me out of my misery here.'

'Jess, Mum's agreed to meet your father.'

'She's what!' I saw, not red, but rainbows as my thoughts recoiled and bumped around inside my skull in horror.

'Exactly. I told her not to – told her to cut him off when he got in touch via Facebook, but you know how she is.'

Our mother was a sucker for any sob story or any chance to forgive. She was too good for this world in so many ways. That was why we both worried about her.

'Can the situation be salvaged? Stopped? Do you want me to talk to her?'

'What can you say that I haven't? It's bloody hopeless. No, I'm just warning you. Apparently,' her tone was dry, 'your father's been to counselling and is making amends.'

Otherwise known as the perfect story to pull in my mother. 'Shit, shit, shit.'

'You don't think that maybe ...?'

'No, I don't,' I said flatly. 'He won't change. This was how he got to her in the first place – pretended to be the strong man she needed after your father died. He knows it's her catnip; she'll roll around in ecstasy on the chance that all might be sweetness and light in her world.'

'She told me that she isn't going to do anything foolish and that there's absolutely no chance they'll get back together.'

'Oh God.' I fisted my hair in my free hand.

'But he apparently wants to be on good terms with her.' Miriam paused. 'And with you.'

I should've known that was coming. 'Not a chance in hell.'

'I thought I'd warn you so that you can be prepared when Mum starts on the emotional blackmail. She's already said that if their first meeting goes well, then she'll see if she can bring you two together to mend fences.'

'That man doesn't know what a fence is. He is a steamroller – no, a category five hurricane!' I was so tempted to punch a parked car I had to move further off before I started setting off alarms.

'She's muttering something about daughters needing their

father, some sentimental nonsense about who's going to walk you up the aisle.'

'Oh my God, the woman's insane. A – I'm not getting married; and B – I'd not let my father anywhere near me; C – he'd be struck down by a bolt from on high if he tried to enter a church.'

'Then maybe you should set a date so we can all toast the charred remains of the lightning-struck father of the bride.'

This was why actually, at the end of the day, I loved my sister. 'Thanks for the advice, sis. I'll get right on that. When's this disaster of a meeting supposed to happen?'

'Coffee, tomorrow morning. In a bookshop.'

'Where exactly?' I wondered if there was any chance I could kidnap my mother before then.

'Cheltenham.'

Too far for me to get to in time, not having my own car. 'Can't you stop her?'

'How?'

'Tie her up in the basement? Slash her tyres? Fabricate a false charge and get her arrested?'

Miriam sighed. 'If I thought that would stop her, I'd do it, but Mum is surprisingly stubborn, as you well know.'

I did. Mum had the appearance of someone soft and gentle, but she had the ability of a limpet to stick to the rock she'd decided upon. Meeting my father was her latest boulder.

'Would you please at least ask her not to make any promises to him, or to forgive him on first meeting, or, for that matter, to tell him how to contact me?'

'I can try, but she has this religious code. She's pretty unshakeable about forgiving.'

That was a lost cause – I knew that really. 'OK, forgiveness I can live with, but not forgetting. Ask her not to forget what he is really like under all the flannel he'll be giving her. She's not to believe in his transformation, not unless he's lived without reproach for over a decade, sacrificed himself in any way for someone else, adopted and nursed stray animals, and has a reference from the Pope, or another respected religious leader of proven worth.'

Miriam snorted. 'With your father, that would be Satan.'

I returned to the bar but the thought of my mother meeting my father had sent a ice scalpel slicing down my spine. It was hard to explain why I was still so scared of him – I was thirty-one now, not sixteen – but the old instincts were humming. I wanted to rush to the farm, wrap my mother up in a blanket and bundle her away to some safe house where he'd never find us.

I tried to be rational. What harm could come to her in a bookshop cafe?

It was the fact that she wouldn't see the damage that really worried me. He'd hook his nasty bloodsucking tentacles into her heart and start taking her over again like some Dr Who alien. All he had to do was find the right words of apology, flash the same smiles, make her feel like she was ever the only one for him and I would predict she'd make all the same mistakes all over again.

People didn't really learn from disasters; they just had fewer excuses for repeating the same mistakes. At least, that was my experience.

'Everything all right?' asked Jago, handing me a cocktail glass with an olive balanced on the rim.

I felt exhausted but summoned up my inner party animal. 'Wow. What's this?'

'A Martini, shaken and not stirred,' he attempted a Scottish accent.

'That's perfect!' Unlike his Sean Connery impression. 'Thank you!' I kissed him.

He smirked. 'It was Kieren's idea.' He nodded to the barman. 'Seeing how we're rubbing shoulders with film stars.'

I raised my glass to Kieren. 'Thanks!'

'Your guys are in the back room,' the barman said, with a nod behind him.

Jago took my hand. 'You didn't answer me.'

'Your totally rocking choice of drink sidetracked me. It's just something about my mum.'

'Serious?'

'Nothing I can do anything about so let's leave it for the moment.' And I didn't know Jago well enough to start pouring out all the family history. Maybe Drew would listen later?

Don't think about him. You're with Jago! I mentally gave myself a telling off for being so inconstant.

'Sorry we're late!' I called with a fair impression of my usual happy tone as I spotted my smoking gang. They'd cornered a prime spot in a booth and had already had a round from the evidence of the empty glasses.

'Here's Princess Jessica!' said Leanne. 'Shine worn off the magic kingdom yet?'

'Nope – and I hope it doesn't. Guys, this is Jago. Jago – Leanne, Ben—'

'Len!' Len the lighting gaffer corrected me. Oh well, that sorted that out.

'Elijah, Roman, Pete, and gosh, I forgot your name?'

'It's all right, love, I don't think I ever told you. I'm Neil, and this is Margaret, my better half,' said the designer, whose name had so far escaped me.

'Don't I recognise you?' Leanne narrowed her eyes at Jago. 'You're the wild swimming man. You were on TV last month – I caught a few episodes.'

Jago puffed up a little. 'That was me. Did my sales the world of good.'

'Then you can get the next round.' Her quip was well received by the others. Jago took it in his stride and did a little table round to take orders. I tried to pass him a twenty as a contribution but he brushed it away. 'It's fine, Jess. Really.'

I then remembered Michael had hinted at a trust fund behind Jago's lifestyle and felt a little less guilty.

As we were waiting for Jago to return with the refills, a girl sidled through the tables to put her hand casually on Roman's arm.

'Hey, Dad.'

He turned around and grinned. 'Angelica! How was your day?'

And, of course, my attention was immediately riveted to the girl. She was a gangly teen, features a little too big for her face yet, pale hair highlighted in the usual mid-shoulder length style favoured by so many girls. When did conformity become such a thing for hair? It was like they were all recruits for *The Handmaid's Tale*, minus the funky hat. I couldn't see much of her mother in Angelica, apart from the nervous way she had of hovering at her stepfather's shoulder and shooting us looks.

'My day was fine. Saw some friends. Are we eating here tonight?'

He didn't try to introduce us to her. 'Are you hungry?'

'Starving.' She gave him a real smile.

He patted her hand. 'Then go ask Kieren for a menu and get us a table in the restaurant area for seven-thirty.' He waited for her to go. 'My stepdaughter.' He caught my eye. 'Angelica.'

Yes, Roman, I saw how she said she was hungry. No sign of an eating disorder there.

'Nice kid. What's she doing with herself this summer?' I asked.

'I haven't got any leave left so we're just hanging out in and around Oxford. She's made friends locally thanks to Pete's daughter. Same school year.'

'It doesn't take much to give them something in common at that age,' said Pete, proving he knows nothing about girls.

I thought of Angelica's Instagram feed and knew that the men were either lying or were blind to the truth. She wasn't posting pictures of any of her new friends. I suspected she was feeling fairly isolated, moving to a new village on the edge of a city where she had no friends.

Jago returned with the drinks and joined in the conversation. I watched Angelica, waiting for my chance. After a few minutes, she looked around awkwardly, not seeing anyone she could chat to now her stepdad was occupied, so sloped off to the Ladies – a familiar move to anyone who has felt out of place.

'Excuse me a moment.' I grabbed my handbag. 'Look after him for me,' I said to my work colleagues and patted Jago on the shoulder in passing.

I made it into the toilets as the door swung back from Angelica's entrance. She'd already disappeared into one of the cubicles. Fishing in my bag, I got out a lipstick and made a fuss preening in the glass, all the while watching the closed stall door behind me. There were only two sinks so when she came out she had to stand next to me. I smiled blandly.

'Hey.'

'Hi.'

'I was with your stepdad when you came over.'

'Oh yes, I remember.'

'I'm Jess. So, how's living in Elsfield? Your stepdad told me you just moved here?'

She reached out for the hand dryer but it didn't appear to be working. She kept waving her hands though as if she could force it to switch on for her.

'I think it's broken.'

She wouldn't look at me, determined to have things her way.

'Here.' I passed her a paper towel from the stack on the window ledge.

'No thanks. I'm fine.' She wiped her hands on the seat of her jeans instead.

I didn't have long for this and she was being less than forthcoming, which was fair enough seeing as how she didn't know me. 'Angelica, I wanted a chance to talk to you.' I couldn't mention her mum's name; I could tell it would be kryptonite, sending her flying out into the bar in protest. Instead, I handed her a business card. She didn't know what to do with it.

'What's this?' She turned it in her fingers. I guessed it might be the first card she'd ever been handed.

'My business card with my phone number.'

'Why do I need your phone number?'

'I look for missing people. One of my jobs is to act as a go-between. I pass messages for people who don't want to be directly in touch.'

She was no fool; she quickly made the connections. 'Did my mum put you up to this?'

If I said yes, she'd go straight and tell on me to her dad. 'Put me up to what?' I smoothed the lipstick over my top lip again.

'Approaching me! If I wanted to contact her, I would. But I don't. I never want to see her again.'

'I know how you feel.' I tucked my lipstick away and zipped up my bag.

'No, you don't!' She was quivering with righteous anger in a quite splendid teen funk.

'Interesting.' I leaned back on the sink and crossed my arms. 'You think you are the only person to live estranged from a parent?'

She scowled.

'Lots of us fall out with our parents. I've not spoken to my father for over a decade.'

'So?'

'So you might find a go-between a useful person to know. I can pass on messages from your mother, and ones from you to her, and that will reduce the drama in this situation.'

'Drama?'

'Angelica, if you keep stonewalling her, she'll end up going to court to get access to you, social services will become involved, judges, solicitors, your stepdad will be questioned, the nature of your relationship put under the microscope – none of it will be pretty. He's no blood relation and they'll listen to your mother, who is. And that will all happen because you wouldn't use the channel being offered to you.'

She didn't look as though she was listening until I mentioned Roman, which in itself was not reassuring. I wasn't getting a sexual vibe between the two but she certainly seemed more protective of him than was normal. 'You don't understand what she's like.' She fixed me with her intense gaze, willing me to see things her way. 'She makes me ill.'

I wasn't going to fall in with her version of events when I knew so little about the facts. 'What does she have to do to make it possible for you to see her?'

'There's nothing she can do.' She looked up at me, a hint of cunning in her expression as she prepared to bargain. 'But I do want to see Pawel.'

There was the one thing both sides had in common. 'That's where I might be able to help then. Do you want me to ask your mother if that can be arranged?'

'She won't. She's stopping Dad seeing him. She hates him
– but it's her who's to blame for all this! Why can't Pawel see
his dad?'

'Because she's scared. If you reduce the tension in the family
by agreeing some ways forward, then the barriers will begin
to drop.' This was common sense, of course, but I didn't hold
out much hope for a fifteen-year-old to go for the reasonable
when she had the drama-filled option.

Angelica thought about it for a moment. 'You know what?
I don't want you or anyone interfering. This is my life – my
brother!'

A woman came in, glanced at us, and went into one of the
stalls.

Better to beat a retreat before Angelica started making more
flamboyant gestures, such as ripping up my card. 'OK, let's
leave it for now. But the offer stands.' I lowered my voice,
hoping the woman couldn't overhear. 'Let's keep this just
between the two of us at the moment? I won't tell your mother
your address, you can trust me on that; and in return you
don't mention this to your stepfather.'

Angelica snorted. The toilet flushed so I at least had some
cover for the next thing I wanted to say.

'No, really, I won't tell. It's in my code of practice if you
want to check it out on my website. I was a runaway once so
I do know what it's like.'

'I haven't run away.'

'No, but there are parallels between what you're going
through and what I experienced. If – when – you are ready
to talk, then just call.'

I left as the other woman emerged. I could feel Angelica following me but she headed off in the opposite direction, towards the restaurant. I knew I'd taken a big risk, confronting her like this. She was what my mother would call 'an awkward customer'. I thought it was a chance worth taking, even if it did get back to her stepfather. I probably couldn't go much further with Roman: he'd dished his dirt on Amy so not much lost if he did turn his back from now onwards. Now I had to find out what Amy had to say. If she was as Roman painted her, then I'd not help her mess up her daughter's life any more than she had already.

Chapter 34

Jess

'How did you like my new friends?' I asked Jago as we headed down the A-road to Windsor. The world here was postcard England, rolling hills, slow rivers, hedgerows.

'I though they seemed a nice bunch. You're enjoying your job?' He overtook and cut up a lorry which was never a good idea in my book. I mean, who was going to win if the driver decided not to pump the brakes? Not a Leaf.

'I'm having a really good time. It's a shame I've only got another week.'

'Maybe you should see if they've got something more permanent for you. One of the guys said you should angle to keep your current job as you were good at handling your film star.'

'Hmm. Maybe.' In my usual fidgety fashion, I opened the glove box and found a pair of swimming trunks and goggles.

Jago flashed me a grin. 'Be prepared. Dig deeper.'

Dutifully, I pulled out the trunks and found a minuscule bikini. I held it up by one finger. 'Who does this belong to, Jago?'

275

'Me. In case I can persuade my lady friend to come with me later.'

'I thought we were going to Hinksey Pool tomorrow?'

'We can go tonight.' He had his fanatic's smile, the one that told me he was determined to convert me to his lifestyle. 'Come on, Jess, you've barely scraped the surface of what I can offer you. I want to show you the places where you can swim under the sky rather than in some climate controlled, chlorine filled leisure centre – that's what wild swimming is all about. Hinksey is the only open-air pool in Oxford. It's all very well during the day, but there's nothing like swimming at night, the moonlight, the peace and quiet ...'

I'd messaged Inspector George that we were going tomorrow. I wasn't convinced I would be a hundred per cent safe with Jago. 'Isn't it against the rules?'

'Completely. If we slip in just before closing we'll have the place to ourselves for a few hours. I know one of the lifeguards. He'll turn a blind eye. It's been hot and the water will be lovely. No one to watch us whatever we choose to do.'

'Hmm. Maybe.' I was getting hot in all the right places. I was tempted – so tempted. This kind of rule-breaking impulse move was right up my street.

'There's no chance anyone can be following us – not going via Windsor.'

Oh hell, why not? 'I'm in, if we can get back in time. I've got a couple of people I need to see tonight.'

He indicated that he was taking the turn for Windsor. 'A couple? I thought it was just your client?'

'Actually, um, look, it's a little complicated.' The pleasant flush of anticipation subsided as I remembered where we were. 'I got the client because she lives opposite my ex's parents – and Drew is back this weekend. I thought I'd just check in with him – see how he is.'

Jago went very quiet. As usual I had done my open mouth insert foot act. How to salvage this?

'It would be odd not to say "hi" seeing how I've come all this way.'

His hands were clenched on the wheel. 'I must be an idiot.'

'What? No! You're very far from being an idiot.'

'Here am I hoping we'd spend the night together but instead I'm just your glorified taxi driver bringing you to your what ...? What is he exactly? To you, I mean?'

'To be honest, I've no idea. I really like you, Jago. We have fun together. God, I'm not explaining this very well. Remember I told you I was free to see other people – and that's the truth. I think Drew just got worried when he heard about the murders. He's just wanting to make sure I'm OK. We're still friends, whatever else we are.'

His hands relaxed a little. 'Sorry – I was just feeling stupid.'

'Why don't you have a quick drink somewhere while I'm seeing Drew, then come back and get me?' An olive branch was required. 'I'll even wear the bikini – or not.'

That made him grin. 'Fine. That's a deal. I suppose I'm OK with all of this as long as I'm the guy going swimming with you tonight.'

Jago dropped me at the entrance to the cul-de-sac, then accelerated off, promising to return in an hour. That would have to be enough for the conversations I needed to have.

I knocked on Amy's door.

'Jessica, thanks for coming.' Her voice was lowered. 'Pawel is watching the TV – still a little early for bed. You'd better come through to the kitchen.'

I could see the little boy lying on his tummy on the sofa, hand bouncing a Lego robot along the carpet as he half watched a Transformers film. His pyjamas were decorated with planets and rocket ships. I was relieved to find he struck me as absolutely normal and in no need of immediate rescue from a Munchausen mother.

Amy put on the kettle. 'What would you like to drink?'

'Coffee, thanks.' I sat down at the kitchen table, pleased to have a closed door between us and Pawel for this conversation. 'Amy, I saw Angelica this evening.'

She spun around, hands to her mouth. 'You did? Is she OK?'

'She's fine.'

'Did you persuade her to come home?'

I shook my head. 'I have to earn her trust. It was just a preliminary conversation. She's got my contact details now.'

Amy sat down opposite me, forgetting all about the drinks she was supposed to be making. 'Thank you. Thank you.'

'I haven't really done anything yet.'

'You've talked to her – that's more than I expected so soon. You can't know how it is – how wild my imaginings have been – about her being locked up by him, or silenced in some way. I've thought of her being trapped, wanting me but not able to get out. Of being dead.' She sobbed and put her face in her hands.

I made allowances for her as a worried mother but clearly her mind had been spinning fantasies out of nothing. 'She's none of those things. Whatever story she's telling herself about you, it's not because Roman is doing any of those things to her.'

Amy sniffed and pulled a fraying tissue from her sleeve to dab her nose. 'I suppose not. He's too clever. He twists reality so you believe his version. It's a kind of trap, just one you don't notice. But she looked OK?'

'She looks well. She wants to see Pawel.'

Amy nodded. 'She must be missing him. He misses her too – some of the time.' She smiled slightly, remembering some family joke. 'Mostly they fight like cat and dog, but underneath it all they're brother and sister.'

'It's a difficult age gap, so few interests in common.'

'Yes – yes, that's it, I suppose. Right, coffee.' She got up again, pulling herself together like the Scarecrow refilling his empty shirt in *The Wizard of Oz*. I knew how that felt getting back up after life knocked you down.

'Amy, I have to ask you something – it's going to come up if you go to court with Roman.'

She put the instant coffee down in front of me and pushed the sugar bowl in my direction. 'Ask away.'

'Roman has found out about Cancun.'

'Oh. That.' She absently dropped three spoonfuls into her own drink and stirred. I was shocked she took any sugar at all. Maybe it was her go-to crisis concession, like me with my cigarettes?

'Do you want to tell me what happened? He's going to use

it as evidence that you falsify allegations and health problems, make it seem like a pattern. It's pretty toxic to be tarred as an unreliable witness.'

She twisted the handle of the mug around, staring down into the steaming surface. I wished she'd just look at me.

'It was too much to hope that it would stay buried.'

'Usually works out that way.' And I should know. None of my skeletons had ever stayed in the cupboard but leapt out and did a rumba just when I least wanted them to.

'It's not what it looks like.'

'Then you should tell me the truth. I might be able to help.'

'Help?' She gave a hollow laugh. 'No one can help – too much water passed under that bridge, thanks to that bastard.'

I waited for her to clarify which particular bastard she had in mind.

'Richard Garland, my first big crush. Did you ever do something as a student that you knew was completely idiotic?'

'Oh, many times. I haven't stopped.'

'I was at college, working part-time as a barmaid, and fell for this local boy, an army lad from the Colchester garrison. Total stars in my eyes time. We dated for over a year and I thought, you know, that he was the one? I saved up big time to go to Mexico on holiday before he was deployed, took all the shifts I could in the pub to earn the airfare, almost failed the course because I was doing so much overtime. But I thought it was worth it. I thought he was going to pop the question.' She gave a shudder. 'What a bloody awful judge of character I was – probably still am.'

She went quiet for some time.

'Amy, did he rape you, like you told the Mexicans?'
Silence.

'I can understand why you might not want to face a trial. I mean, God, I would've wanted to run and just forget about it. Is that what you did?'

She sighed. 'It was much more complicated. He filmed us, you know, having sex? Then the bastard posted it online on a porn site.' Now I understood her anger. 'The internet had only just got going then – I don't think YouTube even existed – but the porn sites were well ahead of the game. A complete new world to me. I wouldn't even have known what he'd done if he hadn't told me about it, the prick. He laughed and told me that he'd had lots of views and positive comments. That I was a "hot babe" and he was proud of me.' She looked down at herself. 'Not much of that girl left now but, believe it or not, I used to be quite glamorous, made an effort. Ha!'

'He told you while you were in Mexico?'

She blinked back furious tears. 'Yes. While we were sitting in this beachfront restaurant. It was gorgeous – sun setting over the white sand, a few sailing ships on the horizon; I think there was even a mariachi band playing somewhere in the distance.'

'Better than close by. Mustachioed guys in sombreros – real mood killer.'

She gave a wry smile. 'Probably would've been better if they'd invaded our space. There was I thinking "this is it – this is the moment he'll propose" and instead he downs four too many cocktails and blurts it all out, how he and his mates filmed each other having sex. The feelings of the girls involved didn't register with them; it was all some bloke club thing, who could get the most porno lay. I couldn't believe my ears. We didn't have smart phones then so I couldn't do anything – couldn't even check if it were true. I walked out and back at the hotel looked at his computer – he had the footage right there on a CD, like he needed it with him. I felt violated. He'd put a private moment out there for anyone to see like I was some peep show dancer. It hid nothing.'

A loud explosion echoed in from the living room reminding us of Pawel. Amy gulped her coffee and grimaced.

'I had no idea what to do – I was wanting revenge but didn't know how to get it. I should've waited until we came back, complained to the army, got myself lawyers, but all I could think about was getting him away from me right then. That's why I reported it as rape to the police. I'd never consented to be filmed. But I didn't want to hand over the CD – not have another load of men watching it all – so I destroyed it and Richard's computer. I threw that in the sea after bashing it with a rock. Not very sensible but it felt right at the time.'

I could imagine acting the same way – panicked, driven to get this away from me even if I knew I could never really escape the images. Knowing that Michael and sundry police officers had seen grainy photos of Jago and me was bad enough.

'And they arrested him?'

'Yes.'

'And you ran home to England?'

'Yes, I ran home. And a few weeks later, I met my lovely

John. I was in pieces and he put me back together. In the end, he knew everything – he even tracked down Richard and got him to take down as many of the links to the video as he could manage with an agreement that he'd let him live if he did so. Richard also promised not to raise the Mexican allegations again. John said he'd ruin his career in the army if he so much as squeaked about them.'

'I like the sound of John.'

'He was a good man.'

'Where's Richard now?'

'God knows. We didn't exactly try to keep in touch. I thought I'd put it all behind me. He paid for what he did – not enough, but he paid a little. Now?' She shrugged. 'Now I tell myself I'd handle it better, but I wonder if I would? I was so young – so bruised. I did the best I could in a shitty situation.'

'You might have to explain this in court.'

She made an effort to straighten her bowed shoulders. 'You know what? Maybe it's a good thing nothing ever really goes away online. If it comes to it, I should be able to dig up that video to back up my story.'

'Or get Richard to testify?'

'That would be an ironic twist – that bastard coming to my rescue!'

'Did anyone else know about the video – other than John and yourself?'

'Richard's mates at the time. Apparently they all did it – a little group of sex pests, all admiring each other's conquests. Scum.'

'Sound delightful people – but one or two will probably

crack if put on the stand. He can't count on them to stay silent, would be afraid of the hard evidence being produced, so I think your solicitor could persuade him to explain the background. It'll certainly be enough to debunk the idea that you make up allegations – you had a serious charge to lay against him, you just panicked and went for the wrong one.'

'I don't think he'll help. With the honourable exception of John, all men are pigs,' Amy concluded.

'Not all.' I could hear Pawel chuckling at something next door.

'OK, not all,' she said with a fond smile at the outburst of untroubled hilarity. 'But most.'

With that sentiment ringing in my ears, I headed out to meet my own man. Or not my man. I knocked on Glenda and Ron's door. Glenda answered and folded me into a hug, treating me as if it was years rather than days since we'd last met.

'Jessica – lovely to see you again! Drew, Jessica's here!'

Drew came out of the kitchen – my bearded buccaneer, looking lean and tanned in his tight black T-shirt. This house was built to the same plan as Amy's but everything in reverse, slightly disorientating me for the moment. Or was that the swell of longing?

'Hi, Jess.'

I hung back, not sure of my welcome. Hands dug into jeans pockets as I wasn't sure what to do with them. 'Drew! How was the flight?'

'Good. No hold-ups.'

It was like we were almost strangers. Glenda took one look at us both and vanished upstairs.

'I was just having a sandwich. You want something?' Drew stood back to let me pass him into the kitchen.

'Er, maybe some toast?' So far I'd only had a packet of crisps at the pub and an apple.

'You should eat better than that.' He set about slicing some bread and putting it in the toaster. 'Tea?'

'No, just water. If anyone else offers me a drink, I'm going to explode. Speaking of which, I'll just dash to the loo.'

I reversed course to the toilet by the front door and shut myself inside. It was a welcome sanctuary. This was awful. We'd spoken better on the phone. Was it me? Was it him? I should've at least given him a hug, not stood across the hall as if he had the plague. OK, I'd go out there and reset the mood. Time was ticking away and Jago would be back very soon.

'Drew, how's the yoga?' I said breezily as I wafted into the kitchen. 'I imagine you're a great student.' No snarky comments about bending every which way Nel tells you, nope, not from me.

He handed me a plate of honey on buttered toast, one of my favourites. 'Sit down, Jess.'

That sounded ominous. 'Thanks – you remembered!' I took a bite and crunched away as if nothing was wrong.

'Of course I do – it's only been a few months.'

'It'll soon be four months. And you're planning on staying away longer.'

He watched me eat. 'You're looking well.'

'I'm not pining away if that's what you mean.'

'I should hope not. And from what you told me, you're filling your time.'

Was this code for having sex with another man? 'I'm making new friends and discovering new interests – like you.'

'I'm pleased. I want you to flourish, Jess – always have. I think this time apart is proving really good for us.'

I abandoned the crust as my mouth was suddenly dry. 'Is there an "us", Drew? I don't feel very much like there is.'

'There is when we're together.'

'That doesn't answer my question, does it? I slept with another man. Do you mind in the least?'

He rubbed his neck. 'Yeah, a little. Can't help the odd primitive urge now and again. I try to overcome that. But that doesn't mean what you've done was wrong.'

'And you? Have you remained a vestal virgin while in Austria?'

He shook his head.

I pushed back from the table. 'I knew it! Nel and her peach bum!'

'It's just a casual thing. No commitment on either side.'

'But that's the problem right there! I thought we had a commitment – you and me – but then I found out that we didn't and I'd been the only one not to know!'

He looked surprised by this accusation. 'I thought you'd realise – I mean, you had a relationship with Max Tudor when we first started seeing each other. I never made any fuss about that, did I? Except that it wasn't what you wanted.'

I was tempted to throw the plate at him. 'That wasn't a

relationship – that was some twisted blackmail thing, and you know it!'

'I just meant that the sex wasn't important to me. It's whether you love me that matters. You have to be free to do that.'

'Oh, I see, so a relationship to you is love which keeps checking on the taste of the grass on the other side of the fence.' I lowered my voice to an approximation of his. '"Hmm, I'm getting a little tired of Jess. I wonder if I still love her? I know: let's try Nel. Hmm, nice but I still think it's worth keeping Jess just in case I want to go back to that side."'

'It's not like that.'

'Then what is it like?'

'We're both adults. We should not be kept together by a ball and chain but by attraction.'

'Not manacle but a magnet: got it. Sorry I didn't understand. I sort of thought feelings were unreliable in the long term, leaving the other partner always worried they'll not be good enough to keep the old magnetism going. I thought that the point of relationships was to be like your parents, in it for the long haul and not just day to day.'

He ran his hands through his hair. 'I'm not explaining this very well. Look, just come here.' He got up and pulled me to my feet to hug me. I felt a momentary panic: I wanted to give in and rest my head against his chest but that would be just wrong, a surrender. Instead, I pushed him away.

'You're trying to have this all on your terms, thinking that's clearly the only right way. You're confusing me, Drew. I thought you loved me but I find I'm just a ... a doll you can pick up and put down, leave in the bloody play park if you feel like it.' My shoulders started to shake but I refused to cry. I wanted to be incandescent with anger – strong – I felt so cheated! But as usual I was even making a hash of my big moment. 'Just finish with me if you don't want me – don't play with me like this!'

There was a ring on the doorbell. Oh God, what timing.

Drew went to answer before I could stop him. 'Yes?'

'Hi, I'm Jago Jackson. You must be Drew.'

'Yeah, er, wait there. I'll get her.'

I'd followed him into the hallway so I grabbed my things and gave a little hiccup of laughter. 'My lift home.'

'Via a swim so we'd better get our skates on,' added Jago.

Drew looked sceptical. 'Really? Jess going for a swim? Volunteering for exercise?'

'I've changed,' I said defensively.

'Maybe we both have.' Drew's shoulders hunched.

I took a pained breath, dangerously close to tears.

Only Jago was unaffected, twirling the car key on its loop. 'Coming, Jess?'

'Yes.' My voice was a whisper.

'Can we speak later? I fly back Monday,' asked Drew.

'If you think there's any point.'

'I'll call you.'

I nodded and followed my ride.

Jago was grinning, oblivious to my distress. He was probably thinking he'd won. 'Ready for another wild swim?'

Chapter 35

Nathan Parry-Jones enjoyed his final length at Hinksey Pool. Past closing time and he had the enormous pool to himself as the last swimmers climbed out to get changed. He would just throw a hoodie over his head and wrap a towel around his middle when he left so he didn't miss these final few moments of peace. Harried all day at his city job in finance, trying to pretend he understood what the hell he was doing moving money around the world when really he was just a slave to his computer's prompts, he lived for this brief perfect bubble of physical calm. The bloody algorithm couldn't chase him down here. The lifeguards knew him well so didn't spoil the mood with whistle-blowing or announcements over the tannoy system. His favourite one was on duty today so there should be no problem. All was well. It was just him, the water, and this blue oasis in the south of a busy city.

His fingers touched the tile at the end and he reluctantly got out. Dripping on the still warm concrete as he towelled off, then waved to Kyle at the far side. The attendant was hauling in the lane markers so didn't have a hand free.

'Have a good one!' Kyle called instead.

A good what? mused Nathan, enjoying the play of Kyle's biceps in his tight polo shirt as he reeled in the floats. Presumably Kyle meant a good night but Nathan chose to apply it to his week ahead. As cox to the Oxford City rowing club, he anticipated a busy training schedule in preparation for the Maidenhead regatta at the weekend. His eight had really come on since the two brothers from KPMG had joined the team. Both Oxbridge blues when they were at college, they brought a competitive edge to the crew that had been lacking, not least because the others were now worried that their place in the boat would be taken by yet more friends of the newcomers.

Nathan wasn't worried. He knew his skill and weight made him very hard to replace. What did worry him was the crush he'd developed on one of the new guys – very unprofessional for one of the country's leading coxes. He weighed up his dilemma. Joel was out but Nathan wasn't. It shouldn't matter these days but he still found it odd having to declare his preference for something so personal. Maybe he should just say something to Joel, sound him out. *If I were … and you were … would you even be interested?*

Nathan threw his goggles into his sports bag, a gesture of frustration. Wise up, asshole. The man looks like a god; and you …?

I look like Mr Tumnus, James McAvoy style, funny skinny legs and what I hope is a cute beard but might just be trying too hard. I've no idea if that floats Joel's boat. See what I did there? he told his imagined inner audience, who promptly rolled their imagined eyes at him.

Nathan bowed out of the debate and headed for the exit. *Quit while you're behind.* His flat was only a short way across Grandpont near the station but he'd brought his new motorised scooter to try out tonight, rather than the bike he usually used. He was not entirely convinced he was a natural at motoring while standing up on a moving board and far better to make the mistakes in the park where no one could see him than in front of his teammates tomorrow. They wouldn't let him live that down if he took a spill before them – all hair-trigger set to mock anyone for anything. That was the deal if you joined a rowing eight.

A young woman was fiddling with her bike lock, having a problem getting the key in the D-Lock, long brown hair falling over her face. A bit of WD40 should sort that out. Maybe he'd say something. But it was tricky, striking up a conversation with a female stranger; she could either think him a creep or accuse him of patronising her because she was a woman. He decided to say nothing and leaned over to undo his own combination lock. The number – what was the bloody number? He was shit with numbers. He'd only just set it today when he'd bought the lock. He thought it was his birthday backwards but that didn't appear to be working. He'd written it down somewhere in case he did just this – goldfish brain misfiring as his brother always teased him. Frustrated, he stood up to check his backpack.

And that was why the crowbar missed his skull and hit the bike rack instead. The clang shocked the peaceful sounds of the park at twilight. It took him a precious millisecond to realise he was under attack.

'Fuck!' Nathan leapt back, stumbled over his backpack and only avoided a second strike because he was on the ground. He got a brief impression of angry dark eyes and gritted teeth. Instincts took over. As cox, he was often seized on by bigger and stronger men than him, usually to throw him in the river. Instead of moving further away, he rolled into the legs of his assailant – a man, he realised – and knocked him down. He made a grab for the wrist holding the tool. The man punched him, power diminished by being on his back, but still enough to give Nathan a moment's disorientation as fist connected with his chin. But he was determined. This was a fight for his life. He flailed wildly, grabbed hold of something, pulled. It came away with a rip.

'Hey!' A man's voice – from a distance.

Nathan's assailant gave up on the crowbar, leapt to his feet, and jumped on the bike. He cycled off, standing up to power his exit and avoid the arrival of Kyle, who fortunately had chosen to leave the swimming pool by the public exit.

Nathan looked down at himself as he lay on his back, propped half against a bike rack. He had a crowbar in one hand and a wig in the other.

'You all right, mate?' asked Kyle.

'Yeah, I think so. Why the fuck would a trans chick attack me?' He tried for a joke as his teammates would expect. Never show weakness.

Kyle was dialling for the police. 'That wasn't a chick; I think that was that psycho killer.' He rattled off the details to the dispatcher, then turned back to Nathan and offered him a hand up. 'We've been told by the management to look out for a female impersonator. But I didn't think ... God, I never expected ...'

'You mean the one that killed the others?' All the news stories came rushing back, leaving him feeling quite sick. 'Oh God.'

'Head between your knees,' said Kyle. 'You're OK, Nathan. He didn't get you.' His hand was gentle on Nathan's neck.

If I hadn't straightened up just then, if I hadn't rolled in the right direction, I would be dead, thought Nathan. He started to hyperventilate.

'Look at me, Nathan. You're fine. You fought him off. You'll be able to help the police catch this fucker.' Kyle gently tipped his chin so Nathan met his steady gaze. Kind hazel eyes were looking at him with real concern. 'Just hang in there. I won't leave you and he won't get through me to harm you. I promise.'

Chapter 36

Jess

Cory was giggling. Not exactly the response I'd expected when I unloaded to her about my evening. We were sitting in the lounge, sprawled in front of her big TV on the L-section sofa, Olivia Colman frozen mid-speech as Cory had hit pause on the remote when I returned.

I waved my empty glass ironically in salute. 'Well, thanks, Cory, for the sympathy.'

'You asked Jago to drive you to see Drew? I have to say, you've got whatever the lady equivalent of balls are.' A snort sneaked out. 'Sorry.'

I had to smile. 'Yeah, well, I suppose that was a bit cheeky of me. But it just seemed ... efficient.'

'And poor Jago didn't even get a chance to swim up your channel?'

I grimaced. 'That's gross.' I sighed. 'But also true. I didn't feel like it after talking to Drew. I thought Drew was my one – you, know the big one?'

She topped up my glass of wine. 'I don't believe in that

– it's an idea sold to us by books and films, but real life isn't lived like that. It's love at first, then that mutes to everyday affection.' She waved her hand in the air, dismissing her words like a bad smell. 'No, that's not right. If it is real love, it is more about commitment over the bumpy times. That mad feeling that your great love has finally come into view? That's passion, a flush of hormones, not love.' She paused, no doubt remembering things her ex had said and done. 'Maybe I should have that made into a fridge magnet?'

'Too many words.' We shared a grim smile. 'OK, I'm expecting too much of Drew, is that what you're saying?'

'He's a man – flawed, conflicted, changeable.'

I liked men – most of the time – so was forced to be fair. 'Men sound just like us women.'

'Except women know that when you've kids there's no storming out just because your hormones are tricking you into thinking happiness lies elsewhere.' She downed her drink, and toasted me with the empty glass. 'To be fair, some men manage that too.'

'I've known a few. Not personally, of course.' I thought briefly of my father meeting my mother tomorrow. The man was a scary bastard. He'd broken into my student digs once and ripped up all the photos that showed me with a boyfriend, or even just a male friend. At least, I'd always assumed it was him. 'And sometimes a bit more ability to change would be welcome.'

Cory picked up the remote and exited from Netflix. 'I think I'll call it a night.'

The TV reverted to the channel it was normally programmed to and we caught a glimpse of a reporter standing in front of flashing blue lights.

'... third attack in two weeks.'

'Don't!' I said to stop her turning it off. I was reading the ticker tape of news along the bottom. *Wild swim killer in new attack.*

'The victim managed to fight off his attacker and was able to give a description to police. Hinksey Pool and the surroundings will be closed until further notice so a fingertip search can be made of the area in daylight. The police are appealing for any witnesses who may have seen what they might have assumed was a dark-haired woman on a light blue bike cycling to the pool earlier this evening – the individual was wearing a distinctive white and green running outfit. Or a person cycling away, in the same clothes, at around eight-thirty.'

'He got away.' I rubbed my eyes.

'Yes, very lucky. The killer made a mistake with him.'

I'd actually been thinking of the attacker, but Cory was right – the victim had had a very close shave.

'And at least that breaks the link to you,' she said, switching off as the news moved on to the next item. She sounded relieved, having hidden her worry about that as best she could.

I had to be honest in return, didn't I?

'Cory, do you remember where I said I turned down the swim tonight?' My voice was tentative. I was never sure when I reached 'too much' with people.

She paled. 'No!'

'I'm afraid so.'

'Who knew ...?'

'No idea. We weren't exactly posting updates on social media.'

'Coincidence?'

'I suppose it could be that.' But the shivery feeling I had inside suggested otherwise. 'The police wonder if the killer is using Jago's book as a guide, though the last place – the boatyard – didn't actually appear in the book. Parson's Pleasure and Hinksey Pool both do, though.'

Cory wrinkled her nose. 'I remember. He complained that the outdoor pool was too full of annoying kids from round there.'

'That's Jago: never one to miss a chance to piss off potential readers.'

'We agreed at book club that he's built his career on it.' Cory hovered. 'Seriously, I'm worried about you. These attacks are far too close to you.'

'I know. I'm sorry.'

Cory threw a cushion at me. 'That's not what I meant. I don't want to switch on the TV and find it's you they're talking about.'

'Believe me, neither do I.'

Cory went upstairs to look in on the children, the scare making her even more protective than usual. I carried the glasses into the kitchen and downed a mug filled from the tap. I might've been a little woozy from wine, but I felt too disturbed by the news story to go meekly to bed.

I might as well work on something that had nothing to do with wild swimming.

I got out one of my notebooks and made some entries on what Amy had told me. I found that her account was credible and I could imagine behaving like that myself when in a panic – any woman would feel so angry and violated to find the most private moments broadcast without consent. As the world was hardly short of pornographic images, then it had to be about the sick power play of the man involved and I agreed with Amy that it was a kind of rape – if not the sort as defined by the law. I was still Team Amy.

I had to ask though, didn't I? Had that early blow damaged her mental balance and led her to become someone who would take out their anxieties on their child? I guessed it was possible. I was sometimes too quick to trust people – part of my impulsiveness – but, deep down, I thought Amy might have outstanding issues from this experience, but I couldn't see her knowingly torturing her daughter with fake illnesses. She might be blind to her behaviour, of course; or she might be telling me the truth.

Perhaps I needed to understand more about the other half of this equation – Roman Wolnik. One of the colleagues I'd cultivated as part of my missing persons work was a guy who worked for a debt collection agency – Marek Baranowski. He sometimes did a run on a person for me – strictly under the table and as a favour – and I sometimes helped him track down an elusive debtor, not something I liked doing but it was how the world works. We actually met first when he knocked on my door to collect a small debt. I lured him inside and we had a hilarious conversation where I was trying to propose this arrangement and he thought I was offering him sex. Hey-ho. We cleared that up and Marek decided that my little problem of failing to pay off a store credit card could be settled in another way. (Anyway, just for the record, who would let a woman like me have one of those? It was like providing a opioid addict with a repeat prescription for Codeine.) And as the name suggested, Marek was originally from Poland so I thought he might just be the perfect person to dig into Roman's history for me. See what the old homeland had to say about him.

We did all our transactions over the phone so there was no written record to catch us out. I hoped he wasn't on a hot date or my call was going to be very unwelcome. Fortunately, he answered on the third ring.

'Jessica Bridges, my favourite private eye!' He always teased me about this – a title I could hardly claim, given my on-off relationship with my career.

'Marek Baranowski, my favourite knee-capper. Thrown any widows and orphans out on to the street this week?'

'Only a few. It's been a slow week. So, what can I do for you?'

'Is this a good time to call?'

'Yeah. I got stood up. Back home with just me and Solidarność.'

Solidarność was his sheepdog – said solid-dar-nosh, after the movement that brought down the Communist government. Weird choice for a dog's name, but I thought that was rather the point. Marek was a pretty odd guy – had to be to be friends with me.

'Bad luck.'

'Not at all. I always look on it as many evenings saved on a relationship that was going nowhere.'

I wondered how many evenings he got stood up? I supposed his facial piercings might strike some as alarming, particularly the spike through his nose which gave him a slightly nasal tone. He usually had his hair bleached white – those two features a little odd with the bodybuilder stature and the three-piece suit he wore to work. He was all about confounding your expectations. He was like one of those flip books I had as a child – fireman head, caveman body, astronaut legs – though in his case it would be punk, weight-lifter, businessman.

'Good attitude, Marek.'

'So what can I do for you, gorgeous tits?' Marek had not heard of equality – no one dared whisper the word 'feminism' near him. He larded his conversation with the most un-pc terms, meaning no disrespect, he said, but I thought he just didn't care if you took offence.

'Well, big balls,' he honked with laughter, 'I was hoping you'd give me the low down on the partner of a client of mine.' I read out the details I'd gathered on Roman.

'OK, leave it with me. I'll shoot over a report by the usual means.' That meant a call or, if more substantial, couriered.

'What'll it cost me?'

'A lap dance?'

'Dream on, Marek.'

'So sad. You, me, we could be beautiful together. OK then, how about you follow up a couple for me? Absconded from a ground floor room in Reading without paying the rent and I can't trace them.'

'OK, put the details in an envelope and I'll do my magic.'

'You do that, sweetness. It's good working with you.'

'As always, Marek.'

Chapter 37

Leo

Nathan Parry-Jones had recovered from his initial shock and was now quite enjoying his experience of the undivided attention of a group of sympathetic police officers, at least, that was what Leo judged from the young man's body language. He was sitting forward, alert like a greyhound at the track. They were in an airless interview room, painted gunmetal grey. The chairs had been arranged in a non-confrontational circle as suited a witness debrief. Nothing, though, could hide the smell of misery that pervaded such places.

Rather than see Parry-Jones in his own home, Leo had decided to stage the interview at Kidlington HQ so Michael could join them – and Nathan was more than willing to let the psychologist sit in, particularly because he recognised him from TV.

Parry-Jones took a long gulp of water from the plastic cup he'd been given. 'Single use?' he said.

Leo gave him a questioning look.

'Sorry. When I get nervous I make stupid remarks.'

Leo could understand that and he'd put up with much more than that from the only person to survive an attack so far. This had turned into a well-resourced investigation, attracting media attention, which in turn brought the brass behind it with the scaled-up budget. Leo was keeping his interview team tight, but he had many other officers busy tracing other leads, following up forensics, CCTV footage, and the other minutiae that might clinch this. The buzz among the team was constant; with this new lead, they'd not yet had enough time to get disillusioned or frustrated, so all were putting in the overtime without complaint. The murderer was giving them so much evidence, there was a general feeling that it was only a matter of time before he was caught, but it might not be quick enough – there still might be yet more victims before they got him. At least Jago was alibied this time. The officers who had been keeping an eye on Jess Bridges' house saw him dropping her back not long after the attack. His car registration had been tracked on the motorways and they had spent the evening in Windsor.

In this interview, Leo was leading the questions, Boston observing, and Wong making notes. Michael's job, at Leo's request, was to draw out as many details about the killer as he was able to help build a profile.

'Thanks for coming in, Nathan,' Leo said. 'You should know that your actions will likely save lives.'

'Really?' The young man looked up, hesitant smile on his face.

'We're hoping for DNA from inside the wig you got off your attacker. Even if it doesn't match any on record at the moment, it will help make the case when we arrest him.' Leo was worried, though, that the wig they'd recovered was ex-theatrical or belonged to a former cancer patient. It was far better than a party shop brand and inside the mesh showed wear and sweat stains. It could've sat on other heads before ending up with the murderer. Leo kept that thought to himself. He had some of his team looking for recent online purchases of second-hand wigs of this type but that was a needle in a haystack. Had to be done though. A lot of police work in a murder inquiry is elimination.

Nathan had already given them a blow-by-blow account of what had happened immediately after the event. Now they needed to find some more telling details.

'Dr Harrison here will tell you,' said Leo, 'that humans are very good sizing up others in the first few milliseconds, Nathan.'

Michael took his cue smoothly. 'All of us do this all the time – it's a reflex, something we might not even realise we're doing. Often it gives a clue about something integral to the other – are they our adversary, our friend? Can you remember what you thought, just in passing, before he made his move?'

Nathan rolled his shoulders. 'Right, OK, I'll give you the unexpurgated version. I thought, nice hair; whoa, not so blessed in the curve department, blocky, poor woman. I mean it's not like I was checking her out or anything – not my type, so to speak – but I empathise with people who don't check all the boxes, you know?'

Michael nodded and made a note. 'Anything else?'

'I guess ... I guess I thought she – he – seemed angry, maybe a bit defensive? I was going to offer advice on the bike lock but kinda decided she wouldn't like it. Like she'd snap back at me?'

Nathan had picked up on the pent-up energy, the prepared-ness. Leo found this helpful as it meant the killer ran hot, not cold.

'Nathan, would you say you were a creature of habit?' he asked.

'Well, yeah, I suppose. I'm cox to an eight, did I mention that?'

Only about five times. 'Yes. The city team, wasn't it?'

'That's right. We're good – serious about training. Our schedule means I have to carefully timetable all my other activities.'

'And swimming on a Friday is on that timetable?'

'Yes – unless I'm travelling for work or going away for the weekend, which I don't do much when we're training, and certainly not in the summer. In fact, I won't be able to make Archie and Rowena's wedding tomorrow because they chose an August weekend – can you imagine? An all-day affair, penguin suits at Blenheim.' He realised this comment might have misfired in this room. 'He's a second cousin.'

Harry only half-swallowed a snort.

'OK, so your attacker knew that nothing short of a royal command would change your routine on an August Friday?'

'I suppose that would be true.' Nathan frowned. 'Am I that predictable?'

'Being predictable isn't your fault,' Leo said. 'None of this is.'

'We think your attacker is attracted to people successful in their field,' explained Michael, doubling down on the 'not your fault' theme.

'So it's a weird kind of compliment?' Nathan gave a little hysterical laugh, almost cartoonish – Shaggy caught in the kitchen with Scooby. 'Wow, he's got me so wrong. I've not a clue how to do my job, barely hanging on there, like surfing the data before crashing on the shore. It's always a relief to get back to Oxford from the City of London. Feels calmer waters here, though I suppose that's ironic considering.'

Leo liked him better for this admission. 'It's the impression he's after and, from what I've heard from you, he would be thinking mainly of your rowing prowess. We already know he's medium build so going after one of your teammates wouldn't work so well. He was probably intending to turn up as you at your next training session and see what the rowers would do.' He self-corrected. 'Or find some isolated member of the team and try it on him. Yes, that would fit pattern better.'

Nathan's face took on a mulish scowl, his loyalty button pushed. 'Then he'd have to have his running shoes on. Any of my guys would've beaten him into the dust.'

'Were you planning to meet any of them on your own?' Leo asked. He liked this theory – he wanted to see if it would hold water.

'I'd arranged to spot for Joel – Joel Driver – at the weights room tomorrow morning.' He glanced at the clock. 'I mean today.'

Another lead. 'Did anyone else know?'

Nathan shrugged. 'It's regular. His brother doesn't like getting up so early on Saturday – not when he doesn't have to – so I volunteered.' He looked a little sheepish. 'I suppose I'd better tell him I'm cancelling.'

'I believe he knows,' said Suyin. 'I've had multiple messages passed to me from teammates just checking you're OK. I said you were holding up well and you'd be in touch as soon as we're done here.'

'The guys were worried about me? Can I text them now?'

From his gratified tone, Leo realised that, in terms of social maturity, Nathan wasn't much more than a boy despite being in his mid-twenties.

'Of course, Nathan,' said Leo. 'You're free to do whatever you like – leave if you want at any time – take all the breaks you need. You're just helping us get a fuller picture of your attacker to help us stop this killer – and we appreciate that.'

'I want to do everything I can.' Taking out his phone, Nathan shot off a quick message to his group. 'Do you have more questions?'

'Following up on the question about routine, can you tell us if you've noticed anyone watching you or any strange encounters over the past few months?'

'Months?' His voice squeaked in alarm.

'We don't know how long these attacks have been planned for so we're casting the frame quite wide.'

Nathan scratched his chin. 'I only started going to the open-air pool in June.'

'OK, that's helpful. Let's think about the last two months then.'

'I found out about it from that new book by Jago Jackson.' He grinned at Suyin. 'Bought it because of the name, you know? Sounded cool?' She nodded encouragingly. 'Found I really liked swimming in the open air. Not noticed anyone out of place when I'm out and about. But then, I'm usually head down over messages when travelling, listening to music or podcasts. I've got some really good noise cancelling earphones I picked up on a rowing trip to Hong Kong. I reckon an alien spaceship could land and I'd not notice.'

The bane of modern policing – people disappearing into their own personal space, thought Leo wryly.

'Is it OK with you if we crosscheck the followers on your social media accounts with our other victims?' he asked. 'He's been getting his information from somewhere.'

'No problem. Anything to help. Do you think he'll try again?' Nathan directed this question to the psychologist.

'You're the first one to escape him, so it's hard to predict what he'll do now,' said Michael. 'On the current information, probably not. He's careful about how he approaches people and he hasn't yet struck when anyone was expecting him. Sorry I can't be more definitive than that.'

Leo agreed with a cautious approach. The attacker would be spinning in confusion, all his clever plans wasted; he'd be like an upended turtle, flippers flailing as he tried to get his feet back under him. He'd be very hard to predict right now.

Nathan appealed to Leo. 'Still, the advice is: don't walk down any dark alleys on my own, right?'

'Correct,' he confirmed. 'Is there anyone who can stay with you – or where you can go?'

'I'll go to training then go home for a bit. Take a few days – the team can absorb that. Crap, Mum is going to be unbearable.' He face-palmed, mostly for Suyin's benefit.

'I can imagine,' she murmured.

'Home?' asked Leo.

'My parents live in the Cotswolds. Chipping Norton.'

Of course they did, probably next door to the ex-prime minister Cameron and Prince Charles.

'That's a good idea,' said Leo. 'I suggest you don't talk to the press – don't draw any more attention to yourself just in case we're wrong about the killer's interest passing on. We'd also be grateful if you'd make a note, as detailed as possible, of your routines for the last two months. This man has to be seeing you and the other victims somewhere; if there are connections that lead to him, we need to find them.' None of them wanted this to be a truly random target killer. Such a thing was almost unheard of but it did happen.

Nathan shuddered. 'Sure. Yes, I'll do that.'

'Leave your contact details with us and let us know when you come back to Oxford. We'll make sure you're safe in your own home – we'll run a security check and keep the local beat officers in the loop. Is there anyone who can stay with you tonight?'

'Kyle has volunteered.' Nathan now blushed even more furiously.

'The pool attendant we spoke to earlier?' Leo glanced to the waiting area outside where the other witness was waiting after completing his own interview.

'Yeah. He saved me. Without his intervention, I think this psycho would've got me.'

'Well, if he's offered, I'd encourage you to take him up on it.'

'Good. Great.' Nathan laced his fingers together, stretched them out in front to relieve the tension in his shoulders. 'Finished?'

'We have for now.'

Nathan got up. 'Oh, er, I suppose I have remembered one thing. It seemed a bit odd at the time but I dismissed it. My bike was stolen – hardly news, I know – but then it came back. Just appeared outside my flat no worse for wear.'

Leo's interest flared. 'When was this?'

'About three weeks ago. I only mention it because the one the attacker rode, it was just like mine, same light blue, an all-terrain bike. I only got a quick glimpse but I'd say it was the same make and model. I normally would've been on mine but went for the scooter instead.'

'That's helpful. He may have been practising,' Michael said.

'Well done me – psycho target.' Nathan waved his hands, mock cheerleader pose. Leo could see how he fitted in his team – the boat clown.

'You're not the only one and it was nothing you did, Nathan. It could've been much worse.'

If you were breathing, there was always worse.

Chapter 38

Jess

It had been a long night of trying not to think how close we'd come to the attacker again. Only my falling out with Drew had stopped us being right there in Hinksey Park, during or moments after the attack. Would he have gone for us too or had he meant us to find the body, as we had on that first occasion? And where was he going with this? Were we his end game?

I did not like to be in the sights of a killer. No way was I going to any riverbank or swimming pool for the foreseeable future. I'd just have to persuade Jago to do likewise. That would be tough as he lived for his wild swimming.

I only fell asleep at dawn when Cory and the children got up. Knowing they weren't lying in bed and vulnerable at least allowed me finally to give in to sleep. Surfacing groggily at eleven, I texted Jago to invite myself over for brunch.

I rushed into his rooms and dumped the bag of croissants I'd picked up in Summertown on his breakfast table.

'Good morning to you too?' he said, standing in his bathrobe. He looked amused by my lack of normal greeting.

'Jago, I think we should tell the police that we had Hinksey Pool on our schedule for last night.'

He frowned. 'You mean because of the attack? But we weren't there.'

'But we'd planned to be. Don't you find that ... well ... suspicious?'

He nodded. 'If you put it like that ... Can you call them? I've only got some switchboard number. I couldn't get through last time.'

I got out my phone. At least that explained why he hadn't reported the boatyard before the police got back in touch with him. 'I'll do it now.'

From the bleary tone that DI George used to answer, I guessed that I was waking him up. 'Sorry, it's, er, Jessica Bridges here.'

The inspector cleared his throat. 'No problem. Long night.'

Of course it had been. 'I apologise for disturbing you, Inspector. I'll be quick. I'm with Jago. I thought you should know that we'd planned to go to Hinksey Pool last night.'

Tiredness evaporated. 'I thought you'd messaged a few days ago that you were going this morning?'

'We changed our plans last night. It was an impulse thing.' God, that sounded terrible. I hadn't realised what a risk we'd been taking.

'And who did you tell?'

I held the phone away from my mouth. 'Jago, did you mention it to anyone?'

'Only in passing. I mentioned it down the pub yesterday

when we talked about weekend plans.' Light dawned. 'Oh, and I reposted a link on my blog to my article about Hinksey Pool last week. I do that every summer Thursday just before the weekend.'

I sighed. 'Did you get that, Inspector? Jago told the world – or drew the world's attention to it.'

George didn't sound surprised. 'Can you ask him when he first posted that article?'

This was foolish. I thrust the phone at Jago. 'You talk to him.'

Jago took my phone in hand. 'Inspector George? Hi, Jago here. I first wrote it last year, during that heatwave we had, if you remember that? I updated it and reposted it last week as part of my usual site maintenance.'

I couldn't hear George's question but I could make out what it was about from Jago's answer. 'Yes, I do put new places on there, ones that don't make it into the book.' So basically our suspects had just ballooned into anyone with an internet connection. I could feel George's despair. At this point they wanted enquiries to be narrowing down. That set Jago on the defensive. 'It's my business. I get sponsorship. I can't stop just because someone is exploiting the knowledge I'm making available to everyone.'

George asked a follow-up.

'Yes, all the sites where there have been attacks have been mentioned on the blog this summer,' Jago confirmed. 'Only the boatyard wasn't described in detail – I left it a secret. Could someone work out where it was? I suppose – if you know the area. You'd still need a code to get in there. No, no,

I'm not planning any more blog updates now. Yes, I'll stay away from the river. I understand. Yes. No guarantees. I'll be careful.'

He handed me back the phone. 'It must be a digital stalker. I mean, how else would they know what I'm thinking?'

'That's the problem with modern life: we put far too much out there. For which I am grateful as it gives me a job.'

'If you did what you do,' he twirled his hand in a general approximation of my sleuthing through online profiles, 'would you be able to predict my moves?'

A good question. Was it that simple? No one watching us, or at least not directly. If Jago shut up for a bit, would this person's interest move on? 'Maybe he has all kinds of targets lined up and what you post online just helps him select which he goes for next.'

Jago pinched the bridge of his nose. 'I'm thinking some mad back-bedroom deal here – photos, notes, coloured string linking people and places.'

'Interesting. You're showing your analogue roots, Jago, 'cause I was thinking computer files – lots of them.' Having done everything I could for the moment, I began setting out the brunch. 'Tell me: do you write longhand?'

'A first draft. Sometimes.' He sounded defensive. He filled the kettle. 'Laptops and water don't mix.'

'God, I can see you now. Wearing that bashed up denim jacket of yours, sliding into a waterfront cafe, notebook in your pocket, or sitting in a station on a duffle bag, penning your impressions as the city rats race around you on the hunt for more financial cheese.'

He gave me a familiar look. 'Jessica, has anyone told you you've got a weird imagination?'

'Everyone usually does eventually. Congratulations, you're early to realise the uniqueness of my interior world. My brain is one big soup of images which stick inappropriately to the spoon of my imagination when I give it a stir.'

He pointed a teaspoon at me. 'That right there proves my words.'

Chapter 39

Michael

Michael made some more notes on the profile he was generating for DI George after the interview with Nathan. The outline of the killer was clear: reckless, sociopathic, thrill seeking, compulsive; the problem was filling in the detail to catch the man before he struck again. It was bloody frustrating to know so much and yet still have no suspect.

It didn't help his concentration that his flat felt airless. He opened the garden doors, hoping to coax some breeze through the stifling living room. His computer added to the heat, fan whirring as it battled to keep its cool. He wanted to lie down and sleep but pride, coupled with a sense of urgency, kept him on task. Sweat trickled down his back, gathering at the point where the seat cushion met his buttocks. He was so hot, and longed for a swim in any of the pools Jago rhapsodised about, even with the threat of catching a water-borne parasite.

Michael's mood didn't help his patience. He hadn't liked

the guy – he was talking about Jago, not the killer obviously – before taking this on; that dislike had baked into loathing after knuckling down and watching the documentary last night. He even had the completely outrageous thought that watching Jago enthuse over another grubby bit of Thames would drive anyone to violence.

He tapped his lips with his steepled fingers. Was this evidence of a neurosis? He'd considered Jago as a possible stalker; such unbalanced judgements would fit the vicious person sending Jessica and him parcels. Unless it was a pose and there was more to Jago than met the eye? Jessica seemed to like him enough to sleep with him so he couldn't be quite as awful as Michael found him.

Couldn't he though? Jessica wasn't always the best judge of character.

Maybe there was another clue in there? These victims were the people Jago brushed up against, briefly intersected with in that way of so many of our city encounters. Was the attacker circling ever closer? Was Jago actually the real goal?

Michael added that to his email to the inspector. There wasn't much that could be done about what amounted to a hunch, not with the killer eluding them. He couldn't even get a clear grasp of his character, other than this hunger to be someone else. Serial killers – and as he was the author of a short chain of linked murders, he could be given that title – usually had some rationale behind their actions, even if it sounded insane to the rest of us. 'They needed killing' didn't fit here, because he admired his targets. Michael was thinking he was working along the lines of 'it should've been me' – that successful job or relationship, that profile or prowess. Could he be motivated by nothing more complicated than envy? Coveting, that was a better term. It was one of the original sins in the Ten Commandments. And there was no more ultimate takeover of someone else than to steal their life and lifestyle too.

But the takeover didn't work, did it? How long would it take the killer to realise that this fantasy of being Ken, Ruby or whoever was just that – a fantasy? If he was moving so fast to new victims, Michael predicted this was going to be a short and not sweet killing spree. He wouldn't be surprised if the murderer ended it all by killing himself, even before or shortly after his arrest. Serial killers often went that way, choosing death rather than submitting to justice.

He might die, but not, Michael was afraid, before taking more with him. Nathan escaping was going to enrage him, maybe spook him, and he'd want to get back on what he saw as his track. Where would he strike next?

It really was too hot to think straight today. Michael decided to take a break – perhaps even get in a late siesta. He wasn't going to call it a nap because that just sounded so old. He tried to summon up the energy to move. The curtain billowed a little in the breeze. Leaves rustled outside. Blossoms bobbed on the neighbour's climbing rose that had sprung up into Michael's trees – a benign yellow invader laced through some pears that last year had never quite got ripe enough to eat, according to the woman from whom he'd bought the flat. Perhaps she just hadn't waited long enough? If he just went and opened up a window in his bedroom, he would have a through draught, and that should help.

He wheeled into the bedroom and wrestled with the window. It stuck but with a thump, delivered from an awkwardly low angle, he managed to get it to shift. It was shady in here, a little cooler than the big expanse of sunlit lounge. He could maybe just allow himself five minutes.

He woke up thirty minutes later stretched out on the bed where he'd flopped after an exhausting transfer. He knew instantly that something had changed in the house – that something was wrong. There was a presence in here with him. His mind sprang to the open garden windows. He never usually risked ...

Never mind that now. He could hear a person moving around. There was a muffled cry, like a kitten. Had he got Colette?

Cursing his slow body, he shifted to swing out of bed. Never had he felt more frustrated by his disability – not since lying at the bottom of his cellar steps, cursing his would-be murderer. Fuck this – FUCK this!

Phone the police, you idiot! his more intelligent brain shouted at his inner ape who just wanted to drive an interloper off his territory with some chest thumping.

He groped for the nightstand, but realised he'd left the phone by the computer.

Of course he had: he almost deserved this for being so stupid. He knew better than to let his guard down even for an instant.

There came the sound of sirens outside but they went past and stopped somewhere nearby with a final whoop.

Had that scared off his housebreaker? But, shit – if he got his computer ...!

Rage filled him. Finally – thank God, finally, he'd managed to haul himself into his chair. It was the heavier electric one, so at least good for ramming into someone. He grabbed a weighty metal doorstop in the shape of a hare and got it ready on his lap. He kept going down the corridor – the whine of the motor would have clued the intruder into his approach if the noise of him getting up hadn't already done so. Pushing the chair to its top speed, he bumped from tiled hall to wooden lounge floor, brandishing the hare held upside down by its ears like a torch.

And found the room empty.

Or almost.

A Moses basket had appeared on the dining-room table – wicker affair with frilly cotton sheets. These were moving, and the distressed cat noise was even louder now.

He was almost too sickened to look. Was that Colette in there – eyes gouged out like Jessica's doll? That was the next logical escalation. He'd have to put her down immediately if that was what had been done. He eyed the hare statuette, putting it in his lap just in case it was needed for a mercy killing.

Then two things happened at once. Colette slunk in from the garden, completely unharmed, and the strangled kitten noise resolved itself into a full-on baby wail. He reached inside the basket and touched soft, slightly damp, warm flesh.

The troll had left him holding the baby.

Chapter 40

Jess

I abandoned Jago running the Jacuzzi to answer my phone. It was Michael – more distraught than I'd ever heard him.

'Michael, slow down, please. What's happened?' I could hear voices behind him and, oddly, the shrill cry of a baby. He was still not making sense and then, even more alarming, the line went dead.

Jago came out of the bathroom, a beard of bath foam overlaying his neatly trimmed one. 'Bath's ready.'

I looked at the phone in my hand. Michael wasn't answering.

'Jess?' Jago wiped off the beard.

'Crap on toast.'

He winced. 'What's wrong?'

I poured metaphorical cold water on my libido. 'You're going to be so, so mad, but I've got to go.'

He grabbed my hand as I put my things back in my tote – bikini, massage oil, purse, phone. 'Hey, you can't go now! The bubbles are already on full.'

'I'd like nothing better than to play with you in the Jacuzzi but that was a friend – he's in trouble.'

'What kind of trouble and which friend?'

I shoved my feet into my sandals. 'In reverse order, Michael Harrison and I don't know.'

Little white anger lines appeared at the top of Jago's nose and bracketed his mouth. 'Really? Another of your exes muscles in on our time? Is this to be a regular event?'

'They really do have extraordinary timing, don't they?' I said with inappropriate cheerfulness, my knee-jerk response to serious situations.

'He's not your responsibility, Jess.'

'No, he's not. But we are friends and I help all my friends if I can. That's the deal on friendship with me. You'd get that too if you were in a fix.'

He captured me in his arms and pulled me closer. 'And I can't change your mind?' He began to kiss his way down to my breasts, mouthing them through the T-shirt material.

I squirmed. Loyalty was an inconvenient instinct. I tried a new argument. 'Look, Michael isn't the same guy you knew. He's vulnerable. His social circle has shrunk because he can't get out so easily and is too proud to invite people home. I need to check up on him.'

Jago pressed his forehead against mine and heaved a put-upon sigh. 'All right; I'll take you.'

'You don't need to do that. It's over in Jericho.'

'There's still the killer out there. I don't want to send you out on your own.'

He did have a point and having a car might be quite useful.

I'd no idea what I was walking into. 'If you're willing to drive, then I'd be grateful.'

We arrived at Michael's address and my heart turned over in my chest. There was a policeman on the door – never a good sign – and a group of neighbours gathered further up the street, behind some tape. They had the pitchfork look to them – scowls and crossed arms. I leapt from the car, ducked under the tape, even before Jago had finished parking. I dashed up to the policeman.

'What's happened to Michael? Is he OK?'

The policeman fielded me so I couldn't pass him. 'Miss, you can't go in.'

'Michael? Where is he? Is he OK?' I repeated.

'Mr Harrison ...'

'It's Dr Harrison – he consults for the police – a celebrity psychologist.'

The constable clearly didn't know anything about this but faltered only for a second. 'Dr Harrison is at Cowley police station, helping us with our enquiries.'

'Enquiries into what?' What had happened now?'

'Child abduction.'

The answer was so unexpected I laughed. 'You've lost your mind! The last thing Michael wants is a kid. This is all some ridiculous mistake. Didn't you notice he's in a wheelchair, for Christ's sake?'

'Miss, I must ask you to step back or I'll have to have you removed.' This officer was low on the food chain; I'd be better off not angering him and getting myself arrested.

'Fine, fine. At the station on the Cowley Road, you say? I'll go there then.'

I got back into the car and issued the new instruction. Jago accepted the new directions with no snide comments.

'I take it something bad has happened?' He checked his dials. 'I'm going to need to look for a recharging point. Google one for me, will you? Near the police station?'

'Will do – just need to call someone first.' I placed the call.

'What?' George's reply was nearly a growl. He sounded like he'd been asleep too after a long night on duty.

'Sorry – so sorry – I feel bad that I keep ringing but I think you'll want to know about this but it's Michael. He rang me – in a bad way. He's just been arrested and I couldn't get much sense out of him. There's some crazy child abduction charge made against him. They've taken him to the police station in Cowley. I thought, what with the stalker leaving stuff for us with a baby theme, that it has to be him, right? But the beat police might not connect the dots. Can you help?'

'I'll get down here right away. I'll ring the duty officer – make sure he's got the full picture.'

I ended the call. 'The inspector is untangling things at the police end but I'm still worried about Michael. He didn't sound right. Do you mind if I do some outrageous lying to get in to see him, Jago?'

Jago grinned. 'Not at all.'

We parked at a charging station – having an electric car was almost as good as a disabled blue badge, I realised. Jago followed me. Neither of us looked either official or important so this was going to have to go on force of personality.

'I'm here to see Michael Harrison,' I said boldly. 'I'm from Renfrew and Jakowitz. He called me in.' See, I didn't say I was a lawyer, just let her assume that. And it was true that I was from there (though no longer employed) and he had rung.

'And this man?' The woman on reception looked somewhat dubiously at Jago.

'My partner.' I didn't specify which kind. 'But he'll wait out here as we're expecting Inspector George from Kidlington CID to join us.' And if Michael was in a bad way, the last person he needed to see was Jago.

'Do you have some ID on you?'

I fished in my bag and came up with my driver's licence and the lanyard with my employee's pass on it, which I'd accidentally-on-purpose forgotten to return on my last day at Renfrew and Jakowitz.

'I'll take you back there now so Mr Harrison can confirm your story,' she said.

'Dr Harrison,' I reiterated. 'And believe me, there is so much more to the story than you know. You'll need to tread very carefully with Michael – he's been mistreated by the police once already. I'm surprised you don't know.'

She pursed her mouth, not liking to be told she was ignorant, which was what I'd basically just done. To give her her due, she took me to the interview room without further complaint and rapped on the door.

'A Jessica Bridges for Michael Harrison, his lawyer.'

I pushed past her. 'I never said I was his lawyer. Michael, are you OK? It's going to be all right – I called DI George: he's on his way.'

Michael was looking rough – in shock, I'd say. His shirt was rumpled and drenched in sweat but he was shivering. 'Jessica?'

I turned on the two men interviewing him. 'You do realise that a paraplegic has special medical requirements, don't you? He's clearly having difficulty regulating his body temperature – and he looks dehydrated. Have you called a medic?'

'He didn't want one when we offered,' said one of the officers, a weaselly looking man in his late thirties.

'But I can tell within two seconds of getting in here that he's not tracking well. Call the medic and while you're at it, look up the cock-up the Met made of the last time Michael was attacked. You should be treading very carefully right now.'

I was feeling good on my gust of indignation – Boadicea rolling over the Romans in my chariot. Well, Michael had the chariot, I just had the attitude to jump onboard.

Weasel guy got up. 'Miss Bridges, you can't just charge in here and take over!'

There was another knock on the door and a constable put her head around the door. 'Viv, Neil, you're wanted upstairs a.s.a.p.'

That must be George getting through to speak to a senior officer. The two policemen reluctantly left the room. I got Michael some water from a jug on a side table and held it to his lips. He tried to take it but his hands were shaking. I hated this – Michael should be strong, disdainful, not ... broken.

'What happened, Michael?'

'I found a baby on my dining table.' His hair was falling over his eyes and I smoothed it back.

Oh God. I had a horrible image of a dead baby left on a plate. 'How did it get there? Whose is it?'

He managed to sip some water. 'Snatched from a local garden just shortly before and left in my house. I was asleep – heard it crying.'

Oh, thank God: it was alive.

'Came out and was just reaching for it when the police busted down my door. Tip-off that I'd been seen taking it. They didn't believe me when I said that was impossible. Something about baby stealing that gets the police hyped. To be fair, they did find me with this crying kid in my arms wondering what the hell to do with it.'

I hugged him. He was hot – not for once in the sexy sense. 'Don't worry – Inspector George will explain all about the stalker. There's no way you could physically steal a baby even if they want to carry on with this ridiculous idea.'

'Back gate apparently. Runs down an alley to my garden.'

'It's all just nonsense. Just sit tight. We'll get you sprung.'

He leaned into me. 'It's a fucking mess.'

'It is that. Someone is playing us – someone we're not seeing.'

'I think it's fucking Jago Jackson. He hates me – I hate him.'

'It's not him, Michael. I've been with him since this morning.' I decided this was odd behaviour even for Michael. He would normally be turning on the charm, then if that hadn't worked tried the 'don't you know who I am?' routine. I reached for his forehead. 'Michael, do you know you're running a temperature?'

He shook his head. 'No, no, it's just a hot day.'

'Then why are you shivering?' I got out my phone and texted Inspector George. *Michael is ill. Need doctor at once!!!* I didn't need to point out the fallout if Michael collapsed in their custody. George would know.

'I'm fine – just shaken. I didn't predict this.'

'Michael, you're not fine. You've got a fever. Tell me the truth now: have you been looking after yourself?'

'I don't know, Jess. I've been consulting for CID – sat in on the interview with the victim from yesterday.'

'In other words, you've been going out at all hours, probably skipping meals and sleep. You need to go to bed.'

'I've got things to do.'

'Like get better.'

'I can't get stranded at home – it'll kill me.'

'I'm not talking about you taking to your bed permanently – just till you beat this. You don't want this to become pneumonia.' But he had no one to look after him; he'd need nursing. Shit. 'Look, I'll stay over – until you're recovered. Let's get you sprung from jail then we'll take you home.'

'We?'

'Jago's outside. He brought me in his car.'

Michael just nodded, surrendering what happened next to me. That proved we needed a doctor urgently.

George hadn't let the grass grow: he arrived exactly as promised with the station's doctor-on-call at his side.

'Dr Harrison, I'm so sorry for all this. I've explained to the officers in charge of your case about the stalker and they are now returning to your house to look for traces of the intruder. They thank you for your cooperation and you are free to go.'

From the tight expression, I could tell that George had just had a professional disagreement – aka a shouting match – with his colleagues and he'd won. 'Dr Grayson here will give you a quick check over.'

The GP was a reassuring older man with iron grey hair and a hint of pipe smoke. He gently pressed Michael's glands, took his temperature, checked his throat. 'A virus,' he declared. 'You need to be in bed, Michael, and keep up the fluid intake.' He then turned to me. 'Hopefully he'll shake this off after bedrest. Paracetamol should be enough but if his temperature rises any further, or if the fever lasts more than another twelve hours, call his local doctor for further advice.'

'I live alone,' growled Michael.

'Oh, er ...'

'Don't worry, doctor, I'll see that someone is with him till he's better. I can do the rest of the day and tomorrow.' And Monday was too far away to worry about. 'Let's go home, Michael.'

'I'll arrange for a lift,' said George.

It was a strange procession heading back to Michael's flat: the inspector, Michael and I in a police car; Jago following us in his Leaf. The police were dusting surfaces for finger-prints, but I shooed them out of Michael's bedroom on the very good grounds that the intruder had not gone in there. Michael was slumping in his chair by the time I helped him into a fresh T-shirt. I looked at the bed wondering how I could lift him. It would be so much easier if he let me call for aid.

'Michael, can I ask Jago to help?' I knew he wouldn't want

a professional colleague involved. 'You can keep your eyes closed.'

'I might just do that,' he muttered.

Jago displayed his better nature, making no quips and helping me lift Michael onto the bed.

'I'm sorry you're not feeling well, Dr Harrison,' he said.

'Thank you, Dr Jackson. I apologise for being a burden.' It was a weird kind of detente but I'd take it.

'Not your fault, Michael,' I said briskly. 'Blame the baby-snatcher and the common cold.'

'Just a cold, is it?' Michael shivered under the covers. 'Jessica has declared it thus, therefore it is so.'

If he could sass me, then he wasn't at death's door. 'Exactly. No gloomy diagnoses from me. I'll chase the police out and come back with a Lemsip.'

I ushered Jago out.

Once in the corridor, Jago looked at me. 'He isn't as formidable as I remember.'

I shrugged. Now was probably not the time for my theory that they were too like each other to get on. 'You remember the professor with whom you locked horns. Michael's just a guy whom life has kicked in the balls a couple of times.'

'I guess.' He hugged me. 'You're sweet – looking after him like that.'

'Well, as I said, if ever you need bailing out, who you gonna call?'

He chuckled and we went to battle with the police in the lounge.

Chapter 41

Jess

It was late Saturday evening and I was on my own in Michael's sitting room. Fingerprints had been lifted and I'd hoovered away the mess left by the powder the forensic team used. We didn't yet know if the stalker stork had been careless when he delivered this particular baby bundle, but somehow I doubted it. The child had arrived untouched in its Moses basket and been handed back to his distraught parents from the house two doors away, none the worse for the experience. Unlike the rest of us. Michael was still sleeping, though I did manage to get him to drink some chicken and tarragon soup – made by Jago, no less – at around seven. Jago had resigned himself to a further delay on our Jacuzzi plans and gone home, promising to return tomorrow.

Finally I could take a breath. Finally I could pick up the messages on my phone that I'd been ignoring. Finally I could try to make sense of an ugly hectic day.

A real baby placed in Michael's home – but unharmed. The result? Major hassle for Michael, no lasting trauma for the

335

kid. The parents might have panic attacks later thinking of what might've been, but I didn't think their feelings factored into this calculation. If the police hadn't already had their fingers burned believing a slime attack on Michael's reputation, he could seriously be in the frame for child abduction. He lived alone and so had no alibi beyond the difficulty of achieving the physical task of removing a child from one garden and placing it in a house a few doors down. Thank God he'd reported the earlier parcels.

I went to his laptop and entered into the guest area he'd created for me so I could work from his apartment. I called up the messages he'd screen-shotted and flagged from his social media – Duckweed58. People rarely chose numbers at random. Did that mean that the stalker was born in 1958, making him in his sixties? I could imagine him as that typical angry white guy, the sort of person who voted for the current crop of idiotic political leaders, and finally felt his kind of people had their hands on the levers of power, God help the rest of us. Or that he lived at number 58 somewhere? It might just be his lucky number, taken from his first number plate or some such association that I wouldn't be able to track down.

My phone jiggled. Mum. I'd been avoiding her calls all day, mainly because I just didn't want to think about her meeting my father. Bad daughter. I needed to reverse some of the damage he no doubt had done.

'Jessica! At last! I was worried.' She sounded pumped up on happy hormones. My heart sank.

'No need to worry. I've been busy helping a friend – couldn't pick up.'

'Oh? A *special* friend?' For Mum, hope springs eternal.

'Just Michael. He's ill.'

'Oh.' Mum had never been entirely sure what she felt about Michael ever since his injury. He appealed to her wounded creature empathy but she also knew he wasn't the nicest boyfriend to me. 'Poor dear. Is it bad?'

'Any illness is a challenge for someone in his condition.' I made myself ask. 'So how was your day?'

'Your father and I had a lovely little talk in a cafe this morning. Just a quick half hour, though it flew by – to break the ice, he said.'

'Define "lovely".'

'Well, he bought the drinks and one of those muffins that I like. And he was very polite. Told me what he gets up to in his retirement – driving for a special needs activity club, taking the elderly to hospital appointments.'

I snorted. I just didn't believe it. That list was concocted for my mother's benefit.

'It's true! He showed me photos.'

'Brian Bridges does not drive little old ladies to have their hips replaced – not unless he wants to be mentioned in their wills.'

'He might've changed, Jessica. You haven't seen him for fifteen years – how do you know what he's like now?'

Because leopards couldn't change their spots. Because fool me once, shame on you; fool me twice, shame on me. 'Mum, I can't talk about this with you.'

'He was very interested to hear how you're doing. He worries about you – as is only natural.'

No, he wanted to strangle the life out of me, taking over so I could only function in a way he approved. He wanted a whipped dog, not a daughter. 'I hope you told him nothing?'

'But he knew so much already.' A sensation like icy fingers brushing the back of my neck chilled me. 'He followed what happened last year in the news – was quite incensed at how your trust was abused.'

I choked on my horror. 'Incensed? On my behalf?'

My mum wasn't hearing my warning signals, or was closing her ears to them on purpose. 'He wants to meet – no pressure – anywhere you pick with whoever you want present.'

'Erm, let me think. That would be never, nowhere and no one.'

She sighed. 'Jessica, you're grown up now. I really think you should try harder to progress from where your teenage years left you. You won't heal until you make peace with him.'

She was making me feel physically sick. 'I'm not you, Mum. This isn't right for me. Please respect that.'

There was a pause. 'I haven't chosen a good time, have I? You're worried about Michael. I'm sorry. Let's talk about it when you're feeling less emotional.' She was seizing the upper hand with her oh-so understanding tone, making me out to be the hysterical one.

I moved to the counter, picked up a carving knife, and stabbed the loaf of bread left out from my supper. My mouth was in an open but silent scream.

'Jessica? Are you still there?'

I breathed through my nose. One and two and three. 'Mum, I've got to go. Michael's calling for me.'

'All right then. Give him my best wishes.'

'Will do.' I ended the call, put down the knife, swept up the crumbs into my hand and chucked them in the food bin. I hoped Michael didn't begrudge me one loaf of his artisan bread supply.

The handset buzzed again. If it was my mum or Miriam wanting to talk to me about my mum, I wasn't going to answer.

Marek's face came up. Relief swept me. Just my vulgar-mouthed contact, not my blood family.

'Hey, big guy, how's it hanging?' I asked.

'Excellently, thank you, sugar cube.'

I wasn't going to ask to which part of my anatomy he was referring. 'I followed up those names you gave me but I need a bit more time to pin them down.'

'No problem. I just wanted you to know that I've found out something very interesting about your Roman Wolnik.'

'You did? Marek, I think I love you.'

'I know, I know, all the girls do eventually. First, Roman Wolnik is not his actual name – that's his cousin living inno-cently in Szczecin. I believe your man is really Tadeusz Wolnik, wanted for arson and insurance fraud involving his graphics business in Poznan back in the day.'

'You'll have to send this to me on paper – I've no idea how to spell the names.'

Marek tutted. 'Show you Anglo-Saxons a few Slavic conso-nants and you all panic. It's a very logical language – much more so than your crazy English.'

'Yes, I know, sorry. My brain is just failing to compute. Go on about the fraud.'

'He was too optimistic at the business opportunities in the early 2000s, borrowed money from the wrong people and they wanted to be repaid more quickly than his turnover would allow. He tried to find the money by burning down his own business after hours but the police suspected foul play and the insurance company refused to pay up. Fortunately for him, we joined the EU so he could steal his cousin's passport and travel to the UK with none the wiser.'

'And he remade himself here?'

'Exactly. It's very good you've brought him to my attention. There are people who are still interested in his whereabouts.'

Meaning Marek could rat him out to the people holding his debt.

I'd have to bargain as he scented a way of making money. 'Marek, I know you love me really so you won't mind holding off on that for a few weeks, will you?'

He harrumphed.

'There are two kids involved – one living with Wolnik at the moment. If some guys come over to rough him up, the kids could get caught in the crossfire.'

'Sugar cube—' Marek wasn't sentimental about children. I'd have to find another argument.

'Plus this is the information my client needs. If you sell him out too soon, it loses its potency – and there would've been no point in me swapping this for a favour.'

He thought for a moment. 'You deliver the information on the two names I gave you – on my lap while wearing a French maid's costume.'

I rolled my eyes. He never gave up. 'No to the last part.'

'Aw, you're no fun.'

'I'm lots of fun, as you well know. Dream on, Marek. Professional favours, not sexual ones, is how we jive.'

'I'll hold back what I know until you say it's fine to use it if, *kochana*, and only if, you get me the details on my runaways by Wednesday. If you still don't have anything for me, then ...' He let the implied threat hang.

'I'll work up the profile on your guys before then. Trust me.'

'I do. I just don't want those losers getting too far away for me to follow them. Nice doing business with you.'

'Yeah, you too.' When I put the phone down, I imagined Marek chuckling away in his three-piece suit, telling Solidarność how he'd got me over a barrel. I didn't think he'd ever push this beyond very vivid teasing; in fact, I thought he'd probably be shocked if I did turn up in a maid's outfit. I had to admit I was a little tempted just to see his face. He was an honourable man in his own way.

At least, that was what I was banking on. He hadn't yet proved otherwise.

Let's concentrate on the important news though. Roman aka Tadeusz thought he had dirt on Amy. I now had a whole barrelful to upend on his head. It should certainly be enough to get him to back down from revealing Amy's Mexican debacle in court. The biggest remaining problem was Angelica. If he was a gaslighter, as Amy claimed, then he'd done a bang-up job on the girl as she seemed more devoted to him than was healthy for a fifteen-year-old who should think at that age that all adults suck. That was how gaslighting works though:

the one who told the lies persuaded you that the world was as he described it, even if you could see evidence to the contrary. It could happen to whole countries – you didn't need to go back to Nazi Germany, just look at the world today. If adults fell for it en masse, I could hardly expect a teenager to snap out of it.

Still, I'd made progress. I summarised my findings and sent them off to Amy, cautioning her to keep her cards close to her chest until we could work out how to turn this to our best advantage.

Double-checking the doors and windows were shut, I then switched off the lights. I could go to bed on the pull-out sofa with the satisfaction of not having wasted my time today.

Chapter 42

Jess

I sat out in the back garden to sneak a cigarette and phone Cory. This undercover role at Linton College had brought back the old habit just as I feared it would, but I'd deal with that once this case was over and things went back to normal.

Not that I ever seemed to live in the normal zone. Twilight was more my natural milieu.

'You stayed out all night then?' pried Cory.

'Who are you, my mother?' I wished she were. 'Get your dirty little mind out of my private affairs. I stayed over at Michael's. He's got the 'flu the proper sort, not man 'flu. The doctor even paid a house call this morning—'

'Michael must have some influence to get that treatment.'

'I think the police are worried they'll be sued for dragging a sick man into custody without getting him the right attention. Kinda been there done that in Michael's case.'

'Poor good-looking guy. Handsome, soulful, vulnerable doctor, in need of some female companionship ...'

'Cory, stop it. We are not in Dr Who territory. Michael does

343

fine on his own normally.' Though I had to admit there was something David Tennant-ish about him. 'The doctor said he might have to be hospitalised if I couldn't stay on so I promised to make sure he had someone with him until he's better.'

'Of course you did, you sucker.'

'I haven't got to the good part yet.' I blew a plume of smoke out over the wall in the direction of the rescued baby family.

'There's more?'

'Yeah. Jago came round, bearing groceries. He's still here. Cooked us all a lovely Eggs Benedict. With chopped chives.'

Cory snorted. 'Yum.'

'I didn't tell Michael who cooked – he'd probably spit it out on principle. It's quite funny really, how they bristle around each other like hedgehogs.'

'Jessica, I totally adore you. Anyway, the book club has agreed we need an emergency meeting to savour your latest exploits.'

'I'm not a book.'

'Jess, you are far more entertaining than any of our most recent reads. Of course, we'll pretend to discuss Miss Havisham, but we all really want to hear about Jago, and your complicated love life. Tomorrow night at mine. No excuses.'

'I might still need to be with Michael.'

'Would he mind if we came to his?'

'What do you think?'

'Get Jago to babysit.'

'I'm hanging up now, Cory.'

'Do lots of things I wouldn't!' she trilled as I cut off the call.

I found a call from Drew waiting for me. He picked up immediately I rang him back.

'We didn't get to finish our talk,' he said.

'Do we need to? I think I understand your position.' I scowled at the nearly empty cigarette packet. How had I managed to smoke my way through all of those? Oh yeah: stress. 'You don't want to be trapped – want to be free to pick up and put down relationships.'

'I don't want to trap you either. It goes two ways.'

I took out the final cigarette. 'Problem is, relationships are more like smoking to me – addictive. I can't pick up and put them down so easily. For you, they're more like a musical instrument, to be played when the mood strikes.' I smiled sadly. 'And if that's true, I'm getting the feeling that I'm a tuba – a bad choice to pick up in the first place.'

'I'm not sure that's fair.'

'To tubas?'

'No! To me – to you! I love you, Jess.'

'Conditionally, I imagine you do. And I love you too, but for me that means sticking together, maybe planning for the future, considering kids eventually.' The silence spoke volumes. 'Be honest, Drew: am I the partner who you see as the mother of your kids? In a few years time, obviously.'

'I'm not sure I'll have kids. The world has too many people already.' That was the usual excuse of our generation when we didn't want to be forced into a decision.

'But if you change your mind? Just imagine that for a second. Am I good enough?'

'Jess, you are a lovely, caring woman. Fun. Compassionate.

But do you really think you could handle a family, with all your issues?'

'Wow, that's a bit blunter than I imagined.' Stupid tears threatened so I drew deeply on the cigarette and blew a stream of smoke in front of my face to give an excuse for watering eyes. 'Thanks for that.'

'I don't mean to hurt you. I'm just trying to be honest, like you asked.'

'Super. Much appreciated. Now fuck off, Drew.' I ended the call, got up and strode to the gate. I opened it and stomped down the alleyway, needing a breathing space. I got to the end, turned around, and walked back. Then I repeated, but this time I kept walking. Jago could look after Michael. I needed this. I'd been keeping a firm grip on my impulses for the last few days; if I didn't keep walking, I was going to explode. My spirit felt too big for my stupid body – it wanted to burst out and fly away like a release of doves at the Olympics. Better to be scattered than trapped.

The number I'd been given for emergencies swam before my eyes and I stabbed at it.

Charles Haslam, my psychiatrist and Michael's friend, answered. 'Jessica?'

'Charles, I need a session.'

'How's Michael?'

Shit, shit, Jessica. Remember that this wasn't just about you. 'He's not so great – 'flu on top of the stalker stuff. You heard about that?'

'Isn't that why you're calling?'

'Kinda. Sorta. Maybe.' He knew that meant no.

'Jessica, I thought I explained. I don't think you need me any longer.'

'Just a little pick-me-up session? I'm a bit stressed, what with nursing Michael, springing him from jail and everything.'

'You're nursing Michael?'

'Well, there's no one else, unless you've got the time?' A man actually taking on caring duties over his career for a friend? Will pigs fly?

'I ... I'm afraid I can't right now. But I could come round later – after golf. See you and Michael together.' He gave a dry cough. 'I won't even charge.'

It was better than nothing. 'Great. When should we expect you?'

'Eight?'

'OK, it's a date.'

I wasn't sure why I kept going back to stuffed-shirt Charles, but he did usually provide me with new guard rails when I'd ripped them up for some reason. I guess he stood in for my weak prefrontal cortex, the brain's policeman. Mine misfired frequently, sleeping on the job, doing the crossword when it should be paying attention to the robbery in progress; Charles blew the whistle, got out the little notebook, and gave me my warning before I did something really stupid.

Like fall in love with someone who didn't really love me. Too late.

Chapter 43

Pawel

Pawel jumped on the trampoline, feeling the water he'd just drunk slosh inside him.

'Angelica! Look at me!' He did star jumps to show how good he'd got at it since she'd left but his sister was watching Mum and Dad. They were arguing, as usual. Angelica refused to come into the house, so the row was happening right on the street by Dad's car. Uncle Ron from over the road was trying to ignore it while he mowed his lawn. Pawel waved at him and Ron waved back. He always had a smiley face even though he buried dead bodies for his job. Maybe, thought Pawel, he'd go over and see if Auntie Glenda had any chocolate chip cookies? Mum didn't believe in refined sugar but Auntie Glenda thought it was the best thing since sliced bread. He preferred it to sliced bread himself, because fresh baked cookies smelled fantastic and that always cheered him up. Angelica might like one too. She was looking cross.

Pawel stopped bouncing and climbed off the trampoline.

Mum was screaming something about Arsène in Poland, which didn't make a lot of sense because Arsène Wenger had retired as a football manager.

'Do you want to get a biscuit with me?' he asked his sister.

'Not one of Amy's?'

'What? Mum's? Course not. From the lady over the road.' She glared at Mum's back. 'She'll see.'

'Not if we go out the back and round by the playing field.'

Angelica looked down at him, finally paying him some attention. 'You've done this before?'

'Might have.'

'I wanted to get some things, anyway. That's why we came. Let's go inside while she's arguing with Dad.'

They went into the house. Angelica headed upstairs and stuffed some clothes into her old backpack. He noticed that she put in some of his things too.

'Hey, that's mine!' He made a grab for his favourite T-shirt.

'I'm not stealing it. I thought we'd go camping. Spend some time together.'

Pawel wasn't sure he wanted to spend time with Angelica. She didn't like him much. But he'd always wanted to go camping so ...

'With you and Dad?'

'Just me. An adventure. There's this really cool den in the woods I know, near the river. Amy and Dad will be arguing for hours. They won't notice.'

Pawel decided that a den in a woods sounded much more fun than more hours bouncing in the front garden. 'We could leave them a note?'

'Good idea.' She scribbled something in joined-up writing that he couldn't read but got him to sign it.

'What does it say?'

'Just that we've gone to the woods and we'll be back before it gets dark.'

Pawel thought that his mum might still be worried. 'Have you got your phone?'

She smiled at him, making him feel really little compared to her. 'Of course I've got my phone.'

Pawel still hesitated. 'Maybe we should just ask?'

'Where's the adventure in that? Come on, slow coach. You're not going to be a baby about this, are you?' Angelica took his hand in hers, squeezing too tightly. He'd forgotten these moods of hers, the ones where she got really angry if you disagreed with her way of thinking. So he let her lead him out the back way. His mouth was watering. They passed the turn to Auntie Glenda's.

'What about the cookies?'

'Later. I want to show you the den first.'

But cookies would've made the den even more fun. 'I'm thirsty.'

'I've got some water. We'll have it when we get there.'

They walked on. Pawel was getting tired going at the rapid pace Angelica was setting. He wasn't enjoying this adventure. Angelica's adventures, he now remembered, were never nice. She enjoyed scaring him, leaving him in places he didn't know so she could find him again for his mum and get the praise. How had he forgotten about that?

'I wanna go back.'

'Can't. Not till we get there.'

'Please!'

'No!'

'I'm telling!'

'No one to tell. Besides, I'm rescuing you.'

'Rescuing me? From what?'

'From Amy.'

Pawel didn't feel like he wanted to be rescued but he knew from experience that Angelica would be really mean if he tried to run back now. She'd make something up about him to get him in trouble. 'Only as far as the den, then we go back?' he asked, trying a new tactic of making a deal.

'As far as the den,' agreed Angelica. But she was silent on the second part.

Tripping over an untied shoelace, Pawel followed.

Chapter 44

Jess

I was barely holding it together but, thank God, Charles arrived as promised. I'd spent the last few hours since my final conversation with Drew walking around Michael's little garden. I know I was freaking Michael out, but I couldn't stop myself. Drew leaving had flipped something in me – I'd finally given up hope we'd ever be anything. I was crawling out of my skin. When I feel stressed, like now, the best way I can describe it is that I'm like Alice at the end of the Wonderland adventure when she gets pelted with a pack of cards – so many things whirling around in my head that I needed a gentle sister to shake me awake from the dream. Not having one of those at hand, Charles would have to do.

Charles had a steadying manner. Six feet tall, golfer's lithe build, with little wings of grey in his dark hair, he reminded me of Benedict Cumberbatch playing Dr Strange. He had no magical powers though, unless you counted his voice. In his 'trust me, I'm a doctor' tones, he told us both that we were managing well with our various challenges – Michael's physical and mine ... being me. Michael had perked up on that news. And me? I guess I felt a little affirmed too. After some boring talk about golf that seemed to satisfy Michael and then send him into a doze, Charles sat me down in the sitting room and led me through a visualisation session. He told me to imagine looking at each item in my chaos and placing it in mental filing boxes – not to ignore but to organise so I didn't get overwhelmed.

There was a shortcut for mental exercises. I asked for him to put me back on medication.

'You don't need pills, Jessica. You need persistence,' he said.

I got the impression I wasn't the first patient he'd said that to. 'Telling an adult with ADHD to persist is like telling a person with depression to cheer up.'

He shook his head. 'You underestimate your own resources, Jessica. Give it another two weeks. If you're still struggling, we'll reconsider.'

At least he did manage to help out with cover for Monday, phoning Fernanda and asking her to spend the day in the house. She'd even agreed to stay the evening so I could go to book club as long as I could come back to sleep over. Charles encouraged my participation in the book group; he thought female friends were healthy for me. Little did he know my crew. I think he was thinking of the ladies who lunch that he saw out and about in his circle, not my scurrilous bunch.

Once Charles left in his new Mercedes Benz, I settled down with Michael to watch some TV, him on his bed, me in the armchair, feet propped on the covers.

'Have you seen Charles's car? Pretty swish.' I quelled the impulse to take the controller away from Michael as he flicked his way through the channels. Nothing seemed to suit and I doubted he'd go for my *Love Island* suggestion. He settled on a news discussion programme. What joy.

'Charles changes partners only a little less frequently than he does his car,' said Michael.

That tactless comment reminded me of my day and my recovering spirits plunged back into despair. I was tempted to raid Michael's bathroom cabinet to see if he had anything to take the edge off my mood.

'What the fuck!' Michael's abrupt cry dislodged me from my nefarious plan.

'What?'

Michael pointed at the screen. Some woman called Anushka Kapoor was on a *Newsnight* panel, talking about the stalker baby stealer targeting Michael. She said in so many words that Michael had brought this upon himself, that he invited weirdoes with his provocative stances on violent offenders, and that we all needed to sit and sing 'Kumbaya', rather than stir up such feelings.

'What an idiot,' I murmured.

Michael threw me a furious look.

'You see, Jerry,' she said with false concern, 'some people say that he might've even orchestrated it himself to attract publicity for his comeback to public life.'

I had a new public enemy Number One. 'The bitch!'

The host shut her down on that pretty quickly, but Michael and I both had the experience to know that that kind of mud sticks. The tabloids liked their celebrities to have clay feet.

'I could murder her!' Michael hissed.

'Do so and I'll bury the body.' I pointed to myself. 'Ex-undertaker – I know the right people.' That was probably the best thing I could have said because he gave a rueful laugh. The programme ended and he switched off the screen.

He put the controller back on his bedside table. 'Today is now officially the third worst day of my life.'

I knew him well enough to know what the other two were: the day his wife died and the day he broke his spine.

'Who the hell is she?' I asked.

'Just some commentator I've crossed recently. I thought better of her.' He lay back and closed his eyes, looking exhausted and clammy.

I bit my lip, still worried for him. He didn't need me to stir up strong feelings against her. 'Forget the bitch. Try and sleep.'

He nodded. 'Yeah. Thanks for staying, Jessica.'

'No problem.'

Michael slept after that, too tired to feel all the anger he normally would. I felt it for him, my new hate figure mixing with my bitterness over Drew. If I knew witchcraft, she would've had pins stuck in her like a hedgehog.

At two o'clock in the morning, I gave in and raided Michael's bathroom cabinet. No sleeping pills. I stared at my reflection for a long moment, considering more drastic action. His pain meds. The razor.

I checked. Impulse controls were fried. Shit, this was dangerous.

My hand went to the packet of pills.

Boxes. Put things in boxes. My inner Charles kicked me in the behind just in time.

Right. I began the painstaking process of putting my head back together.

Chapter 45

Jess

I arrived at work on Monday, expecting some light relief with Jonah after my turbulent weekend, and walked straight into a crisis.

Jonah leapt up as I entered and backed me up against the door. I'd not yet seen this angry, threatening side to his character, not away from the film set. For the first time in his presence I felt scared.

'When were you going to tell me?' he roared to my face.

I had a horrible flashback to my father. 'What have I done now?' was my first thought. 'Tell you what?' was what I actually said.

'That Amy Mason is accused of abusing her daughter!'

Alarms rang. I knew this was a sore subject for Jonah with his past. 'Nothing's been proved against her.'

'Fuck that! The kid's run away – with the little one – Pawel.'

'What?'

'If nothing was wrong at home, why did they run?'

This information was coming too fast for me to compute.

'Back up: Angelica and Pawel have run away? That doesn't make sense. Angelica was with Roman.'

Jonah was shaking with anger. He was taking this very personally. 'Why didn't you tell me? I helped you with her! I helped push a kid back into abuse.'

OK, Jessica, deal with Jonah's meltdown first. 'Jonah, nothing is proven – in fact, I don't believe Amy's done anything wrong other than be an anxious mother.'

'Fuck that! They pretend to care! It's all lies!'

Not touching that with a barge pole. 'Go back to the beginning. Roman is the villain of the piece – taking Amy's kid from her.'

Jonah realised he'd do something he'd regret if he continued to threaten me physically like this. With an effort, he pulled back. 'Oh yeah? If you're so sure about that, why leave a message, signed by both kids, that she's a monster and needs to be put in prison?'

'A message? Hang on, how do you know all this?' Clearly everything had gone to hell yesterday, but why? Oh God, the email update I'd sent her after talking to Marek! What if Amy had confronted Roman about the arson despite my warnings not to? Was Roman spinning some new tale to divert from his own sins? But she didn't know where he lived – I'd made sure of that. How did Angelica get to be with Pawel?

'The news is all over the set – Roman's asked for volunteers to help look for the kids. They went missing from the house in Windsor last night – or didn't come back, or something. They're combing the meadows around the river. I'm ditching filming to help, fuck the director.'

360

'No thanks,' I said absently, while my mind spun. This made no sense: Angelica gone off with Pawel, but not back to Roman's. Something had taken Angelica over to Windsor. Had she been trying to reconcile like I suggested? No, I was fairly sure she wouldn't have changed her mind since Friday. And why run with her brother? I hadn't got the sense that the children spent much time together and Pawel seemed perfectly happy at home – wonderfully normal to tell the truth.

I thought about the girl I had confronted in the Ladies, the stubbornness, the arrogance that only she knew what it was like to have issues with a parent, the hint of cunning as she bargained. What if ...?

No ... it's hard to credit a kid with this much deviousness.

I had been fairly devious at that age though, hiding things, mainly from my dad, but also from my mother, until I ran away.

OK, think the unthinkable. What if I'd had this upside down from the beginning, got my victims and my perpetrators around the wrong way? Fifteen-year-old kids weren't angels, even if named after them.

'Jonah, can you give me a moment?'

'I don't feel like giving you anything but a kick out of the door. You fucking lied to me.'

I glowered at him. There was enough distance between us now that I no longer felt afraid. 'I fucking did not. I kept client confidentiality over what is mostly likely a false accusation.'

He glowered back, ears flushed red as temper still stormed inside. 'You've got thirty seconds. Make it snappy.'

'Angelica did it.'

'What the fuck are you talking about?'

'Amy assumes, Roman assumes, that the other is gaslighting their daughter. Amy thinks Roman poisoned her against her mother; Roman is convinced Amy was medically mistreating Angelica. It's the other way round. Neither has done anything but the usual flawed parenting. Angelica is playing them off against each other.'

'She's just a kid.'

'She's fifteen, knows her parents better than anyone, and has decided this is the way she gets to do what she wants.' I flopped on one of the sofas, coming down off the spike of adrenaline my reception in the trailer had given me. 'Kinda admirable in a Machiavellian way. She didn't want to be taken to a specialist for an eating disorder, can't bear to be told she wasn't managing her mental health well – it's a blow to her pride. What does she do? She turns it on her mother. She's the one with the problem, Daddy – Munchausen by proxy. She probably googled it.'

Jonah sat opposite me and rolled a cigarette. 'Kids can be little shits. I was one. Why involve the brother?'

I lit up a cigarette. 'Because it adds to the drama. Look what's happening: her mother labelled a monster, half of Windsor drafted to look for them, probably local news putting out alerts.'

'You think she'll just turn up, Pawel in tow, continuing her story of woe?'

'That would be a good move for her. It forces the authorities' hand, doesn't it? They can hardly send Pawel back to the home where he purportedly signed an appeal for help. That's her doing – I'll put good money on it.'

Jonah tapped the roll-up on the lid of his tobacco tin. 'You don't like her much, do you? The kid?'

'Not much. I met her on Friday and I guess even then I thought she was enjoying the drama rather too much. But then she's a teenager – they do the most ridiculous things to keep themselves the centre of their own big deal story.'

Jonah reflected for a moment, joining his smoke to mine. 'Sorry, Jess. I didn't mean to leap on you like that.'

'Yes, you did – and you were scary.'

'You can pummel me if you like.'

'I'll save that till later. I think we'd better get over to Windsor.'

'You still think we should go?'

'I only said a good move for Angelica would be to turn up with Pawel after one night away – just enough to show everyone she's serious.'

Jonah grabbed his jacket. 'And a bad move?'

I squeezed the bridge of my nose. OK, so we were going there. 'Jonah, do you know what little sociopaths look like?'

'No. Should I?'

'They look a lot like Angelica.'

Jonah's driver was summoned to take us to Windsor. Sharing the back seat, I filled Jonah in on my understanding of the brother and sister dynamic.

'The main thing I know about her relationship with Pawel is that they're not close.'

'So he's what? A prop?'

'Or a weapon.'

'Will she hurt him?'

'You need my ex for that kind of prediction – he's a psychologist.'

'I thought you seemed well-versed on mental issues.'

'Yeah, well, we had a run-in with our very own deranged killer – I'm perhaps quicker to suspect than others would be. I might be wrong – Angelica might be having just a normal teenage pout, and she'll flounce right back in.'

'But you don't think so?'

I patted my stomach. 'I'm going with my gut here.' I tried Amy again but she wasn't answering. A better source of information occurred to me. I rang Glenda.

From the heavy breathing, it sounded like Glenda was outside.

'Glenda, it's Jess here.'

'Oh Jess! You've heard then? About the children?'

'Yes, just heard. Where's Amy?'

'I think she's still in the house but the police are questioning her.'

'Alone?'

'She distraught – yes, alone. Roman is out searching.'

She needed a lawyer like yesterday. I'd call Renfrew and Jakowitz next. 'How did it happen?'

'Ron thinks he saw the kids leave together yesterday afternoon. Amy and Roman were having words out on the street and the children went indoors. He thinks he saw them heading across the playing fields. He didn't think anything of it at the time. He thought Angelica might be taking her brother to the play park to get him away from the argument.'

That would've been the right kind of story to persuade the boy to leave without protest.

'Glenda, can I ask you something?'

'If it's about Drew, I have to say I'm disappointed in him.'

'No, it's not about Drew.'

'Stepping out with that yoga woman while he was still with you – that's just not how we do things in our family. I told him as much when I dropped him at the airport. He owes you an apology.'

I wasn't so sure about that myself, finding my love life rather entangled just at present. 'It's not about Drew. It's about Angelica.'

'What about her?'

'Glenda, do you like her? I mean, do you trust her?'

'I ... I like Pawel. He's a cutie.'

'Glenda.'

'I know what you're asking, but she's fifteen. She's supposed to be obnoxious at that age.'

'Tell me your impressions.'

'I'd say she's a little cold. Ron agrees. He actually said he was surprised to see her take her brother to the park; she normally ignores him. Why are you asking?'

'No matter. I just wanted a second opinion. You've confirmed something for me. We should be arriving in a few minutes – to help.'

'Who's we?'

'My employer is bringing me. Jonah Brigson.'

There was a short pause. Then Glenda came up trumps. 'I'll put the kettle on then.' Even a film star didn't faze her.

Chapter 46

Jess

Jonah and I were barred entry to Amy's house. The police were treating it like a crime scene, going through the children's rooms to see if they could find any clues as to where they might have fled. She was allowed out though, so crossed the street with us to have tea with Glenda.

'You stay here, love,' said Glenda, patting her shoulder. 'Until the children come home.'

Jonah had already gone to join the search, news crews trailing after him like ducklings. He tried to tell them to fuck off so he could get on with searching but they weren't listening. Might not have been such a good idea to come. Jonah wasn't yet used to being an A-lister rather than an ordinary mortal. Everyone from the shoot at Linton College was out searching – Leanne; Joseph, Roni's assistant; the lighting crew, Len, Elijah; the guys from Roman's department, Pete, Neil and his wife, Margaret; even two of the younger porters had abandoned their post, Simon and Bernard. There were many others I recognised from around the college. The locals were also out in force – Ron helping the police coordinate. I'd go and join them in a moment. Only Amy had been told she couldn't go: apparently her presence might be 'counterproductive, Mrs Mason'. I could slap the officer who'd told her that. What a way to disempower a mother!

'But why would Angelica say those terrible things about me?' said Amy, truly bewildered. 'I've never done anything to her – never! Never really told her off – just tried to set a few boundaries and, God, those were hard to maintain. She usually rode roughshod over them. I've never abused her – not for one second. I'd rather cut off my right hand than do that!'

The real workings of family life came tumbling out: the hapless mother trying to keep up with the strong-willed daughter; the repeated best efforts that got brushed back; the reverse power relationship with one side having all of it – and not the side you expected from the relative ages.

'Amy, does Angelica have any favourite places around here – somewhere from when she was younger? A hang-out?' I asked.

She shook her head wearily. 'I've told the police all of this, Jessica. She worried about having an asthma attack so wasn't an outdoorsy kind of girl growing up, not till Roman came along and changed her mind. Then they mostly did sports together. I thought it good for her to get out.'

'Did she and Pawel do any outdoor things together? Cycling?'

Amy sniffed and blew her nose on the Kleenex Glenda handed her. 'No. Pawel's only just learned to ride his bike.'

I remembered the fishing trip on the Instagram feed. Was that something they did regularly? 'Fishing?'

'We only did that the once – on holiday in Scotland. Pawel hates the river. He can't swim yet so it frightens him. I forbade both of them to swim there – so dangerous.'

Where would a girl with sociopathic tendencies take her little brother if this was all some big performance to punish the mother? Why: the place that she'd banned. My money was now on the river – and that made me feel very, very scared for Pawel. Drew was sitting on a plane back to Austria, but at least I knew who else to ask. I walked into the hallway to make the call.

'Jago?'

'Jessica. How's Michael?' I could hear him tapping away on his laptop and the sound of coffee being made in the background. He was cafe-crawling to get inspiration from the people he so despised.

'OK, but there's another emergency.'

'I'll be right there.'

'Not with Michael – in Windsor. Two children have gone missing. My client's: fifteen and seven.'

'Missing kids. It never rains but ...'

'Yeah, I know. This time they went off on their own accord – or at least, with the older one leading the younger. I've a question. If you were going to sneak off swimming round here, where would be the best, most super-secret place that feels like adults wouldn't know about it?'

'There are quite a few. I'll just look at my map.' I could hear a few more taps as he drew on his database. 'You think that's where they've gone?'

'It's a hunch.'

'There are some places that spring to mind. They're a bit hard to find.'

'Any suggestions where to start?'

'Try the Chapel of Saint Mary Magdalene, near Boveney Lock. It's set in the fields and manages to feel quite wild even though it's only a few miles from town. There's a place near the chapel to get to the bank, and a second a bit further on where you can get through the bushes to a little inlet. It's pretty cool actually, might appeal to kids.'

I could see a chapel chiming with Angelica's instinct for drama, particularly if she was planning some punishing gesture. I'd just have to hope she wasn't going to go so far as to harm her brother – or let harm come to him. 'That's really helpful – exactly what I wanted to know.'

'In that case, if you think I can be useful, I'll drive over to help in the search. Let me know how you get on at the chapel.'

We could do with his expert knowledge of the river. 'Thanks, Jago. Appreciate this.'

I joined the searchers and told Ron to expect Jago. I asked if anyone had checked the chapel. It had been visited last night apparently, when they were looking for the kids sleeping rough, but I thought it worth a return visit to check out this path down to the riverbank. I invited Jonah to come with me. I didn't feel I could quite manage Angelica on my own, but if we took too many she might hear us coming.

In the cul-de-sac filled with volunteers, Elijah separated from the rest of the team and came over. He'd got his red hair tied back in a bandana style which I was sure he had copied from Roman. 'Can I join you?'

I really didn't want to deal with my puppy follower. He showed zero initiative and, frankly, just bugged the hell out of me. 'Actually, Elijah, can I ask you to do me a favour? I'm expecting Jago to join us. Will you look after him for me, till we get back? I'm thinking this will be a wild goose chase, so we won't be long.'

'Jago? Of course!' He looked delighted by this new task. 'Len and I will see to him. Hey, Len,' he shouted, 'want to wait for Jago Jackson with me?'

Len nodded and gave a thumbs-up, separating from the design team clustered around Roman.

'Jago's got expert knowledge of places along the river – the kind of places children might go,' I explained.

'Of course he has! Wild swimming.' Elijah did an enthusiastic bob on his toes like he was about to dive in himself.

'Send him over to the police officer in charge of the search.'

He saluted me – and I didn't think it was ironic. 'Will do.'

Jonah had finally managed to shake his press following so I got a lift with him – it was much longer that way round but we got there more quickly than we could've done walking the two miles through search parties. We drove as he lay propped up on the back seat so he wouldn't be spotted, checking his iPad for updates.

'Don't you find that guy annoying?' I asked Jonah as he scanned the police Twitter feed. Windsor Castle sailed past the window, untouched by our crisis.

'Who?'

'Elijah – the lighting guy.'

'Len's sidekick? Can't say I've noticed him. Seems OK.'

'There's just something that annoys me about him.'

'He likes you and you don't like him – that's why he annoys you.'

'Maybe.'

'Welcome to my world of adoring fans that you can't satisfy.' He grinned at me.

'I doubt very much you'd have any adoring fans. Maladjusted females living alone with their cats who fantasise about you, maybe a few.'

'You'd be surprised.'

Actually I wouldn't. Though I saw it as my job to keep his feet on the ground, Jonah did have something to him that made you want to look, and look again.

The driver pulled over in the lane near the chapel. Jago was right: the little building was very romantic, set apart in fields. It looked genuinely old: a barn-like structure with red roof and little wooden tower thrusting out of the roof. If I'd had more time, I'd have liked to know why it ended up here all alone. It wasn't derelict but looked after, according to a sign outside, by a wonderful sounding organisation: Friends of Friendless Churches.

Jonah snorted, not taking the same message as me from the sign. 'I can think of a few friendless people who could do with that money, not a chapel that no one wants.'

'But we do want it – we just don't know we want it until it's threatened.'

'Bleeding heart liberal.'

I tried the door. Locked. 'I'm not the one saying give your money to the poor, but spend on heritage. That makes me a bleeding heart conservative – with a small c.'

Our banter didn't stop us circling the chapel looking for any sign that children had come here last night. I couldn't see anything. They'd locked it up pretty tight to stop vandals.

'Riverbank?' I suggested.

Jonah nodded. The first spot Jago mentioned was in the open, but no one was there so that was a negative. We headed down the track to the spot where Jago said it was possible to push through to the bank. The opening was not much bigger than a rabbit run, but that was part of the pleasure, he'd said. Those that used it kept it like that so the uninitiated wouldn't find it.

I wriggled through the opening and slithered under some persistent brambles to reach the little inlet I'd been promised. I suppose I'd been hoping to find the children waiting down there like some latter-day *Swallows and Amazons* tale, bottles of pop and a little campfire. However, I wasn't too surprised to discover it was deserted. Jonah joined me.

'Sweet,' he said.

And it was – a tiny private swimming spot with a shallow slope into the water hidden by weeping willows. It looked inviting and I had to remind myself not to follow my impulse to strip off and dive in. I was on a mission here. Jonah meanwhile had picked up a branch and was poking the thick mat of brambles that tumbled down the bank. Some of the blackberries were already ripening. After a few whacks, he hooked the strap of a bag and pulled out a backpack.

Our hopes rose.

I unzipped it. It contained some of the items Amy had noticed were missing from her clean washing pile. 'Score one to Jago. He's right. The kids have been here.'

'I think they're coming back,' said Jonah. 'Why else leave this here?'

I glanced into the river. No, this wouldn't turn into some wretched drowning then suicide case – I wouldn't let it take that turn. 'So we wait?'

'Yeah, we wait. I imagine they've gone scavenging. Must be hungry by now.'

'But won't someone see them if they go into a shop? Everyone is on the lookout.'

'She won't go anywhere like that. I was thinking more of stealing from picnics – there are plenty of people on the banks today. Or bins.'

I'd done that once upon a time when I was homeless. 'I don't think Angelica would lower herself to that. Not yet.'

'Allotments then – pick your own.'

True, there were quite a lot of options for free food if you knew your own area.

'What do you want to do, Jess?' asked Jonah.

'I'll text Ron an update but ask the police to keep away for an hour. I can't imagine she wants to be out in the open for long – not unless this is the moment she's planned to make her dramatic return. If so, problem solved. I'm just worried for Pawel and what she might do if she brings him back to the river.'

'You think she might hurt him?'

'I've no idea – but I can imagine a scenario where she puts him in danger to heroically save him. This is all about her, remember. And what if she can't save him? What if she miscalculates?'

'What if she'd prefer him gone?'

I didn't reply to that. 'If she sees too many police hovering, she might get spooked and decide not to return. Let's sit tight, keep quiet, and see if they just walk right back to us.'

Chapter 47

Leo

There was an emergency further down the Thames – two children missing – so Leo found most of his officers redirected to help with the search. That left him in an almost empty incident room. Harry and Suyin were interviewing Nathan's boat crew in case the killer contacted any of them – a slight chance now but they had to cover their bases.

He spread the files generated during the inquiry out on a conference table. He'd read everything once already but sometimes circling back brought new things to light. He picked up the list of members who belonged to the gym where the second appearance took place. There were a few names that crossed with those at the college. Jago had been a member but let his membership lapse. New recruits came from the crew – a sound technician, a makeup artist and a lighting rigger. Interesting. What about the link to the visit to the food bank woman at the church in Headington? It's very specific local knowledge to know that church's routines. He'd have to go back and check where each of the crew lived. What link could there be there or had that been picked purely because it was last on the circuit? Rereading the statements from the film crew at Linton College he came across a mention from the wardrobe department that they'd experienced a number of thefts, more than usual for a location shoot where everything got locked down nightly. He'd not noticed because he'd read this before the attack on Parry-Jones but one of the items that had gone missing was a long-haired woman's wig. Brunette.

He went back to the evidence log of the hairpiece left behind when Parry-Jones pulled it from the attacker's head. Brunette.

It clicked into place. Checking the wig out of the exhibits officer in charge of the evidence, Leo drove back to the college. It was much quieter than before, no sign that any filming was taking place. The head porter gave him a wary welcome.

'Are they having a break?' Leo asked gesturing with his thumb over his shoulder at the empty quad.

'I thought you'd know – being police.'

'Know what?'

'One of the crew – his kids are missing. Most folk jumped in their cars to help with the search. Even Simon and Bernard went, leaving me holding the fort.'

'The children from Windsor?'

'Yeah, that's them. Any news?'

'Not that I've heard.' But he'd certainly check. 'I was hoping to speak to someone from the wardrobe department. Do you know if they're here?'

The porter shrugged. 'They don't answer to me, but if they

are, they'll be in the Old Laundry – that's where they've set up shop for the duration.'

Leo followed signs to the oldest part of the college near the student bar. Opening the door to the Old Laundry he could see why they'd chosen this place as it had long scrubbed tables and good light. When the students were up, it was used as an events venue, now it was full of fabric.

A woman sat sewing in the window at the far end, bathed in light like a Renaissance Madonna. She looked up, shoulder-length black hair slipping backwards. 'Can I help you?'

'Hello, I'm Inspector George.'

'Miranda Melrose.'

'Miss Melrose, I'm investigating the murders of three people and the attempted murder of a fourth.'

She put aside the blue silk dress she had been working on and stood up, holding her hands in front of her neatly. Leo was reminded of a ballerina, waiting for the next instruction from her choreographer. 'I've heard. Terrible business.'

'A wig was left at the scene of the last attack. I was wondering if you could identify it?' He pulled it out of his messenger bag still wrapped in its plastic bag and spread it on the table.

Her eyes widened and her fingertip went to touch the strands. 'May I take a closer look?'

'I'm afraid I can't take it out in case of contamination,' Leo explained. 'But do you recognise it?'

'Yes, yes, I think I do. Or it is identical to one that went missing right at the beginning of the shoot. It belongs to the main character – Ronnie's part. Diana.' She tipped it to look at the webbing. 'I'm almost positive it is the same one. Look, the staining is the same. It's already been used in earlier scenes on our London location during that really hot period we had a few weeks back.'

That was good enough for Leo. 'Who has access to this room?'

'Wait – you think the murderer was in here?' She looked about in alarm. There were plenty of places to hide among the racks of costumes so Leo didn't blame her for feeling spooked.

'You have a key?'

'Yes, as does my assistant. She went off to help with the search. And the porters of course.' She picked up the blue dress as if to save it. 'But to be honest the door is often open as we go to and from the set so much.'

But it solidified the link between these attacks and Linton College. They weren't dealing with a random person following Jago's blogs; the attacker came from here. It was just a question now of narrowing down the list. They'd almost got him, Leo could feel it.

Only problem now was that most of his suspects were down at Windsor. By a river. With children missing.

Realising the implications of that, Leo spun on his heels, heading for his car. He phoned the commander of operations at Windsor as he went.

Chapter 48

Michael

Thankfully, he was feeling a lot better. Jessica had made him excellent chicken soup yesterday which steadied him – not a skill he'd known she had. He realised that he'd not eaten properly for a few days, which hadn't helped fight off the fever. Too caught up in the excitement of being part of something again. She was a real friend through the nightmare – and even Jago showed he wasn't entirely worthless. He'd kick himself for throwing her away – if he could kick, that is. Bloody soul-destroying form of comeuppance.

Fernanda was in occupation, bribed by Charles to babysit. Cleaning was accompanied by singing along to some music he didn't recognise – possibly Brazilian pop but he wouldn't be able to tell. It could be a Korean boy band for all he knew about that end of music. That was if you could call it music.

She tutted when he said that he wanted to get up, but his plan was only to go as far as the sitting room so she could change the sheets.

'Dr Harrison, you should stay in bed!' Her hands were on her hips, chin tipped up like a matador about to give battle.

'I will – but on my armchair. I'll stretch out there,' he told her. He wasn't going to surrender any more of his independence.

Fernanda insisted on helping him with the transfer to the specially adapted chair that he could manipulate by remote. It was an ugly but useful addition to the house. He would've loved playing with this when he had been a child – going up and down, tilting forward and back. He could remember thinking he wanted to be a dentist just so he could have the chair. What an irony that he had the chair and detested both it and the reason for its presence in his house.

Fernanda placed fresh orange juice beside him. He didn't feel like anything so acidic so asked for a coffee instead.

She shook her finger. 'No coffee. Bad for you.'

The tyranny of women. 'Please coffee. I'll even drink the juice if I get one.' He didn't specify when.

Satisfied with that bargain, she went over to the kitchen area and poured him one from the filter. She drank it all day and made a pot each time she came. Fernanda's coffee was strong enough to make dead men wake – he was hoping it would work on this semi-living one too.

The doorbell rang. He checked the monitor but didn't recognise the man on the steps. Late middle age, large, thinning hair. His features looked distorted on the camera but there was something of a bulldog about him.

Fernanda headed to answer.

'Just find out who it is,' he called after her. 'If it's the press, send them away. If it's a parcel, leave it on the step – I'll tell the police so they can take it into evidence.' After a baby, he hated to imagine the next move the stalker would make.

On the monitor, he could see Fernanda had kept the chain on as he'd impressed on her earlier and she was having a short conversation with the man. She closed the door and he was left waiting.

'Dr Harrison, you have a visitor. He says he is your Jessica's father, Brian Bridges.' Fernanda had met and liked Jessica, though Jessica was daunted by her. 'I tell him that you are ill but he says he wants a quick word.'

Now? After all these years? How bizarre. Michael had once thought that he'd been badly treated by his daughter. Jessica never had a good word to say for him, refused all contact, and Michael assumed she had exaggerated his awfulness as she did about everyone she disliked. He wasn't so sure about that these days, his judgement where she was concerned had always been a little off.

He looked back at the screen. Brian was waiting patiently. He couldn't see any of Jessica in his face; she looked more like her mother and shared many of that lady's character traits – kind, a little too soft for this world, chaotic.

Suddenly, he turned and looked up into the camera. It was then that Michael's gut kicked in to tell him exactly who else he was – in addition to being Jessica's father. He was the stalker.

Babies in cradles. Cradle snatching. Destroyed toys a punishment – that had probably been Jessica's own doll, though she hadn't recognised it in its mutilated state. This had always been about Michael taking her from him – or that's how he misunderstood their relationship. He was well behind the times, but if he hadn't communicated with her for years, taken his cues from the media, then he might well believe they were still connected. They hadn't exactly publicised their split at the end of the Jacob West case.

Michael's mind went into overdrive. If he'd felt well, if he could have stood up in his old body and been sure he'd outwrestle him, then he'd have let him in. As it was, he was weaker than normal, stuck in a bloody armchair. No, he couldn't see him on these terms. But the man had tipped his hand, coming to gloat in the aftermath of his most outrageous move. Michael just needed to think of a method to make him lay down his cards in such a way as they could trap him.

'Fernanda, please send Mr Bridges my apologies and explain that I have 'flu. I should be better in a few days and would be delighted to see him.' No, not delighted – that sounded too eager. 'Say I should be *able* to see him on Wednesday afternoon if that's convenient. Suggest he comes back at four.'

Fernanda went to deliver the message and Michael checked that he left after hearing it. He didn't feel safe, though, knowing he was in the area. The man had too many screws loose in his head.

'Can you close the doors to the garden, please?' Michael asked Fernanda when she returned.

'But it is a lovely day, Dr Harrison! The sun is shining. There is a lovely breeze.' She moved with a swing to her hips, dancing to the faint burble of her music.

Why couldn't she just do what he asked? 'Nevertheless, I'm sitting in a draught.'

With bad grace she closed the door.

'Lock it, please.'

'But I'm here, Dr Harrison.'

As if she would be any protection against a man as big as that. 'For my peace of mind. Thank you.'

Task completed, scorn trailing her like a scarf, she went back into his bedroom to finish changing the bed. He immediately tried calling Jessica but she didn't pick up. His next call did go through though.

'Inspector George?' From the sounds behind him, the inspector was in his car. 'Yes, I'm feeling better. I think I may have a break in the stalker case. Let me lay it out to you and you can tell me what you think.'

Chapter 49

Jago

Jago parked in Ron and Glenda's drive, mentally preparing himself for his public. He checked his expression in the mirror, trying for 'concerned'. But maybe rehearsing made him a bit of a media whore? Jess would say so. He snapped up the mirror and gathered his bag of maps. He sincerely did want to help find the missing kids, but he also was aware, hotfooting it down here from Oxford, that it would make a great piece for his blog. Plus it helped answer that nagging little voice, the one that compared him to Dr Harrison and asked him what he was doing with his life. His knowledge had just become useful in a real world way, and not merely as entertainment.

A familiar man of about his own age got up off the garden wall where he had been waiting, messaging on his phone – the guy with the red hair. What was his name? He'd been down the pub on Friday, a friend of Jessica's, the one with a crush on her. Eliot? No, something biblical. Elijah. Yes, that was it. Not that Jago could blame him for his crush. Jess was something else. True, she could be annoying and scatty, with terrible timing, but, wow, she was smoking. For all his bluster, Jago was acutely aware that he had always felt his counterpart in popular media was the spotty nerd who never got the girl. It had been like that at school, and university hadn't been much better with mature men like Dr Harrison pumping out the alpha hormones. Travelling had helped break that pattern but only in a series of casual hook-ups with women who were frankly too self-absorbed in their own journey to think much of his. *Eat, pray, love* yourselfers. For once, he had landed whatever the British equivalent was of the curvaceous captain of the cheersquad, one who was mind-bogglingly sexually uninhibited, and he had no intention of giving up that just yet.

'Elijah, thanks for waiting for me.'

The guy smiled. 'My pleasure, Jago. I'm impressed you remember me.'

'Friday's not that long ago.'

'And we met when you filmed your TV series, I was on the crew.'

Jago didn't remember this. 'Oh yes, of course. Thanks for making me feel welcome.' He vaguely recalled chatting with some of the crew while filming but his clearest memory was of some makeup girls pressing him to say which were the best swimming spots. They'd been flirting with him, which he'd rather enjoyed, so he'd mentioned a few of his favourites, some of the special spots like the boatyard and how to get in. Oh, he should tell the police about that when he'd finished here. 'How can I help?'

'First, how do you take yours? Len has gone to get us coffee from the volunteers' canteen and will meet us on the way.'

'Coffee would be great. White, no sugar.'

Elijah texted the order to Len. 'The policeman in charge of the search team asked me to bring you to him. This way.'

Jago looked back at his car. 'On foot?'

'It's not far.' Elijah started walking so Jago fell into step. 'No news?'

'Jessica and Jonah – that's Brigson, the actor, her boss – found a bag belonging to the girl – Angelica – so they are staking out that spot. We're all keeping clear, and carrying on searching elsewhere.' He pulled a face. 'The police aren't so optimistic. Don't tell Jessica, but they're dragging the river below the lock.'

They were cutting across some playing fields. Jago wasn't so sure of this part of town. It wasn't somewhere he'd explored. 'Why not tell her?'

'Because she's convinced this is going to end happily. You know what she's like.'

That seemed quite a personal thing to say about someone. No wonder Jessica was finding the guy annoying. 'Know her well, do you? I thought you only met last week?'

'Doesn't take long to get to know her though, does it?' His smile asked for Jago to agree. 'She's an open book. I mean it was pretty obvious she was cosying up to Roman for Amy's sake, trying to find out where Angelica lived. I didn't say anything though.' He tapped the side of his nose – a gesture that Jago had only ever seen on stage before, and never in life. There was something phoney about Elijah; worse, something just not right. 'It was fun to watch – she's pretty transparent – as well as pretty.'

'And taken.'

Elijah held up his hands. 'I know. I was just wondering what it was like to be her.'

Jago looked up and realised he really wasn't sure where they were. Elijah had led him to the rougher ground by the racecourse but that was as far as local knowledge took him.

'Do you know where you're going?' he asked.

'Oh yes. It's a shortcut to Boveney Lock. I told you the police are focusing their search there.'

They would end up on the southern bank away from the chapel, but maybe that was the plan. 'OK.' Jago thought there should be more police around, even this far back. Two missing kids surely demanded more than a scattering of searchers?

'Do you think Jessica would like me more if I were you?' asked Elijah as if this was something he'd been thinking about for some time.

'That's a weird question.'

Elijah laughed. 'I get that a lot. They tell me I'm on the spectrum – say whatever's going through my head.'

'Right. Might need to add a filter or two, mate, if you want to get on with people.'

'But do you think she would?'

Alarm levels rose that Elijah was not dropping a clearly inappropriate question.

He prevaricated. 'I ... I'm not sure how much she likes me, so I've no idea.'

That seemed to be the right answer, for Elijah just nodded.

'Thought as much. She's really hard to predict when it comes to men – not much taste. You're much easier to guess. You've got your routines, your favourite places.'

Jago stopped. This guy had gone past creeping him out to scaring him. 'Actually, you know, Elijah, I think I'd better turn back. I'd prefer to wait at the house.'

'But they want you at the river.'

'And I want to go back. You don't have to come with me.' *Please don't come with me* is what he actually meant.

'If you're sure?' Elijah stopped a few feet ahead.

'I'm sure.' Jago glanced around. No one in sight. His heart was banging against his ribs but he tried to act calmly.

'You know the way?' Elijah seemed oddly cool, using an almost singsong tone.

'I'll work it out. You go on. Tell them where I am.'

Jago knew it was a risk to turn his back, but he took it.

Chapter 50

Jess

Jonah took to sitting with nothing to do much better than me. He lay back, listening for the telltale sound of the children returning. I found it hard not to fidget, throw stones in the water, or talk.

Jonah opened one eye. 'For fuck's sake, Jessica, make a sandcastle or something.'

That wasn't a bad idea. It wasn't really sand, but river mud, but it gave me something quiet to do. Having ADHD was like permanently sitting on an ants' nest. The only way to forget the itch was to keep moving. Eventually Jonah rolled over on his stomach and joined in, making an outer wall of bent twigs.

'Never did this as a kid,' he admitted.

'I did – but it was always terrifying. Dad would tell me how I was doing it wrong.'

'Your dad sounds a —' And he used a word that I didn't think I'd ever been able to say.

'Don't malign female body parts,' I whispered back.

He sniggered.

'Thanks for waiting with me.'

'No problem. You certainly keep your promises. Life is much more peppery with you in the mix. Want to stay on?'

'I can't do Amy out of a job!'

'Yeah, well, she might not want to come back after this.'

'Let's cross that bridge when we come to it, OK?'

I think it was only because we were being so quiet that we both noticed the disturbance on the other bank. Someone was dragging something down the brambly slope towards the water, lanky red hair dangling. He was having difficulty as his burden kept getting caught.

'Is that ...?' I suddenly realised what we were seeing. It made so much sense, but yet was completely insane. Why?

'Fuck. Can you swim that far?' Jonah kicked off his shoes.

'Yes.' I followed suit, wriggling out of my jeans, dumping my phone on the pile.

We both ran into the water. It was usually a busy stretch but the guy had chosen a moment when there was no river traffic – of course he had: he was trying to dump a body. Fortunately we were watching a little upstream so could use the current to take us down and across. The man – Elijah – saw us coming. He gave the body a final push and made a run for it.

'You get that, I'll get him,' said Jonah, striking out for the bank.

The body was floating – if Elijah had planned to weigh him down, then he hadn't had time. I grabbed a handful of hair and recognised Jago. He'd been knocked out and stripped.

Oh God, oh God. I towed him to a clear patch and hauled him ashore. He'd got a wound to his head but I thought – yes – he was still breathing. What I really needed now was my phone – left on the other side. I looked up and saw two children watching us from the little beach.

'Angelica!' I bellowed. 'Call for an ambulance – he's dying!'

She looked doubtful but I saw Pawel pick up my phone. I shouted out the code to unlock it, though maybe you could make emergency calls? I'd never tested it.

'You can be the hero of the hour!' I yelled over to her. 'Save a man, catch a killer – is that dramatic enough for you?'

She snatched the phone from her brother. I thought for one terrible moment that she was going to chuck it in the water, but I saw her talking to the operator. That gave me the space I needed to see what I could do for Jago. He hadn't been in the water for more than a few seconds and was breathing so I didn't think I needed to do CPR. He was just unconscious. Remembering the first aid course I'd once done as a teacher, I tilted up his head to check his breathing. Seemed OK. Next step, recovery position. I rolled him over onto his side. His eyes were moving behind his eyelids.

'Jago, you're OK. It's Jessica. We've got you.' I carried on this stream of reassurance, helping him surface.

'Elijah,' he muttered.

'I know, I know. It's OK – we've chased him off.' If Jonah didn't get him, the police surely would. And where were they? There should be scores of policemen within reach with the hunt going on. I knew they'd swept this area earlier but they couldn't be too far away.

As if my thoughts summoned it, a red air ambulance flew low overhead. I waved and got a thumbs-up from the medic in the open door. She pointed over my head in the direction of the racecourse. On the other side of the river, I could see a yellow-jacketed police woman push her way through to the kids. Pawel immediately clung to her leg. Angelica tried distraction, pointing to me and claiming her part in the rescue. Great. I had been worried she'd try to take off again but she must have realised the jig was up.

Suddenly, everything went pear-shaped. Elijah burst through the bushes. He must've evaded Jonah and circled back. He'd got what looked like a crowbar in his hand. I misjudged his intentions, thinking he was back for another go at Jago, so stepped between him and his victim. But it was me he was after. He barrelled right into me and we both ended up in the river; I landed under him. I grappled for the hand holding the weapon but the guy was powered by insane energy. His hair blinded me. He knew this was a fight for his freedom, and I for my life. He ducked me. I managed to get a knee to his groin but there wasn't much force behind it as I was squashed and half drowning.

Then something lifted him off me. I surfaced spluttering in time to see Jonah drag him backwards up the bank, throw him on the ground and drop on him like a rugby ball. Elijah's hair – no a wig – was askew, showing his shaved scalp beneath.

'Jess, you ... OK?' Jonah panted.

I was too breathless to reply. I staggered out of the river to take the crowbar out of Elijah's hand before he recovered enough to use it.

And finally, law enforcement arrived, escorting the stretcher bearers.

'Everyone all right?' barked the first officer on scene.

'We're fine but he's hurt,' I said, pointing to Jago. 'That guy did it – Elijah Ellwood. He's your killer.' Two policemen were already taking over from Jonah, getting cuffs on Elijah. They read him his rights and then carried him off. Elijah had completely lost it. He was shouting how we'd attacked him, how we were the crazy ones. Like anyone was going to believe him when there had been a police officer watching from just across the river.

But then, he'd revealed himself as a psycho killer so I guess he wasn't thinking straight right now, if he ever had been.

More police arrived. In fact, the bank was soon swarming with them, including a river patrol.

'Are you all right?' one asked me. The boat had provided us with blankets and someone – bless their hearts – had rustled up a cup of tea from a flask. 'Anything you need?'

'A lift over to get our stuff?' I suggested, pointing across to the little beach. I saw that Pawel and Angelica had already been led away. Come to think of it, I couldn't see our stuff either. 'Oh, it's gone.'

'I'll check with my colleagues what's happened to it.'

I followed Jonah's example and stripped off my Thames scented T-shirt. I wasn't going to feel good about myself until I'd had a hot shower. I looked down at myself. 'Hey, go me.'

Jonah raised a brow. 'Obviously always, but why this time?'

'I'm actually wearing underwear – and they match.'

He looked puzzled. I didn't think I'd ever told him the full gory details of the University Parks incident.

'I'll explain later.'

'I'll keep you to that.' The boat circled closer to shore so we could board. I thought I recognised the man next to the pilot. 'Captain?'

The police officer turned to us. 'It's inspector, Miss Bridges. I thought you knew?'

I grinned at Inspector George as he stood next to the wheel. 'You're here too?'

'I got a break in the case and realised, a shade too late to stop him, that our attacker would be here.'

'And you rushed down in time to see him almost claim his fourth victim?'

He grimaced at that. 'But you stopped him.'

'Yeah, thank God. Jonah, this is Inspector George.'

Jonah nodded curtly. 'Will the press be waiting for us when we disembark, Inspector?'

'I'm afraid so,' said George. 'Do you want a blanket or something to put over your head?'

'Fuck no!' Jonah looked aghast. 'And look like the nutter you arrested. No, bring 'em on. My agent is going to love this.'

So barefoot we did our walk between the massed ranks of the news crews, me with my blanket demurely tucked under my armpits, Jonah with his slung precariously around his waist, his arm across my shoulders.

'Is it true you apprehended the river killer, Jonah?' someone called.

'Ask Inspector George here,' said Jonah, with a 'hell yeah, we did' grin.

'Is this your new girlfriend?' called another, showing what they were really interested in – a story where Jonah two-timed his gorgeous Jenny and managed to end up solving a crime.

'No, she's my new bodyguard,' lied Jonah cheerfully. 'Saved my bacon, she did.'

The story was so outlandish considering I was only a few inches over five foot and looked like a drowned rat so it threw them.

'She's small but deadly,' he added, enjoying himself rather too much. I couldn't elbow him or I might've lost the blanket and make the front pages.

By the time the press recovered, we were in the police cars heading back to Glenda and Ron's.

'How's Jago?' I asked Inspector George. 'Do you know anything yet?'

'Mr Jackson is on his way to hospital. Last we heard, though, he was awake. I take that as encouraging.'

'Any chance of getting a lift to where's he's been taken?'

'You don't need to ask the fuzz,' said Jonah. 'I'll take you. Car and driver, remember?'

Oh yeah. I'd forgotten how the other half live. Or the other half a per cent live.

'We'll need you both to make statements,' warned the inspector.

'I refuse to do anything before a hot shower and some dry clothes,' I replied.

'What she said,' grinned Jonah.

'Stop enjoying yourself so much,' I hissed.

'Why? One killer caught, one boyfriend type saved, two little kiddies back home – what's not to like about this?'

He was right. It would be churlish to harp on about the three dead people – Jonah didn't know them, nor did I for that matter. I just felt bad because I knew that even an arrest and a conviction wasn't going to end the sentence of those grieving for them. But it was the best we could do.

We got out at Ron and Glenda's house. Across the road, I could see many people crowded into Amy's living room. Hopefully the kids were there, upstairs somewhere.

'I'd better go over. She is my client after all,' I told Jonah.

'I'll come with you. They won't let you in without me,' offered Inspector George.

I needed to help Amy by telling the police my suspicions about Angelica. If the girl was as I thought, she'd be crucifying her mother some more right now.

With a word from the inspector, I was allowed into the kitchen. Amy was sitting huddled at one end of the table, Angelica and Roman on the other side, two police officers separating them. There was no sign of Pawel so I hoped he was in bed, being kept out of this.

Roman looked up as I came in.

'What's she doing here?' he asked, anger mixed with suspicion.

I ignored him. 'Amy, how're you doing?'

Amy gave me a ravaged expression that said everything. 'They're back at least. Safe and sound.'

I sat down beside her. 'Roman, there's something you

need to know. Amy employed me to check up on Angelica
– and on you. She was worried you were gaslighting her
daughter.'

'Gaslighting?' Roman didn't know the word but he was
taking it as an insult.

'It means persuading her of something that isn't true.'

'But that's what she did! She got Angelica thinking she was
ill.'

Angelica hid a dry-eyed face on her stepfather's arm.

'That's not true,' I said. 'It wasn't Amy and it wasn't you,
was it, Angelica?' I let that question hover.

Roman was the first to break the silence. 'Angelica, you
don't have to listen to this. You've been through enough.'

'Oh really? What exactly has she been through? I agree it
was a horrible break to lose her father so young, but after
that, all she had to deal with was a mother trying to help her
cope with her problems. Then you came along and she had
the rivalry of a little brother. Made-up medical emergencies
got her quite a lot of the family attention, I'd guess.'

Angelica's head shot up. 'I was ill! I didn't make anything
up!'

'Get your story straight, Angelica: either you weren't ill and
your mother is a monster forcing treatment on you; or you
were ill and she was doing her best to help. Which is it?' I
knew that tone would annoy her but unless she let her temper
speak she'd find a way of turning this back on me.

'You don't know anything!'

'I know that you didn't want to see a specialist who might
work out how much you were fabricating in your illnesses,

not now you are old enough to realise someone might guess what you were doing. You worked on your stepfather so you could gain his sole attention. I'm not sure you really wanted Pawel with you but it pleased you to take him away from your mother, didn't it? Made for a bigger drama with you as the lead.'

'You're lying!'

I turned to Roman. 'What did Pawel say about why they went missing?'

'He said ...' From the expression in Roman's eyes I could see that he was putting it together. 'He said Angelica took him to her den and wouldn't bring him back.'

'Oh, Angelica!' said Amy. 'How could you?'

'Pawel told me he was scared of her – I thought he was confusing Angelica with their mother, but he meant his sister, didn't he?' He was looking at his daughter with a completely new expression.

'Angelica, I don't understand!' Poor Amy. She held out a hand but her daughter snatched her own away.

But Roman did. 'I think you have some explaining to do, Angelica.'

Angelica turned furious eyes on me. 'She's lying. I don't know why you're believing this woman and not me: I'm your daughter!' Angelica pushed her chair back and stormed upstairs.

Amy rose as if to follow.

'Let her go, Amy,' said Roman.

'But—'

'I think she's had enough attention, don't you?' Roman got

up. 'Thank you, everyone, for bringing the children back. Now if you don't mind, Amy and I need some time alone. There's a lot we need to talk about.'

Inspector George followed me back outside. 'You knew?'

'I guessed earlier today. There was something off about the girl when I met her last week. It was only when she went for the little brother that I was sure.' I sighed. Would Angelica have hurt her brother? That suspicion was one that, thank God, hadn't been tested. 'I've done all I can for them. The rest is up to them.'

I discovered, as I probably already suspected, that both Jago and Jonah were media hussies. Jonah's offer of a lift to the hospital in Reading wasn't so selfless as it gave him time to set up a photo opportunity with his chosen tabloid. Jago was all too ready to agree to the idea. I kept well out of it, despite their attempts to cajole me into the frame. So they just got a picture of a bandaged swimming celebrity shaking hands with his famous rescuer. The less said about my part, the better, if I wanted to carry on with my job, including the undercover aspect of it.

And I found that I did. It had been a wild ride these last few weeks, but that was maybe what I craved. I was less likely to start getting itchy and hanker after a prescription if life was going to hell around me. I was funny that way.

The press left, escorted out by Jonah. He promised to return bearing coffee and snacks.

'So,' said Jago, 'Elijah. I guess he's our killer?'

'Looks that way. When did you know?'

'Rather late in the day. Just before he took a blunt instrument to my head. He's deceptively strong.'

I remembered the thrashing about in the water. It had been like wrestling a man made of wire and steel. 'His job is very physical – must build muscles.'

'He told me he first met me on the documentary. I didn't remember him to be honest. I guess that was when he started obsessing about me – where I swam, the people that use those places.'

'They're not going to be the first crimes he's committed,' I said. 'You don't just wake up and say, "hey, I know, let's murder someone today."'

'I suppose not.'

'I think he'll have been imitating other people for a while – trying on their lives for size. I did notice how he was copying me, but I had no idea what was motivating it. Thankfully, I didn't make the grade for a target.'

'I don't want to even imagine that.'

'You, my friend, were his top pick. He was working his way up to you and we happened to give him the perfect opportunity. Sorry about that. It was my fault – I asked him to wait for you.' As to why Elijah did what he did, I wondered if anyone would ever know. What tipped a man with an interesting job, successful in other people's eyes if not in his own, to lose himself so far in fantasy that he killed for it?

Jago waved my apology away. 'Really, not your fault. I think you bounced him into making his move. If he'd been better prepared, waited for somewhere less public, I might not have survived.'

'He missed his last victim, so I'm thinking he got reckless – jumped to his end game before he was ready.'

Jonah came back with a takeout tray of drinks, a bag of muffins, and a familiar policeman.

'DI George, what have I done to get the top guy to visit me?' asked Jago.

'He bought the snacks,' said Jonah, in an over-the-top aside.

'You caught me my killer – suspected killer,' said George.

'That's right, officer, innocent until proven fucking guilty,' said Jonah with some heat. He wasn't a fan of the police, as he had told me many times.

George's sexy little smile did not dim. He'd heard it all before, I was sure. 'And I've brought you your phones and personal belongings. With the compliments of Thames Valley police.'

'Great.' I reached for mine and saw that Michael had tried to get in contact. Crap: I was supposed to be back there tonight after book club. And yes, look: Cory had been ringing me too.

I sent her a quick text. *Just to update the girls: found lost kids, caught killer, got photographed in my undies, now sitting with Jonah Brigson and Jago Jackson. My I-Spy book of celebrities is fast filling up. Please fill in the blanks with your own wild speculations.*

I checked I'd got the phone on mute because I could imagine what that would do to the WhatsApp group.

'Have you charged Elijah?' Jonah asked.

'Not yet. He's being evaluated,' said George.

'I can save the taxpayer the expense. The guy is a nutcase.'

'Still, we have our procedures.'

I got up. 'Will you excuse me a moment? I just want to check in with Michael.'

DI George held me back. 'About that, Jessica. There's something you need to hear first.'

Chapter 51

Leo

Leo didn't think any of them would forget the experience of searching Ellwood's flat in Headington. His grandmother, his last living relative, had died in 2014 and he had been alone and able to indulge in his obsessive behaviour since then. A normal two-bedroom apartment in a newly-built block by the petrol station had been turned into a shrine to his fantasies. There was copious evidence that he had had previous fixations before the wild swimmer. He had had time to amass heaps of articles and clippings, and Leo dreaded to think what his computer would reveal. He was going to keep the police and the psychiatrists busy for a long time.

It would appear that the spark of his last and most deadly obsession was lit when he first read Jago Jackson's book on cycling. Leo found that by his bedside, along with the one on wild swimming. Both were heavily annotated. From the three bikes stacked in the hall, Ellwood was a keen cyclist and Leo imagined that they would discover that he'd moved between attack sites on his own bikes. There were so many cyclists in

Oxford, this would have made him blend. He could travel up and down the towpath numerous times and no one would notice. Only idiots begging to be caught, like Lucas Crouch, stop to take photos and act suspiciously.

'Here, sir, you might like to look at this.' Suyin took down from a pinboard in the kitchen a parish magazine for the church in Headington Quarry where he'd first impersonated Ken Kingston. The date was January 2014. 'Looks like his grandparents were parishioners. There's a mention of Mrs Ellwood in the recently departed section and notice of her funeral. I wonder why the witness Mrs Busby didn't recognise him?'

'She's fairly new in Oxford. Moved here on the death of her husband. She wouldn't have known the Ellwoods.' He sealed it up in an evidence bag.

'But it was a massive risk for him to take. What if someone who did know him saw him?'

'He likes risk. He would've adapted, or abandoned his plan to go in. But he also watched and knew everyone's routines so could be fairly sure she'd be alone.'

On the kitchen counter, in a pile of unopened post for his grandparents, Leo found a letter for the gym in Temple Cowley asking if Ellwood was going to take up membership after his free month's trial – another link confirmed. Ruby Lonsdale's boyfriend had worked as a personal fitness trainer there. Had Danny met Ellwood, told him too much about his talented girlfriend and how they kept fit? Leo suspected this was the case. It was certainly something to ask during interview. He had already made the connection running the membership list from the gym against the suspects – but this speeded things up as he could put it in front of Ellwood.

Suyin and Leo could hear Harry crowing in the grandparents' bedroom. 'Fucking pervert. The guy must've been a transvestite along with everything else. Look at all these clothes! He's got scores of wigs in here and enough makeup to do a RuPaul.'

Leo went to look at what he'd found. The room still had that old lady scent of lavender talc. The wardrobe was bursting with male and female clothes of many different kinds. Among them would be a green-and-white ladies gym outfit and a smart white shirt and dark trousers belonging to the victims. 'Bag them up.'

Harry checked a label on a slinky 1930s nightdress. 'Naughty boy! Someone's been stealing from the costume department.'

Leo was pleased to note he'd been right about that too. 'The least of his sins, I'd say.'

Satisfied that there was enough evidence here to tie Ellwood to the murders, Leo handed over to his colleagues and returned to make his report to the superintendent. Though he had been frustrated by the slow pace of the investigation while living through it, Leo realised that only two weeks had passed since she'd first called him. That was a very quick turnaround for a murder case. The long haul really started now as they had to ensure a secure conviction. The team were left in no doubt that they mustn't slip up on any details.

'Good work, Leo. Please pass my congratulations on to your team,' Superintendent Thaxted got up to shake his hand as he came in. 'You'll make yourself available for the press conference, I trust?'

He hated these moments, the top brass wanting to trumpet that an arrest had been made, he just wanted to get on with his job, but he knew what was expected. 'Yes, ma'am.'

'I'm wrangling with Windsor to get Ellwood transferred to our care but that should all be sorted by close of play today.'

'Good. I'm eager to interview him.'

'But you've got the evidence to nail him?' She offered him a coffee which he refused. He'd drunk enough coffee to convert his bloodstream to pure caffeine.

'Without a doubt. The only question is over his fitness to stand trial.'

'Let the shrinks handle that. You look as though you could do with a night off. After the press conference, consider yourself ordered home. You won't be able to question Ellwood before tomorrow at the earliest.'

This was exactly what he'd told his own team to do once they finished at the flat. 'Yes, ma'am.'

In his garden, enjoying a solitary beer as the sun set behind the poplar trees, he contemplated the tasks ahead. A bee hung precariously from a purple cranesbill, its work ethic putting Leo's to shame. There would be a full day of questioning tomorrow, if the psychiatrists allowed, and then the arrangements for the final loose ends to be tied on Wednesday. As he was in the superintendent's good books, and because those involved were instrumental in capturing the killer, he didn't anticipate any difficulty getting the required manpower.

Goldemort swam out to receive his tribute of fish food. Was that how he saw Leo: an acolyte coming to worship at the dark pool he dominated? Or was he the god of his world, coming at regular intervals to hand out blessings? Leo's reflection rippled as a breeze disturbed the surface, a smudge of shadows. The waterlilies were closing for the night. He'd barely been here during the hours of daylight to appreciate their colours: scrambled egg yellow, soft pink and crocus purple. And from the looks of his diary this week, it would be a few days yet before he could catch up on the gardening. His work was not done until both men were put away where they couldn't harm anyone.

And then what would he do? There was always another case, of course, and much more to achieve in the garden, but he was thinking rather about Jess Bridges. It would no longer be unprofessional to seek her out outside work if he so wished. He knew she was involved with ... well, with various people, but there was just something about her that made him want to circle a little closer, be within the sound of her laughter. It'd been so long since he'd had anyone like her in his life.

He imagined her here, enjoying a drink in the garden. Yes, he thought that he'd like that. The question remained, though, whether he'd have the courage to ask.

Chapter 52

Jess

My father had done it. I supposed I had always been waiting for those words, never mind the crime that they accompanied. Brian Bridges had been wired to explode for years now. I was just lucky it had happened when I had people on my side. George had stressed that it was just a suspicion, nothing certain, but as soon as he told me Michael's theory, it had felt right.

This was why I was at Michael's on Wednesday, hidden with George in the bedroom as we waited for my father to call round. A good-looking guy and a bed – my mind just had to go there. Behave, Jessica. There were uniformed officers in the garden, out of sight of the open doors, ready to swoop in. Michael's job was to get my father to talk.

I shivered. I hadn't actually seen Brian Bridges for years. I'd caught a glimpse of him once when I was at college, watching me from the opposite platform on the London Underground. I'd told myself it was a coincidence but in my heart I'd always known that he was keeping tabs, what with the break-ins and

413

the sense of being watched. That was why I didn't want my mother to tell him anything – an attempt to keep him away but it had always felt no more substantial than the walls I'd built around any childhood sandcastle.

How was Mum going to react to the news that his rapprochement had been all some twisted plan to get at me? She shouldn't be surprised but her faith in the basic goodness of humanity would be shaken again. And that might be a good thing if it protected her.

The doorbell buzzed. Michael checked the screen.

'You're good to go,' said George softly from the inner room.

Michael released the lock to let in his visitor. I was impressed by Michael's courage. I'd always known him as a confident man, a boxer when at college, so sure of his moves, but to retain that after his accident was impressive. We were close by to help, but there were still risks involved in this. The police needed at least some admissions that would allow them to get a warrant to search our old family home, where my father still lived. His lair, as I liked to call it. I was sure they'd find plenty of material to link to the parcels – he'd be too arrogant to dispose of stuff.

George had rigged up a monitor so we could see what was going on in the sitting room. Michael had a tea tray set out, pretending that this was a social call.

'Mr Bridges, it's great to meet you at long last,' he said as if nothing was wrong and there was no posse ready to pounce.

'Harrison.' My father's voice – that deep bass that liked to boom, shout till the windows rattled, scream in my face as I covered my ears. I wasn't sure I could do this.

I jumped. Colette had just slithered onto my knee from the middle of the bed where she'd been sleeping, and, after a few exploratory prods, curled up. Thanks, puss.

'I've made us tea. How do you take yours?' asked Michael.

This civility was intentionally disarming. Brian could not be sure of his welcome here – but this pulling out of all the stops to make him feel at home was confusing.

'Is Jessica here?' he asked bluntly. His only mode was rant and demand – nothing had changed.

'Not at the moment.' Michael pushed a mug towards him. We had debated if we could risk hot tea and decided against it – too obvious a weapon – so if my father did sip it, he'd find it disgustingly cool. It was just window dressing. 'I understand from her that you've not spoken for years. Is that right?'

'Her decision, not mine,' Brian said tightly.

'I see.' Michael splashed some milk into his mug. 'I guess that's her prerogative – her right,' he glossed in case my father didn't understand the longer word.

I'd already told Michael that this was the hottest button to press with my father and he'd gone right there. 'It's not her right!' My father was steaming even if his tea wasn't. 'I'm her father. A child owes her father her respect. Says so in the Bible.' He'd never been to church in his adult life outside weddings and funerals.

'Jessica is thirty-one, Brian. Not a child.' Ah, the patronising tone now. Be careful, Michael.

'And you're what, fucking fifty?'

'Not quite there yet,' said Michael, staying infuriatingly calm.

415

'See, that's my main problem with you.' The finger was out, pointing right at him. 'What's a man of your age doing running around with a girl like her? Seduced her when she was your student, didn't you? Dirty old man! You should be chemically castrated!'

My father had lost any finesse he might once have had. Too many lonely days putting out his social media messages in full caps lock had eroded his control. George was worried. He'd moved nearer the door, but held position, watching the screen intently.

'Was that why you sent me those tasteful gifts?' asked Michael, as if this was a convivial meeting, not a confrontation.

'What gifts?' growled Brian.

'The dead bird. The baby. Jessica was perplexed by the eyeless doll – you see, she'd forgotten all about that toy.'

'You lie. She loved that doll. It was her favourite.' Michael had tripped him into the confession we needed. I hugged Colette.

'And you thought she'd get the message to come back. How does that work exactly? Come back and I will gouge your eyes out, or come back and I won't? We were confused.'

'You can't have her!' Spit flew from my father's mouth and he banged the table, overturning his tea. God, he depressed me as much as he frightened me.

George took this as the signal and strode in. The officers waiting outside blocked the window. One moved swiftly to stand between my father and Michael.

'Brian Bridges, I'm arresting you on suspicion of stalking

and harassment, under the Protection of Freedoms Act.' George then reeled off the additional charges, complete with the relevant legislation. I guess he'd had time to prepare. I entered last when I saw that my father was secure.

'Jessica!' He lurched towards me but he had already been handcuffed so didn't get far.

'Hi, Dad. Goodbye, Dad.'

'We need to talk!'

'I don't think we do.' I moved behind Michael and put my hand on his shoulder, mainly because I knew that would rile my father.

'You don't need him. Come home.' His eyes were popping in his sockets. Maybe I'd get lucky and he'd have a heart attack.

'No way. Anyway, you're not going to be there for a while.'

'Jessica!'

But the uniformed officers escorted my father out to the waiting police car, and his wails were cut off as the door closed. DI George stayed for a few words then followed to help with the processing at the station. He warned us that stalking didn't come with much of a sentence, but if they could get him on kidnapping, I might be able to sleep easy for quite a few years. He was hopeful. My father had shown he had triggers; if they could get him to admit to stealing the baby to leave on the table, then they could add that to the charges.

'I think that's about it,' he said, looking around the now emptied room. 'River killer and the troll both apprehended. It's been a pleasure working with you, Michael. And you, Miss Bridges.'

'Jess – or Jessica if you absolutely must.'

'Jess.' And then he unleashed a devastating smile on me, just for me. Oh my God, where had that come from? He'd gone before I could fully process what I'd seen. Hearing him say my name felt like he had changed the rules of our inter-actions. But I suppose we were no longer involved in official business, were we? I suddenly very urgently wanted to know what Inspector George would be like off-duty.

But too late: he had gone before I could ask.

Soon there was no one left in the apartment but Michael and me. I leaned down and kissed his cheek.

'Well done.'

He patted my hand. 'Thank you. I apologise I ever thought you'd exaggerated about him.'

'I know. He's something else, isn't he? Sort of like a rancid mackerel stuck behind the radiator and stinking out the house.'

'Is that a common problem, in your experience?'

'You obviously never shared freshers accommodation with a prankster. Shall I make us a fresh pot?'

'I think we've earned something a bit stronger. I've got your favourite wine in the fridge.'

'And I know where your Scotch is – good thinking.'

I served us drinks and set them down on the table. 'Cheers.' We toasted each other.

'That's got to be it for the crazies, don't you think?' I asked. Michael nodded. 'George told me that he doesn't think Elijah will emerge from secure accommodation again. A trou-bled man – social disfunction made worse by disrupted childhood, thanks to parents who rejected him and he ended up living with grandparents. When they died, he lived alone in their old flat and that's turned out to be full of mementoes from the victims and of costumes stolen from film sets he's worked on. He learned the makeup techniques there too.'

'You'd think they'd keep a better inventory but apparently not.' I was rather sad my stint on the production was over at the end of the week. I'd been hoping Amy wanted to spend more time away. She, Roman and Angelica were taking family mediation and they were getting professional help for their daughter.

'I can see how a fantasist such as that man might want to work on films.' Michael took a bracing sip of whisky. 'Moth to the flame. A failure at life wanting to cling on to the superficially successful.'

'Lots of us want to work in the industry,' I said a little defensively. 'Not because we're failures.'

My phone buzzed. I looked down to see Marek's name and my promise to the debt collector came crashing back.

'Shit, shit, shit. I totally forgot!' I slapped my forehead and picked up the call. 'Marek, don't do it! I've just got the family back together; you can't send around the knee-cappers.'

Michael rolled his eyes. He thought I was exaggerating.

'But you promised, *Kochana*,' said Marek gleefully.

'French maid's costume – Friday – with the information and I'll buy you a drink too.'

Michael spilled his drink.

'Hmm. I think that will be ...' he made me wait '... acceptable. I'll text you time and place. Good doing business with you, *Kochana*.'

Michael had wiped up the spillage by the time I ended the call.

'Do I want to know?'

'Yes. No. Maybe. It's complicated.'

Michael was amused rather than shocked. I wasn't his any more so he didn't feel the need to disapprove of me. 'Does Jago know you're seeing other men wearing costumes?'

'Obviously not, because I've only just made the plan and he's still in hospital.'

'But he'll be fine with it?'

'No, he will not. But I probably won't tell him.' I saw Michael's expression. 'What? We aren't officially an item.' He didn't have to say anything. 'OK, I probably will blurt it out while trying very hard not to tell him. Does that satisfy you?' I couldn't imagine the thing with Jago lasting. He'd be too busy milking his close brush with death for his next book and I'd be too busy trying to distance myself from it. A private investigator could do without that kind of notoriety.

At least Amy and the film people had paid me so I wasn't flat broke for once.

Michael grinned. 'Actually, Jessica, I was wondering. If you want somewhere to look forward to, how would you like to be my Plus One at the Frankfurt Book Fair? I'm collecting a prize – at least I've been told I have a good chance of winning one.'

'Your Plus One?' *What's the catch?* I meant.

'Just as a friend. Or bodyguard, if you like.'

I hid my face. So he'd seen the clip of Jonah and me emerging from the police launch, had he?

He laughed. 'Jessica, I know I messed up with you so badly that there's never going to be an "us" again, but I do think we're close enough to be friends. You'll like Frankfurt. The locals dress up on the days when it's open to the public. Cosplay, isn't it called? It sounds like you're into that.'

I looked at Michael and he was smiling at me over the rim of his special tumbler. Yes, surprisingly, after everything, we'd circled around to be friends.

'All right, captain. Make it so.'

'Good. Thank you. But why "captain"?'

'You've the big ass chair like in *Star Trek* so you might as well work it. I'm getting you a Captain Kirk costume.'

'Don't tell me: you're coming as Spock?'

'I can't come as anyone else in the OGs without offending multiple ethnic minorities, so yeah, I'll come as an alien.'

'You want me to collect my prize dressed as Kirk?' Michael was looking bemused – an expression I often prompted him to assume.

'Obviously. You mentioned costumes so that's my condition.' Michael needed to lighten up a little.

'It's a deal.'

We shook on it.

'Why did you agree?' I asked later, after several glasses of wine and reruns of *Star Trek* on his streaming service. I was sitting beside him in his funky moveable chair. He'd even let me handle the controls. Colette was stretched across both our laps.

He rubbed her behind her ears. 'Because, oddly, despite everything we know about each other – or maybe because of that – I feel safe with you in a way that I don't with other people.'

'Good enough,' I said – and started to plan. Where could I get my Vulcan ears?

THE END